THE SHORTLIST

A DCI LOMOND THRILLER

ANDREW RAYMOND

HUNTERHILL BOOKS

SRS

Copyright © 2023 by Andrew Raymond

All rights reserved.

No part of this book may be reproduced in any form or by any electronic or mechanical means, including information storage and retrieval systems, without written permission from the author, except for the use of brief quotations in a book review.

All characters in this publication are fictitious and any resemblance to real persons, living or dead, is purely coincidental.

andrewraymondbooks.com

CHAPTER ONE

WILLIAM MACRAE TOOK up his usual spot on the bench at Kelvingrove Park, crying gently for the man he had killed the night before.

No one paid much attention to the sixty-four-year-old, oblivious to his silent tears as he sat back, admiring the view of the city he loved so much. He took out a silver hip flask and took a long swig. 'Well, Billy...I guess it's over.'

The man MacRae had killed had been his best friend, DCI Bob Roxburgh. In many ways, other than his ex-wife Claire, Roxburgh had been MacRae's only friend for the last thirty-seven years. The fact that Roxburgh was fictional didn't make any difference to MacRae's grief. After writing twenty-four books in the million-selling Roxburgh crime thrillers, the maverick Glaswegian detective was as real to MacRae as anyone else walking around the park on that freezing January afternoon.

After a night of hard frost, the west end of Glasgow was a postcard image. The trees and grass and surrounding hillside all covered in the purest twinkling white. The sort of weather that makes you hug yourself as you walk. Hot air from chimneys and factories and industry curled gently into the air like smoke or steam, reminding MacRae of a JMW Turner oil painting.

There was a steady hum in the air. Glasgow was always moving, always working. But the only ones that saw it all were the crows, the pigeons, and the seagulls who circled and swirled above the tenements and office blocks. The ones who perched on chimneys and slated roofs were the lighthouse masters of the city. Keeping an ever-watchful eye.

From MacRae's bench at the Lord Roberts Monument, he had a panoramic view of the city with crystal clear visibility. Out past Kelvingrove Art Gallery and Museum, and Glasgow University, their rooftops thick with frost. Beyond the old Yorkhill Hospital he could see as far afield as Glennifer Braes on the outskirts of Paisley. And farther west, along the River Clyde, he could even make out the outline of Dumbarton Rock.

It was two in the afternoon, and it seemed that the sun had barely risen. Its light weak behind the grey clouds covering the city. Snow wasn't far off.

MacRae had spent many idle hours on that bench, constructing plot lines and thinking up ways to kill people. He had killed so many people on the page over the years, it was automatic now. Darkness, death, and murder had been at the forefront of his mind for so long. Yet all it took to penetrate MacRae's gloomy, grieving heart that day was the sound of a little child's laughter as they frolicked on the freezing grass far below his elevated position. MacRae wiped his tears away with a gloved hand, rising from the bench and craning his neck to see the child, shielded from the cold in their thermal snowsuit. MacRae remembered playing with his daughter Liz at that same spot. It reminded him that, much as it pained him to kill off Roxburgh, he had done it for his daughter Liz. Soon, everyone would understand that.

In the short term, there would be hell to pay. Not least from his publisher Hathaway. Then there was his editor Seth Knox, who had been reading MacRae's final draft since dawn.

MacRae looked down at his phone screen as it lit up yet again.

SETH KNOX CALLING.

He had now called nine times in the last hour alone.

Had MacRae really been sitting there in the freezing cold that long? Although now he thought of it, he hadn't really been aware of his arse cheeks for quite some time.

On the evidence of his phone call history, Seth had recently become the second person in the world after MacRae to find out he was killing off DCI Roxburgh. And if Seth knew that Roxburgh was dead, then it wouldn't be long before Seth made arrangements to see him. Such drastic changes to an editor/client relationship demand at least a home visit or some kind of personal intervention. It would be within twenty-four hours at the latest.

Seth might even just drive north through the night. He could already be closing in on Birmingham if traffic had been kind.

There was no way of putting it off any longer.

MacRae scrolled through the "Favourites" in his phone.

They weren't so much "Favourites" as "Necessaries". A doctor he didn't call often enough. A dentist he called far too much. Then, of course, there was his ex-wife, Claire.

He only called her when he absolutely had to. And this was one of those times.

Except Claire wasn't answering. Whether she had taken one look at his caller ID and looked the other way, or was genuinely unavailable, was unknown to MacRae.

Either way, the only option left to him was voicemail. Which he hated. It was like having a conversation with a wall.

'Claire, I need you to listen very carefully. I don't have much time to explain. And before you sigh and wonder if I've been drinking, I have not been drinking. Okay? I promise. I know this probably sounds strange. And the rest of what I have to say will sound strange too...I've found something out. About another writer.' He paused. 'The sort of thing you would kill to keep secret.'

CHAPTER TWO

MacRae warmed his hands by the fire, still smouldering after his time out in the cold. The study was lined with towering bookcases rammed with foreign editions of his Roxburgh books. A monument to his own success.

He stood over his desk, surveying a large paperback novel that had no cover art on it. It was an advance proof copy of a forthcoming title.

The Shortlist by AD Sullivan.

Popular authors – especially bestsellers like MacRae – were deluged with mail bags full of proof copies every week. They all came with letters from the publisher showering MacRae with flattery in the hope that his giving a pithy quote for the book would lend it credibility.

The marketing blurb in front of MacRae proclaimed the book 'This year's most exciting thriller'.

Neither MacRae – nor anyone else – had ever heard of AD Sullivan. But it was being published by Hathaway, and MacRae had felt pressure to have something to say about it

– however faint the praise might be. He did actually like the sound of it. The blurb called it one of the most ingenious whodunits since *And Then There Were None* and *Murder on the Orient Express.*

High praise. But surely hyperbole, thought MacRae, comparing it to not one, but two, of the greatest murder mysteries of all time.

The set-up was perhaps unoriginal, but had just enough of a twist to prevent him throwing the book away: a group of bestselling crime writers who have been shortlisted for a prestigious prize, gather at a remote country mansion for a crime-writing festival in the north of Scotland. But they are left stranded by a blizzard. Over the course of a weekend, the shortlisted writers find themselves being killed one by one, in the same way that characters are killed in their books.

When it came to proofs, MacRae could be in possession of a book for weeks before he even attempted the first page. From there, he would normally toss it aside after the first few paragraphs. He could barely read anything in his genre anymore. The mechanics of everything the author was doing seemed so transparent to him. All of those subtle clues that were so well hidden to everyone else, honked like a ship's foghorn to him. Outside of non-fiction, reading for pleasure had been stolen from him years ago.

But this thriller was different.

A week earlier, when he had taken the book out of the cardboard envelope and read the blurb, he knew he had to start reading straight away.

After page one, he kept turning the pages.

Then chapter two.

And on. And on. And on...

He churned through it.

Four breathless hours later, MacRae had turned the final page at two in the morning. It was indeed one of the most ingenious solutions to a whodunit that he had ever read.

He was aghast. Horrified. And trembling with anger.

When it was over, MacRae knew that he would never be the same again. And not in a good way. He didn't eat for two days. Couldn't sleep.

His own writing ground to a halt. He felt sick. A knot in his stomach twisting and tightening, that had remained there ever since.

And there was only one way of getting rid of it.

CHAPTER THREE

UNABLE TO AVOID his editor any longer into the evening, MacRae called Seth back, who picked up before the first ring had even finished.

Seth's voice was urgent and reeked of expensive English public schooling, followed by the inevitable Oxford masters in English literature. When people first met him, they found his model good looks, deep intelligence, and boundless enthusiasm for literature either an impressive or nauseating combination. It seemed unfair that one man under thirty-five could have so much going for him. He even *sounded* handsome. His writing and emails were handsome.

MacRae's first impression of him was *lucky bastard*.

Meanwhile, MacRae had been left pockmarked and scarred after a frightful and persistent bout of teenage acne. The scars had since combined with deep wrinkles that left his face looking like the surface of the moon. He had bushy eyebrows that required regular gardening, along with ear and nose hair that was growing at an alarming rate. He looked weathered. Lived a hard life but had plenty to show for it.

Seth's first words to MacRae were simple and to the point. 'You killed him!' he exclaimed, still in disbelief that the whole situation wasn't a prank.

MacRae put Seth on speaker then poured himself a stiff Lagavulin from a bottle that had arrived a few days ago in the post. The sender was anonymous, other than describing themselves via a Post-it note on the bottle as "Your Number One Fan".

MacRae swirled the whisky in the glass as he spoke. 'I'm afraid I did.'

'But William...it's...it's DCI Bob Roxburgh! You can't just kill him.'

'In fairness, in twenty-four books, poor old Roxburgh's been shot, stabbed, burned, suffocated, and driven off a cliff. I don't think he could say that it's not been coming.'

'In your draft two weeks ago, Roxburgh survived a bullet wound to the shoulder. What happened? What changed?'

'What does it matter?' said MacRae with resignation. 'I'm sure someone at Hathaway will find a way to bring old Bob back from the dead once I've popped my clogs.'

Seth wheezed, 'That would be quite a task considering he's been decapitated by a train after being tied to a railway line!'

'I'm writing according to your own rules: no cliffhangers at the end.'

Seth scoffed. 'Yes, congratulations. Now what am I supposed to do?'

'Publish it!'

'And after that? I don't understand. Is this your way of retiring?'

'Heavens no. I've got a few more mysteries left in me yet.'

Seth paused.

MacRae could hear the dry gulp from his end. Nerves. Tension.

'I don't know how delicately I can ask this...there have been rumours. From Charlie.'

MacRae waited. 'Is there a question there, Seth?'

'Okay, I'll just say it. Apparently, Charlie has been going around town telling anyone who will listen that you're leaving Hathaway. That you're going to self-publish instead to keep more of your royalties. I've got people upstairs telling me that there's no way William MacRae would ever do that. Now I'm reading this manuscript, and I'm not so sure anymore.'

MacRae replied, 'You and I both know that Hathaway will hire some other writer to keep the series going.'

'But–'

'He's dead. Yes, I know. That hasn't stopped Hathaway in the past. They'll just start some "Roxburgh – The Early Years" prequel instead to get around it. Then they'll beat the horse long after it's dead like ITV did with *Inspector Morse* and *Lewis* and *Endeavour*.'

Seth tried not to make it sound like a threat. 'She's going to call you about this.'

MacRae paused. 'You told her?'

'Of course I bloody did! I had to. You can't turn in a final draft like this and expect me to go to print without telling my CEO of a major change to a major series! Hathaway's share price dropped five per cent the one year you failed to deliver a book to them. What do you think's going to happen when investors find out the series that's bringing in millions in sales every year is ending?'

MacRae sniffed. 'They've still got twenty-four other books to flog. I'm sure no one on Hathaway's board will be queuing at a food bank anytime soon.'

'You know that nothing sells the old books like a new one. This time next year, backlist sales will be half what they are now. And in five years?'

'That's not going to be my problem any longer. I'm a writer not an accountant.'

'You have no idea what she's talking about doing, William.'

MacRae brushed it off. 'Oh, please. Zoe Hathaway is a spoiled trust fund brat who has no business helming a major publisher. She's an embarrassment to her father's legacy.' He stabbed a finger on the cover of *The Shortlist*. 'And if she publishes this AD Sullivan book, she'll regret it immensely. You'll regret it too.'

'What is that supposed to mean?'

'Oh no, Seth, dear boy. We don't have to play that game, do we? We're too intelligent for the feigned ignorance.'

'I honestly don't know what you're talking about.'

'I heard a rumour that you're the editor of that book.'

Seth said nothing for what, in his head, seemed like a full minute, but in reality was closer to three seconds. 'Where did you hear that?'

'There's not very much in this industry I can't find out. Not with an agent like Charlie Whelan.'

Seth snorted. 'Old Wheelin' and Dealin' Charlie strikes again. You know, I really will dance on that bastard's grave when he finally dies from the massive coronary he's long overdue.'

'Don't deflect.'

'Okay, fine. I edited the book. What's this all about, William?'

'I need to know who the author is.'

'You know their name.'

'Not their pen name. I want their real name.'

'Hang on,' Seth replied. 'You've got to understand, William. I've never even spoken to them on the phone.'

'What are you talking about? How is that possible?'

'Well, take us. Until today, when was the last time we spoke on the phone? Did we even talk before *A Wee Grave* came out?'

'No,' MacRae replied, remembering now. 'It was all email.'

'Which I can tell you is not atypical these days. Most writers have never met their editors: publisher staff all live in London. I don't even know if AD Sullivan is a man or a woman. The manuscript was sent to me by Max Hathaway directly, shortly before he died. He told me that he had a standalone thriller from one of the trade's biggest properties, but that they were going to remain anonymous. It was even a condition of signing them that Hathaway wouldn't know their real identity until publication. All I knew was that it was someone who wanted out of their existing contract. Someone big. Someone with clout. Someone who wanted more money, and Hathaway was willing to pay it.'

'A name, Seth. I need a name!'

'I can't do that, William. I'm sorry. I just don't know! What I do know is that Sullivan is appearing at the Lochinver Book Festival this weekend.'

'I'm well aware.'

'Hathaway's been planning it for months. Why are you so keen to find out who they are?'

'I know a thing or two about AD Sullivan. And my lifetime achievement speech at the festival is the perfect place for me to tell the world about it. In a few days' time, Sullivan is going to go viral. And not in the good way that people use that word these days.'

Seth took a moment to compose himself. 'You're not thinking clearly, William. I don't know what all of this *Shortlist* stuff is about, but we need to talk about Roxburgh. I'm coming over.'

MacRae tossed his copy of *The Shortlist* aside, then turned his head slightly towards the window. 'Coming over?'

It was a curious phrase for someone supposedly in London.

'Yes, I'm getting in a taxi and I'm coming over.' He paused, waiting for MacRae to realise. 'I'm in Edinburgh.'

MacRae's eyes narrowed. What was he doing in Edinburgh? His editor came to Scotland during the final draft process and he was only telling him now?

'You told me a few days ago you couldn't make it up here to discuss the book.'

Seth said, 'I know. I'll explain when I come over. Just hang tight. We're going to figure this out. All of it.'

MacRae hung up the phone then swore, 'Shite.' He picked up the only photo he kept displayed on his desk. Him with his arm around his daughter Liz. It was the last photo of them together, taken when she was twenty-one. It was a rare moment catching her with a smile on her face. She looked reluctant, almost embarrassed, at appearing happy.

Just two weeks later, she was dead.

MacRae said to the photo, 'I hope you can forgive me, Liz. I'm doing this for you.'

THE PHONE that had made the 999 call would later be found in the cobbled gutter of Park Terrace Lane that backed onto MacRae's street. A pay-as-you-go phone bought a few days ago with cash. No fingerprints would be found on it. The caller long since disappeared into the bitter, sleety night.

Police cars pulled up outside MacRae's address, their flashing lights illuminating the ceiling of the study. The two constables first to the main door pressed the intercom with urgency, alternating between sharp calls of 'Police!', and thunderous side-fists on MacRae's front door.

More constables from the car behind made a dash to Park Gate to access the rear, but it wasn't required. The constable at the front door called them back.

The front door had been opened.

A man with blood on his face was flecked by the blue

lights outside. His face was ghostly white. Eyes wide but seeing nothing.

The cops fired a hundred questions at him. He heard them all, but listened to none of them.

A constable stepped forward and spoke with increasing volume and urgency. 'Sir...can you tell me your name?'

The man could barely talk.

The constable looked beyond the man, into the vast hallway where there was a chef's knife in a small pool of blood on the floor. The blood crept out slowly across the black and white tiles, like Death itself sneaking away from the scene.

'Can you tell me your name?' the constable repeated.

The man's eyes scoured the floor in confusion. 'Seth. My name's Seth Knox.'

The constable approached slowly, holding a hand out defensively. He didn't know yet if he was talking to a victim or a murderer. 'Okay, Seth, is there anyone else in the house?'

Seth looked towards the stairs, then up to the second floor. He pointed vacantly, eyes haunted. 'Up...upstairs,' he croaked. 'He's dead. William's dead.'

Terrified at the looks he was getting, he croaked, 'I didn't do it.'

CHAPTER FOUR

DCI JOHN LOMOND sat in the dentist's waiting room, clutching his jaw. Everyone else was on their phone, but all Lomond could concentrate on was the pain that had been building up in his gums in the past week.

He was already in a rotten mood because the appointment for routine fillings had meant travelling back a second time in as many weeks to his old dentist in Paisley. He still hadn't got around to changing to a dentist nearer his flat in Maryhill, now that his transfer to the Major Investigations Team in Govan had been finalised. Each time he thought he was done with Paisley, somehow the town kept dragging him back.

When Lomond's name was called, he made no attempt to raise a hand and call out affirmatively. He just trudged to the surgery room still holding his jaw, awaiting his dentist's inevitable round of small talk.

Lomond couldn't stand small talk. Didn't care to hear it. Didn't care to speak it. In his line of work, all talk mattered. Sometimes it was life or death. A little comment here or there by a witness or suspect could turn a case. Lomond had learned the hard way that when Dennis the dentist asked you a question, you smiled politely and told him everything was fine. Otherwise he would talk you into an early grave.

Before Dennis could move on from the current state of St Mirren Football Club to enquiring about Lomond's home life, Lomond decided to get ahead of it for once.

'Look, I know you're just doing your job. And all this chat is meant to put wimps at ease about being at the dentist, but I don't need it. I've got a shit-ton of fillings to get done the-day, and it's going to hurt. So let's crack on.'

In the chair, Lomond kept catching sight of the reflection of his own mouth in Dennis's protective visor. He kept telling himself not to look, but it was either his own bloody gums or a very weird thing in Dennis's eye.

Lomond opted for the bloody gums in the end. He was horrified at the amount of hardware that had been scaffolded around his mouth. Mostly because he couldn't feel any of it and hadn't noticed any of it being attached, such was the strength of the numbing injection in his gums. There was a bar that had been clamped onto his gum with a wing nut, like a prop for a supporting wall in a crumbling house.

Then, suddenly, Dennis wheeled himself backwards on his stool and told Lomond he could sit up.

It was only thirty minutes into a ninety-minute appointment. Lomond had a feeling that whatever Dennis had to tell him was either very good, or very bad.

'Okay, John,' Dennis sighed dismally, and handed him

a small mirror. 'If you just hold that there for me. Do you see that big hole there?'

Lomond shrugged as he searched around the bloody crime scene of his own mouth with half-averted eyes.

'That's where your filling is meant to go,' Dennis explained. 'But the hole's much deeper than we originally thought.'

We? thought Lomond. *Now that something has gone wrong, suddenly this is a collaborative fuck-up?*

'The problem is,' said Dennis, 'any filling that goes into a hole that deep has a good chance of pressing on the nerve.'

With his jaw totally numb, Lomond took two attempts at saying, 'What are we looking at?' A long bit of drool spilled out of his mouth, which he mopped up with the back of his hand.

'We don't have any options other than root canal.'

Lomond let his head fall back. 'Come on, there must be something.'

'Well, there's also root canal. And root canal again. Though personally, I would recommend going with root canal.'

'All right, all right, I get it,' Lomond said. Although 'said' is putting it charitably. What came out was little more than a string of consonants. 'When can you book me in?'

Dennis put his visor back on. 'Oh, we have to do it all now.'

'Now? I have to be back at work soon. Is there time?'

'I'll push back my next appointment.'

'No,' Lomond grunted. 'My concern isn't *your* time-keeping. It's the important police work my team need me for in half an hour.'

'John, I've already drilled into your teeth to recce the depth of fillings needed. I can't patch you up and send you out now with nerve endings exposed. We've got to do this now.' He spun around on his stool and took a big needle that the technician had been preparing in the background. The needle looked like something you would sedate a horse with.

'Fine,' Lomond relented with a shake of his head. 'Let's get it over with. But will I be able to talk after this?'

Dennis bobbed his head from side to side in uncertainty. 'You'll be able to talk. Whether anyone will be able to understand you is a different matter. I'm sure your colleagues will be sympathetic to your plight.'

It was proof, if Lomond needed it, that Dennis had no idea what sort of people he worked with in Police Scotland.

———

LOMOND EMERGED AN HOUR LATER, grimacing and light-headed when the freezing air hit him outside. His six-foot-three frame lumbered against a stiff head wind. One of the issues with being so tall that you're known as – among others – Big Yin and Lurch, is that your height turns you into an excellent windsail.

None of the seasons were generally very kind to him. In summer, he had to worry about sunburn on his scalp because of his completely shaved head. Then in winter, making sure you always had a hat with you. He didn't really like shaving his head, but it had turned into a weekly ritual since he discovered his hair thinning on top in his early thirties. There was something about removing himself from the whole charade of "going for a haircut". Back when he still had hair, it was always overly styled when fresh out of the barbers, but the tiniest whiff of wind would turn it into utter chaos.

Then there was a honeymoon period of about five days when his hair was just how he wanted it, before day six when it started refusing to do whatever he asked of it.

Shaving his head removed the whole bloody annoy-ance. He knew that his facial features were a little too large for his face. Which a shaved head accentuated. But it wasn't like he cared what anyone thought of him – another reason why he had now ticked over to about a stone over-weight for his height. If he hadn't detested the sport, he would have made a great rugby player. Though if he kept going the way he was going, he would soon make a really good darts player.

He wasn't happy about his weight gain, and hid it well by wearing a 44-inch chest suit jacket that he left hanging open, rather than the slim-cut 42 he had been rocking with a button fastened. He kept waiting to feel better. But it never came.

Grief has a habit of doing that to you.

HE COULD ALREADY FEEL the first waves of pain working him over, like a boxer softening up an opponent with body shots. The real pain hadn't started yet, but Lomond knew that it was in the mail, and he was going to be in for a terrible ride in a few hours' time. Right when he needed to be in full control of his faculties.

He called Ross on his mobile.

'DS McNair,' came the reply.

'Ross, it's John. Sorry I'm late, I didn't get a chance to call.'

There was a long pause at the other end. Long enough for Lomond to ask, 'Are you there?'

Ross couldn't understand a word he had said. He checked the caller ID, mystified. 'John, is that you?'

Lomond hung up with a huff and resorted to a text instead. He hated texting members of his team. They insisted on using acronyms he didn't understand, and inserting stupid emojis that were so tiny it was impossible to tell what emotion they were actually trying to convey.

'Was at dentist. Can't talk properly (evidently). On my way. Don't start without me.'

CHAPTER FIVE

Donna opened the passenger door to DS Ross McNair's unmarked police car. An unremarkable-in-every-way Skoda that drew no attention.

Donna shuddered as she got out of the cold and handed Ross a weak takeaway cup of tea from Greggs. She told him, 'Don't get your hopes up about that, by the way. I'm sure I saw ice forming on it during the walk back.'

'I'm not surprised,' said Ross, the timbre of his voice suggesting he was gearing up for a quip he was excited about delivering. 'It feels like you left during the last Ice Age. What kept you?'

Donna brandished her sausage roll – still in the wrapping – like she might use it as a weapon. 'Do you want to drink that or wear it?'

Ross turned to face the windscreen again. 'That's what I love about being police. The respect and collegiate atmosphere between colleagues.' He showed Donna the message from Lomond on his phone.

'His texts are so weird,' she said, unwrapping her sausage roll. The pastry might have been chilled by icy winds but the filling inside was still Vesuvius-like. She hung her mouth open and flapped a hand impotently at her mouth.

'I know,' replied Ross, oblivious to Donna's distress. His voice was distant, not taking his eyes from a narrow shopfront across the road.

Three men all in tracksuits were ferrying in cardboard boxes from a flash Mercedes saloon into a rather down-market ice cream parlour. They were all marked as "G1 Gelato" in a poor imitation of *The Godfather* font. The men carrying the boxes looked distinctly un-Italian. The car's suspension had been dropped so that the bodywork was a matter of inches off the ground. Bass thumped so heavily from the car speakers it was a wonder the car hadn't burrowed a hole in the tarmac.

Ross complained, 'Look at the state of this. The middle of winter and you'd think there was a heatwave. They watch a few seasons of *Breaking Bad* and suddenly everyone from Shawlands to Shanghai reckons they can launder money. What kind of numpties do they think we are?'

Donna pulled the lever under her seat to push it back, far more relaxed than Ross. 'The kind to sit in a freezing car all night without turning the heating on.'

'I've told you already, I can't keep the headlights off if I turn on the ignition for the heating.'

'It's half-past five on Great Western Road and it's dark, Ross. There are headlights everywhere.'

'I don't care. We're doing this—'

Donna said, as if she had heard it a million times before, 'By the book. Yes, I know. We've been staking this place out for a fortnight now waiting for their boss to show up. We know this is Frank Gormley's operation. Why don't we just send the gaffer up to Barlinnie to–'

'To what? Beat it out of Glasgow's most notorious gangster? We're too late. Gormley will be out this time next week.'

'I can't believe he's actually getting out for helping us with the Sandman case.'

Ross sniffed. 'Gormley's got some powerful friends in Holyrood. In any case, John gave Gormley his word. And he never breaks his word. Doesn't matter if you're Frank Gormley or the Chief Sup.'

Donna lifted both hands in frustration. 'We *know* that it's Gormley's money being laundered over there.'

'We know it. But we can't prove it. Not yet.'

'And how are we going to do that? We don't have a phone number for anyone, or a single lead on anyone who can point to Gormley. You know the definition of madness is doing the same thing over and over again and expecting different results.'

'I am aware of that, Donna.'

'You said so yourself. We've got a week before Gormley is released. Once he's out, you know we'll probably never get him locked up again. We got lucky once. We won't get lucky twice. Not with him.'

'Tell me something I don't know, Donna.'

She implored him, 'Then let's mix it up. Send me in.'

'What are you going to do differently?'

'Get a result, for starters.'

Ross shook his head.

Donna kept on. 'Ross, the last time you went in to the shop, the guy joked about giving you a loyalty card you've been in so often. You don't think they're getting suspicious about a guy constantly going in for ice cream cones in the middle of winter?'

Ross thought for a few seconds. 'What about sending John in once he gets here?'

'You want to send a chief inspector undercover into an ice cream shop?'

'Ice cream might help with the pain. It's a good cover. And it sounds like he'll be believable.'

'If anyone at HQ hears about that we'll be a laughing stock. And if the Chief Sup gets wind, we'll be sent out to fucking Airdrie or Hamilton or something, picking up bams for shoplifting steaks from Tesco.'

Ross gave her a funny look. 'Shoplifting steaks?'

'They tag those things for a reason. They're six quid a pop, and you can easily stuff a handful of them up your jacket.'

'Are you sure this is from police experience or should I be taking you in to Mill Street for some questions?'

Undeterred, Donna said, 'Look, the gaffer can't currently speak. So unless he's got one of those Stephen Hawking voice computers, I'm our best bet.'

Ross shook his head again, watching the young Chinese owner of the Mercedes close the boot while talking loudly into a phone. 'Tragic to do that to such a beautiful car. Got all the money and no taste.'

'What's wrong with it?' asked Donna.

'That's one of the most elegant saloon cars in the world,

and he's kitted it out like he's going on the World Rally tour.'

Donna pushed out her bottom lip. 'I think it looks pretty cool.'

'Of course you do. You're from Paisley.'

Much of their stakeout time had passed like this. A gentle ribbing was the only sensible way to pass the time in such close proximity. Especially two colleagues who were still getting to know each other.

The Sandman case had been five months ago now. After a period of favourable press and a little grace from the higher-ups at Dalmarnock, it was now very much time for the Major Investigations Team to get back to winning ways. And they hadn't made a significant arrest for six weeks now.

Lacking a headline-grabbing and sensational serial killer on the loose, DCI Lomond had steered the team towards a joint investigation with the Specialist Crime Division into gangland activity that had been flourishing across the city. Drug deals were smaller these days, but there were far more of them. That meant a lot of money that needed laundering through seemingly legitimate businesses. Like G1 Gelato.

During their investigation, Ross and Donna had observed steady streams of deliveries arriving, despite the tubs in the shop having barely been scooped in months. There were all sorts of red flags about the business. It had two high schools nearby, yet the shop never opened at lunchtimes when it could have been making a killing. It had few and lousy reviews online for its deliveries, which often never arrived. That suggested a lot of orders being rung through tills that didn't exist. That missing cash could then be replaced by the illegally acquired kind, and if anyone came asking, G1 Gelato's directors could point to their brisk pace of trade. Trade that no one was ever around to see.

It was a textbook money laundering business. And Ross and Donna badly wanted to make an arrest soon.

Their involvement in the Sandman case had been significant. DCI Lomond couldn't have cracked the case without them, but it was still ultimately his historical case. Ross and Donna wanted to make their mark.

Noticing Ross eyeing up her sausage roll, Donna said, 'Are you really having the gaffer over for dinner tonight?'

'Who told you?'

'He did. Said something about your bird's cooking being so minging that he should have something to eat beforehand. He's over at University Café filling his face. Are you really so ambitious that your idea of a cosy Wednesday night in is dinner with your boss?'

'It was Isla's idea. My idea of a cosy night in is the little fella asleep in his cot by half seven, leaving me free to watch the game on Sky. Instead, I need to sit there for hours with my arse clenched, waiting for something embarrassing to spring up. I only went along with it because the boss seemed so up for it.'

Donna stared out the windscreen for a moment. 'Fuck it. I'm doing this.' She started taking off her insulated jacket, revealing a sporty hoodie underneath that she had put on in an attempt to dress down. Then she held out her hand. 'I need twenty quid for petty cash.'

'What for?' asked Ross.

'Forget it,' she said. 'I'll just keep the receipt.' She reached out for the door handle.

'What are you doing?' asked Ross, his voice loaded with tension.

'What I should have done hours ago. I'll be back in five.'

'Wait!' Ross lunged across to try and grab her, but he missed.

She got out and crossed the street, nonchalantly holding out a hand to pause the flow of traffic in either lane. It wasn't a request and the drivers knew it. She then went into the newsagent three shops down from the ice cream shop, emerging a minute later with a blue plastic bag.

'What is she doing?' Ross wondered aloud. Not wanting to cause a scene by chasing after her, he was left gesticulating and twitching in the driver's seat.

As Donna approached the ice cream shop, Ross took out his phone. There was nothing else for it.

A FIVE-MINUTE WALK and a ten-minute drive away because of the static rush-hour traffic, DCI Lomond was sitting in the University Café on Byres Road, tucking into a bowl of peas and vinegar. Now that the numbing agent was wearing off, he suffered only minor dribbles. Nothing that couldn't be quickly mopped up with a napkin.

The waitress remarked to Lomond, 'This sergeant of yours you're having dinner with. Is the wife's cooking really that bad?'

'They're not married,' Lomond slurred, his bottom lip stubbornly static as he tried to talk. 'But apparently so. He told me he was worried that if I came I wouldn't get fed properly. I'm not sure I could get anything else down me than peas and vinegar to keep me going. It's not half bad!'

The peas and vinegar were the first decent thing to happen to him all day. And it had taken until dinnertime to get to it.

He was right to savour the dish because things were about to get a lot worse.

It all started with a text from Ross.

'*You better get over here, boss. Donna's gone off the reservation.*'

'Why am I not surprised,' Lomond muttered to himself. He swiped at his bowl for a final spoonful of peas before rushing to the door, wincing from the pain in his gums.

CHAPTER SIX

THE THREE MEN in tracksuits who had carried in the cardboard boxes were hanging out behind the counter, huddled around one of their phones.

Donna couldn't see what they were watching when she entered the shop. She didn't need to. The otherwise silent shop was punctuated with the groans of pornography.

The moment one of them noticed Donna, he shut the phone off.

Without missing a beat, Donna barked at them, 'What the fuck is this? A wankers convention? Wankers Anonymous? The Tiny Pecker Shed?'

The men exchanged baffled looks, each hoping that one of them knew who she was.

'You could at least look busy,' Donna went on. She paused, looking up at the security camera in the corner of the ceiling. 'Are you taking the piss?'

The one who fancied himself the leader swaggered

along the length of the walkway to behind the till to get closer to Donna. 'Is there something wrong?'

He had a vaguely Eastern European accent that Donna couldn't place. Which was consistent with what they had seen of the place so far. It had been like a United Nations of organised crime, with new faces every other day.

'Something wrong?' She lifted the counter top and joined the three men behind the till. She pointed at the camera above them, and spoke with a lowered voice. 'We're here to rinse Frank Gormley's money. Do you idiots even know who that is?'

They all looked at each other in confusion.

'We just work here,' said one of them. 'We don't ask questions.'

'Frank Gormley asks questions. And if he sees that camera recording he'll definitely have a question for you three.' Keeping her voice down, she snarled through gritted teeth, 'Like, why are you recording video evidence that the orders we're ringing through the tills here don't fucking exist. Are you fucking stupid or what?' She gestured with disgust at the camera. 'Switch it off and any others you've got. Christ. I miss working with professionals...' Seamlessly, she reached into the carrier bag from the newsagent, and tossed four new SIM cards onto the counter. She held her hand out. 'Now give me your old ones. We're gonna start changing these more often.'

The three men looked even more confused now. Expressions of '*shit, she must be important if she knows Frank*'. With barely a hundred IQ points between them all, nobody questioned her. It was something about the steeliness in her eyes. An unshakeable belief – deep down in her bones – that she belonged there and was part of their gang. It was the only way it would have worked.

And it did.

She looked the part, and she definitely sounded it. You could take the girl out of Paisley, but you can't take Paisley out of the girl.

The men each took out their phones, then handed over their SIM cards one by one.

As Donna picked them up, her voice returned to normal, as if nothing had happened. 'How's business?'

'Slow,' came the reply, while one of them unhooked the camera.

'Then make it look fast,' she replied, glancing in the direction of camera. 'No one's looking.' She turned and walked out with the bag of SIM cards. She couldn't help but smile to herself as she crossed the road again. 'Wankers.'

DCI Lomond met Ross and Donna in the car park of Kelvinbridge subway, right at the back near the children's play park. Once Ross had parked, Donna got out jubilantly, clutching the carrier bag.

'Three SIM cards,' she declared. She showed a tiny gap between her thumb and forefinger. 'I swear they were *this* close to thanking me.'

Lomond looked at her in disbelief. 'How did you manage that?' Before she could answer, he looked to Ross, who was emerging shellshocked from the car. 'How did she manage that?'

'Don't ask me,' Ross replied.

Donna said, 'If you do it with conviction, you can convince someone of almost anything.'

Lomond took control of the SIM cards as if he was holding precious jewels. 'This could be the break we needed.' He nodded his head swiftly. 'Get these away for examination. I think we'll call it a night.'

Donna turned towards the car.

'Excellent work, Donna,' said Lomond.

'Don't encourage her,' Ross added with a grin.

Lomond asked him, 'Get you at yours?'

'Sure thing.' Ross took a step closer to him. 'And did you...'

'Aye. I already ate.' Lomond leaned in, speaking quietly so Donna couldn't hear. 'You could be a little more encouraging, you know. A bit of banter is fine when you're the SO. Tell her she did well on the way back to Helen Street.'

Ross complained, 'She's still running off doing her own thing. She can't be led. And she definitely can't be controlled.'

'Maybe,' replied Lomond, stepping back to leave. 'But we can trust her.'

When Lomond was far enough away, Ross muttered to himself, 'Is that right?'

CHAPTER SEVEN

LOMOND ARRIVED at the McNair household, in a new-build estate in Cambuslang that could have been anywhere in the central belt. The houses were all aggressively close to one another so that the developers could maximise their profit in the land they had. Every house had a tiny square of garden at the front, and tiny windows looking out onto it. It was neither Ross nor his partner Isla's idea of a dream home, but it had quiet roads to safely raise a little boy who would likely want to ride a bike a lot, was close to a school that wasn't outright dangerous, and they got a good deal on the mortgage.

At twenty-eight years old, and settling in to his role of detective sergeant in a Major Investigations Team, Ross was coming to realise that your teens and early twenties were for dreaming, and your thirties were about practicalities. That might have sounded depressing to some people, but to Ross and Isla, there was comfort to be had in it. A sense of responsibility.

Lomond was clutching a bouquet of flowers for Isla. He had once seen a cop in a movie bring flowers for his colleague's wife at a dinner party, and he thought it right to do the same.

As he waited for someone to answer the door, he looked down at the flowers and realised he had left the price sticker on. He tried to peel it off in a oner, but it refused to come off in anything but thin strips. By the time Isla answered the door, he had only succeeded in removing some of the price, and half of the Tesco logo.

'Isla?' said Lomond, as if there was some doubt about her name. He thrust the flowers out to her.

Isla put a hand to her chest. 'Oh, John. You didn't have to do that.' She leaned in for a hug, which took Lomond by surprise. 'It's so nice to finally meet you,' she said, still embracing him.

When she let him go, Lomond's attention was drawn to a cacophonous wailing upstairs.

'He's teething,' Isla explained. She put her hands out to take his coat.

'Ah, wee soul.' Lomond shuffled out of his coat to settle into the small talk that he assumed would make up the entire evening. 'How old is the little fella now?'

'Eleven months and three weeks.' She glanced towards upstairs. 'Didn't Ross mention his first birthday party?'

Lomond panicked. He didn't want to land Ross in it when there was a good chance that he had simply failed to recollect Ross telling him. 'Oh, yes, of course. That's *next* week. That's grand.'

Isla showed him into the living room which was nothing short of chaotic. And that was after the pair of them had been running around frantically trying to clean the place up. It was like a toy shop and a launderette had exploded. The clean clothes and dirty clothes lay in overlapping piles that were indistinguishable from one another, and the floor was littered with various sizes and types of plastic balls and shapes that had become detached from whatever toy or game they were part of.

Steam billowed out of the kitchen, suggesting that dinner wasn't far off. Despite Ross's dire warnings of the food to come, it smelled great to Lomond. If Isla was out of her depth cooking anything beyond a Pot Noodle, as Ross had suggested, then she was oddly calm about it.

After a quick exchange of yells between kitchen and baby room, Isla checked with Lomond, 'Is beef wellington okay? And I've just rustled up some potato gratin and a green veg medley. And goose fat roasties, because,' she held a shrug for comic effect, 'well, they're fecking amazing and I'll take any excuse to cook them.'

Surprised, Lomond shook his head quickly, realising he'd gone briefly silent. 'Sorry, yes, of course. Sounds amazing.'

Beef wellington? Surely one of the hardest dinner party dishes even a professional could cook. Dauphinoise? *What the hell is going on*, thought Lomond.

Isla had a Northern Irish accent that was lilting when directed at Lomond, then coarse and direct when aimed at Ross – mostly over a disagreement about exactly how long it should take to change a nappy.

Ross came down the stairs, holding baby Lachlann with great care until he had navigated the final step on the steep stairs. 'Hi, John.' Ross puffed out his cheeks which were red from exertion. Dressed down in more casual clothes than what he wore to work, he looked truly like a dad with a one-year-old, rather than the "lad selling insurance on the street" vibe that his work clothes gave off. Ross always maintained that he knew what the right stuff to buy was, but he could only afford the cheap high-street version of anything. A trait that had led Donna to refer to Ross behind his back as "Discount Daniel Craig."

Little Lachlann pointed at Lomond. 'Dat.'

Ross explained to Lomond, 'Everything's "dat" right now.' He said to Lachlann,'Yeah, that's John. We work together. John's wondering why you're not in bed yet.'

Lomond made a show of checking his watch in an attempt to help things along. 'Wow, it's so late, little man. It's bedtime.'

Ross was amused at the change in Lomond's voice. And how natural he sounded doing it. Altered without going over the top. 'Yeah...it's also apparently time for a pee fountain all over your bed.' He craned his neck, seeking out Isla in the kitchen, who was tending to a tray of roast potatoes, gently steaming veg, and carving into a sizzling beef wellington that looked to have been cooked – and rested – to perfection.

'Ross,' Isla said in frustration, 'how many times? We have to move that changing table away from his bed.'

'I know, I know. I keep meaning to...'

Isla took everything off the heat, grabbed Lachlann out of Ross's hands and took him over to Lomond. 'John, would you mind?' she asked. 'Just for a minute until we get his bedsheet changed. It's so much faster with two of us doing it.'

Sensing what was about to happen, Lomond put up his hands. 'Oh, now, I'm not sure he'll want to...'

Ross started to protest.

Isla didn't notice the desperate looks between the two men. 'Oh, he'll be grand. Look, he loves you already.'

As Lomond took hold of him, Lachlann threw a hand up and let it drop with a splat on Lomond's face. 'Dat.'

'Yeah, I'll hold you while your mummy and daddy fix your bed.'

On the way upstairs, Ross was trying to explain something in hushed tones to Isla, who retorted much louder, 'What's the matter? He's perfectly happy with him...'

Intrigued by his new pal, Lachlann smiled. 'Dat,' he announced again, pointing a finger towards the stairs.

'That's right,' said Lomond. 'They've gone upstairs. They won't be long.' He bounced him gently in his arms in a pre-emptive move to ward off crying that he assumed would come.

Instead, Lachlann cooried in to Lomond, eager to fall asleep now that he had something warmer than his crib's mattress to fall asleep on.

Lomond relaxed a little, making quiet shush noises. 'It's bedtime, little man. It's bedtime.'

Lachlann's blinks were getting more protracted. The gentle white noise from the kitchen of the oven humming and food still boiling nudged him into sleep. His eyes shut completely.

Lomond kept rocking him lightly. It was only then that he realised the last time he had held a baby was when Eilidh was still alive. He had assumed the next time he would be holding a baby it would have been their own.

It was hard not to feel melancholy standing there, holding someone else's. Lomond hadn't felt so alone for a long time. But then he looked at how peaceful Lachlann looked. As if there was no other place he could want to be.

Lomond whispered, 'God, I would have loved to have someone like you.' Feeling himself choking up slightly, he added, softer still, 'I hope your mummy and daddy know how lucky they are.'

In Lachlann's room, Isla and Ross whipped the bed into shape with military efficiency.

She whispered to Ross, 'Why were you being so weird about John holding him?'

'Just do me a favour,' he replied. 'Don't talk too much about parenting or kids.'

'Why?'

'It's a long story.'

CHAPTER EIGHT

ONCE LACHLANN WAS DOWN for the night and dinner was served, talk inevitably turned to work.

Ross steeled himself. Since he heard Lomond pulling up outside, he had known that this moment would come.

'What do you do for work?' asked Lomond.

Isla seemed surprised. 'Hasn't Ross told you? He doesn't tell you much, does he? I do this.' She gestured at the food in front of them. 'In a slightly more stressful environment.'

'You're a chef?'

'Yeah. I'm head chef at Bandini's in town.'

'Oh, hey, I know that place. I ate there many moons ago with Eilidh.' He broke off, thinking aloud to himself. 'She wasn't long pregnant, actually. So that would have been nearly six years ago now. Have you worked there long?'

'When I get back after mat leave it'll be seven years.'

'So you've cooked for me already.'

'Yeah, that's so funny.' Isla smiled, but she had to force

it to appear. She had been tripped up by Lomond's mention of a pregnant partner. *He wasn't a dad, was he? Surely Ross would have mentioned that?*

The only one not enjoying the banter was Ross.

Worried that Isla's tense smile was his fault, Lomond quickly added, 'I didn't mean to sound so surprised before about you being a chef. This beef wellington is incredible.' His gaze lingered on Ross. The same way he did when turning the heat up on suspects in an interview. 'I had no idea what was in store for me tonight.'

Lomond had already worked out what Ross had been up to.

The sheepish look on Ross's face gave away that he knew Lomond had rumbled him.

He was saved by the bell, though. Or, more accurately, the baby, as Lachlann's plaintive cries from upstairs came through via the monitor on the sideboard.

'I'll get it,' said Ross, relieved to have an excuse to escape Lomond's glare.

There was a brief silence when Isla and Lomond were left alone. Just the light clinking of cutlery and a wine glass being refilled.

'How are you enjoying working with Ross, then?' asked Isla. She had a mischievous glint in her eye that normally would come out after a third glass of wine. But given how little alcohol had passed through her system in the last year, the glint had appeared before she had finished her first small glass.

'Ross? He's great,' replied Lomond. 'The Sandman case was obviously very hard, but he did great work there.'

'He talks about you all the time.' As soon as she said it,

she knew she probably shouldn't have. 'I'm sure he would be embarrassed if he heard me saying that, but I want you to know. He really respects you. John says this. John says that. You're like his guru.'

Lomond widened his eyes. 'That's...surprising. Though nice to hear.'

Now the wine really got the better of Isla, as she ventured, 'So is Eilidh your partner, or...' She trailed off, waiting for Lomond to elaborate.

He didn't know how to answer. Did she not know?

'I'm sorry?' he said.

'You said you ate at my restaurant with Eilidh.' Isla could tell she had landed on something sensitive and immediately regretted digging for more information. 'We don't have to...I mean, I didn't–'

'It's fine, Isla. I just...it's my fault, actually. I assumed Ross told you a while ago. Um. Eilidh died. Five years ago. We, uh...I lost her and the baby at the hospital right after delivery.'

Anytime he explained what had happened, he felt fine right up until he had to actually get the words out.

The exact moment was when he had to used the word "died".

'I'm so sorry, John,' said Isla, putting her cutlery down. She reached across the table to him between the candles that were providing most of the light in the room. 'I can't even imagine...'

'Such is life,' Lomond replied. 'A lot of people have it much harder. I've got a home. A job. I do a bit of good every now and then. That's enough to keep me going. I try not to think about it too much. Keep busy with work. But it's always there. In the background.'

Isla nodded. You could tell from her eyes that she was a good listener. 'As long as you've given yourself time to deal with it.'

Lomond kept chewing his food, but his mind was empty. It sounded so obvious, but he had never really thought about it before. He had always assumed he had "dealt" with it. Physically surviving the days and weeks and months after felt the same as dealing with his grief. Now he didn't know what to think.

He was glad that Ross had someone like Isla. It was important to have a good listener at home. For the times you really need one. It was inevitable in their line of work.

Isla said, 'I've said to Ross that the job would be hard enough even if you didn't have your own lives to worry about it. I couldn't carry that weight on my shoulders.'

'I always remember this time I was helping my dad on his allotment. We were digging up old soil and it was my job to take it away in a wheelbarrow. I kept complaining about how heavy it was. He told me that I was tricking my mind into thinking I couldn't handle more weight. I kept thinking about that phrase for years. When things would get hard, I would tell myself *more weight, John. You can take more.* That's what I do as a DCI. I have to shoulder the burden of a murder scene. And when it's over, I have to be ready for more.'

'I don't know how you do it,' Isla said. 'I see it in Ross sometimes. He tries to act tough. Talks a good game, you know. But I can tell it gets to him. I just hope it doesn't change him. I don't want Lachlann's daddy to talk about the world like it's full of bad people. Even if I know that sometimes it is. Is that wrong?'

Lomond shook his head. 'A parent's job is to reassure. Arm your child with the tools and knowledge to make it in the world. Not to rob them of hope. That's what keeps me going. A smarter man than me once said that the world is a good place, and worth fighting for. I know the second part is true. I'm not so sure about the first.'

A noise from the monitor distracted them both. The sound of Ross gently saying, 'Dada. Dada.'

Then immediately followed by Lachlann saying, 'Mama. Mama.'

Ross kept saying, 'Dada.'

Isla and Lomond exchanged a quiet laugh. Lomond found it endearing – how much Ross cared about Lachlann saying his name as well as his mum's.

When Ross returned, he could tell that the air had changed in the room somehow. He tilted his head in Isla's direction, as if to say, *what's been going on?*

He was scared to ask but felt he had to. 'Everything all right?'

'Yeah, fine,' said Lomond, taking out his ringing phone before it got too loud. 'Excuse me,' he said, heading for the kitchen.

Isla and Ross fell quiet while he took the call, conferring in whispers at the dining table.

'Is he alright?' asked Isla.

'Yeah, fine. Just wanted a cuddle, I think.'

Isla nodded in Lomond's direction. 'You never told me about his wife and baby.'

Ross sighed. 'Oh, for...how did *that* come up?'

'Maybe if you actually told me anything about the guy–'

'I didn't think it was my place to say. I thought it should be a private thing.'

Isla pursed her lips. It was some special guy 'code' thing. She got it. She couldn't be bothered pressing him on it further.

'So what do you think?' Ross asked.

'About John?'

'Of course John.'

She pondered her answer. 'The way he looks at you when you're holding Lachlann. He has this whole tough exterior going on, but you can see it just melt away sometimes.' She paused to consider her wording carefully. 'I think he's someone who thinks he has to live in hell so that no one else has to.'

Ross nodded slowly. Then he straightened his back when he saw Lomond returning.

'Isla, I'm really sorry.' Lomond waited for her to assume the inevitable.

'Just you, or do both of you need to go in?' she asked.

'It's both,' Lomond replied, glancing at Ross. 'It's a bit of a big one.'

Isla took some plates to the kitchen. 'I'll pop the kettle on. You'll need a hot drink if you're standing around outside.'

Ross mouthed 'thank you' to her, then asked Lomond, 'What's happened?'

He said, 'Uniform just found William MacRae dead at his home with a knife wound in his chest.'

Ross pushed his bottom lip out and turned his head slightly. 'As in...'

'*The* William MacRae, yes. And if we're hearing about this now, then the press are probably getting the call as we speak. So we'd better make a move before it turns into a circus.'

While the pair got their coats on in the hall, Lomond whispered so that he didn't wake Lachlann. 'I'm really sorry, Isla, we can't wait for drinks. Thanks for a lovely dinner. Maybe an evening soon we'll finish it.'

'You're welcome,' she replied. 'It was lovely to finally meet you.' While Ross nipped upstairs to give Lachlann a kiss, Isla reached out to Lomond. 'Don't be so hard on yourself. Take some time to yourself. Get out to the countryside for a while.'

Lomond nodded. 'That's a good idea,' he said.

She smiled. 'You've already dismissed it in your head, haven't you.'

'No, really,' he lied. 'I'll do my best.'

'You should. Because you know that thing you said about the world being a good place and worth fighting for. The first part is true as well, John.' Her eyes narrowed slightly. 'But I can tell that you can't quite see it yet.'

Seeing Ross coming back down the stairs, Lomond told her, 'I'm trying, Isla. I'm trying every day.'

CHAPTER NINE

It may have been one of the grandest streets in Glasgow, but there was nothing grand about what was taking place on Park Terrace when DCI John Lomond and DS Ross McNair arrived.

Police patrol car lights had been illuminating the cream stucco buildings for an hour since William MacRae's body had been discovered. The lights were visible as far down the hill as where Argyle Street met the bowling green and tennis courts at Kelvin Way. They spoke of something ominous and serious that had taken place on the otherwise quiet, leafy street at the top of the hill, overlooking an uninhabited Kelvingrove Park.

A white truck carrying the vague title of 'EVENTS UNIT' emblazoned on the side was parked across from MacRae's address. Next to it was a smaller white vehicle that said 'SCIENTIFIC SERVICES DEPARTMENT' on the side.

Noting their presence, Lomond said to Ross, 'Moira McTaggart's here already, I see.'

Ross sighed. 'Moira Dreich. God help us.'

'She's not that bad,' Lomond countered.

'Compared to what? A fire at an orphanage?'

Lomond pursed his lips. 'Now, now,' he said, stifling laughter, 'she's very talented at what she does. In a few more years, Ross, you'll learn that mediocrity has a habit of rising to the top in Police Scotland. If you don't believe me, just look at the last three chief constables. Moira might not sound that enthusiastic or crack a smile much—'

Ross gave him a look. 'Much?'

Lomond cleared his throat in a way that Ross recognised. It meant that he was about to make a more serious point. 'Moira's done her job at an elite level for nearly twenty years. She's spent a career in blood splatters and human remains – even of children, as you well know. Let's not make fun of her in the process. I don't know her well, but I know that she's not had much of a life outside of work. To young polis like you and the others, that might seem odd. But we rarely choose to be lonely in this life, Ross. It can happen to any of us at any time. Remember that, eh.'

Stung by the fact that his ribbing of Moira might have also inadvertently reflected on Lomond's current life status of all-work-all-the-time, Ross nodded in acquiescence.

Only a handful of press had made it there. A constable maintained a tape line to keep them back, but it didn't stop them shouting their questions.

Colin Mowatt of the *Glasgow Express* was his usual obnoxious self – oblivious to the human tragedy two floors up. 'DCI Lomond, is it true that there's a message carved into the body?'

Ross monitored his boss's pace, ready to intervene if he slowed down.

'Tell me to keep moving, Ross,' said Lomond, concentrating hard to keep from meeting Mowatt's eyes. If he locked eyes with the little weasel, he would end up having words – the last thing the investigation needed on night one when there were cameras around.

Ross said, 'Keep moving, sir.'

Detective Inspector Willie Sneddon met them on the front steps of MacRae's building, and handed them protective covers for their shoes. Willie said quietly, 'She's still working on the body. Says she needs another ten minutes.'

'Plenty of time to get us up to speed, Willie,' said Lomond.

Ross noted that Lomond kept his hands in his pockets, even though he had put on white nitrile gloves. A habit he had picked up over the years from the older guys. Made it easier to resist the urge to touch things at the crime scene.

The entrance opened out to a wide stairwell that was lined with paintings of various Scottish locations. What drew the eye, though, was a forensic scene examiner in a white suit, carefully taking photos from various angles of a knife on the floor lying in a pool of blood.

While Lomond took in the grand surroundings, getting a feel for the crime scene, Ross swaggered over to the examiner and flashed his badge. 'DS Ross McNair. I'm with DCI Lomond's MIT from Helen Street.' He paused, expecting the examiner to be impressed.

'Oh, aye,' he replied, continuing to take photos. He

didn't appreciate Ross's "I'm-with-the-band" attitude. 'Moira's upstairs. She'll talk you through.'

Ross flipped his badge shut. 'Cheers.'

Lomond strode past the examiner, polite but not overly breezy. 'How's it going, Pat?' he asked quietly. Lomond didn't like officers shouting across rooms or being overly boisterous. Not at murder scenes. Some of the old boys still did it, but it was becoming outdated behaviour. The way Lomond saw it, it was about respect for the dead. Everyone there knew that you were used to being around dead bodies and that it didn't faze you. That didn't mean you had to crack jokes and fool around to prove it.

The examiner perked up when he saw Lomond. 'Not bad, John,' he said, then gave Ross a withering look. 'I was just telling DS McNair that Moira's upstairs.' He added cagily, 'I'd maybe give her another five minutes. Unless you're feeling brave.'

Lomond grinned at him. 'Was born brave.'

As the three men climbed the stairs, Lomond called to Ross, who was striding ahead. 'DS McNair?'

Ross stopped and turned around. He knew straight away from Lomond's face that he was about to get a bollocking.

'The crime campus at Gartcosh might be sprawling on the outside, but word gets around those corridors pretty quick. Do yourself – and this team – a favour. Don't talk to scene examiners like you're a big shot and they're just "the help". It makes you look a right numpty.'

'Aye,' Willie added, unimpressed.

'Sorry, boss,' Ross said, then sought out eye contact with DI Sneddon as well. 'Sorry, Willie.' Ross wanted to shrivel up and hide under a rock. Two tellings-off in as many minutes from men that he looked up to more than any others. Ross knew that he was in the wrong, but it was partly because of the way uniform constables and everyone else at crime scenes gaped at Lomond nowadays. Since the Sandman investigation, he had gone from being banished to Paisley Mill Street, to outright celebrity within Police Scotland, running the country's premier Major Investigations Team at Helen Street. It was hard for Ross not to get swept up in Lomond's slipstream at times.

Eager to move on, Lomond said, 'Right, Willie. What have we got?'

He explained, 'So we've got a knife down here,' he pointed to the floor below, 'and the victim up there.' He pointed to the second floor. 'He's William MacRae. Sixty-four years old. Appears to be a stab wound to the chest. The body's in the study.'

Lomond grimaced. He had eaten too much and too quickly to be climbing steep stairs.

Willie was struggling too. 'I know Moira doesn't want to give anything away to you just yet, but it looks like it was a single direct impact to the heart.'

'Bloody hell,' said Lomond. 'That takes some force.'

'And more than a bit of anger.'

'Aye, and it's hard to avoid the sternum. That's not an accidental scuffle, or an argument that got out of hand. It takes a bit of precision. Any secondary attempts in the chest, or just one clean wound?'

'Moira won't say yet. But there's some other stuff up there you'll want a look at.'

'Like what?'

Willie pondered how to answer. 'I'll maybe just let you see for yourself.'

Lomond stopped climbing. It wasn't that he needed a rest, though. He looked over the bannister, back down at the knife. Then at the bloodstains on the carpeted stairs that had each been marked off with a border of yellow tape. 'Quite small gaps between the stains. They must have been moving slowly.' He pointed. 'The steps are quite deep. You could go at a fair clip up or down these. If you were fit enough, of course.' He gave Willie a knowing smirk.

Willie and Ross waited to see if there was more.

Lomond went on, 'Someone older, maybe? But a knife in the heart suggests someone young. Strong. Or were they just dazed at what had happened? Were they calm?'

Ross suggested, 'If they were calm, why carry the knife all the way down the stairs just to leave it in the hall?'

'Whether there are marks or not on the handle will tell us a lot. No fingerprints means they could have been wearing gloves. They were prepared, and this was premeditated. Or they had the wherewithal to remove them after the fact.'

Ross offered, 'Maybe they stabbed him without wearing gloves, but in the time it took them to go down the stairs they came to their senses and realised they should clean the knife.'

'Maybe.' Lomond nodded a few times, then got moving again. 'Okay. What else?'

Willie handed Lomond an evidence bag containing a phone. 'That's the victim's. Look at the call history for tonight.'

When he saw that it was a touchscreen phone, Lomond

showed Willie the nitrile gloves he was wearing. 'I can't scroll through this.'

Willie pressed a button on the side of the phone through the bag. 'No need. There's no screen lock.'

Lomond pressed the button, then turned his head a little. 'Call history is the last thing he looked at?'

'That was lucky,' said Ross.

Lomond pouted. He didn't believe in luck. He held the screen up for Ross to see.

Ross's eyes widened. 'Those calls must have been damn close to time of death.'

'We'll need to speak to Moira about that,' said Lomond. He indicated one of the caller IDs. 'What about this Claire here? Is she the wife? I've got outgoing and incoming in the last few hours here.'

'Ex-wife,' replied Willie. 'She's on her way in. That was a fun call to make.'

'Yeah, never easy,' said Lomond, relieved that it was rare for him to have to inform relatives of fatalities. Noting several attempted calls in quick succession, Lomond said, 'What about this guy? Seth Knox. What was he so desperate to talk to William MacRae about today?'

'He's MacRae's editor.'

'We need to speak to him.'

Never the most athletic of polis, Willie stopped, struggling for breath. 'He's in a car downstairs waiting to be taken to Helen Street for a statement.'

Lomond paused. 'Why?'

'One of the constables first on the scene thinks Seth's the murderer.'

CHAPTER TEN

LOMOND SAID, 'Willie, next time, you might want to lead with the fact that we've got our hands on a suspect.'

Willie said, 'He's not being arrested, but he's been told he needs to give a statement. His first words were when he opened the door? "I didn't do it."'

'Exact words?'

'Exact words.' Willie pointed towards MacRae's study along the second-floor hallway, where there was a group of white-suited examiners.

Lomond knocked on the door frame. 'Moira? Are you—'

Before he could say anything further, a voice called out in a listless drone, 'No.'

Lomond went on tiptoe to see where the voice was coming from.

'I told Willie to tell you, John. Ten minutes.' Moira stood up, suddenly appearing from behind MacRae's desk. She removed a mask and checked her watch. 'That was seven minutes and forty seconds ago.'

'That's more than enough for an examiner of your calibre.' He held a smile on his face, looking hopeful. 'Or are you expecting some sudden revelations in the next two minutes and twenty seconds?'

'I cannot predict whether or not I am about to have a revelation for the precise reason that revelations refer to something previously unknown. I'm a forensic examiner. If you want an oracle, then someone at Helen Street called the wrong number.'

For someone with apparently no sense of humour, Lomond found it pretty funny. 'No, we definitely want *you*, Moira.'

She consulted her notes which were attached to a well-worn clipboard. Without any emotion, she said, 'Victim is male, sixty-four years old. Single stab wound to the chest with a knife very much like the one downstairs...'

Lomond came around the tattered sofa in the middle of the room for his first look at the body.

She continued in the same flatline voice. 'As you can see from the amount of blood, this wound was catastrophic. Other than a bomb exploding that destroys your entire brain, or severing the medulla oblongata–' She could tell that she had lost the three detectives. 'Part of the brainstem. It connects the brain to the spinal cord. Other than those, a wound like this is as close as you'll get to instant death. But it would still have taken a minute, maybe two, to die.'

'That's instant?'

'In my line of work, yes it is.' She pointed at where the blood had pooled the most on the tartan carpet. 'Bit of an inconsistency here, perhaps.'

Lomond and Willie exchanged a curious look as they

came closer. Moira didn't like involving herself in speculation, raising something only if the science told her she should.

'What's wrong?' asked Lomond.

'The victim's suffered a single, fatal trauma. Presumably he wasn't in favour of it happening, so you would expect some arcing of blood in this area. On the walls or the desk. All things considered, it's pretty tidy.'

Lomond crouched down, turning this way and that to get a feel for how the body would have fallen.

Ross couldn't help but look incredulous at the bloody scene in front of them. Moira's barometer for what was "tidy" had clearly got a bit skewed over the years.

Lomond could see her point, though. 'He looks in reasonable physical shape for his age. He could have handled himself. Put up a fight.'

Ross added, 'And a wound like that, he wasn't taken by surprise. You have to see that coming.'

Lomond pondered the whisky bottle sitting out that had a label still attached to it which read, "Your Number One Fan". 'There's not too much missing from that, but maybe those weren't his first drams of the night. Could he have been too intoxicated to fight back?'

'I thought that,' said Moira. 'But there's only a moderate smell of alcohol on him. We'll test his blood, of course.'

'He might not seem the type,' Ross pointed out, 'but these days you can never rule out pills.'

Moira checked her watch again. 'Anyway, I've got another two minutes and twenty seconds of work to do.'

'Thanks, Moira,' said Ross, overcompensating for his earlier faux pas downstairs. 'Much appreciated.'

She walked across the room to confer with her colleagues, her arms rigid at her sides as she went. Leaning forwards in a way that suggested she was on the verge of tipping over. It was a walk that had been unconsciously cultivated through crippling shyness as a teen, followed by years of trying to draw as little attention as possible when in public. Forget wallflower – what Moira aimed for was total invisibility.

Willie said, 'Well, that's the technicalities. What about this?'

Hands on hips, Lomond turned away from the body to inspect what was lying a few feet from it. He pointed at a book lying on the floor that was covered in blood. Written by a bloody finger on the front cover was a single word.

JUSTICE

Lomond gestured at the book. 'What's with this *Da Vinci Code*-type business?'

Willie folded his arms sternly. It was like two sausages had been twisted around each other. 'A bit theatrical, isn't it.'

Ross stood over the book to read the title on the cover. '*The Shortlist*. Never heard of it.'

'That's not surprising.' Lomond pointed to the words in a smaller font at the bottom of the front cover.

ADVANCE UNCORRECTED PROOF.

He explained, 'It's not been published yet. Publishers send them out to drum up buzz.' He indicated the publication date at the top. 'It comes out in a few weeks.'

'Who do you think wrote this thing about justice? The killer or the victim?'

Lomond shook his head. 'It can't have been MacRae.

Why would he use up his last moments to conjure up that word instead of the identity of his attacker? But it's too self-conscious, too staged, to be irrelevant. And yet it can't be the killer either.'

Willie chimed in, 'Why not?'

Lomond stood up to reassess the whole room. 'Also, they spend the time it takes to write in blood on the book, then carry off the knife downstairs? Look at the blood under the victim. The body was smothering the knife. The killer had to pull the body up with one hand and remove the knife with another, only to drop the knife downstairs. Why bother if you're just going to drop it downstairs?'

'Okay,' said Ross, 'say it was the victim that wrote on the book cover...'

Moira suddenly called out from across the room, face pointing down at her clipboard where she was making rapid notes. 'Impossible.'

The three men looked towards her.

'There's no way someone with a chest wound like that could have written the word as tidily as that. He would have been bleeding out. The pain excruciating.'

Lomond turned towards MacRae's writing desk. 'There's an empty whisky glass, and the cigarette in the ashtray has burned all the way down with barely a drag taken from it.' He then turned back towards the staircase. 'The doorbell must have gone.'

'Why do you say that?' asked Ross.

'Because there's no sign of forced entry at the front door. We can check for marks, but for my money, the killer knew already what they were coming here to do.' Lomond went through the motions as he spoke. 'MacRae lit the cigarette, left it behind and never got back to it. Something distracted him. As Moira says, no one can be stabbed in the heart like that by surprise.'

'So, someone MacRae knew. Or was comfortable having in his house late at night.'

'Like his editor?' Willie offered.

Lomond nodded that it was possible. 'All we're trying to do at this stage is get a sense of who William MacRae was. Was he liked? Did anyone hate him?'

'He's sold millions of books,' said Ross. 'Even I've heard of him, and I don't even read. I mean, Isla got me that *Girl with the Dragon Tattoo*.'

'Oh, aye,' said Willie. 'That was pretty good. What did you think?'

Ross replied, 'I just waited for that Daniel Craig movie of it to come out. There was a Swedish movie of it, but I can't be doing with subtitles.'

'Naw,' Willie agreed.

Lomond rolled his eyes then raised his arms in mock distress. 'What's the matter with you two? Talking about watching movies instead of reading a book in the very room where *A Wee Grave* and *The Last Bloody Dram* were written. I should be arresting the pair of you for crimes against literature.'

Attached to the wall above MacRae's desk, on a whiteboard with various notes and scribblings, was something MacRae had titled simply "The Rules".

The list had been published in a magazine many years ago, and had become baked into the fabric of all modern detective mysteries since.

"*1. The criminal should be introduced early on, and*

must not be a character whose thoughts the reader has followed.

2. Nothing supernatural.

3. No more than one secret room or passage, and these should only be found in appropriate buildings.

4. No undiscovered poisons, or anything that needs a long scientific explanation at the end.

5. The detective must not be helped by an accident or rely on guesswork.

6. The detective must not commit the crime.

7. If the detective finds a clue, then it must be revealed to the reader before the killer is unmasked.

8. The killer's motive must be explained.

9. The reader should stand just as much chance of solving the mystery as the detective.

10. Rules are made to be broken."

Lomond said softly to himself, 'Couldn't agree more, Mr MacRae.'

Willie noticed a photo frame facing down on the desk next to the computer. He turned it over to take a look. 'What do we think of this?'

'That's his daughter,' said Lomond. 'She died...' he puffed, 'I don't know. Five, ten years ago? I remember reading about it in the paper.'

Ross, who had been skimming MacRae's Wikipedia page, confirmed, 'Nine years ago. She was twenty-one at the time. It says here her death was ruled accidental. No further details released.' He put his phone away. 'But, I mean, it's Wikipedia. I'll look into it further.'

'Oh good,' said Lomond, dripping in sarcasm. 'That's

reassuring you would do that, Ross. The last court case that relied on a Wikipedia entry didn't go too well.'

'Question is,' said Willie, 'did MacRae turn it over, or the killer?'

'And why?' added Lomond, distracted by what Moira was doing across the room.

She was in deep concentration with a pair of medical beakers and a syringed sample of the whisky from MacRae's "Number One Fan" bottle. After mixing the whisky with a concoction that turned the whisky blue, Moira shook her head.

'Everything all right?' asked Lomond.

'I did ask for ten minutes. Not seven minutes and forty seconds. This is why you should listen to me.' She held the beaker aloft as if its blue contents were self-evidently revealing. 'He was poisoned.'

Lomond squinted as he made a beeline towards the whisky bottle. 'As well as–'

'As well as stabbed, yes.'

'Jeez,' said Willie. 'How much of a bastard do you need to be to get killed twice?'

'Number one fan,' Lomond said to himself as he looked at the bottle. 'We need to find out where this came from. Moira, any idea which came first? The stabbing or the poison?'

She said, 'It's too soon to tell when the poison was ingested and how quickly it acted. But he was still alive when he was stabbed, if that's what you're asking. The way the blood...'

All heads then turned towards the staircase, as a woman's voice called out.

'Let me past!' she yelled. 'I want to see him! Get out of my way!'

There was a minor scuffle at the study door, as a constable struggled to contain her.

She was in her early forties, with dark hair in a trendy angular cut. She wore what to Lomond's mind was an expensive winter coat, and even from a distance it was obvious that she was wearing an excessive amount of makeup.

A constable knocked on the door frame, and held out an apologetic hand. 'Detective Chief Inspector, I tried to–'

Lomond indicated for the constable to back off.

The lady stalled in the doorway as she saw MacRae's legs sticking out behind the desk. 'Oh, Billy...' She covered her mouth and turned her back on the room.

The constable hurried to Lomond, telling him, 'She's Claire MacRae. William MacRae's ex-wife.'

Lomond fought to keep his voice down so that she wouldn't hear. 'What are you doing letting her up here? This isn't how I run my crime scenes.'

'I'm sorry, sir. I couldn't find an SO downstairs. The thing is, she says she knows who the murderer is.'

CHAPTER ELEVEN

LOMOND TOOK Claire MacRae to a lounge room one floor down, gesturing for her to take a seat which she took some convincing to agree to. She also seemed strangely out of breath for having walked down only one flight of stairs. Even Willie had outperformed her.

Lomond gestured to Ross to get her some water from the open drinks cabinet. It wasn't that there were magical calming qualities within a glass of water. It occupied the hands. And the mind.

It was a mind that Lomond needed to calm down as quickly as possible so he could get the facts that were hiding within it.

'Ms MacRae,' he began, 'or would you prefer Claire?'

'Claire's fine,' she replied, taking a tissue from Lomond's outstretched hand, then blowing her nose.

'I'm very sorry for your loss, Claire. I know this must be difficult.'

She had been on the brink of calming down, when she

got the image in her head again of MacRae's legs. His dead legs. Her eyes filled rapidly with fresh tears, before spilling down her cheeks. 'I just can't believe how quickly it's all happened. We were just talking on the phone a couple of hours ago.'

Lomond had his notepad out, ready to scribble only the most necessary details. Everything else, he could fill in later with Ross's help. He wanted her to think she had his undivided attention.

'I mean, Billy had his moments.' She wiped her eyes. 'God knows he did. We divorced for a reason. But he has never in his life done anything to deserve...' She trailed off, her eyes tracking upwards to the ceiling.

Lomond was regretting taking her only one floor down. The proximity was still affecting her state of mind. But he had been given word that some press were outside, and he wanted to delay that inevitable indignity as long as possible.

People like Claire were fodder to the press at such times. Nothing more than a job. But Lomond saw the real human side of that job. It involved tears. Anguish. And all too often, a lot of blood.

Lomond took a seat on the far end of the couch, while Ross stayed on his feet. 'We saw from William's phone that he tried to call you earlier this evening. Did he leave a voicemail?'

She looked up as Ross handed her a glass of water. She took it with a trembling hand. It was shaking so hard, she spilled some water on her leg. 'I'm sorry...I'm just...my head is all over the place.'

'That's okay,' said Lomond, looking at Ross.

The two men were used to seeing members of the

public reduced to quivering wrecks in their presence. It was the natural authority and powers of being police that did it. Even total innocents could convince themselves they had done something wrong when being questioned by police.

But there was something about how Claire was carrying herself that gave Lomond pause. Was it shock that he was seeing in her? Or was it nerves?

She took out her phone and tapped around the screen, trying to find her call history. 'Here it is.' She scrolled to William's voicemail then let it play on speaker.

'*I need you to listen very carefully. I don't have much time to explain. And before you sigh and wonder if I've been drinking, I have not been drinking. Okay? I promise. I know this probably sounds strange. And the rest of what I have to say will sound strange too...I've found something out. About another writer.*' He paused. '*The sort of thing you would kill to keep secret.*'

Claire waited until the automated voice kicked in with instructions for deleting or archiving the message. 'That's it,' she said. 'That's all he told me...' She broke off and put a hand to her mouth. 'I had my phone off. If I had only got the message sooner, I might have...'

Lomond pursed his lips. It was hard seeing someone in such emotional anguish and not give them a hug. But he kept a clear barrier between himself and victims of crime that way. It could be a slippery slope. To do the job as long as he had, and at his level, you had to keep a certain detachment.

'I'm sorry,' Lomond said. 'You mustn't blame yourself. This was an act carried out by someone very determined.'

Ross felt awkward standing in the room and not saying anything at such a moment. He added, 'I'm sure that whoever did this would have found another time to do it if you'd been here.'

Lomond's mouth hung open a little as he gave Ross a look of *that's really not helpful.*

Fortunately, Claire was too cut up to notice the remark.

Lomond said, 'Did William mention any other writers to you recently? Perhaps someone he's had some conflict with?'

Claire was already shaking her head after the first part of the question. 'No. No one. William never mixed with other writers. That's why it was such a surprise that he won the lifetime achievement at the festival.'

'Really? He seems to be one of those writers who's been around forever. Everyone knows him. His books are still bestsellers.'

'Yes, but it's voted for by a crime writers guild. William's peers. Amongst those, he wasn't necessarily the most popular guy in the trade.'

'Why was that?'

Claire smiled for the first time. A brief flash of memory. 'When you got William at his best, he made you feel like you were the only person in the world. At any other time, it was like he didn't even know you existed.' She put a hand to her chest at the thought. 'Oh, what I would have given for another ten years with the William I knew when we first met. Not the William who became my husband. I won't presume to put words in anyone else's mouth. You would need to ask them. My suspicion, though, is that if you ask ten different writers, you'd hear ten different complaints.' She gave a gentle snort of amusement. 'He was always so creative. Even in the ways he found to drive you up the wall...and now he's gone.'

'What about outside of writing?' asked Lomond. 'Did William have any financial difficulties?'

She balked at the thought. 'Are you joking? We bought this house together for five figures back in the day. Do you know what it could sell for now? Silly bugger wouldn't sell for any price. He could have lived quite happily under the Kingston Bridge as long as he had a typewriter.'

'Has he mentioned anyone new in his life of late? Perhaps being followed, or receiving unwanted phone calls?'

'No, nothing like that. I'm sorry, Chief Inspector. I'm really at a loss. If he was in my shoes right now, he would say that this is the bit in the story where you promise to catch whoever did this to him.'

Lomond looked into his hands. 'What I can promise you, Claire, is that this investigation will have my team's full attention. We'll do everything we can to find whoever is responsible for doing this.' He stood up and motioned towards Ross. 'DS McNair will take you downstairs and, if it's all right with you, we'll get someone to take your statement. It's important that we get every detail we can at this early stage. There's no telling what might prove valuable later on.'

On her way to the door, Claire nodded. 'He would have liked you, Chief Inspector Lomond. I can tell.' Then, doing close to a Columbo *one last thing,* turned in profile. 'Did I see Seth Knox being driven away earlier?'

He raised his hands in reassurance. 'Mr Knox is

assisting us with our enquiries, but right now we don't have any suspects.'

'Thank you,' she said. 'I know this can't have been easy.'

Lomond squinted a little as she left with Ross, just as Willie entered the room.

'What's wrong?' he asked.

'Funny,' said Lomond. 'We've been doing this a long time, Willie. How many times has someone close to a murder victim said thanks at the end of an informal interview?'

'Never, mate. You?'

'As of about a minute ago, just the once.'

Willie nipped to the door for another look at Claire, who was descending the stairs with Ross.

'What are you thinking?' asked Willie.

'I'm thinking coffee.'

Willie didn't often look hesitant, but he did now.

'What is it?' asked Lomond.

Reluctant to raise it, Willie said, 'You must have noticed.'

'Noticed what?'

'How much she looks like Eilidh.'

'Aye,' said Lomond. 'I suppose she does now you mention it.' He patted Willie on the arm, which was as thick as most people's thighs. 'Let's go. I want to find out what Seth Knox has to say.'

CHAPTER TWELVE

By the time Donna had arrived back at Helen Street following the G1 Gelato stakeout, word had spread to the rest of the Major Investigations Team occupying the second floor. Applause broke out as she made her way through the bullpen of desks separated by fabric dividers. Her fellow officers got to their feet when she lifted the evidence bag containing the SIM cards she had covertly confiscated.

Grabbing stray hands for high-fives on the way past, she told them, 'That's how we do it in MIT, boys. Am I right?'

Standing at her window on the mezzanine overlooking the scene was Detective Superintendent Linda Boyle, who wore a grudging smile. She didn't like cockiness or brashness in her officers. But at the same time, she reminded herself what it was like to be in Donna's shoes. Brimming with confidence in your first major gig in a Major Investigations Team, and proving your worth with a stellar piece of polis work to a DCI like John Lomond. It was Linda's job to mould and shape fledgling talent like Donna's – but for now, Linda wanted her to enjoy the win. She knew all too well that you don't get many in MIT.

Donna milked the applause for all it was worth until she clocked Linda up above. Striking a more modest demeanour, she headed for a small, windowless room at the rear of the bullpen.

Inside the dimly lit room were DCs Pardeep Varma and Jason Yang, illuminated mostly by the glow of their computer screens.

Pardeep sprang out of his chair and offered a hand for a high five. 'Nice catch, Donna.'

She slapped his hand with casual ease. 'Cheers, mate.'

Jason turned in his chair, wondering what was going on. Unlike Pardeep who had been making regular trips to the bathroom, the vending machines, and the staff kitchen for coffee and biscuits, Jason had been hunkered down, trawling through spreadsheets of phone numbers, oblivious and excluded from the specifics of any gossip. 'What did you get, then?'

Donna spun around an office chair, and sat down with the backrest facing her chest. 'Three SIM cards used by the ice cream goons.' She handed the bag to Jason.

He pouted as he examined the contents of the bag. 'Phones themselves would have been better. But it's a start.'

'What can we actually get off those things?' she asked.

'Well, there's no photos or internet browser history.'

'Trust me, I wouldn't want to see either.'

'But you can get some text messages as well as a contacts list. Most modern phones back up to a cloud or the device itself. But contacts generally start on the SIM.'

Pardeep chimed in. 'Yeah, but it's all going to be just burners, isn't it. You might get some phone numbers off them, and it'll tell you naff all about whose phone it is, or where they are.'

Jason slotted the SIM cards one by one into a reader device connected to his computer and downloaded all the data from them. The whole process took less than thirty seconds. After a few quick clicks around, one phone number stood out. 'This one keeps coming up across all three phones. There's a good chance that's someone higher up the chain if all three of them were talking to him...' Jason held a finger up to ask for more time. Then, after a few triumphant bashes of the Enter button, he announced. 'I thought so...This number's got a history on HOLMES. It was logged as evidence in a drugs case just last week.'

Pardeep said, 'Whoever it is, they've got lazy. Used the same phone for too long.'

Donna leaned over Jason's shoulder to see the screen. 'Is there any location or ID on the number from this other case?'

Jason pulled it up on the computer screen. A red dot appeared on the map, where South Street turned into Castlebank Street near the Riverside Museum.

Intrigued by Jason's swift progress, Pardeep came over too. 'Where is that? Zoom out.'

Donna stood up straight. She had no curiosity about the location. There was no tension. She already knew.

Her heart sank. Then her stomach turned over. And over.

It was Glasgow Harbour Terraces. Where her dad lived.

She knew in her gut that it was his phone number the goons had been calling so often.

She asked, 'If they get a location on this person, how long before they kick a door in?'

Pardeep was the best-versed of the three on the topic, having been involved in dozens of drugs investigations at Pollokshields CID. 'They won't do that until they've dug up everything else they've got on other phone numbers. They'll want multiple addresses before approving a raid. They prefer to do them all at the same time so no one can be alerted and do a runner. It's happened before. You never know, the one who does a runner could be the one at the end of the rainbow.'

Jason said to Pardeep, 'Wouldn't this get kicked up to Specialist Crime Division?'

'Aye, probably now,' Pardeep replied. 'The Organised Crime boys will make the call on whether a raid gets the go-ahead or not.'

Donna had gone to great lengths to keep her dad's real identity a secret over the years. When word got out around Mill Street station, Donna went from being one of the most popular constables in Paisley, to someone who ate lunch on her own. It had taken her years of graft to get noticed and hoisted out of there by DCI Lomond. He had never raised the subject of her being the daughter of Barry Higgins – the lowlife degenerate drug dealer who had beaten Donna's mum half to death in front of Donna's own eyes when she was a little girl. Police intervention had saved her mum's life that night, and ever since, Donna had felt a sense of duty to become good polis as well.

But since her dad had been critical in securing information in the Sandman case, he had reached out a few times in the hope of starting a relationship with her again. She had ignored his overtures so far, but now she realised he might prove useful.

He was a medium-size operator in the Glasgow drug scene, and if he was involved in the money laundering operation, then he was expanding his business. And in the process, potentially stepping on some very powerful, and very dangerous, toes.

Except, the location data wasn't conclusive enough for her to be sure it was her dad that was involved in the money laundering.

She did have one way of being sure, though. She typed the phone number into her personal phone and tapped out a text message:

"It's Donna. I've been thinking about what you said about meeting up. Can you remind me where you suggested?"

She held the phone with both hands, gripping it tighter than was necessary. It was an involuntary action. She couldn't take her eyes off the screen waiting for a reply.

If it was her dad, he would surely be confused as to how Donna acquired the number of a burner phone of his. But she was sure he would reply.

She kept staring at the screen. Praying that nothing would happen. She didn't want it to be him because it would put her in an impossible situation.

As long as he didn't reply, she wouldn't have to worry about it.

Then a new message notification flashed up at the top of her screen. It was from the burner.

Okay, she thought. Don't panic. It would likely be some random drug dealer telling her 'get tae...'

She tapped on the message.

"*Awrite Donna. Nice to hear from you. Cannae remember giving you this number but aye still be good to meet up sometime. The Laurieston still alright? Let's talk about getting you out of the fucking piggery haha.*"

She silently sighed and looked down. No way would anyone else have replied that way. They knew the exact pub she had mentioned last time. And they knew she was polis. And "piggery" was a Barry Higgins phrase.

There was no doubt in Donna's mind. The money launderer's gang was working closely with her dad on something.

'You all right?' asked Pardeep, wondering why Donna was suddenly slouching.

'Aye, fine,' she replied, pocketing her phone.

She now faced a decision.

If she gave Specialist Crime the address as a tip-off, and it proved successful, she would have to answer all sorts of questions about how she had acquired the address in the first place. And that would break open the totally illegal manoeuvres she had pulled in the Sandman case in order to track Barry Higgins down.

The alternative was saying nothing, which would save her career, and possibly her spot in Major Investigations, but it would kill the investigation and any chance of catching guys on the level of Frank Gormley – Glasgow's reigning Godfather.

The office door flew open, and Donna nearly jumped out of her skin.

Detective Superintendent Linda Boyle appeared. 'Donna. Ross and John are on their way in. I need you to take a statement from someone.' She made a come here gesture with her head. What Linda had to say wasn't for Pardeep and Jason to hear as well. 'Thing is,' she explained, 'there might be something worth having on this guy. Officially, it's just taking a statement. But I need you to get some answers out of him. Off the record. Something to confirm to John that we're going down the right path.'

Donna nodded. 'Of course, ma'am.'

Linda noticed the change in Donna's posture and the whiteness of her face since she last saw her. 'Are you okay?'

Donna replied with clipped efficiency, 'Yep. Fine.'

That was one thing Linda liked about bringing heart-on-their-sleeve officers to MIT. They're terrible liars, which means you generally always know when something's wrong. Linda didn't know what. But she didn't end up a Det Sup in Helen Street MIT without a talent for finding out what people didn't want to tell her.

CHAPTER THIRTEEN

THE MOMENT SETH sat down in the interview room in Helen Street station he regretted declining legal representation. Some of that was down to the intimidating surroundings. The station in the heart of Govan was the most secure in Scotland – there was a reason that major terror suspects were taken there. With its long orange wall forming a protective barrier around the property, it looked closer to a prison than a police station.

There was an ever-present steady hum of traffic on the M8 behind it. Being driven in to the car park in a police vehicle through the secure barrier entrance, as Seth had been, it was easy to feel like you may never leave again.

More than a little of Seth's anxiety was down to the body language of the detective constable sitting across the table from him. DC Donna Higgins might as well have had a lightbulb swinging above his head in a cigarette smoke-filled room, and detectives who looked like they played some rugby in their spare time rolling up their sleeves menacingly in the background.

The last words DCI Lomond had left Donna with were, 'We could be looking at a murder suspect here, but he's not under caution and I don't want him to think he's under suspicion. Don't push too hard, but get *something* out of him.'

Nothing mattered more to Donna than not letting Lomond down. Even if it meant finding a way to get a square into a circle as he had asked.

Donna began by saying, 'Let me start by saying that I'm sorry for your loss, Mr Knox.'

Seth nodded humbly. 'Thank you. It's all such a shock. I can't get my head around it.'

Donna asked, 'Could you tell me what brought you to Mr MacRae's residence tonight?'

Seth's shoulders were hunched. A chilly police interview room was not his environment. His was a world of endless meetings and phone calls in plush modern offices, sitting on leather couches, surrounded by piles of manuscripts and secretaries and PAs who all seemed to be psychological thriller writers trying to break into the industry, and all seemed to be called Hannah, Kate, or Becky. They were all enthralled by him. And captivated by his looks. Almost everyone Seth had met since he was eighteen had been instantly charmed by him. Not so Donna.

Donna was the anti-Hannah, Kate, or Becky. She lived in a world of getting shit done and putting away hardened, dangerous criminals. It would have been tough to put two people less alike in a room together.

The only thing that impressed her was bravery in the

line of duty. Not the symmetrical proportions of Seth's facial features, or easy-going yet roguish smile. She had always found someone with a sense of humour more attractive than anything physical.

Seth answered, 'We work together. I had arranged a brief meeting for this evening.'

'And what do you do?'

'I'm a senior editor at Hathaway Publishing, where I've been working for the last six years.'

'You seem very young for that,' Donna said, head down, taking notes.

Seth leaned forward to try and see what she was writing so much about. He hadn't really told her anything yet. 'I worked very hard. And had a little luck along the way. Fell in with the right people who opened some doors for me.'

Donna knew his type already. 'Uh-huh,' she said.

'I work with some of the biggest names in publishing. Including William MacRae, who I think would rank near the top of any list of the best British crime writers in the last twenty-five years.'

The groundwork laid, Donna pushed on to Seth's actual account of the events that had taken place at Park Circus that night.

Seth took a long, deep breath. He recounted arriving at William's house. After several attempts to get an answer, ringing the doorbell and knocking on the door, he realised the door was unlocked. When he went in, he was immediately confronted with the sight of the bloody knife on the hall floor. The shock of it made him back up all the way against the front door. He remembered hearing the door close over, because the house was so silent.

He called out William's name a dozen times, then raced up the stairs. He had been to the house several times before, and knew that William often conducted work in his study at that time of night. He went there first and found his body on the floor. It was obvious to Seth that William had been murdered, so he was careful not to touch anything. After conducting a check of William's pulse and hearing no breathing, he took out his phone to dial 999. That was when he saw police lights through the study window. Not knowing if they were coming for William or not, he ran downstairs in the hope of catching them. They were already banging on the door by the time he reached the ground floor again, and opened the front door.

The whole time he recounted his statement of events, Seth grew irritated by Donna's refusal to look him in the eye – instead, concentrating on writing the statement.

He already knew that she was unimpressed with him, but foppish charm was his only weapon. He didn't have anything else to try to win her over with. Normally, all he had to do to get someone on his side was show his face. Not so Donna. It rattled him.

'Were you two working together recently?' Donna asked absently, still making notes.

'Yes. Over the past few weeks William and I were working towards the final draft of his next DCI Roxburgh book.'

'They're great books,' she said. 'I've read a few myself.'

'Thank you. Everyone at Hathaway was excited about William's latest, as they always are. William sent me his final draft late last night. I started reading it this morning at dawn and throughout the day.'

'So you came up here to work on the book with William?'

He paused. 'That was *part* of the reason. I was coming up north anyway for the Lochinver Book Festival.'

Donna nodded. 'I've heard of it, but never managed to make it.'

Seth didn't do much to spare her blushes. He scoffed. 'It's becoming one of the biggest crime-writing festivals on the calendar. Every year it's attracting bigger and bigger writers. No one really knows how. The festival organiser pays handsomely, though. I can tell you that. William was due to receive the festival's lifetime achievement award. I wouldn't have missed that for the world.'

'Did anything notable happen during your journey?'

'I read the final draft of the book. That's all. I finished it on the train. When we stopped at Preston, I tried calling William so we could talk about the ending. But I couldn't get an answer.'

'I know that stop at Preston. I've taken that train a few times. It doesn't stop for long.'

Seth paused. 'What's your point?'

'It must have been fairly urgent to call him during a brief stop like that.'

He shrugged dismissively. 'I was keen to discuss some changes William had made since the previous draft.'

'What sort of changes?'

Realising he had said more than he planned to, he added, 'Well, minor ones really.'

'You called him nine times over minor changes?'

Seth took out his phone and tapped through it. He said cagily, 'I don't *think* it was *quite* that many. Hang on...'

'It was,' Donna said with certainty. 'We checked Mr MacRae's phone.'

Now she was looking at him. Unwavering. Determined.

Seth got the feeling that he had horribly underestimated DC Donna Higgins.

CHAPTER FOURTEEN

KNOWING that he would only prove Donna right by continuing to look through his phone, Seth put it down. 'If you say that's how many times I called him, I don't *dis*believe you, Detective Constable.'

'Was Mr MacRae on an imminent deadline?'

'No. Hathaway always worked out deadlines far in advance so that William was comfortable. He was experienced. A book a year was a walk in the park for someone like him. Two thousand words a day was a light day for him. We never had an issue with William and deadlines. Unlike a lot of the other writers I deal with.' He chuckled to himself. 'I referred to them in William's company as The Idiots.'

Unsmiling, Donna asked, 'Why is that?'

'Let's be honest, a lot of Hathaway authors in my stable write what used to be called airport novels. They're rotten but they sell tons.'

'William MacRae sold tons,' Donna pointed out.

Seth replied, 'I'm talking about the sort of thrillers you can skim-read to find out who did it, and then forget by next week that you ever read it. It's my job to turn these wretched potboilers into bestsellers, and turn their characters from dullards into dynamos. I swear they should be giving me royalties half the time.' He leaned back with a satisfied grin on his face.

Donna was struck by how quickly his veil of grief had given way to snarky amusement. Looking at him at that moment, you would never have known he had discovered the dead body of a colleague that night.

He webbed his fingers behind his head, as relaxed as someone sitting in their own living room. 'Not a problem I ever had with William.'

'I never got an answer about those nine phone calls, Mr Knox.'

'And I wasn't aware that this was an interrogation, Detective Constable.'

Donna didn't back down. 'Why so many calls for minor changes?'

Seth didn't panic, even though he had backed himself into a linguistic corner. 'Minor changes to the sort of people who read books by The Idiots. But I know that William's readers are of a magnitude smarter and more astute than that.' He rolled his hand in the air, trying to help himself come up with something. 'William had made it too obvious early on who the killer was. I had an idea of how to hide it. I'm excellent at that.'

'An interesting talent,' Donna remarked.

Seth released his fingers, and tipped himself forward in his chair.

'We're not recording here,' said Seth, 'and I'm not under caution. I also know procedure better than most police officers, so let me confront what you've been driving at with these transparent questions...' His eye contact was unwavering and intense. 'I didn't do it.'

'Mr Knox, no one is accusing you of any–'

'DC Higgins, I have a doctorate in English from Oxford, which I earned whilst nursing my mother at home with terminal cancer, and burying my dad who committed suicide after she died. I'm the youngest senior editor that Hathaway has had in its illustrious seventy-three-year history, and before that I was a senior editor at Cargo Books. I've read every major novel published in the seventeenth, eighteenth, nineteenth, and twentieth centuries, and every novel worth a damn in the twenty-first. Many of which I have edited and greatly improved. I'm not an idiot. I know what a police detective thinks when they look at a young man who answers a door with blood on his face, a bloody chef's knife on the floor behind him, and a recent murder victim known to said young man in the study upstairs, with no witnesses – as I understand it – and a reasonably peculiar murder scene with literary references. That all being said...' He showed Donna his palms as a gesture of innocence. '...I still didn't do it.'

Donna held his gaze without a flinch. His performance was irritating her, and so far she had been convinced of nothing. So she decided to push the envelope a little. 'I'm glad that you can see how it looks. I know that someone of your vast intelligence must understand that there's obviously opportunity there.'

Seth wasn't fooled by the sarcastic compliment.

Donna went on, 'There was a window of time before the police arrived when the killer would have had time to go through Mr MacRae's things. Perhaps a computer. Find or delete something, possibly. It's early days yet.'

Seth took a beat, trying to reset the balance in the room in his favour. 'I was William's editor. When I started at Hathaway, I was one of five junior editors working from a bullpen that churned out fifty titles a year between us. We worked like dogs, from dawn to midnight, on everything from footballers' biographies, to romance novels. Every day. Including weekends. For two years. All in the hope of being plucked out of obscurity. One day, he was mistakenly sent corrections I had made on a spare digital copy of his latest manuscript. I had always wanted to edit him. It was only for practice. Like playing dress-up, if you like. When he saw the corrections, he liked them so much that he demanded I copyedit his next book. The rest is history. I owed everything to William! He made my career. No one wanted him to stay alive as much as me.'

'An Oxford graduate who's apparently read everything? I'm sure you'll survive, Mr Knox.'

'I'm left editing nothing but books by The Idiots. Why would I want to kill William?'

Donna didn't have to think long about it. 'Jealousy. Revenge. Betrayal. The usual reasons. As someone who's read all the classics, you should know better than anyone that the main reasons for killing someone generally don't change much.'

Seth said, 'I can't disagree with that.'

Donna didn't have a huge amount of experience, but she had interviewed murderers before. They all had the same dead eyes. Something that was obviously wrong about them. Something in their wiring. Detached and cold. They could issue denials and no comments for hours. She still knew they did it.

Seth was nothing like that.

So that he had no chance of seeing it, Donna wrote very small in the margins of her notes, '*Smart. Knows it. Wants to be caught?*'

CHAPTER FIFTEEN

DONNA'S TRAINING for taking statements followed a basic five-part model of establishing who the witness is and what they're providing a statement about. Identifying the people they will be talking about within the statement, and how they are known to them. Describing locations referred to in the statement. Giving an account of the actual events that took place. And finally, clearing up any ambiguities.

Donna was now at her favourite part.

Clarification.

If someone was hiding something, this was where a good detective could really tighten the screws.

Donna rolled into her next question before she was done writing. 'We could see from Mr MacRae's phone records that he eventually called you back. How did he sound during that phone call?'

Seth puffed, wondering how to phrase his answer. 'He sounded a little tired. Which is to be expected. He often worked late in the night during the approach of a deadline, but no matter what time he went to bed, he would always get up by seven next morning. He would email me like clockwork first thing if he ever had a new draft or changes for me to look at.'

'And what topics did you discuss during the phone call?'

'Just the changes I advised that he make. As I said before, they were minor. Important. But still minor.'

'Nothing else?'

Seth was so disarmed by Donna's persistence, he questioned whether they somehow had a recording of his and MacRae's final phone conversation, and knew that he was deliberately not mentioning the AD Sullivan topic.

'No. *Nothing* else.' He gestured irritably to the door. 'I could fetch a thesaurus, if you like?'

'That won't be necessary, thanks.' Donna smiled inside.

"Irritation," she noted – she was getting to him.

Trying to emphasise his innocence, he offered up something that the police would already know. 'It wasn't a long phone call. There wasn't time to talk about anything else.'

'Okay...' said Donna. 'And could you talk me through your movements from Edinburgh up to your arrival at Mr MacRae's home?'

'I got the quarter past seven train from Waverley. It was on time. Still pretty busy for that time of night. I got a taxi from Queen Street to Park Circus.'

Before he could get any further, Donna asked, 'Did you notice anyone walking around Park Circus? Anything or anyone that didn't look right?'

Seth shook his head. 'I spend most of my time scrolling

through a phone. I wasn't looking out the taxi window much at all.'

'Okay,' said Donna. 'What time did you arrive at Mr MacRae's home? As precisely as you can be sure.'

'Now...' he sucked in air, trying to remember. Then a lightbulb went off. 'It was eight thirty, almost on the dot. I remember because I was monitoring the expected arrival time on my Uber app in the car. It had been a while since I last visited William at home, and I wanted to check how long it would take. It will all be logged in the app.'

'Thanks,' Donna noted. 'We can come back to that at a later date.'

He ran his hands through his hair in anguish. 'I keep thinking what would have happened had I got an earlier train. Maybe I could have stopped this from happening somehow.'

'I know it's hard, Mr Knox. But right now the best thing you can do for Mr MacRae is help me get down as much detail as you can remember. You wouldn't believe the simple things that can disappear after a night's sleep following a shock like the one you've had.'

Seth nodded.

'Can you describe the house as you found it?'

He breathed in hard. Slowly. It was time to go over things that he didn't want to revisit. 'I rang the doorbell a couple of times, and thought it strange that no one was answering. It was one of those doorbells that you can't hear from outside. So I knocked instead, in case the bell wasn't working. That was when I realised that the door was open.'

'Unlocked or–'

'No, actually ajar. When I knocked, the door just gave

way. That was when I saw the knife on the floor.' He paused. Gulping hard. This was a different Seth suddenly. Confidence diminished. Attitude gone. 'There was so much blood on the tiles. There was a big puddle of it. I just started running.'

'Running where?'

'Upstairs. I checked each floor—'

'Sorry, I thought you said that you went straight to the study.'

He paused. 'No, sorry. Yes. I went straight to the study. I called out William's name as I went. I couldn't hear anything. But I could see the blood dotted on the carpet up the stairs. It led to the study. That's where I found him.'

'The victim William MacRae?'

Seth blinked long and hard, then nodded gravely. 'Yeah.' He had a quick glance at his phone, then looked around the room. 'I'm sorry, can I have some water?'

Donna excused herself to the water cooler in the corridor outside. When she returned with a paper cup of water for Seth, he was tapping out a message on his phone.

He tutted. 'I can't get a 4G signal in here.'

'Yeah, you need to go to the end of the hall.'

'Do you have a wi-fi code I can use? I need to send something.'

'Sure,' Donna said, writing it down for him. She wondered what could be so urgent at such a distressing time for him. 'Are you okay to continue?'

He finished sending his message, then downed the cup of water in one go. 'Yeah. I want to get this over and done with. He was...he was lying face down on the floor behind his desk. I ran towards him. I think I shouted his name. I can't remember. Maybe I just thought about doing it. And in my head it sounded like a shout.'

'That can happen,' Donna said.

'I checked his pulse and there was nothing. He was just...' He shook his head. 'I don't think I'll ever get my head around it. How someone could do that.'

Donna waited until she was finished writing until she said, 'I wanted to ask about the book on the floor next to the body. Can you think why anyone would have done that? Why that book? Is there something about this writer, AD Sullivan, that could be a connection?'

'I can't think of any connection. I don't believe the two had ever met. William certainly never mentioned it. I can't say I was very aware of it at the time. One of your colleagues told me about it. DI Sneddon, I think his name was. He was very nice in the aftermath. I was pretty shaken up, you know.'

'Of course,' said Donna. 'That's only natural.'

'After that is a bit of a blur. I think I put my hands to my face when I realised he was definitely dead.'

'Yes, the first officers at the scene reported there was blood on your face.'

'I ran down the stairs to try and get help from someone out on the street, and–'

'Sorry, can I just clarify: you said earlier that you were about to call nine nine nine in the study. You *didn't* do that?'

Seth shut his eyes, trying to remember. 'Sorry, no. I...I thought...I knew he was already dead. But I thought I could raise the alarm faster if I ran downstairs and maybe found someone.'

'If you knew he was already dead, what were you hoping someone could do for you?'

'I don't know...Call someone or something–'

'But you had a phone.'

Seth was flummoxed now. He had lost track of his own testimony. 'Like I said, I thought it would be faster.'

'By hoping to find someone in the street? Which you reported was empty when you arrived?'

Seth glared at her then gave a gentle snort of contempt. 'Yeah. I think we're done here.'

'I'm sorry, Mr Knox, I'm just trying to clarify–'

For the first time, Seth raised his voice. 'And unless you were in that house at that moment, it's very easy to speculate about what's sensible or prudent or expedient! Unless you were there, you have no idea what it was like.'

'Of course,' she said, lifting her hands in placation. 'I understand. So you ran downstairs? Walked?'

He looked at her like she was mad. 'Walked? I ran. Of course I ran. I opened the front door and the police were standing there trying to get in.'

'I see,' she said. 'And you never touched the knife in the hall at any point?'

'I've watched enough murder mysteries and edited enough whodunits in my time to know you never pick up the murder weapon.'

'I'd say that's decent advice,' said Donna. 'You don't want to make yourself look guilty.' She stared, daring him to hold her gaze.

'That's everything,' he said, looking away.

Donna exhaled with finality. 'Okay. Thank you, Mr Knox. This is obviously the very start of our enquiries, so we may well ask you some follow-up questions about this statement. Would you have a few minutes available for a Scenes of Crime officer to take some fingerprints? It's important for us to compile prints to exclude from our investigation. It makes our job and forensics' much easier when it comes to eliminating suspects. Half a day wasted on these things can make all the difference.'

He paused for a moment, trying to calculate how bad it would make him look if he declined. 'No, of course,' he agreed. 'Anything to help catch whoever did this.'

CHAPTER SIXTEEN

SETH EXITED the station from the main doors at the roundabout on Helen Street and Paisley Road West. He saw numerous buses around, but was damned if he knew where any of them went to, and how long it would take to get back to Queen Street station. All of his luggage for the arduous journey to Lochinver was still in his hotel room at The Balmoral back in Edinburgh.

After the night he had experienced, he didn't care about raiding the Hathaway company expense account. He booked an Uber to take him directly back to Edinburgh. It was going to cost the company £100 at that time of night.

With the taxi still five minutes away, a call came through on his phone.

ZOE HATHAWAY CALLING.

Seth puffed with exasperation. It was never good when the CEO of the company calls you nearing midnight on a weekday.

'I've been trying to reach you for over an hour,' Zoe said. 'You never replied to my message.'

'I'm sorry,' Seth replied. 'I didn't have time. I was giving them a statement at the station.'

'How bad was it?'

'Really terrible. I can't stop seeing his body lying there, Zoe.'

'I'm sorry. He always spoke so highly of you.'

Seth said nothing. He knew it wasn't a call about condolences.

Zoe said, 'I know it might seem ghoulish to talk about this, but we need to make plans.'

'Plans?'

'Hang on,' she said, covering the mouthpiece from background noise drowning her out. 'Sorry, I'm somewhere quieter now. I know this won't be at the forefront of your mind, but I wanted to let you know that William sent through his final draft to me a few hours ago. So you've got some peace of mind.'

Peace of mind. He didn't know whether to throw up or scream. He wanted to reach down the phone and throttle her.

'How do you mean?' he asked.

'I know how hard you had worked on this book with him. I thought it might bring some comfort knowing that he had finished the book. The way Roxburgh escapes at the end is classic William.' She chuckled warmly. 'You know for a crazy moment, I thought he was actually going to kill him off. God, we're going to miss him. The whole book world is going to miss him.'

Seth was in awe of how easily Zoe used the language of loss without conveying a single emotion related to it.

Seeing a car pulling up on the main road, he said, 'That's my Uber here, Zoe. I should probably go.' He held a finger up to the car to indicate he would be a minute. 'There's one other thing I thought you should know. It's about AD Sullivan.'

A long pause at her end. 'What about them?'

'There was a copy of *The Shortlist* next to William's body. On the book cover someone had written "*JUSTICE*" in blood. The police obviously don't know how to contact them.'

'I know,' she said snippily. 'I've spoken to the police. Don't worry about it.'

'I assume you've told them they might be in danger.'

'I've handled it. They're happy to go ahead with the event as planned.'

'What about you? Aren't you worried?'

'Why would I worry?'

'What if Sullivan is next in the firing line? Or worse, what if the police think they're the killer? The police are going to demand access.'

Zoe laughed. 'And I've got a team of twenty lawyers at my end who tell me the police can – what was the legal phrase they used again? Oh yeah – go dangle.'

'They may very well say that. But I'm standing outside Helen Street police station. A murder investigation involving a figure as big as William is probably going to fall to DCI John Lomond.'

Zoe waited for more detail that never came. 'I don't know who that is.'

Seth was incredulous. 'The Sandman case. He caught the Sandman killer a few months ago. I've seen him give interviews. He's not someone to fool around with.'

'We've got nothing to hide, Seth. But I'm sending you something I'd like you to keep to yourself for now. I need your opinion on a some names. I'm sending you them now.'

Seth looked at the message that pinged on his phone. A list of five respected thriller authors that were overdue a break into the mainstream.

Zoe said it like it was obvious. 'Writers who could continue the Roxburgh series. The board is going to want to know we at least have a roadmap in place.'

Because he couldn't tell his CEO that her 'roadmap' demonstrated all the sensitivity of a funeral director pitching for business in a hospice car park, Seth pinched the bridge of his nose and swallowed his protests. 'No, yes, of course. That makes sense. A roadmap.'

Once he wrapped up the call and was in the taxi, the driver made it apparent that he might talk the whole way to Edinburgh.

Seth took out a twenty from his wallet and passed it to him. 'Excuse me? Sorry. I've had a rough night, and I need to figure some things out. Does this buy me silence to Edinburgh?'

The driver happily took the note from him. In a half-Polish, half-Scottish accent, he said, 'That'll buy you silence and a lap dance at Harthill if you want.' The driver grinned into the rear-view mirror. Seeing that his humour wasn't landing, he said, 'Joke.'

Seth said, 'I'll just take the silence, thanks.'

The driver made a zipped-lips motion.

Seth stared out his window in the back seat as the overhead lights of the M8 passed by in a steady, monotonous flow going past the Glasgow Fort shopping complex and Easterhouse. It was a land as foreign as Africa to someone like Seth Knox.

He had only one thought: *if I go to Lochinver I might not come back alive.*

CHAPTER SEVENTEEN

LOMOND TOOK a large mug of steaming coffee over to the long whiteboard in front of the bullpen area of desks that were largely vacated for the night. What few officers were around were so hard at work they didn't lift their heads, but they listened to Lomond's every word. For those not on his direct team but still part of the Major Investigations Team framework, catching a Lomond briefing was one of those things that you always hoped for, and rarely got a chance to experience in person.

Anytime that one happened, the officers present would discuss it for days afterwards in the staff kitchen while the kettle boiled.

Major Investigations was a big unit full of experienced officers, but only a select few came under DCI Lomond's direct supervision. Like a sports team with a large roster of players, not everyone got to take to the field.

Lomond took a long drink of coffee that was a little too

hot. A quick review of the faces in front of him confirmed that everyone was there.

Detective Inspector Willie Sneddon had first worked with Lomond on the original Sandman investigation five years ago, and reunited in MIT when the Sandman killer returned four months ago.

Detective Sergeant Ross McNair, who hadn't exactly got off on the right foot with DCI Lomond. Having proved his natural talents, Lomond had taken on something of a mentor role for Ross.

Detective Constable Donna Higgins, who Lomond had handpicked from Mill Street in Paisley. A constable that Lomond trusted to do whatever it took to get the job done. Even if that meant occasionally blurring the rules and regulations that defined right and wrong.

Detective Constable Pardeep Varma, who had come up through the ranks in Pollokshields CID. A breeding ground for solid polis, as far as Lomond was concerned. Although he sometimes dressed too young for a forty-one-year-old, Pardeep's natural sensibility was that of an old-school street detective.

And finally, Detective Constable Jason Yang. He had worked under DI Sneddon and DS McNair for two years before being brought into Lomond's Sandman investigation. He had an IQ as long as a phone number, and lived a monk-like existence where every element of his life – from his daily gym regime, to meditation and non-fiction audiobook obsession – was designed to make him the best police officer he could be.

In a unit comprised of the very best that Police Scotland had to offer, Lomond's team was the one per cent of the one per cent. Rare among the uncommon.

'Okay, good evening, folks,' Lomond announced. With his six-foot-three frame, he dwarfed the lectern where he set his coffee down. 'I know we've been making good progress on our co-op with Organised Crime on the money laundering investigation, but we've pulled a murder tonight.' Next to a picture of William MacRae taken off the internet, along with a few of his book covers, Lomond pointed to the whiteboard. 'This is our victim. Most of you will probably know his name and probably not know his face. William MacRae. Bestselling crime writer.'

'The Roxburgh books?' said Jason. 'My dad loved those.'

Pardeep was wearing a cheeky grin. 'Is it true, sir? That Roxburgh was based on you?'

Lomond was equally shocked and insulted. 'How fucking old do you think I am, Pardeep?'

Realising that Pardeep was about to hazard a dangerous guess, Willie told him, 'Don't bother.'

Lomond continued, 'I was about to say: killed by a single stab wound to the chest – likely the heart. But also poisoned. We're looking within an hour time window at the moment, but Moira McTaggart is working on tightening that.' He drew a large question mark on the board. 'We have two methods of murder. We don't know if we're looking at one murderer or two. We've got no witnesses so far, and no suspects – though Donna may have something on that in a few minutes.'

For now, Donna stayed poker-faced in her chair.

Lomond went on, 'The body was found by Mr MacRae's editor, Seth Knox. He's up on work-related business from London. As far as we can tell, Mr MacRae was well-liked. No issues with neighbours. Kept to himself.' Lomond hammered the lid on the marker with the heel of his palm. 'The only thing the crime scene gives us, in fact, is this.' He attached a crime scene photo taken from the study, showing *The Shortlist* next to MacRae's body. 'This is a book that comes out very soon, written under a pen name. The real identity of the author appears to be a mystery even to Hathaway, the publisher of both Mr MacRae's books and *The Shortlist*.'

Pardeep, slouching in his seat, said, 'Someone at Hathaway must know who they are, surely. An email address or a phone number or a bank account. Something!'

Lomond looked to DI Sneddon. 'Willie? You were the one who spoke to them.'

Willie shook his head. 'There's nothing. The manuscript was submitted last month to the former CEO Max Hathaway – now deceased. How the book came to him isn't known by the current CEO Zoe Hathaway, Max's daughter. She's told me that all she's got is an email address for this AD Sullivan. What we have in our favour is that Sullivan is booked to appear at one of the big event slots at the Lochinver Book Festival this weekend. Zoe Hathaway was at pains to point out to me that although she doesn't know the actual identity of Sullivan, her dad did. Unfortunately, it was a secret he took with him to his grave.'

'Do you think she's lying?' asked Jason.

'It's possible,' replied Willie. 'What she did tell me, was that Max was terrified of other publishers finding out who Sullivan was. Her theory was that Max had poached someone from a rival publisher. Someone big. A heavy-weight, in her words. The issue is, we don't know from this crime scene whether AD Sullivan is a killer sending some sort of pointed message about William MacRae. Or...' He trailed off on purpose. Like a jazz pianist letting the trumpet player know his solo is about to end.

'Or,' concluded Lomond, 'that the message at the crime scene is a threat. Meaning the person behind AD Sullivan is in imminent danger. Which means, for the first time in my career, we appear to be looking for someone who is either a killer, or a potential victim.' His eyes drifted to the back of the room as Detective Superintendent Linda Boyle appeared. 'Which brings us to motives and suspects. Motives is the hardest one to check off. Mostly because we don't have any yet. The literary media's collective tongue has been attached to MacRae's arse cheeks for about two decades now, and had been showing no signs of abating. He's equally loved by readers the world over, even if he has a temperamental side behind closed doors. No rough stuff. But if his ex-wife Claire is to be believed, William was a bit of a tough hang at times.' He looked to Pardeep. 'Am I using that phrase correctly?'

Pardeep grinned. 'I'd need to check with Suzie, my eldest, sir. But I believe so.'

Picking up on Willie looking like a cat that had been told what E equals MC squared means, Lomond explained to him, 'It means a difficult sort to be around.'

Willie replied, 'Oh, aye.'

Ross felt like he should contribute something while Det Sup Boyle was around. The last thing his career prospects needed was to appear as useless as a Scottish fiver down south. 'I think the nine nine nine call is worth mentioning. Made from a burner. The phone abandoned in the lane at the back of the house. If a witness was diligent enough to call the police, why toss the phone?'

Ever the logical pragmatist, Jason suggested, 'Maybe they were doing something there that would cause embarrassment. Having an affair with someone in the back of a car. Or had told their partner or spouse they would be somewhere else, and didn't want to be part of a police investigation that would expose their lie.'

'Okay,' said Lomond, 'and the award for most surprisingly overactive imagination goes to DC Yang.'

Linda piped up, 'I don't know, John. I've seen it before.'

'It can't be the killer, can it?' said Pardeep. 'I mean, why kill someone then call in the emergency?'

Donna replied, 'It could have been an attempt to frame Seth Knox.'

The room fell silent.

She continued, 'If someone knew he was on his way there, calling the police at a certain time could put him in a vulnerable position.'

Lomond put a hand up. 'Can I just say that this is Donna defending the man who found the body, answered Mr MacRae's front door with blood on his face, and has no witnesses in the building to corroborate what he was up to there.'

Linda asked, 'What did he have to say for himself, then?'

'He had plenty to say,' Donna replied. 'Let me put it this way: I think we should know where this guy is at all times for the next week.'

'You fancy him for this?'

'Ma'am, I would have slapped the cuffs on him then and there.'

Linda and Lomond shared a smile. Linda said, *see the monster you've created?*

Donna added, 'Will I tell you why?'

CHAPTER EIGHTEEN

LOMOND ASKED DONNA, 'What makes you think he did it?'

'For a start,' she explained, 'he called Mr MacRae nine times in an hour today. But when you ask Mr Knox about it, he goes out of his way to make it seem casual and normal. Why? If you or I call someone nine times in an hour you'd say, aye, I was desperate to get a hold of somebody. Because that's what calling someone that often is: desperate.'

Linda asked, 'And what did Knox have to say about this?'

'He said that the calls were about clarifying, quote, "minor changes" to the manuscript of Mr MacRae's next book.'

Like Donna, no one else in the room was buying it.

'That's not all, though,' Donna said. 'If we didn't know from Mr MacRae's phone that there had been nine calls—'

Lomond couldn't help but cut in. 'What else might he be hiding?'

Donna then replied in the most Paisley way imaginable, placing all the emphasis on the third syllable, and making it sound like *net*. 'Defi-*nite*-ly.'

Intrigued, Willie asked, 'What else, Donna?'

'I mean, nothing that you would take into a courtroom.'

'Humour us,' Lomond said.

'He's an editor who loves talking about books, yet he seems to hate writers.'

'What's your point?'

'He's resentful. He never missed an opportunity to big himself up and run everyone else down, or to remind me how well educated he is. And that's fine. I didnae take anything personal from it. But he thinks he's better than the people he works for. Criminals require a few things to justify their behaviour. Opportunity. Financial or emotional pressure. And an ability to rationalise their behaviour. If you resent those around you, you can justify a series of actions that could potentially escalate over time. Who knows what Seth Knox has been up to before this.'

It was called the fraud triangle, and the FBI's field agents used it all the time in interrogations.

Lomond smiled. 'You read that book I gave you.'

'Of course I did, sir. There's also one other thing. He was as confident and laidback as anyone I've seen in that interview room. Nothing was fazing him, even when I was pushing him a bit like you told me to, ma'am.'

Lomond glanced cheekily at Linda, who winked back at him.

Donna went on, 'But when it came time to talk about the crime scene, he seemed genuinely shaken.'

Pardeep argued, 'That's a natural reaction, regardless of innocence or guilt, surely.'

'I disagree. The natural reaction is to be shaken up throughout. He came in and out of it.'

Trying to steer the ship back on course, Linda remarked, 'And if my granny had wheels, she'd be a bike. This is all very clever and theoretical, but we deal with facts and evidence here. I need you to find me some. Don't be fooled by how quiet it is out there on Paisley Road West. First thing tomorrow the news is going to break in a big way about what's happened to William MacRae. The press have got an angle they rarely get: someone in the fictional crime world becoming a victim of the real one. And it's murder, which always jacks up ratings and clicks. We need to get ready,' she pointed at the ground repeatedly, 'tonight.' She nodded to Lomond to finish off, and made her way upstairs to her office.

'You heard the boss,' said Lomond. 'We need to go with what the crime scene has given us. We don't have witnesses, and we don't have much in the way of forensics. What we do have is a man who's been murdered twice in the same night. Are we dealing with one killer or two? And what about this pointed display towards AD Sullivan?'

Willie said, 'Say the killer was Sullivan. Why draw attention to your own book, your own name, like that? It doesn't make sense.'

Lomond looked around the room. 'Anybody?'

Ross answered, 'Unless there's something in that book, *The Shortlist*, the killer wants us to know about.'

'I'm glad someone other than myself got to that.' Lomond went to the lectern and recovered a copy of the book. 'The publisher managed to track down a blogger on TikTok...' He turned to Pardeep to check. 'Are they still called bloggers? Is that what you call them?'

Pardeep shook his head. 'Not really, sir. But I think we get the idea.'

'A reviewer on the internet, anyhow, that Hathaway sent a copy of the book to. I need one of you to read this tonight, and it needs to be the one of you who reads the most.'

All fingers pointed to Donna.

'Really?' said Lomond in surprise.

'Yeah, I read crime books all the time,' she said. 'Helps me switch off from work.'

'Switch off?'

'It's not really about the crimes, though. It's about the characters.'

'Did Seth Knox know you were such a big crime fiction fan?'

'He never asked, sir.'

Lomond handed her the substantial-looking paperback. 'I don't need an essay, you understand. I just want to know about any parallels with this investigation. Anything that stands out. The rest of you are on finding AD Sullivan and picking apart William MacRae's life. We need to start getting fact from fiction.'

Jason raised his hand before asking his question. A habit that Lomond wished all too often the rest of the team would imitate. 'Sir, about Sullivan. How do we find someone like this who doesn't want to be identified? Hathaway might be okay playing roulette with Sullivan's life, but we don't have that luxury.'

'Almost word for word what I said to Superintendent Boyle ten minutes ago,' said Lomond. 'There's only one place we know for sure that the person known as AD Sullivan will be in the next few days. The Lochinver Book Festival.'

Donna sounded a note of caution. 'Isn't that going to be tricky to work out who they are? There must be dozens of authors at a festival like that.'

'Forty-three, in fact,' said Lomond. 'But I've been able to reduce it to ten.'

'How did you do that?' asked Willie.

'Because William MacRae told us. Or, technically, he told Claire MacRae in a voicemail he left for her. He said that he had found out something about a writer who was appearing as part of his lifetime achievement event. It's a bit of a leap, but there has to be some kind of a motive there...'

Lomond went to the board where he had written up a list of ten names. 'Six bestselling authors. Three old friends and acquaintances. This is *our* shortlist.'

RJ HAWLEY
BRAD CARR
TOM ELLISON
JIM PROVAN
NOEL REDMOND
CHARLOTTE FOUNT
CLAIRE MACRAE
SETH KNOX
CRAWFORD BELL
ZOE HATHAWAY

Lomond paused to review the names. 'Actually...I've forgotten one.'

He added the name under the others.

AD SULLIVAN

He pointed to the shortlist, tapping the pen on the board for emphasis. 'One of them is our killer. Or possibly the next victim.'

CHAPTER NINETEEN

A HEAVY SILENCE, full of the weight of their responsibility, filled the room.

Lomond nodded to Willie. 'I need you for a minute.'

The others broke into a huddle to discuss what they had just been told, while Lomond and Willie stayed by the whiteboard.

Lomond said, 'We can't all go, Willie. There's going to be too much to do back here.'

'Aye,' Willie agreed. 'Where do you want me?'

'I want you to oversee things here. I'll go up north with Ross and Donna.'

Willie said, 'I hear nothing but good things about the pair of them from Organised Crime.'

Lomond nodded, then eyed Jason and Pardeep. 'What about Captain Kirk and Mr Spock?'

Willie's eyes narrowed, uncertain and curious. 'Which one do you think's Captain Kirk?'

'Aw, come on, Willie,' Lomond complained. 'Jason's

obviously Spock. I mean, all right, he's carrying a bit more muscle, but there's no way Jason just follows his gut like Captain Kirk.'

'I didnae watch *Star Trek*. Load of shite.'

'I'm going to pretend you didn't say that,' said Lomond. 'Anyway, I need some background on MacRae. Especially the daughter. That photo was facing down on his desk and it can't have been an accident. Either MacRae or the killer did it. I want to know why. And I'm going to need you to be the conduit between them and us up north.'

'I can do that,' he said, watching Donna approaching tentatively.

'Sorry, sir,' she said. 'I don't mean to complain. But this book...' She held it out, her issue all too evident. The book was enormous. 'I'll never get it finished by morning.'

Willie took the book with hands formed from the genes of shipbuilders and welders. Then he pulled as hard as he could along the spine, and held out the two halves. 'There we go.' He handed one half to Donna, and the other out to Ross. 'Ho! Ross. Come here. I've got some work for you.'

Lomond held his hand up to halt Ross from coming any closer. 'Bloody hell, Willie. Give me that,' he said. 'No offence, Ross. If it was the Argos catalogue, I might have considered giving it to you. But I think I'd better take this one.' He turned to Willie so that only he could hear him. 'Let him get home to see his wee boy. He's going to be away all weekend and the wee guy's teething.'

'John Lomond going soft?' Willie wondered aloud.

'Maybe. I also want Ross's head in the game. Not thinking about missing his son.'

'What about Pardeep? He's a dad too. He's got four girls at home.'

'Pardeep's not travelling two hundred miles north for the weekend, and his youngest isn't a year old.'

'Right, then,' said Willie. 'What about this poison in MacRae's whisky?'

Lomond said, 'If we're at this crime book festival up north, there's not much we can do about tracking down where that poison came from.'

'We'll get on that, John,' Willie promised. He pointed at Pardeep and Jason, then thrust a thumb at himself. 'You two! You're with me. We're on background to MacRae and the daughter. And we need to find out where that poison came from.'

Lomond turned to Donna and Ross. 'You two,' he pointed at them, then turned a thumb to himself. 'Looks like a road trip.'

CHAPTER TWENTY

LOMOND ALWAYS HAD the feeling that you were leaving Glasgow once you had passed under the Provanmill Railway Bridge that crossed the M8o. It wasn't long after that before Robroyston gave way to long flat swathes of open land. Every time Lomond drove through there another housing development seemed to have popped up. They were all the same. Eventually, the city would just be everywhere, and it would be impossible to tell when you had left.

Eventually, the city finally lost its grip on the country-side after Cumbernauld, and greenery took over around the vast farmland around the outskirts of Stirling. It reminded Lomond of what Scotland had been for so long. And still was. A green and mostly wild country.

Lomond, Ross, and Donna were making the trip in Lomond's car. A car so anonymous and average, Ross couldn't even tell what make it was. It was also spotlessly clean.

They had left Helen Street at seven a.m. on the button, when it was still dark. Lomond wanted to be clear of Perth and the central belt by the time rush hour came about.

It had been a long night for everyone. Donna and Lomond were up for most of the night reading their respective halves of *The Shortlist*, while Ross ended up sitting on the living room couch, watching *Top Gear* reruns with the sound off and subtitles on, cradling Lachlann to sleep in his arms. In truth, he could have put him down in his crib far sooner than he did. With the knowledge that he wouldn't be seeing his baby son all weekend, Ross wanted to get in as much physical contact as possible – as well as to let Isla get some much-needed sleep.

Ross hadn't spent more than a single night at a time away from the pair. Doing a whole weekend was a leap – one that he wasn't entirely ready to make. But he didn't have a choice. If the morning papers were anything to go by, the MIT had caught their biggest investigation since the Sandman murders.

'Jeez...' Ross groaned at the map on his phone. 'Still four hours to Ullapool.' He had taken on the role of unofficial navigator sitting up front with Lomond.

Donna grabbed the back of Ross's seat to pull herself forward. She felt left out sitting in the back on her own. 'Tenner says you'll be asking "are we there yet?" by Perth.'

Lomond said, 'How about we get some work done.' He sought out Donna via the rear-view mirror. 'Tell me about your half of *The Shortlist*.'

She said, 'I'm not surprised the publisher's making such a fuss about the book. I couldn't put it down. When I could feel myself getting closer to the end of my half, I started to slow down. I didn't want it to end. It left me a nightmare of a cliffhanger!'

'Yeah, sorry about that,' said Lomond. 'On the flip side, picking up a book from halfway through is a bit of a bastard. I kept asking myself "who's this guy?"'

'Although I did have an idea that the publishing industry should totally take up.'

'What's that?'

'Sell books in two halves. The first half costs ten pence. The second half costs a tenner.'

'That's what a drug dealer does,' Ross remarked. 'Gets you hooked for cheap, then charges you over the odds for more.'

Donna squirmed at the mention of a drug dealer. She hadn't made further contact with her dad since her last text message.

'I mostly skimmed it,' said Lomond. 'I couldn't see much in the story that was familiar with what we've seen so far. Nothing instructive, anyway.'

'What's it about then?' asked Ross.

Donna replied, 'It's about a bunch of writers attending a book festival, and they start getting picked off one by one in this big country pad.'

Ross looked like he'd seen a ghost. 'Are you serious?' He turned to Lomond, 'Is she serious?'

'Is something the matter?' Lomond asked.

'You're not at all worried about us driving into the plot of a murder mystery?'

'We're staying in a hotel in the village, not some country mansion. In any case, it's the writers getting bumped off in the book. Not the police.' With a sly grin on his face, Lomond asked Donna, 'Did you guess the killer?'

She felt some professional pressure. She wanted to impress Lomond with her detective skills, even if it was only fiction they were talking about. 'I think it was the first victim.'

Lomond flashed his eyebrows up, failing to suppress a grin.

'How could it be the first victim?' asked Ross, then noted Lomond's grin. 'What is it?'

'She's right,' said Lomond. 'It was the first victim. He wasn't really dead.'

Donna whooped with delight. 'I knew it! There were all these little clues right from the start.'

'But it's not much help to us, is it,' said Ross. 'William MacRae is definitely dead. Killed twice, for god's sake.'

'Yeah, we don't need to be checking with Moira on that. If there's nothing there in the story, then it must be about the writer. AD Sullivan.'

Donna kept holding on to the back of Ross's headrest. 'Remind me how we're going to sniff them out?'

'It's not anything very sophisticated,' Lomond admitted. 'It's just a process of elimination. Talk to everyone. Gather as much evidence as we can. But we'll need to be smart about it. And we might have to keep a few wee tricks up our sleeves. Whoever we're dealing with is a step ahead of us already.'

THE JOURNEY north really began at the Keir roundabout, where the M9 became the A9, and you were undeniably heading north. The land west around Gleneagles and the heart of Perthshire started to rise and roll. Once you hit that pair of major roundabouts at Perth, you were no longer surrounded only by cars, and other standard vehicles of the Central Belt. There were articulated lorries full of livestock or logs or other massive cargos. The liveries on their flapping sides declared far-flung places like Stornoway. Thurso. Aberdeen. Even bloody Kirkwall on Orkney, and Lerwick on Shetland. These places might as well have been in Norway or the moon.

The trip up the A9 through Perth to get to Aviemore and Inverness and beyond, was a journey Lomond had made dozens of times in his life. He and Eilidh would take long walks in the Cairngorms and the surrounding forest trails. Away from phones and Netflix and distractions, it was the perfect opportunity to make big plans for their lives. Where they wanted to live at what point in their lives. Where they might like to retire. What they each wanted from their careers and how they were going to get it.

It was on a walk around Loch Morlich at the foot of the Cairngorms that the couple decided they would try for a baby. Lomond wondered now if he would ever be capable of walking in the area again, such were his emotional ties to the place.

By the time they reached that monotonous slog of single carriageway around Dunkeld – everyone at the mercy of whatever caravan or motorhome was puttering along at fifty miles an hour up ahead – Donna was fast asleep in the back. Knackered after a twenty-hour-day and reading fifty thousand words in a few hours when she was already beyond exhausted.

Ross had watched her head drooping since Perth and prayed that she would somehow stay awake. He thought about putting his window down to blast some cold air in her direction, but thought better of it. He just didn't want to be left alone with Lomond, because he knew what was coming.

'Good effort, Ross,' Lomond said.

Feigning having been lost in an innocent daydream, Ross said, 'I'm sorry?'

'Good effort. In trying to put me off coming for dinner.'

For a moment, Ross thought about denying it. 'I can explain...'

'I've got to hand it to you. Even up to a few hours before, you were encouraging me to eat at the University Café.'

'It's not what it looks like.'

'What does it look like?'

'Like I don't want you to be a part of my social life.'

Lomond paused. 'I was going to say it looks like you hate your boss.'

Ross chewed on a fingernail, looking out his window. 'You wouldn't understand.'

'Try me,' Lomond said, clearly not taking offence at any of it.

'I know you think I was a bit of a...I don't know...'

'A bit of a fanny?'

Ross's face froze in shock. Was he serious?

Lomond cracked a smile. 'Ross, you don't have anything to prove to me. And you don't have to worry about me looking at you any differently as a sergeant in my team because I've seen you being cute with your kid at home.'

'That's what you think it was?'

'What was it then?'

Ross stared out the windscreen. 'I was worried that you being around a family with a wee baby for hours might be upsetting. I didn't want to flaunt all that stuff in front of your face.'

Lomond was taken aback. 'You know, Ross. You might dress like a Second Division footballer on a night out, and you might have a swagger that's got its own postcode...' he turned to him for a second, 'but sometimes you're a right fucking softie.'

'Thanks a bunch.'

'It was a compliment, son.' In typical Scottish male fashion, using the excuse of checking what traffic was in his mirrors currently, he looked away while delivering the final compliment. 'And thanks, by the way.'

CHAPTER TWENTY-ONE

Around Blair Atholl, Lomond announced. 'Right, the pair of you. We've worked together for nearly five months now and I don't have a clue what music you both like. So god help me, Ross get Spotify opened up on your phone and let's take some requests.'

'Amazing!' said Ross, already tapping out a search for his choice. He turned the volume up before the music started. Which was a mistake. As it was twice as loud as he thought it would be.

What sounded like a synth quickly gave way to a driving guitar-and-drums rhythm.

Drumming along on his legs, Ross said, 'Love this song, man...'

Lomond didn't want to admit that he didn't know what it was yet. Donna knew. She just didn't care and rolled her eyes.

'Such a lad's song,' she complained.

It didn't take long to get to the chorus, at which point

Lomond leaned over to see Ross's phone. 'What's that?' He asked, trying to sound disinterested.

Not wanting to miss a second of the song and still leg-drumming, Ross said, 'It's "Dakota" by Stereophonics.'

Donna reached forward and grabbed Ross's phone to choose the next song. 'You think that's a banger? I'll let youse listen to a proper banger.'

She waited patiently for Ross's song to end then hit play on her choice.

'God help us,' Lomond muttered.

As soon as the intro started with a rumble of thunder, lightning, and crashing rain filled the car, Ross cackled and clapped his hands. 'Oh my God, classic...'

It was "Set You Free" by nineties rave band N-Trance.

Donna ignored him and belted out the opening vocals. Arms were outstretched, feeling every note of the euphoric rave beat that took over the song.

Lomond looked at her in the rear-view mirror. 'What... the fuck...is *this*?'

Ross was giddy with laughter. 'Man, this is every high school disco ever for me.' He started air-drumming appreciatively. 'Good choice, Donna!'

Lomond thought his eardrums were going to explode.

At the synth break after the chorus, Donna broke into her trance dance moves, not giving a single damn about anyone or anything in the world.

Lomond chuckled at Ross. 'Is she all right?'

'Seems fine to me,' Ross replied, recovering from his own laughter.

When it was over, Lomond appealed for calmer heads. 'Right, right. You two have no idea how to do a road trip compilation. You're gonna wear yourselves out with stuff like that.'

Catching her breath, Donna called forward. 'What do you want, boss?'

Lomond said, 'Punch in Duncan Chisholm. Farley Bridge.'

'Oh, man,' Donna groaned. 'Sounds like teuchter music.'

'It is,' replied Lomond. 'Take a look out your windows, listen, and tell me this isn't the really good stuff.'

Ross and Donna were primed to hate it. The fact it started with a fiddle didn't help Lomond's cause. But then they did as he had told them and looked out their windows.

The music took them to the black clouds in the distance over the Pass of Drumochter, the road flanked on either side by towering hills, opening out to a vast expanse.

A minute or so into the track, Lomond pointed out where the River Garry, that had been snaking alongside the A9 since Killiecrankie, joined the mouth of Loch Garry to their left. 'You know, I went up this road I don't know how many times with my wife. And every time we saw that loch we'd say, we should stop one day and go walking over there. It looked so inviting. Like you'll reach the edge of the world if you only walk far enough. But we always found a reason not to. We had to get to whatever accommodation we had booked. Or the weather looked bad. We should have made the time, you know. Planned to come a day early or something. Such a shame.'

'You should come back, then,' Donna said.

'Aye,' Ross added. 'It's not like you can never do it.'

'Aye,' Lomond agreed reluctantly. He knew that deep

down it was like all the other times. He said he would. But he wasn't going to drive a few hours out there to go for a walk. He didn't have the gear. He didn't know a crampon from a tampon.

After he lost Eilidh and the baby, he had been told to try some 'proper' walking as a means of recovering from the grief. To give himself time to 'process'. Christ, he hated that word. It was just a fancy way of saying 'get on with it'. Lomond's nan didn't have time to 'process' when she had a stillborn baby on the kitchen floor of her tenement in Govan. She still had five other mouths to feed, and a list of chores and clothes-washing that was never-ending. It may have been faulty logic, but Lomond figured if she didn't need to 'process', then neither did he.

All the same, he thought he'd give the walking a bash.

He bought the first pair of leather walking boots he tried on in the shop, assuming that because they were expensive they would be comfortable. How wrong he was. After a walk halfway up Conic Hill in the pouring rain, his feet were covered in blisters like he'd been kicking about hot coals. He had hobbled back down like a leper, then left the leather boots sodding wet in the boot of his car. A few weeks later, they were so foul-smelling and cracked, they were beyond any use or repair.

He vowed to make a change and do it properly this time. Even if he didn't really believe it. It was easy making promises or resolutions. Lomond needed someone to boot his arse at home if he didn't do what he said he would.

Ross thought about Lachlann, wondering what he was doing. He was already missing his face, and his laughter.

Meanwhile, Donna was in a world of anguish, deciding

whether to give up her dad's address to Specialist Crime Division, or say nothing and protect her career.

But as the music played, all their collective troubles frittered away. In their current surroundings, it was hard not to feel just a little bit proud to call Scotland home. Or at least incredibly lucky.

With the music and scenery, and the sun shining in that weak winter way, it was easy to make the mistake of thinking they were on a field trip, or even a holiday.

But what was waiting for them at Lochinver would be far from either of those.

CHAPTER TWENTY-TWO

It had been a long time since Lomond had last been north of Inverness. He had always meant to explore the remote north of Sutherland, but had been so seduced by the wild beauty of the west coast he found it hard to entertain spending time anywhere else. Aesthetically, it didn't get more dramatic and beautiful than Skye and the mainland directly across the water from it, so Lomond hadn't tried very hard to explore farther north.

He had always been a west coast guy at heart. Unlike that solid, predictable east coastline from John O'Groats to Inverness, there was something about the jaggedness of the west that offered much more variety. From Mallaig, past Applecross and Skye, to the network of coastal villages around Poolewe, offering consistent views across to Uist, and Lewis and Harris on a clear day.

Once through Inverness, the popularity of the North Coast 500 route was evident all the way to Ullapool, judging by the number of motorhomes and camper vans clogging up the road. Many of which were bound – like Lomond and co. – for the Lochinver Book Festival.

Situated on the coast just north of the Summer Isles, Lochinver and the surrounding district of Assynt was one of the most sparsely populated areas in Scotland. Which in Sutherland, in the far north, really took some doing. Barely one thousand people called the area home, and it wasn't hard to see why.

From Lomond's vantage point, he could see weather moving in from miles away. Clouds of squally showers reduced mountains to faint outlines. Smears in the distance. The distance between villages grew ever greater. More remote. Wilder.

After passing through Ullapool, Lomond told Ross to check the map on his phone that he had downloaded earlier. Relying on an internet signal in such a place would have been a laughable townie mistake.

'I can't see anything,' Ross claimed.

'It's coming up, I'm telling you,' Lomond maintained.

Ross showed him the map on the phone. 'Look. There's no road there. I'm not lying.'

'I'm not saying you're lying. I'm saying you're wrong. Zoom in.'

Ross pinch-zoomed the map, and suddenly a thin white line appeared, cutting up through a huge zone of green with nary a village or landmark in sight.

'See,' said Lomond, 'I told you it was there.'

'Are you sure we want to take this route? The A835 looks a longer route, but I think it will be faster.'

'How much faster?'

'I can't tell, can I? I don't have a signal for it to calculate it for me.'

'Then maybe you should just trust me.' Lomond swooped his neck forward, seeing a brown road sign for 'Achiltibuie and the Summer Isles' along with an upcoming turn-off left. 'This is it.'

'If this is wrong, it's a whole lot of nothing for quite a while.' He showed Donna the map. 'This road doesn't even have a name or a letter assigned to it. It's smaller than a B road, and only marginally bigger than a cycle path from what I can see.'

Lomond said, 'Pipe down, Ross.'

But his confidence soon faded when they were presented with a road sign declaring a single track road with passing places. After a tight corner, the road snaked up over a heather and gorse-covered hill, with nothing but the most desolate mountains any of the three had ever seen. They looked like something out of Tolkien's Middle Earth. Spiky and impassable.

Their progress slowed to a crawl. The road constantly rolled up and down, presenting an endless series of tight blind corners combined with blind summits that left Lomond's heart in his mouth. The locals, it seemed – and god only knew where they were coming from – knew the roads inside out, and were quite happy to tear around them at suicidal speeds. They had driven them so often in all kinds of conditions and lighting, every corner was burned into their muscle memory. The one variable they couldn't predict was happening across a saloon car full of Glasgow townies driving at half their speed – which was the only thing keeping both parties alive at certain points.

After half an hour of hearts-in-mouth driving, a sign told them to turn right for Lochinver.

Collective hearts sank. There was still another twelve miles to go. And little did they know that what they had faced already was like a busy motorway compared with what was to come.

Trying to keep spirits up – whilst avoiding any sense of responsibility for picking the tortuous route – Lomond said, 'This is surely the most beautiful road I've ever been on.'

Donna and Ross didn't disagree. The road weaved in and out and up and down through a lochan-strewn wilderness, occasionally broken up by pine woods, and staggering mountains in odd shapes and unclimbable sheer rock faces. Eerie beauty aside, it took them an hour instead of the thirty-five minutes Ross's route would have taken.

'Saving time is overrated,' Lomond said. 'Everyone's so obsessed with saving time these days. Online banking. Do click and collect instead of queuing, or do your Tesco shop online instead of traipsing around the supermarket, doubling back up the aisles because you keep forgetting stuff that you've gone past already. What do we do with all this saved time? Does anyone ever say, you know what, I saved six hours this month, so I've got free time to take my family out for the day? Or, now I can finally watch that ten-part documentary about World War Two? We never cash this stuff out. What does everyone *really* do with spare time? Sitting on their bloody phones all night? Watching eight hundred episodes of some shite on Netflix?'

'That's why I read so many books,' said Donna. 'It's never wasted time if it feels like you're hanging out with some pals. That's what the really good ones do.'

'You know the biggest swindle of the modern age? Corporations convincing us that we're all running out of time.' He gestured at their surroundings. 'Look at this place. Does it feel like time's running out around here? We don't need to find ways of fitting in more shite to the time we have. We just need to stop doing so much shite.'

Ross said, 'I look forward to reading your self-help book someday, boss. *Do Less Shite* by John Lomond.'

'Aye, well...we should.' He was distracted by the sight of a cottage by the side of the road. Then another. Then a house.

'Looks like civilisation,' said Ross.

'And a book festival,' added Donna, as they passed a temporary road sign.

LOCHINVER BOOK FESTIVAL - ONE MILE

CHAPTER TWENTY-THREE

SIGNS for the festival continued to dot the roadside, directing visitors to 'Lochinver Private Estate' a few miles outside the village. The heart of Lochinver itself was the main road that ran along the east side of Loch Inver. But wherever you turned, your eye was drawn to the mountain known as Suilven. Its policeman's helmet shape made it look a more difficult climb than it was, showing you a sheer side of rock on the village side.

'Feels bloody ominous out here,' Ross said, gazing at the mountain through his window.

AFTER CRESTING A STEEP HILL, the festival grounds came into view. A series of white marquees sprawled across a field, next to a magnificent 18th-century Georgian house that would have made a perfect location for a Jane Austen adaptation. An elegant and tasteful sign on the front lawn said "Crichton House".

In the background, teasing a view from behind the roof of the lower buildings on either side of the main house, was a castle perched on a steep cliffside a mile away, its white stone resplendent in the dim light.

Donna remarked, 'If you were going to do a murder mystery, *this* is the place you'd set it.'

'They don't actually let anyone stay here,' said Lomond. 'That's why we've been put up in the hotel back in the village. We need to check in with the festival director first. See if there's any sign of AD Sullivan yet.'

They parked in front of a fence marking off the entrance to the house gardens. Before any of the three could get out, they were descended on by a group of security guards. They marched out of a wooden hut on the periphery of a secure barrier entrance, leading to a winding dirt track that went around the back of Crichton House. The guards were dressed in army surplus uniforms of green woollen jumpers with leather shoulder pads, and black cargo trousers. They all looked like they could handle themselves, and had the steely expressions of men who were determined to secure the site at any cost.

'You can't park here,' said the senior guard, pointing to the official parking zone they had passed.

'We're here to see Crawford Bell,' Lomond said, reaching into the inside pocket of his suit jacket for his badge.

The guard swaggered forward. 'I said, you can't park here.'

Before Lomond could identify himself, the guard put

his arm out, ready to physically direct Lomond back to his car.

Ross and Donna each made surprised exclamations at how quickly the guard had escalated things. They rushed around the car to Lomond's side. While Ross pulled out his badge and called in a frenzy that they were police, Donna had already reached the guard. She grabbed his outstretched arm and twisted it up his back in three simple, firm motions. The guard sank to his knees.

Donna told him, 'And you can't lay your hand on a detective chief inspector.'

The guard yowled in pain, while his colleagues hovered on the periphery, unsure what to do.

With a conciliatory nod of his head, Lomond showed the guard his badge. 'DCI John Lomond. You were about to fetch Crawford Bell for us.' He motioned to Donna to let the guard go.

The guard puffed, grabbing at his aching elbow joint.

A man in his fifties, wearing a tweed suit, came running out of one of the smaller outbuildings adjoining Crichton House. 'What's going on here?' he yelled from a distance. He was definitely Glaswegian, but had affected a slight Highland lilt that was convincing neither himself nor anyone else.

'Crawford Bell?' Lomond called out.

'Yes. Who are you?'

'DCI Lomond. Major Investigations Team, Police Scotland. We spoke on the phone.'

Crawford raised an arm to the guards to appeal for calm. 'Thank you, gentlemen. I'll take this from here.'

The guards withdrew, scowling and muttering among themselves.

'You've got them wound a little tight for a book festival,' said Lomond.

'I'm afraid they're not my responsibility,' Crawford replied. 'They're Inver Castle's staff.' He pointed to the white castle in the distance. 'I have to live with them as you do. I apologise for the welcoming party. I had asked a helper to keep an eye out for your arrival.' He checked his watch. 'I was expecting you an hour ago.'

Lomond turned to Ross and Donna, who introduced themselves. 'We would have got here sooner, but we had a disagreement about what route to take.'

Clapping his hands, Crawford said with a burst of laughter, 'Oh no! You didn't take the single track road, did you?'

Lomond couldn't bring himself to admit it.

'Bit of a detour,' Ross said, attempting to spare Lomond's blushes.

'It's a wonder you're here now. The locals drive like maniacs over there. If you think they're bad during the daytime, try going that way at night. They go even faster because they reckon they'll see headlights coming from farther away. If you get into a car wreck on that road at night, good luck! During a snowstorm that road is no joke.' He looked up at the heavy grey clouds moving in above. 'I believe we've got some weather coming in over this weekend. I do hope it keeps off. Our marquees are strong, but eighty-mile-an-hour winds might be pushing things.' He led them towards Crichton House, taking a narrow gravel path that forced them into single file.

'Eighty?' said Lomond. 'I saw fifty reported on BBC before we left.'

Crawford laughed. 'Sorry, but once you've lived out here for a while, you'll realise how preposterous it is forecasting weather for here from Glasgow or London.' He gestured towards Inver Castle. 'We're basically at the entrance to the Atlantic Ocean. The weather doesn't really follow rules or predictions out here.'

Donna said, 'It's quite a set-up you've got. What happens if the weather gets too dangerous?'

'It's always a possibility we'll have to cancel. Those are the risks of operating here in January. But it's the only time we can do it – the house is open to the public the rest of the year. Most people reach us via the A837 as it's the main North Coast 500 route. It might lead through a total wilderness, but it's a reasonably brisk road to drive on. Nobody would be stuck here, at least.' He paused, letting the three detectives go past an elaborate fountain, squirting water in eighty different directions. 'Do come inside.'

CHAPTER TWENTY-FOUR

THEY ENTERED the grand entrance of the main house, marked by exceptional Rococo plasterwork. Almost every inch of the towering walls on all sides covered in oil painting portraits of various Earls, Lords, and landed gentry from years gone by.

Crawford said, 'We're fortunate to have a generous benefactor within Inver Castle who brokered an arrangement with the Crichton family, allowing us to hold the festival on these grounds.'

'It must cost a pretty penny,' said Lomond.

'Our benefactor is a strong believer in a robust literary culture and they have the resources to protect it. All they ask for in return is privacy. They have no interest in publicity or attention.'

'But you must know who they are.'

'I do.' The admission appeared to be reluctant. Crawford explained, 'I'm not at liberty to divulge that at this time. Let's just say that the festival is totally reliant on their support. Lord knows the government is no help in supporting the arts. There's a lot of unfair criticism of the so-called monied class who own properties like this. But without their funding and support, there would barely be an art gallery or a museum open in the country.'

The three detectives turned every which way at the extraordinary architecture and priceless antiques they were surrounded by.

'It's certainly something,' said Lomond.

'I must say, I can't thank you enough for coming at such short notice. Everyone involved with the festival was devastated to hear about what happened to William. It's a crime how long it took the guild to award him the festival's Outstanding Contribution to Crime Fiction award in the first place, but there's no accounting for taste these days. I don't know why people can't just see past the man and recognise the work.'

'Sorry,' said Lomond, 'what guild?'

'The Crime Writers' Guild. They're a panel of crime writers who nominate and collectively decide a number of our festival awards.'

'What will happen to the award now?'

'It's normally the final event of the weekend, but I've decided to turn the award presentation into a memorial for William and make it the festival opener. He was too important and influential a writer for us to go through a whole programme of events before paying our respects. The people we had invited to speak for his award have agreed to now share some personal memories on stage instead. A tribute event.'

Ross said, 'I thought William MacRae was revered in

crime fiction circles. Why did it take this long to give him the award?'

Realising he'd put his foot in it, Crawford replied in a flap, 'Well, William wasn't unpopular, you understand. It's complicated. A lot of these things become quite political. Especially when awards are concerned. A lot of jealousy and conflicts build up over the years.'

He took them to a large drawing room with enormous tapestries hanging on the walls. 'This is, believe it or not, the Tapestry Room.' He smiled to himself at the joke.

Ross and Donna exchanged an impatient look with Lomond.

They were all on the same page.

Lomond said, 'Sorry, Crawford. This is all very nice, but we don't have time for a tour.'

'Oh, I'm not giving you a tour,' Crawford replied. 'This is a bit like our green room, where the authors come before their events. Prepare notes, maybe. Go over a reading they're giving.'

Lomond waited for a point to be made.

Crawford said, 'I wanted you to see where you would be spending most of your time this weekend.'

'Why would we be spending most of our time in the Tapestry Room?'

'If you're going to be protecting the authors from any threats on the festival grounds, this would be the ideal–'

Lomond waved his hand to be allowed to interrupt. 'We're not here as bodyguards, Mr Bell. We're investigating a murder.'

Crawford paused. 'It was my understanding that you

believe there to be a possible threat against AD Sullivan. They'll be appearing here tomorrow lunchtime.'

'Yes,' said Lomond. 'But we're here to identify them and talk to them. We're not here to–'

'Protect them?'

'Yeah, well, of course we're going to protect anyone who needs it. But our main job is to identify a suspect in our investigation and find out who killed William MacRae.'

The panic in Crawford's eyes was clear to see. 'You don't understand. The only reason I was comfortable going ahead with this Sullivan event tomorrow was knowing that there were three police detectives of the highest order staying on site.'

'We're not staying on site,' said Lomond. 'I was told by your people that arrangements would be made for us to stay in the hotel in the village.'

'Yes, I was informed of that a few hours ago. Unfortunately, it appears that you spoke to someone in our office who is unaware that the hotel in the village has all of ten rooms, and is already fully booked for next year's event, never mind this one's. We survive on hired help and a lot of volunteers, Chief Inspector. I can only apologise.'

Ross said, 'Is this your way of telling me that the three of us are sleeping in our car?'

'Can't we stay here?' asked Lomond. 'If there's a whole room just for tapestries, surely you can squeeze us in somewhere. Is there a Really Impatient and Increasingly Pissed Off Detectives' Room?'

Crawford grimaced through a smile. 'Chief Inspector, this is a stately home. It's not a bed and breakfast. However, I've had a word with the owner of Inver Castle. They've offered to provide accommodation for you and your colleagues tonight.'

Lomond turned to get Donna and Ross's temperature. They both seemed keen.

Trying to sweeten the deal, Crawford said, 'The authors who are speaking at William's memorial tonight will all be staying at the castle too. I would have thought an opportunity to observe them in close quarters, out of the public eye, might be valuable.'

Lomond looked back towards the car, mulling over the prospect of the three of them sleeping in there versus a literal castle. 'We don't seem to have much choice.'

Crawford rubbed his hands together in satisfaction. 'Then it's settled.' He took out his phone and made a show of checking the screen as a segue to leaving.

Before he could, Lomond said, 'We'll need to speak to everyone taking part in the event tonight.'

'Of course,' said Crawford, checking his phone again and taking a few faltering steps towards the door.

'Including you.'

Crawford paused in the doorway. 'Me?'

Lomond looked around with a frown. 'The chairs in here look awfully dear. Is there somewhere a little comfier we can talk?'

The delight vanished from Crawford's face. 'DCI Lomond, I have a book festival to open tonight. There are a million—'

Before he could protest further, Lomond steered him across the hall to another room. 'I'm sure it'll only take ten minutes of your time. Fifteen, tops.'

CHAPTER TWENTY-FIVE

CRAWFORD and the detectives ended up in what was called the Morning Room. What exactly made it a Morning Room wasn't made clear to any of the detectives. From what they could tell, it was a very fancy living room with a view of the fountain in the front garden.

Crawford reached for a rope hanging near the door. It was attached to a bell that rang in the old servants' quarters. 'Can I get tea or coffee for anyone?'

Ross and Donna immediately answered, 'Coffee, thanks.'

'Just water,' said Lomond. There were some people who claimed to never be affected by caffeine – "liars or just fucking wrong", as Lomond referred to them – and he wasn't one of them. His tolerance had increased over the years, but every morning without fail that first mug of the day always got him wired. Caffeine made him talk instead of listen. Want to move instead of stay still. Neither of which was conducive to good interviews, no matter how informal.

'As I said before,' Crawford explained, dropping his hands onto his thighs as he sat down, 'I really don't know how much I can help you on any of this. It's a long time since I last saw William.'

Lomond asked, 'How did you two know each other?'

'Before this role, I was actually a publisher for a long time. Literary fiction, mostly. Scottish authors. We worked out of a tiny office in Trongate. Before they cleaned the place up. Not at all what my family had hoped I would spend a rather large inheritance on. I was convinced we could make a success of it. All the major publishers were in London, but that cut them off from a huge pool of talent that I saw around Glasgow. We were William's first publisher.'

'I thought he only had the one?'

Donna added, 'Yeah, I've got *The Long Dark* in paper-back along with all his others. They have the same cover design.'

'Hathaway bought the rights from us. I use the term "bought" very loosely.'

'How do you mean?' asked Lomond.

'Stole might be a more accurate term.' Crawford looked down for a moment. He appeared to be genuinely pained to discuss it, but knew that Lomond wouldn't take no for an answer. 'William had just left university with a first in English literature, and thought he was going to set the world on fire. He had pitched his first novel to every literary agent in London, then was mystified why none of them wanted it. It's easy to forget now, but back in nineteen eighty-five, you just didn't see Scottish voices on the page. No one cared what a foul-mouthed detective from Maryhill had to say about the world or life. It wasn't seen as proper standard English. All that swearing! All those apostrophes to make the words look the way they sounded. Anyway, the rejections hit him hard. It made him realise that he wasn't Shakespeare or James Joyce. I think you know – deep down – by your mid-twenties whether you're a genius or not. A real genius. For William, the results came in and they weren't good. He could, however, tell a rollicking good story. What he needed was a decent character to hang a full book on. I wasn't long out of uni myself, when I discovered him at a spoken word event in a pub on Dumbarton Road. He blew me away with a story he said he had written in an hour earlier that day. It was remarkable. I told him that I loved his work, and that I was starting a publishing house that was going to take on the big boys in London. He liked that part. He was always up for a fight, William. Four weeks later he submitted to us the next thing that he wrote. That was *The Long Dark*.'

Lomond said, 'You must have been jumping for joy. A tiny publisher getting a book like that.'

'I knew within five pages that William was going to be a star. The problem was, we didn't have any money to give him an advance, and all the big London publishers that William had also sent the book to did. We were trapped: we wanted the book badly because we needed the sales. But we couldn't afford to buy the rights. So I came up with a business proposition that might go down as one of the worst business deals ever made.'

'What went wrong?'

Crawford snorted. 'Everything. In order to secure the rights to *The Long Dark*, I agreed to give William a bigger royalty than normal instead of an upfront advance. It seemed like a win/win. The book would sell well across Glasgow and Edinburgh independent book stores. I was confident of that. Those sales would cover our printing costs, and William would get paid once it started selling. There was just one problem. It sold faster than I thought possible. Which was great for William, but terrible for us. We were getting pennies for every copy sold.'

While a butler brought in a tray of coffee cups, Ross asked, 'How many copies did it go on to sell?'

'About one hundred and seventy-five thousand.'

Ross made an "oh" shape with his mouth, wincing.

Crawford then clarified, 'The first six months.'

Donna and the others recoiled. 'Ouch.'

'Yeah,' said Crawford. 'Ouch. By the end of the first year of sales, we had lost a quarter of a million pounds in revenue in that deal.'

Lomond said, 'Didn't it wipe you out?'

'Close. But not quite. So I went to William and asked if he would review his initial contract for book two. William agreed. That prompted me to spend every last penny we had promoting *The Long Dark* further. And it worked. Then, when it came time to sign the contract for book two, William backed out. He wanted the prestige, you see, of being one of the authors with a publisher like Hathaway. He wanted to go to the parties, the award shows, get on the radio, and we could never do all that.'

'What happened?'

'It bankrupted us. I lost everything. Then Hathaway

stepped in and scooped up the rights to *The Long Dark* from us for buttons. The administrators didn't understand that we would be sitting on an immensely profitable intellectual property for at least another fifty years. It didn't matter. We were out of business. So they were happy to flog the rights for whatever they could get.'

Lomond glanced at Crawford's hands and realised his knuckles were white from clenching them. 'You must have resented the hell out of him for a long time.'

Ross added, 'Yeah, I'd struggle to get over something like that. Like losing a winning lottery ticket.'

'Actually,' said Donna, 'it's more like having the winning lottery ticket in your hand, then having someone rip it up.'

Crawford said, 'This is all very helpful, thank you.'

Lomond asked, 'Did William ever try to make it up to you? I mean, he ended up in that plush pad on Park Circus off the back of that book, while you had to shut up shop.'

He forced a smile. 'William didn't care much about correcting the past. Unless he was the one feeling aggrieved.'

'I can see that it still angers you to this day. Understandable.'

'That's very clever, DCI Lomond. Ingenious word play there. Unfortunately for you, I have about fifty witnesses that can say that I was nowhere near Glasgow last night.'

'Unfortunately for you, Mr Bell, William MacRae wasn't just stabbed. He was poisoned.'

Crawford peered back in confusion. 'Poisoned?'

'A bottle of Lagavulin sent to his house. It had to be

someone who knew his home address. Who knew he would drink it.'

Crawford stood up and buttoned his jacket. 'If I'd known the conversation would go like this, I would have waited until my lawyer was present. I understand that I might look like an easy target to pin your case on.' He pointed to the window. 'But if you take a look at some of the speakers here tonight, I think you'll find several people with much more relevant, and recent, motive than me. If you'll excuse me, I have a festival to run.'

Lomond took a quick look out the window, and saw a convoy of Range Rovers spattered with mud, driving up the gravel driveway to Crichton House.

Ross suggested, 'Has the Prime Minister shown up or something?'

Crawford paused in the open doorway. 'The writers who will be speaking at William's memorial. Did I mention that they were all in Glasgow last night having a get-together?'

'Do you know where?' asked Lomond.

'Hotel Devonshire Gardens,' Crawford said. Before leaving, he added, 'And you didn't get that from me.'

Donna snapped her fingers trying to remember. 'That's Great Western Road, right?'

'Yep,' said Lomond. 'Can't be more than a mile and a half from William MacRae's house.' He told Ross, 'Get me CCTV from that hotel. I want to see if anyone went outside for a cigarette for a few hours.'

Ross took out his phone and called Willie back in Govan.

Lomond followed Donna over to the window, as the first car door opened.

'The best of the best,' she said.

'Take a good look, Donna,' said Lomond. 'One of them is AD Sullivan. And quite possibly our killer.'

CHAPTER TWENTY-SIX

LOMOND, Donna, and Ross arrived for the drinks reception for guests and VIPs in the Grand Library of Crichton House, a shade underdressed for the event. A lot of men were in black tie, and the women were dressed like they were attending a film premiere in Leicester Square.

The weather had continued to move in from the Atlantic, bringing howling winds and sideways rain. The entrance hall was quite a sight, as guests arrived wrapped up in waterproof and insulated jackets, before peeling them off to reveal immaculate smart attire underneath. One of the worst jobs that night was working in the cloakroom, as there were so many similar jackets next to each other.

The Grand Library was richly furnished with Chippendale chairs, a fireplace that was as big as a living room, and shelves of leather-bound books from floor to ceiling.

At one end of the room was a raised platform, with several chairs set up in front of microphones. Adjacent, was a bar area illuminated by LED fairy lights on a string, giving it a spectral, enchanted grotto feel.

Servers glided effortlessly through the crowd, delivering champagne cocktails, fine wines, and rare whiskies. Everyone in the room was either Crichton House staff, an author participating in an event over the weekend, or a guest interviewer. There were also a half dozen members of the public. Some who had won competitions to be there, and others who had paid handsomely for the privilege of rubbing shoulders with their literary heroes for a few hours.

Standing patiently at the bar, Lomond was most concerned with the fact that there were no drinks prices listed anywhere.

He said to the barman, 'Two diet Cokes, and a tap water with ice, please.'

The barman handed over three small tumblers containing the drinks. 'That will be twelve pounds, please.'

Lomond shook his head like he'd misheard. 'Sorry, for a minute there I thought you said twelve pounds.'

'I did.'

Lomond chuckled softly. 'It's two Cokes and a water with ice. Or did you swap out the ice for uncut diamonds or something?'

The barman looked confused.

'Never mind.' Lomond handed over a twenty. When he received his change, he said, 'Someone should call the police. Because I've just been robbed.'

Lomond took the drinks over to Ross and Donna. 'Here,' he said. 'Guard these with your lives because you're not getting another round. Not unless I remortgage my house.'

'Thanks, boss,' they both said.

Lomond remarked, 'It's only when I stand in a room like this that I realise I must get some new suits.'

Ross held his arms out for a cursory inspection. 'I think I look pretty sharp.'

'You look like you've spent a fifty quid gift card on ASOS.'

Donna by contrast couldn't have cared less. She was wearing her usual trouser suit with an open-neck white shirt, and had been wrongly identified as a waitress twice already.

Lomond said, 'Let's just try to blend in here – not look like private security on the lookout for assassins.'

'We're not a million miles away from that, boss,' Ross remarked.

Lomond did a quick recce of the room, looking for some of the faces he had seen earlier getting out of the festival courtesy cars. 'Donna, this is where I need you. Give me the skinny on some of this lot.'

'What do you want to know?' she asked.

'We could start with names.'

Donna turned to a man with a deep suntan, wearing the sort of pinstripe suit a banker would wear. 'That guy there...'

'The one who's too important to wear a tie?'

'That's Tom Ellison.'

'Really?' said Lomond, almost let down. 'It's funny. I've never thought about what he looked like until just now.'

'Who's he?' asked Ross.

'My God, Ross,' said Donna. 'If you don't know who Tom Ellison is then the rest of this is going to be hard work.

Probably the biggest-selling author in the world. He publishes about ten books a year, and every one of them goes to the top of the bestseller charts.'

'American?'

'Yeah. He writes super short chapters, like a page and a half, and they're really hard to put down. Police thrillers and FBI agents, that kind of thing. He's more of a brand than an actual writer at this point.'

'What do you mean?'

'He co-writes most of his books now.' Donna took out her phone and brought up a list of Ellison's books on Amazon. 'See his name on the cover. Then this much smaller name at the bottom? Kind of blends in with the background?'

'Oh yeah.'

'That's the co-author. Ellison comes up with the idea and most of the story, then the co-author writes it up. It happens a lot these days. No one knows how much of his books Ellison actually writes anymore. He gets a lot of flak for it, but people forget that he wrote all the John Carver books on his own. He still does. Those are the ones that made his reputation. Carver's an FBI agent. Those are the best. I still read the first Carver book, *Hush a-bye Baby*, probably once a year. That thing of a book title named after a line in a nursery rhyme? He practically invented that.'

Ellison had five people around him, all hanging on his every word. Lomond couldn't help but notice the way he looked over everyone's heads as they spoke. As if something more interesting was going on elsewhere.

Lomond wondered aloud, 'Chances of him being AD Sullivan?'

'It's hard to say,' said Donna. 'He has so many books already. Why would he need a pen name?'

Ross said, 'But we know Sullivan is a truly big hitter in the trade. Ellison's the biggest there is.'

'What about the guy next to him?' asked Lomond. 'The one drinking coffee.'

The man was wearing a tuxedo and looked awkward in it. He was used to wearing jeans and a t-shirt every day.

Donna said, 'That's Brad Carr. I follow him on Facebook. Seems a really nice guy and, yeah, obsessed with coffee. He's a Brit, but spends most of his time in America now.'

Ross said, 'He doesn't look much like a Brad.'

She laughed. 'It's not his real name. I think it's Henry or something terribly English like that.'

Lomond said, 'Seems a decent bloke. I saw him slip a note into one of the server's pockets earlier. I don't know that many of the people here will bother to tip anyone tonight.'

Carr was thin and had a pensive expression. He was used to being recognised in public, and his radar for it was always on. On a regular day in his adopted home of New York City, he could be stopped upwards of twenty times. If he was popular in the UK, he was a superstar in the States.

Donna said, 'He's only written one character. Jack Law.'

Lomond had a glint in his eye when he asked Ross, 'Can you guess the tagline for his books?'

'Let me guess,' he said. 'No one's above the law.'

'Nailed it.'

Donna added, 'Law's an ex-Navy SEAL turned drifter who's always drinking black coffee.'

'His shirt's untucked at the back,' Lomond pointed out.

'You could tell him,' said Donna. 'But I doubt he would care. I also think it's highly unlikely he's our Sullivan. *The Shortlist* is a totally different genre to his.'

'Maybe he's fed up of the Law books,' said Ross.

Lomond said, 'I've read a few of them. A pen name would be a good way of getting something out there that was totally different without alienating your fans. I'd be interested to find out his connection to William MacRae, though. Who else do you recognise, Donna?'

She paused, scanning the room. 'It's hard. I read on Kindle a lot these days, so I don't see the author photos that much...Oh wait, over there by the fire. You'll know that guy.'

'Which one?' asked Ross.

'The guy who looks really animated. Holding the pint of bitter. That's Jim Provan.'

'Ah, now we're talking,' said Lomond. 'He's good, isn't he.'

Ross looked up and away, trying to remember. 'Right, his name kept coming up when I searched online about MacRae. Who's he again?'

Donna's voice dropped an octave. 'Are you serious?' She looked to Lomond. 'Is he serious?'

Lomond smirked. 'I think he's serious.'

Donna asked, 'Did you not read any books when you were a teenager, at least?'

Ross replied, 'I played football when I was a teenager.'

'What about your twenties?'

'Mostly playing Xbox.' He thought for a moment. 'And five-a-sides.'

Lomond chuckled to himself.

On the defensive, Ross complained, 'Oh yeah, Ross doesn't read books. Ross doesn't even know Jim Provan. Blah blah blah...I've heard of him, all right. I just don't know much about what he does.'

'Right,' Donna huffed. 'Out of everyone else here, Provan is the writer most like MacRae. His main character Inspector Rothes is quite similar to MacRae's DCI Roxburgh. A bit of a curmudgeon. Grumpy. Cynical...'

'Sounds familiar,' he said, shooting a glance Lomond's way.

Lomond shot back a look that said *tread carefully, sunshine.*

Donna continued, 'The differences are subtle. Roxburgh is into Scottish folk music, but Rothes is more of a Rolling Stones kind of guy. MacRae's are set in Glasgow. Provan's are set in Edinburgh. I did read once that MacRae accused Provan of ripping him off. Though that could be down to jealousy. MacRae might have been a bestseller, but he never quite got to Jim Provan's heights.'

Lomond sucked in air through his teeth as he mulled it over. 'Hard to imagine he's Sullivan,' he said.

Donna agreed. 'He's too nice to be mixed up with all this stuff.'

'It's hard to imagine any of them are.'

'Someone has to be,' said Lomond, scanning the room. 'The Sullivan event is tomorrow. If we don't narrow our search down and fast, there's no telling what might happen.'

CHAPTER TWENTY-SEVEN

STILL SCANNING THE CROWD, Donna shook her head. 'Sorry, boss, I don't recognise anyone else that–'

Ross suddenly exclaimed, barely able to contain his excitement. 'No way! That's Noel Redmond. Right over there! Look, look...'

Lomond said, 'Jesus wept, son. Calm down. Who's Noel Redmond when he's at home?'

Donna was spluttering laughter at Ross. 'Of course that's the guy *you* recognise at a book festival.'

Ross made a show of holding his head high. 'He's a smart guy. And it's a funny show.'

Lomond said, 'Will one of you please explain who the hell you're looking at?'

Donna explained, 'The really tall guy in the kilt.'

Lomond glared, not sure whether to believe his eyes. 'Is he wearing that...No, surely not.'

'What is it?'

'Look where his pleats are.'

'I don't get it,' said Donna.

'He's wearing his kilt backwards. Christ, do none of these guys know how to dress themselves or something?'

Ross said, 'Maybe he thinks you're meant to sit down on the flat part rather than spoil the pleats.'

'Who is he?' asked Lomond.

Donna answered, 'Noel Redmond. The host of that TV quiz *Wrong but Right*. Imagine *QI* meets *Pointless*.'

'What's he doing here?'

Donna opened up her Amazon app. 'He just published his first book. Look...' She showed Lomond and Ross the current bestseller chart. 'He's got the number one book in the country this evening. *The Bowling Club Detectives*. Says here it's a cosy crime thriller about a group of retired police detectives who meet once a week at their local bowling club to crack unsolved cases in a sleepy English village.'

Crawford Bell had been watching the detectives for a while from the margins of the room. He made his way over tentatively. 'How is your investigation going so far, Chief Inspector? Nice and quietly, I hope? Mixing with as few people as possible? I can't *tell* you what to do–'

Lomond gave a derisory snort. 'That's very generous of you, Mr Bell.'

'That is to say, if you can refrain from introducing your-selves to everyone as police, I'd greatly appreciate it.'

'You might be able to stop us having to do that, in fact.' Lomond indicated the crowd around them. 'We're trying to work out who else is here that we should know about.' He rhymed off the writers they had already identi-fied. 'We need a shortlist of suspects for who AD

Sullivan is. Who else is speaking at the memorial tonight?'

Crawford craned his neck to look around. He pointed out a woman in her late twenties. Wearing a rather frumpy vintage black dress, the only note of colour on her was a thin slash of red across her lips, which stood out against her pale face.

Crawford said, 'Charlotte Fount.'

'Never heard of her,' said Lomond.

'You probably heard of her first book. *The Woman on the Stairs.*'

'That was her?' exclaimed Donna. 'I loved that book.'

'You and about a million other people.'

Donna explained to Lomond, 'They made it into a film. It was all over Netflix last year.'

'What sort of thing?'

'Psychological thriller. A regular person as the main character rather than a cop.' She turned to Crawford, 'I didn't know she had a new book out.'

Crawford checked over both shoulders to make sure no one else could hear. 'Between you and me, the publisher is rather hoping no one will notice.' Revelling in having a bit of gossip to throw around, he clasped his nose shut with his free hand, then said, 'If you get what I mean...' He knocked back the whisky in his glass. Before he had lowered the glass from his mouth, he grabbed another from a passing server. 'It's taken three years for the follow-up, and the reviews so far aren't good. I know a few writers who were sent an advance proof. None of them wanted to give a quote. They didn't want their names anywhere near it. Take a look at the cover for the hardback when it comes out. Talk about damning with faint praise. I think the most rapturous quote was "This is a book with pages you can turn.'"

Trying to be kinder, Lomond said, 'So she's on a downward trend?'

'Try flatlining. I didn't want her here, but she still has powerful friends in the Crime Writers' Guild.'

Lomond wanted Ross and Donna's temperature on Charlotte Fount. 'Our Sullivan?' he asked.

Donna bobbed her head from side to side, considering it. 'Of all the writers here, she writes most like Sullivan. And *The Shortlist* could absolutely have been written by her.'

Ross said, 'I know I'm not supposed to say this, but...'

Donna already knew what he was getting at. 'What, attractive women don't commit crimes, Ross?'

'That's not what I was going to say.'

'You were thinking it.'

'No, what I was thinking was, I can't imagine someone of her build stabbing a man in the chest.'

Crawford, showing his tipsiness now, said, 'What about poisoning? Hot young woman like her would have been just William's type.'

'He was an old man, for God's sake,' said Lomond.

Crawford pointed with his glass. 'He had a reputation, believe me. When he was a lecturer at Glasgow Uni's creative writing course, I heard plenty of stories. And I'm not talking about coursework. And he's not the only one here with a reputation. Rumour has it, there's an incendiary piece coming out on Monday from someone here, making allegations of loose hands, if you know what I mean.'

Lomond muttered, 'Yes, you've been very subtle so far.'

'Every other trade has had their share of explosive accusations. Cinema, music, sport. It was only a matter of time before the publishing world had to deal with a major scandal. I've begged everyone I can think of to tell me who's involved, but it's a mystery.' Catching sight of Tom Ellison, Crawford excused himself, 'Back in a sec.' He grabbed another whisky on the way, then called out, 'Tommy!'

'His tongue loosens when he's had a drink,' said Donna.

Ross added, 'Maybe we could keep him drunk the whole weekend. We might eventually get to the truth.'

'The last thing he needs is another drink,' said Lomond. 'This article could be something, though.' He trailed off, distracted by something. 'That's still only five, by my count. There were seven booked to speak at MacRae's lifetime achievement. The same seven that are appearing tonight.'

Donna took out a promotional flier she had found earlier. 'It says here that one of them was due to be RJ Hawley.'

Impressed, Lomond said, 'That's quite a coup.'

'It would have been. She's no longer showing up, apparently.'

RJ Hawley was the one author that Lomond or Ross didn't need described to them. There also a few hundred million children around the world who knew her Sally Stroud Mysteries. Sally was a child detective who investigated cases of missing pencil cases, and lost dogs. Critics had described Sally as a one-girl version of *The Famous Five* for the twenty-first century.

Lomond asked, 'What would she be doing at a crime writing festival, though?'

'Didn't you hear?' Donna said. 'She's started writing crime books for adults under a pen name. She went as far as submitting them to a publisher without them realising who she was. It was kept a total secret until someone outed her on Twitter.'

Crawford returned. Notably with another empty glass. 'What did I miss?'

Donna replied, 'We were just discussing RJ Hawley.'

'Oh, yes.' He nodded, eyelids looking heavy. 'She and William were very close. She's too upset to give a speech. Such a shame. She's chair of the Crime Writers' Guild. It was her vote that swung the Outstanding Contribution award in William's favour.'

'That's six,' said Lomond. 'Including Sullivan, Seth Knox, and yourself Crawford, that leaves one more name.'

The other suspects made their way towards a makeshift stage on a raised platform at the front of the room. On either side of it were two large video screens showing an official photo portrait of William MacRae – the same that adorned the back covers of his books.

The crowd parted just enough for Lomond to see Claire MacRae standing near the stage next to Seth Knox – and in intense conversation. When she saw Lomond looking at her, she did a double-take, then waved cautiously to him.

Crawford said, 'For every bridge that William burned down, Claire was there afterward rebuilding it. She's the only reason William survived in this industry, if you ask me.'

The murmur of conversation quickly died down as Claire took control of a microphone at the centre of the stage. The other suspects the detectives had been discussing made their way towards the stage.

Lomond said, hushed, 'I don't quite understand what all of these people have in common with William. How did they all end up on the bill for his award event?'

Crawford replied, 'I'm sure you'll find out over the course of the weekend, Chief Inspector.'

Holding him back from leaving, Lomond asked, 'What do you know about William MacRae that you're not telling us, Mr Bell?'

'What I know about him that no one else does, you could barely fit on all the pages of all the books in this room. But all secrets have a habit of coming out eventually. Don't you find?' He pointed towards the stage. 'That's my cue. Would you mind?' He handed his empty glass to Lomond. 'I should probably slow down if I want to survive the night.'

'I hope that you do,' Lomond replied.

Claire said, 'So then...a toast on this night honouring the memory of our dear friend, William MacRae. Please welcome, some of William's closest acquaintances: Tom Ellison, Brad Carr, Jim Provan, Noel Redmond, Charlotte Fount, Seth Knox...' Claire looked all around, realising that they were one short.

Murmuring broke out across the room again, then heads turned one by one as a young woman in an epic, figure-hugging midi dress in dark red, with sheer bodice panelling that left precious little to the imagination.

'Who is *that*?' asked Ross, picking his jaw up off the floor.

Donna said, 'That's Zoe Hathaway. CEO of Hathaway Publishing. Classic nepo baby.'

'Sorry, what?' said Ross.

Donna said it like it was obvious. 'A nepo baby.'

'Okay, Donna, I have no new information from last time. What does it mean?' He looked at Lomond.

'Don't look at *me*,' Lomond said. 'I thought video streaming meant someone sent you a DVD in the mail. I don't know what anything means anymore.'

Donna explained, 'Nepo as in nepotism. The children of celebrities or socialites that go on to great success mostly off the back of their parents' wealth or connections. She might look like an airhead, but she's got some game, apparently.

Lomond said to himself, 'Ladies and gentlemen, one of these people is AD Sullivan.'

CHAPTER TWENTY-EIGHT

THE DRIVE from Helen Street station along the south side of the River Clyde to Laurieston in the city centre was a familiar one for Pardeep and Jason. They had each made the journey more times than they cared to remember, bound for the Sheriff court to spend – or waste, depending which time you asked them – many hours standing around, waiting for cases to be heard. They could spend an entire morning there only for a case to collapse or be settled.

But Pardeep and Jason weren't going to the Sheriff court. They were going around the corner to the Procurator Fiscal's Office on Ballater Street, directly across the road from Glasgow Central Mosque.

The yellow brickwork and poky windows on the Procurator Fiscal's Office made it look like a budget hotel built in the late nineties.

A security guard stood in reception. It wasn't uncommon for there to be some heated exchanges there throughout the day. The guard was built like a brick shit-house, and spoke with a Nigerian accent that Pardeep recognised from neighbours he once had.

'Good afternoon, gents,' he said in a joyful voice. 'Do you have an appointment?'

'We don't,' Pardeep answered, then showed his badge. 'DC Varma and this is DC Yang. We're looking for some records.'

The guard leaned down to inspect their badges closely.

Neither detective could remember the last time anyone checked them as diligently.

Once the guard was satisfied, he indicated the unstaffed reception desk. 'Okay. Just press the buzzer. You need to be firm, though.' He quoted the laminated sign on the sliding partition on the window. 'Remember: if you can't hear it, they can't hear it.'

On the cusp of being won over by his enthusiasm, Pardeep managed a smile. 'Thanks.'

Jason said quietly on the way to the desk, 'I love a man who enjoys his work.'

Their appreciation was to be short-lived.

After pressing, and hearing, the buzzer on the other side of a secure door, a receptionist came mooching out. Her name badge said "DEBS". Her eyes narrowed at the sight of Pardeep and Jason. 'Do you have an appointment?'

Pardeep took out his badge again, as did Jason.

'We don't, sorry,' Pardeep said. 'We're with Helen Street MIT. We're trying to locate a legacy record that's over ten years old.'

Debs almost rolled her eyes. 'No, you need to go to National Records of Scotland over at–'

Pardeep nodded. 'West Register House. Yeah, we

know. We just spent the better part of the morning waiting around there. They said the file we need must still be here, because–'

She cranked out an even bigger eye roll. 'NRS has been receiving legacy records from us since twenty sixteen. After records are ten years old, they get sent to NRS every January and February. Of every year. Without fail.'

Taken aback at her attitude, Pardeep registered her name badge. 'Okay, Debs? Not this file. This file is still here.' He passed over the identification number. 'Can you maybe check the records room? I've had people do that for me before.'

'You'll need to contact COPFS,' she said it like it was a word, 'in writing with ten working days' notice, and then contact the Court and Legal Records team to discuss and approve your request.' She wrote down a phone number. 'You'll need to call this number.'

Jason leaned in and dialled the number on his phone.

Pardeep locked eyes with Debs, who was chewing gum slowly. 'Happy in your work?'

'Not really,' she replied deadpan.

'You'd never know,' he muttered under his breath. He asked Jason, 'What's happening?'

Jason tutted and shook his head. He held his phone out as if for Debs to hear the recorded message at the other end. 'They're closed,' he complained.

'Oh yeah,' she said. 'They closed at two today. They're getting renovations done.' She flashed a fake smile, knowing full well that they were closed before Jason called.

Losing patience, Pardeep took out his phone. 'I'm

calling Detective Superintendent Linda Boyle,' he said. 'Do you know her, Debs?'

'No,' she replied.

'Then you're in for a treat.' Once the line was ringing, he handed his phone to her.

She was about to take it, when Jason stopped her.

'Whoa,' he said. 'What are you doing?'

Pardeep could hear Linda answering, 'Hello? Hello?' at the other end, when Jason grabbed the phone and hung up.

'What are *you* doing?' Pardeep retorted.

Baffled and exasperated, Debs said to Jason, 'He wants me to talk to his boss.'

'And why are you trusting us?' asked Jason.

Debs looked confused. 'What?'

'Why are you trusting us?'

'Because you're the police. You showed me your badges.'

'Which you barely looked at. We could be under investigation for corruption for all you know. It could be our mate in a car outside you're about to talk to, and we could be looking for information on someone with an Osman letter.'

'A what?'

'It's what you get when the police uncover a threat against someone's life.' Jason picked up her landline and handed it to her. 'Google Helen Street police station, call the switchboard phone number listed, and then ask for Detective Superintendent Linda Boyle. Tell them you're with DC Yang and DC Varma.'

After finding the number herself and getting through, Jason said, 'We'll wait.'

The pair watched as Debs' expression shifted once she was connected to Linda. The men could hear her slightly in the background, and she didn't sound pleased.

'Of course,' Debs said. 'Yeah. Sorry.' She hung up, then told the men a little contrite, 'I think I know where you two get it from now. I'll be five minutes.'

'Great, thank you,' Jason replied breezily. Once she was gone, he shook his head. 'No wonder social engineering scams work.'

Pardeep sighed. 'It's just got to be by the book with you, hasn't it.' He sauntered around at the front doors, stuffing his hands in coat pockets. He asked the guard, 'You not freezing standing here, mate?'

'I'm all good,' he replied. 'I've got layers on.'

Pardeep trilled his lips as he blew out air. 'Tougher than me, mate.'

Before Pardeep could wander away, he said, 'You know, I'm from Nigeria. I would love to join your police someday. To give something back to the community. You know?'

Pardeep asked, 'Have you applied for citizenship?'

'Yeah, I got in eighteen months ago.'

'Good for you, mate. But you'll need to wait another eighteen months before you can apply.'

'Any hints or tips?'

Pardeep said, 'Aye, take a course on infinite patience as soon as you can.' He waved his hand to stop the guard writing. 'I'm joking.' He looked to Jason. 'Jase. Any tips?'

Tapping out a message to Lomond on his phone, Jason replied, 'Yeah. Learn how to drive if you can't already, talk to as many Scottish people as you can, and get a good textbook on psychology. It doesn't have to be a new edition.'

'Psychology?' the guard wondered aloud.

Jason explained, 'If you're going to be a PC around here, a ton of your callouts are going to be mental health-related. Officially, it's twenty per cent. In reality, it's close to double that. And you won't be properly trained to deal with most of them. If you know what's in front of you, you might be able to help them.'

He frantically scribbled it all down. 'This is great. And I work hard. I come in early and go home late.'

'Then you're already in the top twenty per cent of the general workforce in the country.' Jason flicked his head up. 'What's your name?'

'George,' he replied.

Debs returned and said nothing as she handed the file over to Pardeep.

When he returned, Pardeep handed George his card. 'Give me a call in five years. I'll be a detective sergeant by then.' He motioned to Jason. 'Not so sure about him, though.'

George smiled, realising that they were ribbing each other. He put out his hand to shake. 'Thank you, DC Varma.'

Pardeep pointed at him. 'I'm going to be waiting for that call, George, you hear me?'

George smiled.

Jason shook his hand, then held on. 'Be so good that they can't ignore you.'

George nodded deeply. 'Thank you, DC Yang.'

Once the pair were outside, Pardeep said appreciatively, 'This city, man.'

'This city,' said Jason.

JASON THUMBED through the file in the car on the way back to the station. 'So how come none of this was on HOLMES?'

Pardeep replied, 'Liz MacRae's death was ruled accidental. It was investigated initially because the cause of death wasn't immediately obvious. Protocol was followed, crime scene photos taken, etcetera. But SFIU ruled that no investigation was needed.'

'Remind me,' Jason said.

Jason was so competent in every area, anytime he didn't know something Pardeep was reminded how new a detective Jason was. 'Scottish Fatalities Investigation Unit,' Pardeep said. 'They're a specialist team within COPFS. They investigate all sudden, suspicious, accidental and unexplained deaths. Which Liz MacRae's very much was. When cause of death was agreed with the doctor who had been on the scene and SFIU's forensic scientist who conducted the post mortem, the investigation was shuttered and shipped off.'

Jason asked, 'Then what is John expecting us to find?'

'A reason why Liz MacRae's photo was face down on that desk.'

Jason stopped to ponder the basic details, then recoiled. 'Poor woman...listen to this, Pardeep. She was a suicide. She drowned in the bath – get this – by weighing herself down with a bag full of books on her chest. Yet the death was still ruled accidental.'

'How could that be?'

'I have no idea. But guess whose books were in the bag.'

'William MacRae?'

'Yeah. God, that must have been heavy for him.'

'Sounds like it was heavier for her.'

'Aw, come on, Pardeep, man. That's rank.'

Realising he had overstepped the mark, he held his hands up a bit off the steering wheel. 'You're right, you're right. Sorry, Jase.'

A few more pages in, something caught Jason's attention. 'Huh.'

Pardeep was eager to take his eyes off the road. He couldn't stand finding something out even ten seconds later than Jason. 'What is it?' he asked.

'No, it's just...This part here. There was a flatmate. The one who found Liz. She gave a statement.'

Pardeep waited for a conclusion that didn't come. 'And?'

Jason frowned at the file, troubled by something. 'I think we need to speak to this woman.'

CHAPTER TWENTY-NINE

WHEN THEY RETURNED to Major Investigations, the two detectives found DI Sneddon holed up in a windowless room. The only light source was the glow of his laptop screen.

As soon as Willie registered Pardeep holding a file aloft in the open doorway, he exclaimed, 'Bloody hell, it's Captain Oates. What kept you?'

Pardeep looked confused. 'Sir?'

Willie said, 'I'm just going outside and may be some time...? The Antarctic explorer?' He waited for some sign of recognition from them, but got none. He sighed. 'Forget it. What have you got?'

'Liz MacRae was a suicide,' said Pardeep, laying the file down for Willie to see.

Jason clarified, 'But ruled accidental.'

Willie pointed to the part about the bag of books laid on her torso. 'Despite this?'

'That's what I said. Though it could well have been

done by Liz herself. To stop her body floating to the surface and finding air. I did a quick search online, and it may have been a reference to Virginia Woolf. She walked into a river with stones in her pockets to keep herself under the water.'

Pardeep said, 'Sounds like she had quite the leaving do. Toxicology found evidence of a large amount of sleeping pills and anti-depressants, as well as point two-five blood alcohol level.'

Willie said, 'All these pills and a point two-five, and this was classed accidental rather than suicide?'

Jason shrugged ruefully. 'That's what it says, boss.'

'I mean, it's interesting. Say you're William MacRae. You're at home. Having a dram. Why do you not want to see your daughter's photo?'

'Shame?' Pardeep guessed. 'Maybe he didn't want to feel like she was looking at him, for some reason.'

With less doubt, Jason offered, 'Who's to say the photo wasn't always face-down?'

Willie nodded. 'Not bad. Could be.'

Pardeep said, 'But then say it was the killer that did it. Why do that?'

Jason ventured an answer. 'The only possible reason can be that the killer must be connected to Liz MacRae in some way.' He turned a few pages through the file, then pointed to a section of text. 'I think there might be something to this bit here.'

Willie tried to scan as much of the text as he could. 'Whose statement is this?'

'Liz's flatmate, Kate Randall' replied Jason. 'They lived in student accommodation together.'

Pardeep, already familiar with the material, said, 'She

was the one who found Liz MacRae's body. Liz had been dead at least an hour at that point. But on her way back through the building, Kate nearly bumped into someone. Now, their flat was at the end of a corridor. The man she nearly bumped into hadn't reached any other door yet. He had to have been coming from Liz's flat.'

'I'd like to talk to the SO,' said Pardeep.

Willie exhaled heavily and handed back the file. He really didn't want a detective constable asking tough questions of a former senior officer. Especially one as modest and gentle as former Detective Inspector Derek Graham.

'Leave him to me,' Willie replied. 'He's retired and we go back a stretch. Right now, I need to show you two something.'

While Willie clicked and scrolled around on his laptop, then clicked play on one of the many video files he had open.

It showed the reception area of a plush-looking hotel. 'This is from Hotel Devonshire Gardens on Great Western Road last night.' He highlighted a group arriving at the reception area. 'I spoke to John about this, and he confirmed that the festival director told him that a party of writers who are up there met for dinner last night before making the journey north. You can see the time is two hours before MacRae's estimated time of death.' Willie dragged the cursor along the timeline. 'Jump to forty-five minutes before time of death, and this happens...' He hit the spacebar, pausing the video. It showed a woman in her mid- to late-forties in a smart dress quickly exiting through the front doors out to the main road.

Jason and Pardeep both leaned in, wanting to make sure they were seeing the same person.

'Is that Claire MacRae?' asked Pardeep.

'It sure is,' replied Willie. He clicked to another window, showing a freeze-frame image of her returning to the hotel. 'And this is her coming back...' He pointed to the time at the bottom corner of the screen. 'An hour after time of death. She arrived at Park Circus while John and I were there ninety minutes after this.'

'Question is,' said Pardeep. 'Where did she go?'

Jason tutted. 'Someone needs an alibi.'

'That's not all,' said Willie, pulling out paperwork he had printed earlier. 'These are bank records from William MacRae's files in his home. Principally, about the owner-ship of the Park Circus property.'

Pardeep took it but was immediately baffled by the legalese. 'This is Greek to me.' He handed it to Jason to decipher.

'I studied a little property law when I was a student,' said Jason, giving most of his attention to the document rather than Willie and Pardeep.

'Of course you did,' Pardeep rebutted. He asked Willie, 'Is it possible to sack a constable for being overqualified *after* he's been hired?'

Willie smiled.

'It's a straightforward document.' Jason passed it back to Willie. 'It says that the property is co-owned by William and Claire MacRae.'

'But they're divorced,' said Pardeep.

Willie asked, 'Can Claire sell the property now?'

Jason said, 'I'll need to look into it. But if she can, then we're looking at an ex-wife who goes missing at the time of the murder, and about a million quid's worth of reasons to want her ex-husband dead.'

Willie clicked to another page on the laptop. 'And to top it all off...'

It was the Met Office's website, showing the Lochinver area – and a blanket of red that meant hurricane rains sweeping east from the Atlantic Ocean, across the Hebrides, were bound for the mainland.

Willie said, 'John, Ross, and Donna are about to get battered.'

CHAPTER THIRTY

THE ROOM WAS PACKED as the bar closed temporarily, and people who had scattered to various corridors and outdoor smoking spots came together. The mood was respectfully sombre, but with the inescapable excitement of having so many big-name authors on a stage at the same time.

Ross whispered under the anticipatory hush in the room to Lomond, 'Isn't it a little soon for all of this? MacRae's body's barely cold back in Glasgow, while this lot are swilling champagne and remembering the good times?'

Lomond cast a sceptical eye towards the stage, pondering every person in turn. 'Funny. I was thinking the same thing.'

First to speak was Zoe Hathaway.

'This should be interesting,' said Donna. 'I've seen plenty of photos of her standing on red carpets. But I've never heard her speak.'

Zoe spoke softly but effortlessly commanded your attention. She had the effect of making you lean forward to catch every word. She said, 'On my eighteenth birthday, my dad took me aside in his office and told me, if I ever wanted to run Hathaway, I would have to read all of the books that captured exactly what it is we do. For readers. For the wider culture. For the business. I prepared myself for a few yards of books to be presented to me on a couple of trolleys. Instead, he handed me one book. *The Long Dark* by William MacRae.' She paused, and some applause broke out across the crowd. 'He told me, *That right there, Zoe, is what Hathaway does.*'

The rest of her speech hit similarly emotive beats. For someone who – as was rumoured – didn't even read books, it was a credible public showing.

She concluded by saying, 'It's been suggested in the press that I don't know the value of anything because I've never had to struggle. That's true. But six months ago, when my dad told me that Hathaway might lose William to a rival, I told him that we should give him whatever he wants. To me, nothing defines the value of something better than a blank cheque. And in the days following my dad's sudden passing, it was a source of great pride to me that the first contract that I put my name to was for another ten DCI Bob Roxburgh books by William MacRae. We might never see those books now, but as long as I have blood running in my veins, William will always be a Hathaway writer.' She gave a small bow. 'Thank you. I'd now like to hand you over to someone who knew William better than almost anyone else in this room. The man who helped sculpt his words, and shape his stories. William's beloved editor, Seth Knox.'

Zoe held on to Seth in an embrace at the mic, offering

encouragement at a difficult time and whispered something in his ear.

'I wonder how he'll play it,' said Ross.

Donna said nothing. Staring Seth down.

Seth waited for the room to return to silence, basking in having so many eyes on him at once.

'Curmudgeon. Cunning. Ingenious. Moody. Bitter. Cynical. Anarchic. These are just some of the things I was told to expect from William MacRae. It was then added that William could be a lot of negative things too.' Seth paused for melancholy laughter which came in abundance.

He went on to give a heart-rending speech that made reference to an acclaimed book or author in every other sentence.

Lomond remarked to Ross and Donna, 'If editing doesn't work out, he could always get a job as a walking quote generator.'

It was as if Seth didn't have any actual thoughts of his own. He could only view life through the lens of other people's observations. But there was also a charm to it. How unashamedly he admired certain writers. It wasn't hard to see how he had managed to ascend to where he had at such a young age.

Next up was Tom Ellison, who couldn't have been more different to Seth. He was flippant and inappropriate. A monologue more in keeping with "having some beers with the guys while watching the game", rather than a eulogy for someone who had died less than twenty-four hours ago. A few minutes in, and most of the crowd couldn't work out why Ellison was there. If there had been any personal connection to MacRae, Ellison didn't state it.

To add insult to injury, he ended by plugging his latest book because 'William would approve of it.'

Brad Carr followed, and was generous and effusive about William's talents, sharing an anecdote about attending a book festival in the States with William. 'I kept looking over at him, thinking, is he unwell? He was hunched over, head down towards his lap. And when it came to audience Q&A he needed every question repeated. It was only as we were wrapping up that I realised, he had in fact been watching the Old Firm match on a portable TV throughout the entire event.'

Ross took out his phone and showed Lomond the message that had just come through.

Willie – "Need to talk asap."

Ross raised the phone. 'I'll take this outside.'

Jim Provan was up next, and spoke with a son's admiration for a father: blinkered to any faults, and exultant about any virtues. 'Without William,' he concluded, 'there would be no me.'

The more Lomond observed of him, the less he believed that Provan could have anything to do with AD Sullivan, or MacRae's murder. He couldn't imagine him so much as underpaying a parking ticket.

Charlotte Fount followed. She started by saying simply, 'William would have hated this. In lieu of having my own words to capture my sadness at losing him, I should instead turn to the words of his favourite poet, Philip Larkin.'

She went on to give a reading of *The Whitsun Weddings* that reduced at least a dozen in the crowd to tears.

Noel Redmond defused the heavy atmosphere with

witty jokes and classic English stiff upper lip in the face of grief. He recounted meeting William for the first time on the set of *Right and Wrong*, where William had been invited for the celebrity guest segment that week. He had given Noel advice about writing a novel, and encouraged him to quit his day job in order to do it.

Claire MacRae was last to speak. It was glowing. Scathing but honest. Much of it Lomond had already heard from her in William's lounge the night before. There was one addition, though.

'The one thing that never leaves you, even in divorce,' she explained, 'is a child. That binds you together for life no matter your differences. You would do anything you could to ensure their happiness. You both would. You would go to the ends of the earth. Even if it meant walking into hell itself. That was one thing William never wavered on. I understand that most of you here tonight want to remember William MacRae the writer. Because that's the William you know. The William I know was a husband and a dad, who would do absolutely anything to protect his family. That's who I wish to remember tonight.'

Cue a standing ovation, and the other speakers taking turns to console Claire – who had succumbed to tears.

Ross returned, phone in hand. He was covering the mouthpiece.

He told Lomond, 'Willie needs a word. He says it's urgent. Something about Claire MacRae.'

CHAPTER THIRTY-ONE

ONCE THE MEMORIAL WAS OVER, Ross and Donna watched as the authors from the stage broke out into various cliques.

Donna asked, 'What do you think the news is about Claire MacRae?'

Ross replied, 'Hopefully something compelling so we can arrest her and get home.'

'You're not enjoying hobnobbing with writers? Sipping Diet Coke?'

'No,' he said, deflated. 'I miss Lachlann, and I was hoping we would make it back tonight.' It was pitch black outside the tall window near them. He knew that they were going nowhere until at least tomorrow.

Ross felt someone brush up against him, then a hand was offered in his eye line.

'Jim Provan,' the man said.

Ross paused, then shook his hand. 'Detective Sergeant Ross McNair.'

Jim then offered his hand to Donna, who introduced herself.

'I'm a big fan,' she explained.

Ross couldn't believe it. She actually blushed. It was hard to imagine Donna blushing at anything.

Jim could tell that the two detectives were wondering why a bestselling author had decided to introduce himself in a room where he was not short of attention. 'Crawford mentioned that you're investigating William's murder. It's terrible what happened. I just wanted to offer my assistance, if I can do anything.'

'We appreciate that, Mr Provan,' said Ross.

Jim looked out across the room. 'Scary to think that someone in this room probably did it.'

'What makes you say that?' asked Donna, wondering how he had come to a conclusion about a fact that they hadn't gone public with yet.

'Well, it has to be,' said Jim. 'Look. Vultures the lot of them. I don't know why anyone would do it, but it had to be personal. That kind of attack.'

Ross said, 'You don't get on with other writers, Mr Provan?'

Jim smiled at the use of his surname. It always made him instantly feel ten years older than he was. 'It's subtle, but there's an entire class system at work in this room.' He indicated the small group with Tom Ellison and Brad Carr. 'Those at the top of their game, the height of their careers. Everything comes so easy to them. They could churn out any old garbage at this point and it would still sell. Look at them. The only people they talk to are their agents or publishers. All they want to hear from anyone now is "yes".'

Donna said, 'I would have thought you could comfortably stand next to writers like them. Number one bestsellers every year. Each book getting bigger and bigger.'

Jim had a sip of his pint of Belhaven. Only his second of the night. 'I'm not quite there yet,' he said. 'I'm probably in between them and the next group down.'

'And who are they?' asked Ross.

'Next you've got the midlist writers. I can't help but feel some kinship towards them, seeing as it wasn't that long ago I was one of them. They earn enough to write full-time, but they scrape by. Writing's an addiction at that level. It has to be. You think the next book will be the one to really break out and bring in some much-needed money. The problem is that books take ages to write. There's weeks or months of research, false starts, outlining. Then the actual writing. The graft. Every day you're dreaming of success. Feel a little wave of jealousy about where others are in the charts. What keeps you going is the hope that when your book comes out, everything will change. Reviewers will sew their tongues onto your arse, and readers will come flocking. But it's always the hope that kills you.'

Donna asked, 'How did you manage to escape?'

'A bit of luck,' Jim said. 'A lot, actually. Some newspaper managed to convince William to name his favourite books of the year. It was one of these end-of-year things, where twenty writers all give a list of three of four books. Not William. He said that my book was the only thing worth a damn that he had read that year. Only picking one book made mine stand out so much more. It was my first real breakout hit. I haven't looked back since.'

'Did he ever find out?' Ross asked.

Jim snorted ruefully. 'I did that stupid thing of trying to get a message from my agent to his, instead of just getting his number and picking up the phone. It put him off me. He thought I was one of the pompous ones. He could be like that. Just take against you because of one thing.'

Donna said, 'Is that what happened when he panned your last book in the *Glasgow Express*?'

Jim's face tightened, the thought of it still raw. 'It was more than that, DC Higgins. It was a personal attack. He never wrote reviews. He actually *requested* to review the book. It was a calculated move to try and hurt me. I think it hurt him more than it hurt me. Most people could tell that it was a hit piece. But let's just say I wasn't surprised when I didn't receive a Christmas card from him.'

'Why the personal attack?' Ross asked.

'He said that I was ripping him off, but sanding down Roxburgh's rougher edges to make Inspector Rothes more palatable.'

'All sounds a bit childish to me,' said Ross.

Jim said, 'It's a childish industry, DS McNair. When I was a student I worked at Waterstones on Princes Street at the weekend. We got all the biggest authors in. They loved to come to the shop when they were there for the book festival. I'll tell you, the real arseholes weren't the Tom Ellisons of this world. It was the midlist guys.'

'Why do you think that is?' Donna asked.

'They're too bitter. Too resentful at not having made it. They make the mistake of thinking the book trade is a zero-sum game. The reader you manage to snag means one less reader for me. But it doesn't work like that. Everything's a struggle when you're at that point. You've got just enough readers to compel you to keep going. It makes trying something new and to take a risk a scary thing.'

'Like AD Sullivan,' said Ross. 'Someone's felt the need to hide behind the name.'

'Could be. It sounds like Hathaway's lured away someone big.'

Ross had a glint in his eye. He just wanted to see how Jim would react. 'Someone like you?'

He smiled. 'No chance. *The Shortlist* is much better than anything I can do.' He nodded in the direction of Charlotte Fount and Seth Knox at the bar. 'If you ask me, the person you want is right around the middle. Tom Ellison and Brad Carr? These guys don't have anything to lose. They walk in between the raindrops. No, you want someone who actually has some skin in the game.' Jim caught the attention of someone across the room and waved. 'Good luck, detectives.'

Ross eyed him. 'I wonder what Jim Provan might have to lose.'

Seeing a break in the queue for the bar, and Charlotte Fount unattended, Donna told Ross, 'Be right back. Do you want anything?'

Ross raised his barely touched glass of Coke. 'I'm fine.'

'Tell the gaffer I'm getting him another water.'

Ross hunted around for sight of Lomond. 'Yeah, he's taking a while talking to Willie. Where is he, anyway?'

CHAPTER THIRTY-TWO

Donna took a spot next to Charlotte, who was in the midst of arranging glasses onto a tray, tallying what she had and what she was still to get.

The barman rang up the bill then told her, 'That's going to be two seventy-five.'

Charlotte's mouth hung open. 'As in...'

The barman's eyes widened expectantly. 'Two hundred and seventy-five pounds.'

'How is that possible?'

The barman indicated the crystal snifter and whisky glasses on the tray. 'That's Remy Martin Louis the Thirteenth cognac, and Jack Daniel's Centennial Gold Medal.'

Donna felt terrible for Charlotte, who was panic-stricken. She was damned if she could help out with the bill, though. Not on her salary.

Charlotte looked impotently through her purse, as if the cash would somehow magically appear. It certainly wasn't in her bank account. She looked back towards the group she was buying 'a round' for. It was Brad Carr who had asked. Not wanting to miss an opportunity to network with someone of his calibre, Charlotte had run off dutifully towards the bar without realising the cost of what she had been asked for. She then realised that Tom Ellison was with the group. If she had known that she would have stayed well away. At least that's what her lawyer would have advised.

Of all the people to come over, the last she wanted to see in that moment was Tom.

Which is exactly what happened.

'Everything all right, Charlotte?' he asked her.

She felt his eyes burning through her. She couldn't bring herself to admit that she didn't have the money on her. But she didn't have an option. 'I'm sorry, it seems I'm a little light.'

'That's a shame,' said Tom, picking up his and Brad's drinks from the tray. 'Maybe you should have thought of that before you wrote that bullshit article.'

Charlotte was too stunned to reply.

Donna turned in profile so that it wasn't obvious she was listening in.

'Yeah,' said Tom. 'I know you wrote it. Word of advice? If you want to take me down, it's going to take a hell of a lot more than two thousand words of a hit piece.' He took a step towards her. 'You wanna play in the big leagues? This is what it looks like.' As he turned, he caught Donna's eye. 'Can I help you?' he barked, then set off with his drinks.

Donna just smiled to herself and nodded slowly. Oh, she was going to make him pay for that, she thought.

By the end, the Charlotte altercation had caught more

than a few people's attention. Including Brad Carr, who looked over in concern. He asked Tom what was going on, but he dismissed it out of hand.

Charlotte looked helplessly at the barman. 'I'm sorry...' She shook her head, almost in tears. 'I can't pay it. I–'

Then, from out of nowhere, Noel Redmond stepped in. 'Hey, I'll take care of this,' he said softly, trying to draw as little attention as possible.

Charlotte was too stunned to reply.

Noel took out his card and passed it over quietly and subtly to the barman. 'And take ten for yourself,' he said.

Charlotte touched Noel's arm. 'I don't know what to say...'

'You don't have to say anything,' he replied. 'I loved *The Woman on the Stairs*, by the way. I heard you've got a new book coming out. You should have your people shoot a copy over to my agent. I'd be glad to give a quote for it, if you want.'

As quickly as he appeared, he then vanished again, swallowed up by several people vying for his attention.

'Thanks,' Charlotte said, in several kinds of shock at once.

Donna pushed her way through the crowd to reach the group of Brad Carr and Tom Ellison.

Tom looked her up and down when she reached them. 'Can I help you?' he snapped.

Donna put on what her granny would have called her "telephone voice". 'Mr Ellison,' she said smoothly, 'I can only apologise for staring back there. I'm a big fan.'

Tom wasn't convinced yet. 'Are you one of the competition winners or the high-rollers?'

'High roller?' asked Donna.

'One of the ones who paid, sweetheart.'

Sweetheart. All the blood flowed to Donna's fist. But professional integrity held her back.

Donna said, 'Money well spent, if you ask me. May I buy you and your friends a round of drinks? It would just make my night.'

Tom held up his cognac. 'This was Louis the Thirteenth...' He looked to Brad Carr.

Some instinct in Brad told him that something was off. It didn't sit well with him, a fan paying for a millionaire's drinks. 'I'm good, thanks.'

'Okay, great,' Donna said, holding the most difficult smile she had ever had to create. 'I'll have them bring it right over.'

The second her back was turned, the smile vanished. She walked with purpose towards the bar. Once there, she leaned across the bar and said to the barman, 'Hey, I'm Tom Ellison's assistant. You know him?'

The barman nodded. 'Sure.'

'Mr Ellison wants to buy the next ten people at the bar a glass of the cognac he's drinking.'

The barman went on tip toes to look over to him. He was sceptical. 'Does he realise that's—'

Donna cut in. 'Trust me. He knows how much it is.' She turned towards Tom's group and waved.

Tom raised his hand, then gave the barman a thumbs-up, then waved impatiently for the drinks he was expecting to be brought over. From the barman's end, it looked like Tom was giving the all clear to what Donna had said.

'Okay,' said the barman. 'As long as he's sure.' Sensing

he had a kindred economic spirit in front of him, he said conspiratorially to Donna, 'So much money they literally have to give it away.'

'I know, right?' she said, this time through a wide – and very genuine – smile. She got out of there as fast as she could, before Tom realised he'd just been scammed into paying a £700 bar tab for a bunch of strangers.

She ran into Ross in the hall. 'Hey, you'll never guess what I just saw.'

Ross interrupted, pointing towards an isolated conservatory with a view onto the house gardens that were steeped in fading sunlight. The blackest clouds moved in from the coast, bringing occasional gusts of wind that had been lacking earlier. 'Look,' Ross said. 'Where do you think they're going?'

Through the conservatory windows, Lomond and Claire MacRae were walking across the grass. Their clothes buffeted by growing winds.

'Beats me,' said Donna. 'But, depending on what Willie had to tell him, I'd love to be listening in right now.'

A storm was about to hit.

CHAPTER THIRTY-THREE

PARDEEP AND JASON had been up and down Old Mugdock Road twice now, trying – and failing – to find the address listed for Kate Randall. It was a twisty tree-lined B road punctuated with occasional massive houses hidden at the end of long driveways. Tantalising glimpses of second floors could be had from the road, hinting at something magical, expensive, and rare behind electric front gates. Running parallel, and almost always within earshot, was the much busier and more dangerous Strathblane Road, with its blind summits and national speed limit. Old Mugdock Road was what Strathblane Road should have been: a chance to potter through the countryside and admire some of the best views to be had between Glasgow and Loch Lomond and the Trossachs.

Jason stared at the live map on his phone. 'You know, with this phone, I can turn my central heating up or down when I'm miles away from home. But as soon as we stray a mile outside Milngavie, I might as well be on the bloody moon as far as Google Maps is concerned.'

Pardeep chuckled. 'All right, Grandpa Yang. Put the phone down and just look for Hunter House. It's around here somewhere.'

'What is it with rich folk – they can't just give their houses numbers like everybody else?'

'They're rich. They get to do what they want. That's the point...' Pardeep broke off, his attention grabbed by a bronze-plate sign nestled among some overgrown hedgerow. *Hunter House.* 'Bingo.' he said.

The gates at the driveway were solid wood, shutting out any view of the house behind unless you were seven-foot tall. Pardeep parked outside the gate and the two men got out.

'How do we get in?' Jason asked.

There was a buzz of static from the hedgerow. A female voice spoke. Clipped, but not unfriendly. Someone who had been interrupted in the middle of a job. 'Can I help you?' she asked.

Pardeep looked at Jason. 'Where do I talk?' he mouthed.

Jason hunted around. 'Beats me.'

'The mic's in the hedge with the speaker, guys. Can we hurry this up?'

Pardeep stepped over to it. 'Kate Randall?'

'Yes.'

'I'm DC Pardeep Varma. I was hoping to ask you a few questions about Liz MacRae.'

A long silence.

Then the gates opened up.

The men were silent as they drove down a long snaking tree-lined driveway. The tarmac was so soft and unblemished it could have been laid the day before. The entire site was barely a year old, and no expense had been spared when it came to building materials. The house had been built at an angle to face the Campsie hills, and the pockets of wildflowers that dotted the gardens towards the back hinted at a private rural haven.

'Whatever this woman does for work, I'm sold,' said Pardeep. 'I'll pack this polis shit in and do whatever she does.'

Jason dipped his head to get a better look at the house. 'Yeah, Pardeep. That's all that's standing between you and a pad like this: choice.'

Kate Randall was standing on her front steps waiting for them. She was wearing an oversize Nordic sweater, baggy pyjama bottoms – the kind that might look terrible but are so comfortable you never want to take them off – and completed her look with fluffy cat slippers.

Pardeep said, 'Kate Randall?'

She folded her arms, resting a coffee cup in the nook of her elbow. 'We covered that part already, DC Varma. What's this about?'

'We're investigating the murder of William MacRae.'

She theatrically put a hand to her chest. 'Oh no. How did you find me so soon? I admit it. I killed him!' Sheepishly, she said, 'Sorry. I've always wanted to do that.'

Unamused, Pardeep said, 'We're here about Liz MacRae. Can we ask you a few questions?'

She nodded towards the hall. 'Come on in.'

Pardeep and Jason held back while she went inside.

'She's quite funny,' whispered Jason, walking ahead.

Pardeep didn't seem to agree.

They went to one of the living rooms at the rear of the house. Everything was showroom-gleaming to the point that it was hard to tell whether anyone actually lived there.

Kate refreshed her coffee, then sat in an armchair that was wide enough to comfortably pull her feet up on. 'You said this was about Liz's dad being murdered? What happened?'

Pardeep said, 'We're not revealing too many details for now.'

'But what can it have to do with Liz?'

For a second, Pardeep and Jason were distracted by the incredible panoramic view of the Campsies. Particularly magical during a winter golden hour of fading light outside.

Pardeep took out his notebook. 'We'll get to that, em... would you prefer Ms Randall? Or Kate, or...'

'What I would prefer, detective, is for women to not have to jump through these ridiculous hoops. Am I married? Aren't I? Men don't have to state these things, why should I?' She sighed. 'To save you having to call me lady, Kate is fine, I suppose.'

Pardeep said, 'In light of events last night with Mr William MacRae, we've been looking into the Procurator Fiscal's report into Liz MacRae's death as part of our investigations. We wanted to talk to you about your statement.' Jason handed her a copy. 'I'm sure it's a long time since you've thought about it, let alone looked–'

'I thought you said you read the statement.'

'I did. Yes.'

'Then you know it was me that found Liz. That pulled

her out of the bath with her arms slit open from wrist to elbow. Who blew air into her best friend's mouth and pumped her chest for ten minutes in the hope she would wake up. You read about all that, yet you think it's a long time since I've thought about it? I think about what happened to Liz almost every day, DC...?'

'Yang. I apologise, Kate. I should have been more careful with my words.'

'Apology accepted, DC Yang. Whatever you ask me now, will be accurate and consistent with what I signed as my statement nine years ago.'

'You and Liz were flatmates. Studying Creative Writing at Glasgow University?'

'That's right. For all the good it did me. I should have listened to my dad. He begged me not to waste four years of my life, as he put it. I went there thinking I was going to be the next Zadie Smith or Muriel Spark. I wanted to learn how to write big important novels. Instead, I spent two years on bullshit experiments like "write a short story without using the letter E", and being marked by lecturers who had two failed novels between them. I should have listened to my dad. Four years later I was working as a barista at Costa with three other Creative Writing graduates.'

Pardeep asked, 'Are you still a barista?'

'No,' she replied.

He waited for her to elaborate. She didn't. 'What's your occupation now?' he asked.

'If your *actual* question is how can I afford this enormous house, the answer is that I managed to prove my dad wrong and put my degree to use. I'm a novelist. Though there are some one-star reviews for *Taming the Billionaire* online that beg to differ.' She reached for a packet of cigarettes, then checked it was okay to light up.

Both Pardeep and Jason gave no objection.

'I write romance novels,' she said. 'I self-publish online.'

Jason said, 'I hear more people are doing that now.'

'It pays the bills. It's not nearly as easy as people think.'

Pardeep and Jason were both thinking the same thing: it looks like it pays for more than just bills. Like a seventy-inch TV, and indoor swimming pool adjoining the dining room.

Kate said, 'There was a time that I wrote literary fiction and drama. That all went away after...' She broke off, wondering how best to phrase it. 'What I write now doesn't demand that I pour my heart out on the page. My heart's been empty ever since Liz died, anyway.'

'How many books have you published?' Pardeep asked.

Kate let out a long haze of smoke. 'About seventy-five at the last count.'

'Seventy-five?'

'It's really not as impressive as it sounds,' she said. 'The books are about sixty thousand words a piece. It only takes about twenty days to write one. A week for editing, a few days to design the cover. Then it's HEA.'

'Sorry, I don't know what that means.'

'It means happily-ever-after. In my romance genre, readers always want an HEA. They get mad and post one-star reviews if you don't give them it. It's like writing a western where Clint Eastwood dies at the end. They just love knowing that at the end of the book it's all going to be fine. It's reassuring that the couple always end up together.

I write them under a pen name. Even the picture I use on social media is created using an old photo of me mixed with artificial intelligence. If they knew the real me, they'd never buy another book. There's not so much happily-ever-after around here. Massive house with no one worth sharing it with. Curled up on the couch with a bottle of wine every other night.' She took a long drag again. 'It's a job. What can I say. But if you get it right, it can be a gold mine.'

'What about writer's block?' Pardeep asked.

'I don't believe in it.' Sensing the men's disbelief, she emphasised, 'Like I said, it's a job. An electrician doesn't go to a job and tell someone, sorry, I'm not up to fixing that faulty socket. I'm not inspired today to find the solution for it. When you go on writers' forums and Facebook groups, they all talk about finding motivation. That's a waste of time. Motivation comes and goes. What you need is discipline. Bum in chair every day until you get your words done for the day. Discipline is doing the work, even when you don't feel like it. Got a hangover? Tough. Write two thousand words today.'

'I certainly admire your discipline,' said Jason, seeking to reroute the discussion. 'What sort of writer was Liz?'

'She was a mystery writer like her dad,' Kate said. 'And she hated that. She did everything she could to not be him. She used to say that there are A-writers and B-writers. A-writers are all about just telling a story. Thrillers. The books that sell loads. B-writers are the ones that are in love with language. They win all the prizes. You can usually tell which ones they are by the blurb. They're always about "the haunting power of memory", or some other bollocks like that. She couldn't stand it, you see. That she was an A-writer, just like her dad. She once wrote a thriller, and hated every word of it.'

Pardeep asked, 'Did you read it?'

'Yeah. It was good. Liz trusted me to tell her the truth, that it needed some work.'

'What was it about?'

Kate shuffled forward in her chair. 'What has this got to do with Liz's dad being murdered?'

'I know it might seem odd.' Pardeep said. 'But anything you can remember would be a huge help.'

Both Pardeep and Jason held their breath, wondering if Kate was about to recount the plot of *The Shortlist*.

CHAPTER THIRTY-FOUR

KATE TOOK another puff of her cigarette. 'From what I remember, it was about a young woman who works as an assistant to a famous writer. The writer dies, but the woman steals his last manuscript and passes it off as her own. But the more successful she becomes, she has to go to ever greater lengths to protect her secret.'

'Did the book have a title then?'

'Yeah, it was called *Shattered Glass*.'

While Pardeep scribbled it down, Jason said, 'You've got a good memory. I can't even remember books I read last year, let alone nine years ago.'

'When your best friend dies, DC Yang, you tend to remember the book they wrote.'

'Do you know if anyone else read the book?'

'She told me she let her mum and dad read it. But her dad's lukewarm reaction sent her spiralling into a dark depression. He said it was too similar to *The Talented Mr Ripley*. She always was too sensitive to criticism. I'm glad she never got it published. She couldn't have handled the online reviews.'

'Did anyone else read it?'

'No. She told me that after her dad's criticism, she was done. She locked the manuscript in a box file above her desk.'

'What about boyfriends who were on the scene?' asked Pardeep.

'Even when it came to them, Liz's dad got in the way. I mean, you must have seen pictures of her. She was beautiful. Just like her mum. But there would always come a point a week into a relationship when the guy would casually drop into conversation, oh yeah, I've written this novel. And do you think your dad would give it a look over...It drove her mad. They didn't want to go out with her. The only relationship they wanted was with William MacRae. Again, something she liked about me: I never asked about her dad, because I was never interested in him. Unlike everyone else. Especially one guy near the end.'

Jason unconsciously leaned forward. 'What was different about him?'

'She was always trying to impress him,' Kate said. 'She would spend hours getting dressed, then undressed, trying on outfits. After a few months, she started reading books by writers that she hated but that he loved, and turned herself inside out to convince herself she really *did* like them. He sounded so pompous. He told her that he had read every major novel from the seventeenth to the twentieth century. Can you believe that horseshit?'

Jason looked over at Pardeep, as if a memory of something had been sparked.

Pardeep asked, 'Did you ever meet him? Or get his name?'

Kate said, 'I never met him. All I could say about him was that he changed Liz. She stopped going out, afraid she would miss a phone call from him. She would upend an essay or short story the night before it was due based on a single text message from him, or some throwaway thing he would tell her. She started having trouble sleeping. That was when she was prescribed the sleeping pills.'

Pardeep leaned forward to highlight a sentence in her statement. 'Kate, you mentioned here that on the night Liz died, you nearly bumped into someone in the corridor where your flat was. But we couldn't find a description of the man anywhere in the report.'

'Yes,' said Kate. 'That was a principal reason the whole investigation fell apart in the first place.'

'How do you mean?'

'The night Liz died, I had been out on the lash. It was the end of term, and we had both failed in various ways with our final term pieces. Mine stank. I knew it. And my lecturers knew it. So I had gone out to drink on my own and forget about it. I came back. I had my head down in my phone trying to text Liz to see if she was still awake, and whether I needed to worry about making noise coming in. That was when this guy barrelled right past me.' Kate stubbed out her cigarette and stared vacantly out the French windows. 'After I found her, the police came. I told them that I had passed someone. That he must have come out of our flat. I gave as good a description as I could, but it was too vague. Then when the post mortem came back with an accidental death ruling, it was all academic by then anyway. Even if it had been ruled suspicious, I had been out at a bar all night. I would have been torn to shreds in the witness box if a case ever made it to court.'

'Sorry, Kate. I just need a quick word with Pardeep.' Jason pointed towards the hall. 'May we?'

'Sure. I'm going to stick the kettle on. Do you want anything?'

Pardeep was about to accept, when Jason pulled him away.

'No, we're grand, thanks,' Jason told her.

In hushed conversation at the edge of the living room, Pardeep asked, 'What's going on?'

'I think I know who the boyfriend was,' Jason said. 'Do you think I can show her a picture?'

'If you think you've got it. Who are you thinking?'

Jason hesitated. 'Can you let me see what she says first?'

'Yeah, all right. But Jase. Show the picture before mentioning any names. This all happened a long time ago. I don't want us to plant any false memories.'

They reconvened where they had been sitting.

'Kate,' Jason said cagily. 'This might be pie in the sky. The man you saw that night, I know you said you struggled to describe him. But would you be willing to look at some pictures to see if any stand out?'

'I can try,' she said, assuming it would all be for nothing.

Jason took his laptop, then he did a search for Hathaway Publishing's website. He navigated to a page showing their current senior staff.

Pardeep leaned over to see. He was as much in the dark as Kate was about what was going on.

Jason showed her the laptop screen. 'Are there any faces there that you recognise as the man you saw that night? There's no need to pick someone if you're not sure.'

Pardeep and Jason waited anxiously, watching for Kate's eyes to slide downwards towards the picture for the Senior Editor. Seth Knox.

She lingered on him, then moved on. She shook her head. 'I don't recognise anyone.'

'You're sure?' Jason checked.

'It's not him. None of these are him. This guy was older.'

'Okay,' Jason said, closing the laptop. 'It was just a thought...'

Pardeep was about to move on, when Jason had an idea.

'Sorry, Pardeep,' said Jason. 'One more thing.' He reached into his bag and took out a paperback copy of *The Long Dark*. He showed her the back cover, where there was an author photo of William MacRae at the bottom corner. 'Kate, would you mind taking a look at this photo, and seeing if you recognise–'

Kate's posture straightened the moment she saw it. 'Holy...' She grabbed the book for a closer look. She couldn't quite believe it herself. She covered her mouth. 'That's him,' she said quietly, lowering her hands. Then, with mounting intensity and volume, she said, 'That's *him!*'

Neither Pardeep nor Jason knew what to think.

'How did you know?' she exclaimed.

'To be clear,' Pardeep said, remaining sceptical, 'you're

identifying him as the man who passed you, leaving your flat the night that Liz died?'

'Yes!' She turned the book over, realising who it was. 'It was Liz's dad?'

'You never saw his face before now?' asked Pardeep.

'I never met him before,' Kate said. She looked at Pardeep and then Jason in horror. 'You don't think that he was involved in Liz's death somehow, surely?'

The detectives were thinking it, but didn't say it.

It's possible.

CHAPTER THIRTY-FIVE

ELDERSLIE GOLF CLUB was in the heart of a residential area on Main Road. The clubhouse had been converted from one of the large detached villas that lined the road, and had acquired a number of extensions and additions over the years. It now looked like a Lego building that a child had got carried with, and slapped on a few too many extras.

The course itself was a reminder of what the area had been before: sedate woods and rolling grasslands near the foot of Glennifer Braes. Foxbar at the far end of the course, out by the ninth hole, had been built up around the course outskirts. So much space taken up in a busy town that so few people would ever enjoy.

Willie pulled into the car park, which was nearly empty. Daylight was fading fast and the temperature had dropped to a point beyond anything that was comfortable for hitting a tiny ball around a field.

A solitary golfer stood on the practice ground with a

mound of practice balls in front of him. He took vicious swipes at each ball, followed by a grumble of 'shite...'

Willie braced himself against the cold, and called from the side of his car.

After the man hacked at another ball, he dug up a rug of dirt and grass that went farther than the ball.

Willie called out, 'I thought they say that golf's just a good walk spoiled. You're not even getting the walk in, Derek.'

Derek turned around, vaguely recognising the voice. 'Willie Sneddon?'

'How are you doing?' Willie asked, hunching his shoulders to try and keep warm.

'Wasting retirement on this fucking game.' He tossed his club aside. 'But I'm addicted, what can I tell you. Golf and sex are the two things you can enjoy without being any good at either of them.' He gave Willie a moment to crack a smile. When he realised it wasn't going to happen, he dropped the niceties. 'So it's about work, then.'

'I'm afraid so,' Willie replied.

'How much shit am I about to eat?'

'That depends.'

Derek picked up a long plastic tube to collect the golf balls he'd hit. 'Walk with me,' he said, wandering around. Most of the balls hadn't gone very far.

'It's about Liz MacRae,' said Willie.

Derek made no sign of recognising the name. 'Remind me.'

'Young woman who drowned in the bath in student digs. Nine years ago.'

Derek started nodding. 'Oh aye. I remember.'

'It was ruled an accidental death. Despite her having a blood alcohol of point two-five and a suitcase full of pills inside her.'

Derek stopped walking. 'There it is. I could always trust you to get right to the point, Willie.'

'What happened, Dez? Did someone lean on you?'

He huffed, letting out a thick cloud of vapour. He turned to face Willie. 'Tell me you're not trying to dangle my pension in front of me, Willie. I'm retired already and this place costs a pretty penny for someone like me.'

'No one's coming for you, Dez. Or your pension.'

Derek's breathing was erratic. Panicked. 'Fuck,' he wheezed to himself. 'What have I done...'

'I don't know, Dez. What *have* you done?'

'You've got to help me, Willie. For old time's sake. Tell me what I can do.'

Willie looked back towards the clubhouse, where a warm orange light emanated from the bar above the pro shop.

'Take me for a pint at the clubhouse and tell me everything you remember.'

CHAPTER THIRTY-SIX

THE CLUBHOUSE BAR WAS QUIET. The only evidence of activity was the insistent pinging and electronic jingle from the puggy machine. Long banks of tables were set up with no one sitting at them. The ever-present television screens were turned to Sky Sports News. A channel that stretched the definition of 'news' to breaking point. Another TV showed Sky Sports Golf, which had on a golf tournament being played in the Middle East. The course was almost void of spectators, and there were advertising hoardings everywhere. January was not a month for golf, but commercial imperatives demanded that there always be a tournament somewhere in the world for golf junkies to tune into.

The nearest members were at the bar to have a better view of the TVs. Groups of twos and threes sat for minutes at a time without saying a word to each other. Watching the latest football transfer news, inert. Their only thoughts were of delaying the inevitable in going home. Of desperately wanting a cigarette, but equally wanting to avoid the freezing cold outside in order to have one.

Derek took a seat far from anyone else, giving a view from the first-floor window out across the first hole and the practice ground.

Derek and Willie each had a pint of Tennent's.

Willie said, 'I just need to know what happened.'

Derek took a sip of beer first. 'It was a suicide. Plain and simple. Except the family had this lawyer involved. This expensive guy from Edinburgh. Knew everyone at Tulliallan. Played golf with half the executive team. There was a lot of pressure to wrap up the case, on compassionate grounds. The dad was in bits over it. A real wreck.' He picked at the edge of the paper drinks mat his glass sat on. Just needing something to do to distract his mind from the pain of the memories. 'They knew I wanted to retire early. Because of Shirley. She'd been in remission, but then...it came back. They leaned on me,' he put his hand up to stop Willie interrupting, 'and I won't say who. Someone senior.'

'Leaned on you to do what?'

'Class it an accidental death rather than suicide.'

'Were you concerned about the investigation being wrapped up too quickly? Before all the facts were in?'

'The toxicology was clear,' Derek said. 'It was Moira that did it. Moira Dreich. Is she still around?'

'Aye,' Willie said with a rueful snort.

Derek was pleading now. Desperate to be believed. The notion that he could have signed off an investigation as accidental death, when there may have been suspicious circumstances, was too dreadful to comprehend. 'You've got to understand,' he said, 'there were only two options in front of us. Did the lassie kill herself, or was it an accident? There was never anything suspect.'

'Dez, there was a witness right outside the flat of the deceased who saw someone leaving around the time of death.'

'Aye, and she was drunk! She couldn't give us anything to work with. Average height. Not too old, not too young. Dark hair. Dark clothes. Were we supposed to go on *Crimewatch* with that or something?'

'But there was still evidence of someone being there.'

Derek was arguing for his life. He could sense his future hanging in the balance. 'And no evidence of forced entry to the flat. No evidence of a struggle. No blood anywhere else in the flat. No bruises on her body. So even if you say she was drugged before she reached the bathroom, there was no struggle. The walls were paper thin, and the neighbours up and down and through the door heard nothing all night.'

'You never suspected foul play?'

'Never! Willie, we've all known those guys through the years, and you know that I'm not one of them. All I did was sign the report that classed the death as accidental. Come on, we've all done it. A wee favour for someone that hurt nobody.' For his own sake, his own sanity, he had to dig his heels in now, to convince himself he hadn't done anything wrong. He maintained, 'I would never have signed off on the report if there were suspicious circumstances.'

'Derek, my guys have identified a person of interest. They're exploring culpable homicide.' Willie could practically hear Derek gulping from across the table.

'Jesus Christ,' Derek said to himself. He looked out at

the course. A heavy squall was moving in. 'What have I done?'

'I'm not asking you to land anyone in it,' said Willie. 'To be honest, after the Sandman case, the last thing either me or John wants to do is having another sit down with Reekie.'

'Christ, he's still around too, eh. What did they make him?'

'Chief Superintendent.'

Derek scoffed in disgust. 'Of course they did...'

'Dez, man to man. Where was the pressure coming from?'

After a long pause to think, Derek said, 'It was the dad, all right. The dad was all over us.'

'William MacRae?'

'Aye. He was the one demanding it be ruled accidental death. Was threatening all sorts if it wasn't. Reekie was my SO back then. He just wanted it to go away and keep the lawyer happy.' Resigned, and unburdened, he asked Willie, 'Tell me how I can fix this? To make sure I didn't make a mistake.'

'Let's start with the investigation materials,' said Willie. 'Forensics photos from the scene.'

'We didn't know what we were dealing with when we showed up, so forensics photographed everything. They'd be in Dalmarnock now.'

'Good,' said Willie. 'Because I'm going to need to see everything you saw that night.'

CHAPTER THIRTY-SEVEN

THERE WAS ONLY one thing you could say to a detective chief inspector who has just pointed out that you've been caught on video fleeing a hotel alone, soon before your ex-husband's murder a short walk across town.

'I know it doesn't look good,' Claire agreed. 'But I *can* explain.'

Lomond said, 'I'm all ears.'

They were walking through the house gardens, illuminated only by the warm light inside emanating from the Grand Library. The only other people outside were working in the car park in high-vis vests over stormproof jackets, and the Inver Castle security staff prowling around with high-power torches.

Lomond added, 'If for nothing else than getting on with the work, I need to eliminate you from our enquiries as quickly as possible.'

Claire was caught off-guard. There was a hint of

displeasure in her tone, too. 'Aren't you supposed to interrogate me and get to the bottom of everything?'

'Not when I saw your reaction to seeing William's body last night, and sitting in a room in close quarters with you for a while. I've been around a lot of death in my time, and more than enough grief to know what's genuine. That was no act I saw last night.'

Claire shoulders dropped. Relaxed a little. 'I'm relieved to hear you say that. Because there is an honest explanation for the hotel incident.'

'Firstly, what were you doing there?' Lomond asked.

'Crawford Bell had put it together. He loves nothing more than playing the host.'

'I had noticed.'

'Throwing parties with other people's money. There's obviously not very much up here, so he decided to throw a little pre-festival get-together for the authors lined up for William's event. He had to do it in Glasgow. He couldn't stomach the thought of Tom Ellison asking some rural-pub waitress if they had kobe steaks or coq au vin laced with Grand Cru Chambertin.'

'Perish the thought,' Lomond said, not knowing what any of it was. But he got the idea: it sounded expensive. 'Why were you roped into this?'

'Crawford had asked me to try and convince William to come along. People travelled hundreds of miles and took multiple plane trips just to speak publicly about how much they admired him. And William couldn't even get in a taxi ten minutes from home to have dinner with them. When the others found out, you can imagine how pissed off they were. Call it loyalty, or sentimentality, but I wanted someone to be at the table defending him. Because I knew he would need it. Yes, we were divorced. That doesn't erase all those years struggling. Building the Roxburgh empire. We did it together. And I wanted to make sure that a lifetime achievement award event was done right. So I came to the dinner to get a sense of what everyone was going to say.'

'Which was what?'

'Perfectly lovely for the most part. Until some old wounds started weeping.'

Lomond looked down at the immaculate grass they were walking over, then turned his face to the increasingly brisk breeze. 'What I don't understand is, everything I've read about William until today has been nothing but generous. Then I come to a memorial in his honour...and everyone seems to be hiding some resentment or bitterness.'

'Don't let that lot in there fool you,' Claire warned. 'They agreed to say a few words in memory of William for a reason. They're playing an angle.'

'Even someone like Noel Redmond? Or Jim Provan?'

'Especially Jim Provan,' she replied. 'Did you know he's been siphoning royalties to William for years?'

'I didn't. Why?'

'I probably shouldn't be telling you this...' She did a quick shoulder-check. 'It was all hushed up. Even William didn't tell me the full details. There was a non-disclosure signed as part of the settlement.'

'What settlement?'

'Between William and Jim. He sued Jim successfully for plagiarism. Jim hasn't made a penny from the first three books in his DI Rothes series for about four years now.'

'I'm no literary expert, but isn't plagiarism a hard case to prove?'

'It is. Ordinarily. But William had proof. Discarded pages from works in progress that ended up wholesale in Jim's books. Entire paragraphs at a time. It's remarkable when you look at the side-by-sides.'

'You don't think...'

'God, no. Jim doesn't have it in him.'

'Claire, I'm afraid I have to press you about the–'

'The hotel, yes. This is all by way of saying that, in a private dining room, with the wine and whisky flowing, they were all perfectly cruel and ghastly about William the moment I stepped away from the table. I excused myself to go to the bathroom, and held back around the corner. They were all sneering and raging at him. I couldn't bear to hear any more of it. So I ran. I just ran right out and went home. That's it.'

Lomond knew that he had to tread carefully with his next line of enquiry. It had the potential to destroy any goodwill he had built up with Claire. 'I understand that you have some suspicions about various people here. And we'll look into them all. But my colleague back in Glasgow has been doing some digging around the events of Liz's death. In particular, the Procurator Fiscal's report classifying it as accidental.'

Claire hugged herself as the wind picked up.

'Are you cold?' he asked.

'A little.'

He took off his coat and put it over her shoulders. He gestured to the insulated vest he had on over his shirt and tie. 'I'll be all right in this.'

'Thank you,' she said. She sighed. 'I told William it was a mistake at the time. He knew the officer in charge. Detective Inspector Derek Graham. He had helped William with some research for a Roxburgh book, and been paid way over the odds. So when William came to him, asking for help in classifying Liz's death as accidental, Derek felt indebted.'

'Why did William want it done?'

'Shame? Guilt? Imagine your own daughter uses your books to...' She could barely comprehend it even now. 'Weigh herself down so that she drowned.'

'William must have been beside himself.'

'He had nightmares for months. He couldn't write. That year was the first he ever missed a deadline. He barely got out of bed the first six months. Drinking himself silly every night, every day. He'd sit on this same bench in Kelvingrove by the Lord Roberts Monument, drinking a quarter bottle of whisky. Just him, and his guilt.'

Lomond said, 'It might not have been a calculated attempt to hurt him. Maybe it brought her comfort in her final moments.'

'That's what I said. But William wouldn't hear of it. If it was an accident – officially – then it would be easier to live with himself. Because he *did* blame himself. He had said some cruel things to Liz about a book she had written. *Shattered Glass*, it was called. A fledgling attempt at a thriller. The worst thing was when Liz told her boyfriend about William's criticisms of the book. And the boyfriend sided with William. She basically stopped writing after that. William never forgave himself. Yes, William's lawyer was well-connected. And yes William asked him to put political pressure on Derek wherever he could. But the reality is, whether or not William was ashamed or embarrassed about it, Liz killed herself. She was depressed and had been for a long time. I know there was the boyfriend on the scene, and her flatmate Kate thought that the relationship was intense and possibly unhealthy for Liz.'

Lomond asked, 'Did you or William ever meet the boyfriend?'

'No,' she said. 'She never let us in to that part of her life.'

'The problem,' Lomond explained, 'is that we have a statement from Kate who has identified William as the man she encountered near their flat around the time of Liz's death.'

Claire shook her head. 'That's impossible. What you're saying is impossible.' Angrier now, she raised her voice. 'What you're *getting at* is impossible.'

Lomond didn't let up. 'Did he have an alibi for that night?'

'I was in Edinburgh.'

'And William?'

'He was working. At home.'

'So he didn't have an alibi.'

Claire was still shaking her head. Tormented and in denial. 'He didn't need one.'

Lomond pressed on. 'William was exerting pressure to have the death classed as accidental. Was it an attempt to cover up something more sinister?'

'But it was accidental rather than suicide. Murder wasn't even on the table. The post mortem was definitive.'

It wouldn't have been hard for Lomond to strip away

everything Claire had believed about her ex-husband. He could have reminded her that William was a crime writer who had all sorts of books on anatomy, poisons, and forensic science. They were all in his study. If anyone knew how to cover up a murder, William was up there with serial killers as far as knowledge went. The scariest thing Lomond encountered on the job was when intention was combined with competence or ability. A William MacRae with his knowledge set and a motive to inflict harm would have been a frightening proposition.

Claire stopped walking now. She wanted to concentrate her energy on gesticulating at Lomond to emphasise her point. 'You're talking about the possibility of William killing our daughter?

Lomond understood. It took a lot of gears to turn to contemplate such a thing about the father of your child. 'I am. I have to. I wouldn't be doing my job if I ignored such a possibility.'

CHAPTER THIRTY-EIGHT

CLAIRE RETORTED, 'Why would he hurt her? How could he have removed any hint of a struggle? This was all investigated!'

Lomond said, 'By someone who's been proven vulnerable to manipulation in a police investigation.'

'John, please don't go after Derek. Promise me. That man's been through hell losing his wife. And...' She broke off and turned away. Tears forming. 'I know we were divorced...But he was the only husband I'll ever have. I know that. And now I know how Derek must have been feeling...'

Lomond looked up into the dark sky as it started to spit with rain. 'I've been there, Claire. Where you are now. I won't say that I know how you're feeling, because everyone is different when someone close to them dies. But I can understand...how it feels to lose a child.'

If anyone else had said what Lomond just had, Claire may have resisted. But since their talk in William's kitchen the night before, she had found Lomond and his world-weary ways invading her thoughts. There was a confluence between them that she couldn't ignore. Lomond had recently turned forty-four; Claire was fifty-two, though she looked much younger – they wouldn't have looked lopsided as a couple. There would have been no head-turning as they walked along a street, prompting thoughts of 'how did *he* get *her*?', or vice versa. They would have made sense. Not that she had been thinking of him beyond his professional duties. But when she *did* take a moment to think about Lomond and his sad, narrow eyes, that promised an abundance of something if you put in the time to discover it, there was no resistance there.

Thinking about Lomond was easy.

Thinking about William had always been difficult.

It was hard not to compare.

Lomond turned his wedding ring between thumb and middle finger – a tic that had developed from his ring being slightly too big when at rest at the bottom of his finger, as he had wide knuckles but slender finger flesh. 'I was married and we were expecting a baby boy. But Eilidh got into trouble after delivery. There was a bleed that they couldn't fix. And the baby wasn't breathing when he came out.' Lomond paused, as a flood of images from that moment stacked on top of another. 'He was ten centimetres away from the world. Ten centimetres away from living a life. Seventy, eighty, ninety years? Of seeing the world. Travelling. Working. Sleeping. Eating. Walking. All of this stuff that we do without giving it a second thought. I lost them both.'

The tears in Claire's eyes spilled over and ran down her cheeks. 'I'm sorry, John.'

He nodded appreciatively. It was the first time they had looked into each other's eyes with anything other than the tragic business of William's death in mind.

They each felt like something had changed between them. That there was no going back from. A connection.

It had happened only a couple of times since Eilidh's death. Tiny glimpses, fractions of a smile, or passing glance, where Lomond felt *seen* by someone else. Appreciated. Maybe even fancied. He had long since stopped thinking of himself in any way a sexual being. He was just a machine to solve puzzles now. And that was fine, because he didn't want to find anyone else. Eilidh had been it for him. Although he didn't necessarily buy into the poetic notion of there only being one person in the world for you, he absolutely did buy into the notion that once you make vows you remain loyal and true to that person for the rest of your life, even if it means remaining loyal only to their memory. He didn't *not* go out on dates because he worried about Eilidh looking down on him from the heavens and being disappointed in him. Lomond had never behaved well simply because he thought someone was watching. He behaved well because it was the right thing to be as a person. To have empathy. To listen. To truly try to understand people.

But above all else, to do the right thing.

Despite all that, he still had moments where he felt wanted, and he wondered what it would be like to be with someone else. It went away as fast as it appeared though. He had once heard a colleague at Mill Street talking about the death of her husband, and how she now felt free in a way – terrible as it was to admit. But Lomond had never felt free. All he could do was try to make peace with his grief. Finding love again would be like cementing over a grave. The body was still there in the ground. There was no getting away from that.

As he saw the tears fall from Claire's eyes, Lomond was sure that in anyone else's company he could have cried too. But he wanted to be a professional. This wasn't about him. It was about Claire. And the killer he was trying to find.

He said, 'Without a change in the evidence around your daughter's cause of death, I don't have anything else to go with yet. But if someone knew that William was involved in her death, however tangential, that's a powerful motive. That word "justice" written in blood. That's not random. Someone was trying to point us in the direction of something. Something we're not seeing yet.'

Claire looked upwards now, the rain getting heavier.

'We should go back,' Lomond said. He waited for her to turn around, but she stayed where she was. 'Claire?' He leaned forward to see her face, which had turned a ghostly white. He touched her arm and she flinched.

'What time is it?' she asked weakly, then pushed her sleeve up to see her watch. 'Oh no...'

'Are you all right?' Lomond asked.

'My pills.' She rummaged underneath Lomond's coat over her own jacket, and patted at her pockets. 'I'm late for my pills.'

'Where are they?'

She pointed towards Crichton House. looking cosy and warm with its golden light inside. 'In my bag back in the cloakroom.'

He took her arm and led her back to the house. 'Come on. It's not far.'

She worked hard to steady her breath. 'I have this problem with...my blood pressure...sometimes it drops too low.'

Lomond guided her under a huge pine tree that was being rocked by gusts of thirty miles an hour. He covered her head as small twigs and debris of old foliage showered down on them.

Ross and Donna were waiting by the conservatory, holding their collars up against the wind. Back where Lomond and Claire had just been standing, a branch ripped off and tumbled down through the other branches before landing on the grass with a thud.

It was just a taste of what was to come.

Seth Knox suddenly appeared behind, as Lomond and Claire struggled towards them.

Noticing Claire's pallor, he asked, 'Are you all right? What happened?'

'My pills...' She pointed to the cloakroom.

Seth reached for her arm.

To Lomond's surprise, she accepted it.

Seth said, 'I'll take you. Come on. Let's get some water as well...'

Lomond stayed back with Donna and Ross.

'How did that go?' asked Ross.

Lomond replied, 'William MacRae has no alibi for the night his daughter died. And now Claire has no alibi for last night. Any progress on Sullivan?'

'Nothing yet, boss,' said Donna.

Ross said, 'I think we need to talk to Linda and Willie. Things are picking up pace back home.'

They went back inside, but the three of them didn't make it past the reception hall, where Crawford Bell was waiting for them.

'DCI Lomond,' Crawford said. 'Could I have a quick word?' He put his arm out to lead Lomond off to one side.

Lomond cast his eyes down to where Crawford was touching him.

Feeling like he had poked a bear at the zoo, Crawford quickly retracted his arm. 'I've been informed by our generous benefactor that they have come into certain privileged information about AD Sullivan. Information even I don't know about.'

The pause that followed told him that Lomond was at least intrigued.

'What sort of information are we talking about?' asked Lomond.

Crawford said, 'The language I've been instructed to use is, a matter of life and death.'

Lomond looked inside, seeing the ten suspects getting their coats and jackets on in preparation for the walk to the castle in the pouring rain and in the dark. He then turned to Donna and Ross. 'Get our bags, guys.'

CHAPTER THIRTY-NINE

'SHITE,' said Pardeep. He and Jason were approaching the turn on Argyle Street for Kelvin Way, in between the bowling green and tennis courts that were overlooked by Glasgow University – as well as William MacRae's house high up on Park Circus.

'What is it?' asked Jason.

'I forgot this road's still blocked off. It forces you into the museum.' He sighed heavily. 'Now we're going to have to go all the way to Charing Cross and around Woodlands Road...'

'Let's just park in the museum,' Jason said. 'It's only a wee walk up the hill. Nip up the South Front, then through the Cloisters. Alumni Office is around the corner.'

Pardeep huffed. 'A walk?'

Jason, still hyped from his morning weights workout at six a.m., was brimming with enthusiasm. 'Yeah, get the blood flowing. Bounce some ideas around.'

Grudgingly, Pardeep turned left towards the museum car park. He grumbled, 'Bloody freezing out there...'

As they marched up the pedestrian walkway leading to the Gilbert Scott Building – the striking main university building with its iconic tower – Pardeep struggled to keep up with Jason's infernal pace.

'Gonna slow down, Jase,' Pardeep puffed.

'Sorry,' he replied.

'You know, I wish I'd got into this uni instead of Caley. I forgot how nice all the trees and that are.'

'It's an inspirational environment, I think. There's something in the air here.'

'If I'd come here, I might have kept my head down and actually done some work.' Pardeep chuckled.

Jason said, 'I liked the work. I never went out much. Watched a lot of *Countdown*.'

'God...I bet you're one of these people who still posts their Wordle games on Facebook every morning.'

Jason shook his head adamantly. 'Nah. Wordle's too easy. Give me a samurai suduko any day of the week.'

'Sudoku's, like, my nightmare – shite, I've done it again!'

'What?'

Pardeep remonstrated, 'I keep saying "like" all the time! Listening to the girls at home, every second word out their mouth is like. "And like I was like, what? And she was like..." It's fucking maddening. Anyway, what's a samurai sudoku? I didn't think anyone did those anymore.'

'It takes five regular nine by nine sudoku grids, and overlaps them to make one giant sudoku. It's mega and totally ace.' Jason couldn't keep a massive grin off his face.

'That's it. I'm making you a Tinder profile, mate. I can't hack this anymore. I can't work you out. You've got biceps bursting out your shirt. You've got that...' Pardeep sucked his cheeks in, 'super skinny face that birds love. It's fucking mad, mate. You look like one of those guys off Love Island, except you've actually got brains. And you're not a total arsehole.'

'It's always nice to hear from your colleague that you're not a total arsehole.'

'You know what I mean, though. The problem is you've got too much brains. Or too many. Whatever. If I was on a date with you, I would be like, yeah, looked good until he opened his mouth.'

'I don't work out to be more attractive, Pardeep. It just makes sense from an evolutionary standpoint. It maximises utility as well as increasing my lifespan by releasing endorphins when I lift heavy weights.' He raised his hand to stop Pardeep who was about to interrupt him. 'Also, you've just found three different ways to call me attractive in the last thirty seconds. Maybe you should be focussing a bit on that.'

'Jase, *objectively*, you're a good-lookin' guy.'

Jason showed him four fingers. 'That's *four* times now!'

'Whatever, mate. My point is that you need to relax a bit. Especially in this job.'

'That's *why* I workout. When we were working the Sandman case, I added twenty pounds on my deadlift, and five reps on my bench press. That's how I relax.'

'Me? I put my feet up, watch a bit of telly.'

'I watch telly!'

'No, you watch quizzes, Jase. There's a difference. I'm

talking about normal TV that normal people watch. *East-enders*, yeah? *Strictly*. Normal TV.'

'I can't do it, Pardeep. I just sit there thinking that I'm wasting time.'

They were close to the top of the hill now.

Pardeep sighed. 'Fuck it. I tried, didn't I? One of these days you're going to fall over or something in the staff kitchen, and your head's going to break open and reveal all these wires and goo like the android guy in *Alien*.'

Exhausted by the exchange, Jason said, 'Maybe our walks should be a time for quiet reflection from now on.'

THE UNIVERSITY GROUNDS were much quieter than normal with it being a Saturday. Groups of Italian and Spanish tourists walked around looking for the Hunterian museum, wrapped up as if they were in the Arctic. Conversely, some local wedding guests were milling around in kilts. Women in dresses, holding onto their hats to stop them blowing away.

It started pelting with rain just as Pardeep and Jason reached the fluted columns and grand archways of the Cloisters. They dashed in for cover, flapping the water off their coats.

'Jeez, that came on fast,' said Pardeep.

Jason pointed across the quadrangle to Professors' Square, comprising thirteen townhouses which now operated as departmental offices. 'The Alumni office is over there. Come on.' He threw his jacket up on his head and made a run for it.

Pardeep tutted, and followed after him.

The administrator that Willie had managed to convince to open the office up on a Saturday morning wasn't in the best of moods. It was the nature of their work that detectives often ended up on the unpopular side of requests.

'Who is it you're looking for?' the administrator asked, opening up the office which was almost as cold as outside.

'No one particularly,' said Pardeep. 'We're looking for a list of Creative Writing students from nine years ago. Basically everyone on that course.'

The administrator sighed. 'Two buses. An hour and a half each way, for a thirty-second job.'

Twenty seconds of it was waiting for the computer to boot up.

A handful of clicks later through the matriculation records, and they had their list.

The administrator printed it for them. Relative to, say, the phone book, it wasn't a long list. But it wasn't nothing, and would need some time to be gone through carefully.

As the administrator locked up, Pardeep slid a tenner into her hand.

'That's for your time,' he said.

Dashing back to the car in the rain, Pardeep put his coat over his head. Jason was using his to protect the list, not bothered about getting wet.

'Are you going to tell me about this hunch of yours, or not?' asked Pardeep.

Jason replied, 'Kate said that the boyfriend had told Liz that he had read every major novel from the seventeenth to the twentieth century.'

'Doesn't that mean he's more likely to have been studying English Literature rather than Creative Writing?'

Jason shook his head. 'You never read Donna's notes, did you?'

'No. You know why?'

'You knew that I would.'

'Of course. There's the old saying, if you're good at something, never do it for free? There's another saying. If you know Jason will do it, then Pardeep doesn't have to bother.'

'You're just a regular Glaswegian Plato, aren't you. Let's get back to the station and have a look at the list. I really hope I'm wrong.'

'Why?' asked Pardeep.

Jason replied, 'Because if who I think is on that list, then it means we've been looking at a major part of this puzzle completely upside down.'

CHAPTER FORTY

In the reception hall of Crichton House, Tom Ellison was two minutes in to a full-on meltdown with the bar manager.

'It's not my bill to *pay!*' Tom yelled, practically stomping his feet.

Looking on from the conservatory, about to venture outside, Donna couldn't help but laugh.

'What's so funny?' asked Ross.

She zipped up her jacket. 'Tell you later,' she said.

The pair trooped to the car for their Police Scotland laptop, turning their faces against the dagger-like, sideways rain.

'Are we sure this is a good idea?' Donna asked.

'Crawford's got us all torches, Donna.' He turned his face away from the rain. 'It's just a bit of rough weather.'

'I meant holing ourselves up with William MacRae's potential killer.'

Ross countered, 'Or giving ourselves the chance to save

their next victim. It's a public safety issue, Donna. We don't have a choice. We still don't know if AD Sullivan is someone to arrest, or to save. This mystery castle owner is worth talking to.'

'Especially if it's an attractive woman.'

'What are you on about?'

'Oh come on, you must have noticed how John looks at that Claire MacRae. I mean, I'm no' a forty-something guy, but I can imagine if I was one that I would find someone who looks like her very attractive.'

'He works angles,' said Ross, defensively. 'John Lomond's no lech.'

'I never said he was. Trust me. Five years in Mill Street? I know a lech when I see one. All I'm saying is, if this millionaire's a woman and she's hot, I'll bet you we'll be on the margins.'

'The man lost his wife, Donna. He's empathising with Mrs MacRae. Not flirting.'

Unconvinced, but willing to let it drop, Donna acquiesced. 'If you say so.'

The last car from the visitor car park was trundling out of the Crichton House grounds, wiper blades working overtime to maintain some sort of visibility, headlights on full beam. Now it was just festival staff, authors, and three detectives on the grounds.

'At least we don't have to worry about driving in this crap,' Ross said.

'Yeah,' Donna replied. 'Just a quarter of a mile walk, crossing a dodgy moat in howling wind on the edge of a cliff. Much easier. Much safer.'

They reached the conservatory of Crichton House,

where the authors who had spoken at the memorial had assembled with their coats and hats and gloves, dressed like townies. Except for Noel Redmond, who had changed out of his kilt. Now he was dressed like he'd done a *Supermarket Sweep* through an outdoor clothes shop, grabbing anything and everything. He had on more layers than an onion, with a woolly fleece underneath a waterproof shell jacket, waterproof overtrousers, hiking boots, and ski gloves.

In the calm of the conservatory, it might have seemed like overkill. But once outside, everyone was wishing that they had brought some more practical clothes.

The only other person moderately ready for the weather, in head-to-toe tweed shooting gear, was Crawford Bell, who had taken on the role of troop leader, and handed out torches before they set off.

Zoe shuddered from the cold. 'Have the drivers gone home or something?'

Crawford answered, 'I'm afraid the owner of Inver Castle won't allow any unnecessary visitors onto the grounds. Above all else, they prioritise privacy over convenience.'

Crawford was the first in a line of Brad Carr alongside Tom Ellison; Noel Redmond and Jim Provan with Zoe Hathaway; Seth Knox on his own; Charlotte Fount also alone; then Donna and Ross, and Claire MacRae next to Lomond bringing up the rear.

Everyone held their hoods up against the wind, leaning at forty-five degree angles when it really gusted. The driving rain felt like pinpricks on their cold faces. The only one coping with the conditions was Noel Redmond.

He yelled over the howl of the wind to the group, 'Not looking so foolish now, am I?'

Zoe turned her torch on him. 'That's debatable,' she yelled back.

Brad, holding the collar of his leather jacket up around his neck, retorted, 'I'd die quite happily out here if it meant I didn't have to wear that clobber, Noel.'

Tom, wearing a heavy Armani overcoat more suited to a dry day in the city rather than a Highlands storm, barked, 'We should go back!' He stopped walking, hoping it would encourage the others. 'That's it! I'm going back!' he yelled more insistently.

Jim, arms linked with Zoe for stability, replied, 'You won't have any argument from me on that.'

Inver Castle stood on a rocky peninsula overlooking Loch Inver, which met the north end of the Minch – a strait separating the mainland from the isles of Lewis and Harris. Beyond that was the Atlantic Ocean.

In the daytime, the castle stood like a gleaming white sentinel. The cliffs lashed it on three sides where it protruded into the water. The castle had been greatly modernised since its days as a fortified tower in the thirteenth century. It now had a symmetrical face, giving it a clean aesthetic as you approached along the arrow-straight driveway. On both sides of the driveway were raised steep banks that gave the effect of walking through a tunnel, as trees on either side – bent over from years of punishing winds – formed a kind of roof.

The trees were being brutalised by gale-force gusts, spraying the driveway with twigs and seeds and leaves. It was a claustrophobic place to walk through at the best of times. But in the darkness, it was scary.

At the end of the driveway, the lights from the small windows of the castle promised sanctuary, warmth, calmness.

But also isolation.

Perched on the end of the peninsula, the castle was helplessly exposed to the elements. Behind the castle, the loch stretched off into a murky gloom of rain like some infinite oblivion awaiting. It was surely one of the most dramatic approaches to any house in the world. One that also offered perilously few options of escape should anything go wrong.

The moat bridge was a treacherous path, dangling fifty feet above a river that had been transformed by flood waters from the nearby mountains into a raging torrent full of rocks and shards of trees. Lomond couldn't ignore the danger lurking below. But the trees behind them were just as threatening. Their creaks grew louder, groaning under the relentless battering of the wind. The group was at a crossroads: either cross the bridge or retreat to the safety of Crichton House.

'We should pick up the pace a bit,' Lomond suggested.

He pushed Claire forward, urging her to quicken their pace as they left the shelter of the trees. From behind, the woods echoed with a drawn-out creak, as if the tortured bark of a tree had finally snapped. The violent winds had battered it relentlessly for over an hour, but now it had reached its breaking point.

Lomond couldn't pinpoint where the sound had come from. He flicked his torch to his left. Nothing. Then, as pointed the torch right, it illuminated a colossal black mass looming towards them. He shoved his hand onto Claire's back, propelling her forward as he bellowed at Donna and Ross, "Run! Quick! It's going to..."

Ahead, the group had halted at the moat bridge, all pointing their torches back as the tree began to topple. With a sickening crack, it crashed to the ground, leaving the others helpless as Lomond and Claire hurtled towards safety.

If Lomond hadn't pushed them forward just moments before, it would have flattened them.

Ross and Donna motioned for them to hurry across the bridge, but a groan from behind them grew louder, rising from the forest floor. The toppled tree had ripped up the roots of its neighbours, and now three more trees leaned precariously, stripped of their usual shelter. In mere seconds, they succumbed to gravity, slamming down across the driveway, blocking it entirely.

The group sprinted towards the bridge, their torchlights jerking and flicking left and right as they ran.

Jim pointed upriver, 'Holy shit!' he shouted.

A wall of wood and earth and water raced towards them, gaining momentum by the second.

'Quick!' Jim yelled, urging Donna and Ross over.

They looked back at Lomond and Claire, who were sprinting as fast as they could, but still far behind.

Donna and Ross braced themselves for the impact, watching the landslide barrel towards them, expecting the bridge to be pulverised any moment. With just twenty feet to go, the bridge shook violently, knocking Ross off his feet. He grabbed for his torch a few feet away.

'Leave it!' Donna yelled, as she hauled him up. Her eyes were fixed on Lomond and Claire, who were still too far away.

'Stay back!' she screamed, not believing they could make it.

But Lomond wouldn't give up. 'We can make it! Come on!' he shouted to Claire, and they charged across the bridge, now rocking like a bouncy castle.

Just ten feet from safety, Lomond felt the bridge give way beneath them. They both dropped their torches trying to keep their balance. Lomond shoved Claire forward, sending her tumbling into the waiting arms of Donna and Ross.

The others in the group watched in horror from the front steps of the castle, sure they were witnessing the death of DCI John Lomond.

CHAPTER FORTY-ONE

THE BRIDGE LET OUT an ominous creak, a sound that made Lomond's skin crawl. Suddenly, there was a deafening crack, and the wood boards snapped like flatbreads.

Lomond's stomach dropped as he felt himself go weightless for a split second before plummeting downward towards the river.

Ross cried out, 'John!'

With no thought for his own safety, Ross hurled himself towards the edge of the moat, and threw an arm down to Lomond.

Claire lay sprawled on the driveway, eyes wide with horror as she saw Lomond falling down below ground level.

Somehow, Lomond managed to grab Ross's arm and hold on. But he was already slipping.

'Quick!' Ross groaned. 'Your other arm...'

Lomond swung his other hand up and found Ross's wrist. Ross now had Lomond's full weight on one arm. It

was all he could do just to hold on to him, never mind pull
him up.

'I can't...' he groaned. 'I can't...'

Lomond looked up in horror. Legs swinging and
finding only fresh air, he screamed back, 'Yes, you fucking
can!'

Donna and Jim were desperately clinging to Ross,
using all their strength to keep him from falling. Even with
the three of them straining, the weight of Ross and Lomond
threatened to overpower them. Brad, Noel, and Charlotte
were quickest to respond to the emergency, sprinting back
to help.

Brad and Charlotte were lightning-fast compared to
Noel, whose numerous layers slowed him down. Together,
they grabbed onto Donna and Jim, grunting with exertion.
The combined weight of Ross and Lomond was more than
they could manage. They only had the strength for one last
desperate effort to pull them both to safety.

'Don't let go!' Ross begged them, picturing Lachlann's
face.

'I was thinking the same thing,' Lomond groaned.

Brad, who knew Ross was a father like him, urged them
on. He shouted a countdown from three. With adrenaline
surging through their veins, they made one final effort they
managed to drag Ross and Lomond to safety.

As soon as they hit solid ground, Ross and Lomond
collapsed, gasping for air. Jim and Donna rushed to help
them up.

Despite not facing death head-on, the terror of the
moment had still shaken Ross to his core. Lomond was

equally stunned, barely able to mutter a grateful "thank fuck for that" as he surveyed the wreckage below.

Slowly, Lomond struggled to his feet, his legs wobbly from the shock. He turned to the group and declared, 'We're definitely staying the night, then.'

CHAPTER FORTY-TWO

WILLIE WAS FIRST BACK to Major Investigations that night. He stood at the coffee station, pouring his sixth cup of the day. His sixth was his favourite – though it wasn't every day he had as many as six. The first of the morning was merely to ensure he could physically move and get out the door without feeling like a pig had taken a dump in his head. The second was one he could savour – actually feel the caffeine kick in. If he had a sixth it came after dinner, around early evening, when he committed to working deep into the night.

He had sat at his desk with the coffee when he noticed the whiteboard at the front of the room. 'What the...' He looked at in confusion. Then walked slowly towards it. He stood in front of it, hands on hips.

The centre part of the board had a list written in black marker in huge letters.

SUDOKU

GOLF

JIGSAWS
BAKING

Each word had a crudely fashioned box next to it.

Then a voice called out from the mezzanine. 'Pick as many as you like!'

It was Linda.

'What's going on, boss?' Willie called back.

Linda descended the stairs, hair still soaked from the pouring rain after nipping out to Asda for a microwave dinner. She had improvised a hairstyle by scraping it all back. It laid her face barer than usual. The snarl of her mouth more prominent than usual. Eyes wilder.

She was pleased to see the office empty. It meant that she could go off on him the way she had rehearsed in her head in the car on the way in. 'I was having a rough day, anyway,' she said. 'Then I come back to find that instead of investigating the murder you were given, you've gone out with DC Tweedle Dee and DC Tweedle Dum to find me another one. A suicide, no less...' She was all the scarier for how quietly she was delivering it all. 'It made me so sad. I thought: fuck me. Poor Willie. He's so bored in Major Investigations, he's finding new murders to solve on top of the one he already has. So rather than fuck my department stats, I decided to find you some new hobbies instead.'

'Linda, I can explain,' Willie began.

'No, I don't think that you can. Investigating cases that the Procurator Fiscal already ruled on? Nine years ago? And now this.' She tossed a brown A4 envelope down on his desk. 'Forensic science photos taken from Liz MacRae's flat the night she died. Are we even polis anymore? Are Pardeep and Jason not chapping on doors?'

Willie protested, 'They're doing that too, Linda.'

'A bestselling author is stabbed to death and poisoned in his own home, and we're spunking our resources up the wall on a suicide that closed nine years ago!'

Willie took out an evidence bag from his briefcase. 'I've actually been looking into the poisoning thing, myself.' In the evidence bag was a flattened piece of packaging with William MacRae's address on it.

Linda was on the cusp of calming down when Pardeep and Jason entered, soaked through as well.

Willie looked to the ceiling. 'Great timing, boys...'

'Ah, here they are.' Linda applauded. 'Butch Cassidy and the Sundance Kid. Laurel and Hardy. The fucking Chuckle Brothers. Well? Do you think you could bring yourselves to investigate the murder that's *not* over a decade old, or what?'

Call it confidence, ignorance, or some heroic combination of both, but Pardeep was the only one seemingly unfazed by Linda's mood. 'Actually,' he ventured, 'we've made a lot of progress.'

Willie implored Jason, 'Tell her what you told me on the phone.'

Jason stepped meekly forward, holding the printout from Glasgow Uni. 'These are the names of every student who studied Creative Writing at the same time as Liz MacRae. Look at the name I've highlighted.'

Linda took the printout, still sceptical it would go anywhere useful. 'Seth Knox? I thought he went to Oxford.'

'That's what he told Donna,' Jason said. 'That's what he tells everyone.'

Not wanting the moment to pass without his colleague getting her due, Pardeep added, 'Seth told Donna that he had read every major novel from the seventeenth to the twentieth century. Kate Randall, Liz MacRae's flatmate, said Liz had a boyfriend around the time of her death that had said the same thing.'

Willie, who had taken ownership of the printout, nodded. 'Nice catch, Jason.'

'Problem is,' Jason replied, 'it doesn't make sense.'

'Wait, what?' said Pardeep . 'I thought we were on the same page on this.'

Jason put his hand out for the list again. 'If I may, Willie?' He showed them all the three instances of Seth's name being highlighted on the list. 'These are three different classes that Seth Knox, Liz MacRae, and Kate Randall all took together. Kate told us that she never met Liz's boyfriend, who we can now say with near certainty was Seth Knox. But they have three classes together. Liz was dating the guy. And Kate somehow never meets him?'

Confused as to why Jason was now turning on the very theory they had only just presented to Linda, Pardeep said, 'What about William MacRae in the corridor? Tell them about that.'

'That's problematic as well,' Jason said. 'Kate had maintained from her original statement that she had nearly bumped into someone in the corridor where she and Liz's flat was located. At a place that meant the man could only have been coming to or from that flat. She tried and failed to provide a description at the time because it was too general in every way. Too broad. This was never a big deal back then, because the investigation ended up ruling it accidental death. Yet this evening she pointed to a picture of MacRae and said that he was definitely the man she saw in the corridor that night. It doesn't stand up to scrutiny.'

'How so?' asked Linda, hanging on to Jason's every word, listening with her entire body.

He said, 'Kate couldn't provide a decent description of the man at the time because she was intoxicated and couldn't be too sure about some details. But William MacRae, even nine years ago, would clearly have been a man of advancing years. It would be the first thing about him that stood out: a man in his fifties wandering around student accommodation late at night. When a witness is struggling to describe someone, it's always the first thing we lean into. How old were they? At the time, she couldn't be sure. Now she can point with certainty to MacRae off the back of a photo a few inches wide? Also, she spoke kind of tenderly about Claire MacRae, yet claimed to have never met William.' Jason handed Linda his phone, which had his Kindle app showing a MacRae book called *Dead Hearts*. It was on the page for acknowledgements. 'Look at the third name listed.'

Linda read it aloud. '"Special thanks to Kate Randall for all the walks in Kelvingrove and giving me notes on an early draft." What the merry hell?'

Jason was nodding away. 'Not just one walk. But "all the walks".'

'So she met MacRae several times.'

Jason was getting excited about the clincher. 'Look at the copyright page at the start.'

Linda swiped the progress bar to the relevant page. She smiled. 'This was published nine years ago.'

'It came out two months before Liz died. She knew MacRae, she met him more than once, they had a relationship that was close enough to merit a mention in his book, and she's lied to us about all of it. Why?'

Pardeep said, 'Maybe she was too drunk to recognise him that night.'

'Say we accept that, Pardeep. How, then, could she possibly recognise him nine years later in a matter of seconds?'

Linda said, 'Well, which is it? Was she lying then in not telling us MacRae was there? Or is she lying now?'

Pardeep suggested, 'Maybe they were having an affair and it ended badly. Now she's trying to tarnish his reputation?'

Willie asked, 'What do you think, Jason?'

He replied, 'I think one of two things is happening here. One, she saw MacRae that night but covered it up. Or two, she didn't see MacRae that night, and is now lying in saying that he was there.'

'If she's lying and MacRae wasn't there at all – then who was?'

Jason lifted his shoulders, uncertain from a proof perspective, but convinced on instinct. 'I think there can only be one person in the mix. Seth Knox. I don't buy for a moment that Kate never met Seth when they and Liz had three different classes together.' He already knew Pardeep's objection and added before Pardeep could get to it. 'I get that she was a secretive person, and she may have kept the relationship a secret. But by all accounts, Kate was Liz's only real friend at uni. She never saw Seth come to the flat even once? Saw Liz and him together, not even once in a relationship that had lasted months, by Kate's own account? That's not credible to me.'

Linda handed back his phone. 'What's not credible to me is how you just happened across this in a random MacRae book.'

Jason said, 'It wasn't random. When we got the job, I downloaded every book MacRae ever wrote and checked the acknowledgements in each one. I'm not much of a reader of crime fiction, but I thought any names that popped up there might be valuable.'

'Christ, I wish I could bottle you, Jason. I should let you have the rest of the night off to "Netflix and chill", as the kids say.'

Jason tried hard to not react.

Pardeep spluttered laughter. Realising it probably wasn't a good career move to laugh in the face of his Det Sup, he rushed to explain himself. 'Ma'am, I hate to say this, but you might not be using that phrase correctly.'

'What?' asked Linda. 'Netflix and chill?'

Just hearing the words coming out of her mouth again was enough to set Pardeep off a second time.

He waved his hand in an *I-can't-even...* motion.

Taking the diplomatic route, Jason said, 'Ma'am, I feel obliged to check that you know what that phrase means.'

A pause followed. Linda knew that no matter what she said it would be wrong. She said, 'Inviting someone over to watch Netflix. And relax?'

Willie didn't have a clue what they were talking about, and Pardeep had since got a grip of himself.

'Ma'am,' Jason explained earnestly, 'it's a euphemism for inviting someone over for, em, carnal...' he cleared his throat, thinking that the more he talked around it, the worse it would be. 'Sexual relations,' he said.

'Really?' she said, thinking back through every instance she had used the phrase. 'Aw, shite.'

Willie asked, 'What's wrong?'

She winced, but without embarrassment. 'I was at a conference last week at Tulliallan. I was talking to three chief supers from down south.'

'Linda, tell me you didn't...' Willie couldn't bring himself to picture the scenario, let alone say it aloud.

'It's just...we were talking about some of the really good cop shows on Netflix. And I said about how good the TV was back at my hotel and–'

Pardeep was already bringing his hand up to his face in horror. Jason knew where it was going too.

Linda confirmed, 'I might have invited all three to, ahem, "Netflix and chill" back at the hotel.' Looking to redirect things, she puffed. 'Oh, well, fuck it. Done now. Anyway, what we think and what we can prove about this case are two very different things. Say we accept that there was something strange going on with Liz MacRae's death that we haven't uncovered yet. Where does that leave us with William's murder?'

Willie picked up the packaging in the evidence bag. 'Putting aside all this stuff about messages written in blood, and authors working under aliases, there are still a few tangibles to this case. One being the poison that William imbibed through the whisky that was sent to him. Moira's confirmed that the poison was fast-acting. The knife wound is cause of death, but the amount of the poison in his blood was more than sufficient to kill him a few hours later. The whisky arrived in this packaging here.' He showed it to them. 'I've been able to reverse the tracking to a drop-off point in a shop in Hackney Wick in London. I just got an email back from the owner of that shop, along with a still image from his CCTV the day that the package was sent to William MacRae's home.' Willie held his phone out first to Linda.

She said in wonder, 'I'll be damned.'

He then showed it to Pardeep and Jason.

Pardeep cursed under his breath, 'Bastard.'

'Pretty much,' said Willie.

Linda looked on, chilled by the scene playing out. 'Well...fuck me sideways on a swing. You know what this means, right?'

'Yeah,' said Willie, as if that was a dramatic understatement. 'John, Ross, and Donna are very much in harm's way.'

CHAPTER FORTY-THREE

LOMOND WAS NURSING HIS LEG, hopping a few steps before trying his weight on the bad side again. It was better than expected. 'Jeanie God...' he wheezed, not knowing where to look first. 'This place is...' He couldn't think of a word to do it justice.

'I know, right,' said Ross.

Donna was more concerned about Lomond's leg. 'Are you sure you're all right, boss?'

'Yeah,' he replied distantly, his adrenaline still pumping. 'Fine, thanks.'

The owner hadn't done the vacuous millionaire thing by buying a medieval castle, then kitting it out with a lot of minimalist modern design. It did, however, have state-of-the-art voice-activated smart speakers that were set into the ceiling. All of which could be controlled from the owner's phone, or the main hub in the library.

It was as warm and snug a haven from the elements as you could hope to find. It was traditional design but with tasteful contemporary furniture. It reminded Lomond of those grand baronial houses that had been turned into five-star hotels. Plush tartan carpets, chandeliers fashioned from stag antlers, and tweed cushions and throws over everything in sight. Lomond had never understood the point of throws. Overpriced blankets that make a sofa look nice, but were always underwhelming when it came to cosiness.

The group shuffled out of their coats and jackets, and rearranged hair matted down with rain.

Tom Ellison strode around the lobby, hunting for a room with a bar. 'Okay...I think I speak for everyone when I say I need a drink.'

He found a sizeable lounge, which prompted the others to follow.

Jim shouldered him out of the way. 'Aye, right. It must have been hard work standing on the front steps holding your—'

Brad pulled him back. 'Jim, calm down.'

Jim kept up in Tom's face. 'I particularly liked the part where you did nothing at all.' He turned to Crawford, Seth and Zoe. 'You lot, as well.'

'I would only have got in the way,' Zoe claimed.

'I'm sorry,' Crawford bumbled. 'I...I...just panicked.' He turned to Lomond. 'Thank God, you're all right.'

Lomond nodded in acceptance of the apology.

Seth didn't bother giving an excuse.

'What about this host?' said Charlotte.

'Presumably,' said Seth, thumbing through an oversize coffee table book on tartans with bored disdain, 'they'll play us a tape reporting on various crimes we've committed, and then we'll all get bumped off until there's only one of us left.'

It was his typical attitude, but the delivery seemed off – particularly to Claire and Zoe, who had spent the most amount of time around him. Underneath it all, Seth looked genuinely spooked and was trying to hide it.

Tom headed for the lounge bar and fixed himself a whisky. 'I think I've paid my tab tonight and then some.'

Once it became clear that the thought of offering anyone else a drink couldn't have been further from Tom's mind, Jim slouched on a tweed sofa with both arms spread out wide across the back. He shut his eyes in relief.

Ross tapped him on the leg and handed him a large measure of Laphroaig. 'Thanks, Mr Provan.'

Jim shook his hand. 'Don't mention it. Glad you're okay.'

Noel Redmond looked at his watch. 'We've been here five minutes, Seth. It's a little soon to be worried we're all potential murderers because we're stuck here for the night.'

'You really think we're stuck here?' asked Zoe.

Lomond said, 'Did you see the size of that thing that nearly clobbered me? It was like a bloody Redwood. Even if someone back at Crichton House could come up with some way of crossing the moat, they'd never get past those trees to get it to us. We're not going anywhere. Not tonight.'

Brad started towards Crawford. 'What about this host of yours, Crawford? Where are they?'

'I'm sure they'll be down shortly,' he replied.

Brad's eyes narrowed. 'We're not here for any memorial. Are we, Crawford?'

Crawford could feel everyone's eyes burning holes in

him. Taking refuge in his phone screen, he said, 'My only concern right now is getting help from Crichton House to clear that road.'

'That's not something you can bump out the way with a Range Rover, Mr Bell,' Lomond pointed out.

Noel asked Brad, 'Why did you say that we're not here for a memorial?'

'Because we're not,' he replied, waving at Lomond. 'Go on. Tell them.'

Claire asked, 'How do you know, Brad?'

Frustrated that he was the only one in the room to see it, Brad replied, 'Because three detectives are here with us for a supposedly private memorial. What are they here for? Crowd control?' He asked Lomond, 'Would you care to deny it, Chief Inspector?'

Ross put his hands out in appeal. 'Why don't we all just calm down. Your questions are for whoever owns this place. Our business will become yours when–'

Then Lomond announced, 'I was told that the owner of this place had information for our investigation.' Aiming his ire at Crawford, he said, 'Where are they, Mr Bell? I was told this was a matter of life and death.'

Noel was first to see her. He turned towards the staircase that swept left and right. Emerging from the gloom of the landing was a woman wearing a dark check suit and a white pinstripe shirt.

She called out, arms aloft, 'I'm right here.'

'Oh my...' said Noel, reaching out to tap someone, but no one was close enough. 'Is that...?'

Jim peeled himself up off the couch. 'Rebecca!' he exclaimed. 'So this is where you've been hiding.'

Brad said to himself, 'Why am I not surprised.'

Everyone watched – both starstruck and baffled – as she descended the stairs.

'Is that who I think it is?' Ross whispered to Donna.

'Sure is,' she replied.

The woman on the stairs couldn't help but smile mischievously at the reaction from the others below.

Zoe snorted with grudging admiration. 'I'll give her this much: she knows how to make an entrance.'

Lomond checked with Donna. 'Is that really RJ Hawley?'

'I'm so glad you can see her too,' she replied in a daze, revelling in some atypical glamour in the job. 'Man, Gallowhill feels a long way away right now.'

CHAPTER FORTY-FOUR

Lomond warned her, 'Donna, if you ask her for an autograph, I'll make sure you can't even get a job as a lollipop woman. Tesco security guard will be something to aspire to.'

Ross couldn't stop staring – along with everyone else. He whispered to Lomond, 'How much money do you think she has on her *right now*?'

Lomond rubbed his eyes in despair.

Jim held his arms out towards her. 'Rebecca! I was just thinking that this would be your kind of place.'

'Grand?' she asked. 'Stately?'

'I was going to say bloody expensive, but yes. Those too.'

Even Tom appeared to be star-struck.

The only one not in thrall to RJ Hawley's celebrity was Charlotte, who made a point of shoving a finger towards her mouth as if throwing up. And she wasn't worried about Lomond seeing her do it.

'Ladies and gentlemen,' Rebecca announced, 'I would like to apologise for dragging you here in such terrible conditions. But in the circumstances, I didn't have much choice.'

Jim said, 'I don't know if you saw the trees falling outside or the bridge collapsing. But other than that, it's looking pretty good out there.'

'My security team have ended up caught on the wrong side of it. They're making their way to Crichton House for a better view.'

Lomond had heard enough, and forced his way to the front of the group assembled at the foot of the stairs. 'Rebecca Hawley, I'm DCI John Lomond.'

'DCI Lomond,' she said. 'I'm so glad you made it. Although I wish the circumstances were better.'

He looked around for an appropriate room. 'Maybe we should have a chat in private somewhere.'

'Actually,' she said, 'I was going to suggest a chat in front of everyone. Seeing as we both want the same thing.'

'And what is that?'

'To catch William's killer.'

Tom barked at Lomond, 'Who exactly *are* you, fella?'

He replied to Tom, then halfway through realised he might as well address the entire room. 'These are my colleague DS Ross McNair and DC Donna Higgins. We're from Glasgow Major Investigations for Police Scotland. We're investigating the murder of William MacRae.'

'What does that have to do with any of us?' asked Tom.

Charlotte scoffed. 'Haven't you figured that out yet? No wonder you need co-authors.'

'Excuse me?'

'They're here because they think one of us did it.' She turned to Lomond. 'Am I right?'

He threw out his bottom lip. 'Seems a fair assessment, actually. Now, if you don't mind, Ms Hawley, Crawford said that you had some important information for us regarding William MacRae.' He didn't want to say that it was about AD Sullivan. Not in front of everyone. Lomond had learned early in his career that you never open your mouth unless you know what cards everyone is holding. As of that moment, he still didn't know what to make of this Sullivan persona. And whether alerting the group to Rebecca having information on Sullivan might even endanger her life.

But for what Rebecca had to say next, Lomond needn't have bothered with such caution.

She said, 'Everyone, I have a confession. You weren't invited here for a private memorial for William. Though, in a way, what I have planned could be considered a tribute to him.'

Clutching her phone, Zoe held her arms aloft. 'What's going on?'

'I told you,' Brad cautioned. 'There's no memorial. Is there?'

'There is not,' Rebecca admitted.

'Then what are we doing here?' asked Claire.

'We have to find out who did it. Someone here killed William. The police know that. We know that.'

'I didn't!' protested Jim.

'Neither did I,' said Charlotte.

'Someone here,' Rebecca explained, 'is AD Sullivan.

Whoever they are, they hold the key to unmasking who William's killer is. We have to find out who they are.'

The penny was finally dropping for Lomond. 'So you've brought everyone here on false pretences? Including three police officers.'

'I'm trying to *help*,' she fired back. 'I thought if I got everyone together under the one roof—'

Lomond interrupted, 'Without legal representation, without being cautioned, under duress...' He threw his arm up in the direction of the driveway. 'We're all stuck here, under the same roof as a killer.'

'Potentially.'

Lomond wasn't interested in her disclaimers. 'Do you have *any* idea how reckless you've been?'

He nearly went on to say that it might yet prove to be a fatal error, but the room erupted in a flurry of outrage and overlapping protests.

How dare you... and *what right do you have...*

Notably, the angriest of the group was Seth. 'This is an outrage!' he seethed. 'We can't stay here. I won't, anyway. Get a bloody helicopter here and airlift is out, Rebecca!'

'Seth,' she replied dryly, 'it's a castle. With turrets. There's no helipad, and we're in the middle of a hurricane. Steel buildings don't go out in weather like this, let alone light helicopters.'

Lomond pushed his lips out, finding Seth's reaction interesting. He made sure to catch Donna and Ross's eyes. *Seth's actually scared*, Lomond thought.

Charlotte turned in desperation to Donna. 'Are we actually at *risk*?'

She appealed for calm. 'We're here conducting routine

enquiries. What happened to William, we think, was an isolated incident. But we can't be sure.'

'So we *are* at risk.' Charlotte fled to the bar and poured herself a large measure of whisky.

The act opened the floodgates.

'That seems like a good idea to me,' said Jim.

'I'll second that,' said Noel, following him to the bar.

Fancying himself the alpha male in the room, Brad told them, 'I'm sure this is all just routine. The best thing we can do is cooperate, and give the police all the information we have. The road will be clear by morning, and–'

'And one of us could be dead by then,' exclaimed Zoe. For once, her phone was nowhere in sight. All of her energies were focussed on the terrifying prospect looming over them all.

Noel called back, 'That's easy for you to say, Brad! You've got decades of special weapons and combat training. I write cosy crime. All I got from *my* research is how to play lawn bowls. Hardly a skillset that could keep me alive when faced with a knife-wielding murderer.'

Tom remonstrated with Crawford. 'Why wasn't I informed of this?' He wheeled away in a fury. 'Man, my lawyer's gonna litigate this goddamn festival into the ground.'

Crawford replied with a series of indecipherable noises meant to convey uncertainty. 'I'm sure we're all perfectly safe. The police are here.'

'Oh yeah, the police,' said Tom, turning to confront Lomond. 'Were you in on this too?' Tom squared up to him. 'My lawyer's gonna can your *ass*, buddy.'

Lomond didn't flinch so much as an optical nerve.

Ross and Donna were quick to put themselves between him and Tom.

'How's about we calm right down, eh?' said Ross.

Donna pushed Tom back. 'And back right up.'

Lomond grinned at her. She always sounded more Paisley when she was manhandling someone.

He told Tom, 'I hate to disappoint you, but in the list of intimidating people I've had up in my face threatening me, you don't even break the top twenty.' He placed a forefinger on Tom's chest and pushed him backwards. 'Keep up the attitude, *buddy*, and I'll lock you to the storm door.'

Ross and Donna didn't move until Tom had backed up.

In the background, Claire was turning on Rebecca. 'Have you any idea what you've done? You've put us all under the same roof as the person who killed William! Are you crazy?'

Having poured herself a drink, Charlotte had since reconsidered and peeled off, walking around the hallway. 'I'm not staying here,' she kept saying.

'You don't have a choice,' Lomond informed her. 'None of you do. Nothing without wings is getting back to Crichton House tonight. We're going to have to just crack on. We have evidence that suggests AD Sullivan could be in danger, or have pertinent information to our investigation.' He held his hands out to the group. 'Sullivan was in Glasgow on Friday night when William was murdered. I understand you may have your reasons for wishing anonymity. But believe me when I say that the potential threat against you is very real and very serious.'

Everyone looked at each other.

'I don't understand,' Jim said, swigging from a bottle of beer. 'Why is no one coming forward?'

'There can only be one reason for that,' Lomond replied.

The most relaxed person in the castle was Seth Knox. Slouched on a couch, looking to the ceiling, he let out a snarky, bored cry. 'I'm on the edge of my seat.'

Lomond ignored him. 'We had been working with two possibilities. Either Sullivan is under threat. Or Sullivan *is* the threat. Now we know which it is.' He didn't think he had to say anything further.

Everyone waited for the answer.

Noel snapped, 'Well?'

'Isn't it obvious?' asked Lomond. 'If Sullivan is here, and they're innocent and worried for their own safety, why *wouldn't* they come forward?'

Charlotte said, 'They might prefer to admit it in private to you. Have you considered that?'

'I have,' said Lomond. 'Except, Sullivan is announcing themselves publicly at their event tomorrow lunchtime. The prospect of being stuck in this castle overnight with a threat against your life isn't sufficient cause to identify yourself a day early?'

Claire staggered back a few paces, hand held at her mouth. 'You mean that Sullivan is William's killer? They're actually in this room?'

Sympathetic to the anguish she would be feeling, Lomond replied sombrely, 'It's almost certain.'

Noel suggested, 'I don't recall the last time a killer was sent down for "almost certainly" killing someone, Chief Inspector. It's not exactly going to stand up in court.'

'It doesn't have to, Mr Redmond. We're not in court. Not yet. You don't jump straight to proof in my line of work. You start by nudging everyone an inch at a time towards the truth.'

'That's it,' announced Tom. 'I'm leaving.'

Jim pointed an accusing finger. 'That's *exactly* what the killer would say.'

In the process of hanging up her phone, Rebecca Hawley said, 'You're welcome to try to leave, Tom. But my security team recommend you check the wording in your life insurance policy. Because unless you can break the world record for the long jump by about three metres, going outside in the middle of a quasi-hurricane might be called suicide. It will be morning at least until anyone can get off the castle grounds.'

Brad strode around, inspecting the surroundings. 'You can't keep us here against our will.' He turned to Lomond. 'Or interrogate us without legal representation present.'

'I wouldn't dream of it,' Lomond said. 'Cooperation is appreciated. Not obligated.'

Noel said, 'This will be the part, then, where you start interviewing the suspects.'

'You mean interrogating,' said Charlotte.

Rebecca sniped from the wings, 'Got something to hide, Charlotte?'

Jim then waded in. He wagged his finger at Lomond. 'Not a bad pitch, DCI Lomond. Anyone who doesn't want to talk will be hanging a big guilty sign around their neck. If everyone else talks, and the one person who's really Sullivan *doesn't* talk, then it will be obvious who they are.

So if anyone wants to continue hiding the fact they're Sullivan, then they'd be advised to talk.'

Suppressing a smile, Lomond said, 'I suppose so.'

'Although you might just end up with a pack of lies.'

'I'm fully expecting to be lied to tonight, Mr Provan.' Lomond turned to Rebecca. 'Ms Hawley. I'm going to need somewhere private to speak to the guests one at a time.' He looked around the cavernous setting, where all sorts of rooms branched off from the lobby. Drawing rooms, study rooms, a grand library...and those were just the ones within his eye line. Lomond said, 'I don't suppose you could spare one.'

Rebecca indicated the library. 'That offers the most privacy.'

'Good. We'll start with you, Miss Hathaway.'

Zoe looked up from her phone, startled. 'Me?'

Lomond nodded towards the library, indicating to Ross and Donna to follow him. He said over his shoulder to the others, 'Make yourselves comfortable, folks. It's going to be a long night.'

CHAPTER FORTY-FIVE

In the grand library across the lobby, there was a quadrangle of seating already set up. A green leather armchair, surrounded by two small couches on either side, and facing another much larger armchair.

A log fire was burning behind the small armchair, but DCI Lomond planned to bring plenty of his own heat to proceedings. He had to. There wasn't much time.

Lomond had Zoe sit in the smaller armchair. She recoiled from the intense heat, trying to shuffle the chair forward a bit. It was too heavy, though.

Donna sat on one couch, Ross the other. Lomond didn't sit down. He paced.

Zoe said matter-of-factly, 'I don't know what you think I know, but I'll bet it's not nearly as much as you think.'

Lomond stopped. He looked up, thinking intensely for a moment, then resumed pacing. 'Boy, that was quite a sentence, Miss Hathaway. Does it come with a map and a trail of breadcrumbs?'

'I mean that–'

He waved her explanation down. 'I'm sure you really don't know who Sullivan is, and if I had to bet on someone being the killer, you wouldn't even break my top five.'

'Oh,' she said, suddenly relieved. 'Thanks.'

Lomond went on, 'I know that I've been banging the drum that everyone is a suspect, but in your case I'm willing to make an exception. From what Donna here tells me about you, it's a wonder that you've even read a book, much less written one.'

Donna interjected, 'Um, that's not exactly what I said.'

'Close enough,' said Lomond. 'I'm paraphrasing.' He returned to Zoe. 'Is that fair to say, that you were not expected to take over Hathaway Publishing?'

If Zoe was intimidated by Lomond and his two colleagues, she didn't show it. She had her legs crossed and was sitting back in a relaxed pose in the chair. 'I've been confounding people's expectations of me since I was a child. You told everyone out there I know who Sullivan is because it suited your needs. I've never attempted to correct the public perception of me as a millennial, spoiled, trust fund brat who could turn pouting for Instagram into an Olympic sport, because it makes me a hundred times more dangerous if the public me doesn't match up with who they get in a board room. Eventually, word will get out that I'm not running my dad's company into the ground – quite the opposite. But until that time comes, I'm happy for people to think whatever they want about me.' She took out a cigarette from a tiny handbag.

Lomond flashed a worried look around the room. 'I'm not sure you're allowed to smoke in here, Miss Hathaway.'

She lit it anyway and exhaled a thin cloud of smoke straight up in the air. 'You can arrest me for smoking if you want, Chief Inspector. But then you'll never find out what I know about William MacRae. I might as well tell you before one of those vipers out there throws me under the bus for trying to keep secrets from you.'

'And what do you know?'

She paused for another drag. 'William wasn't himself the last few months. He had threatened to not renew his contract with Hathaway. There's been gossip about it all over London, and I know someone out there knows.'

'In what other ways was William not being himself?'

'Outlandish things. Outbursts.'

'What sort of outbursts?'

'Like screaming at my dad in a crowded office over contract renegotiations.'

'Why would you need or want to keep that secret from us?'

'Don't patronise me, DCI Lomond. You'll hear it from someone else in the next few hours, I'm sure. William caused my dad's heart attack. The fight was what brought it on. We both know that on the face of it, that gives me a motive for wanting to hurt him.' She reconsidered her words. 'Or get rid of him.'

'Did you blame–'

Zoe pretended to conduct an imaginary orchestra along with parroting Lomond. 'Blame him for my dad's death... No, I never blamed William for that. I blamed his death on forty Marlboros a day and a lack of exercise beyond turning the pages of books for fifty years.'

Ross indicated her cigarette. 'I would have thought that you might think twice about smoking yourself, in that case.'

'I do think twice, DS McNair,' she said. 'It just so happens that my second thought is always, "fuck *me*, I love smoking." Every single one is like strawberries and cream, if you ask me. Plus...' She made a ta-da gesture. 'I look spectacularly cool while doing it.'

Donna flashed her eyebrows up, as she and Lomond exchanged glances. Neither of them would have argued with Zoe's contention. She might have been twenty-six, but she carried herself like she was ten, even twenty, years older.

Lomond asked, 'What sort of relationship did Seth have with William?'

Stumped for specifics, she said, 'Fine. I guess? They went way back, but I haven't had much involvement with Seth yet. He was hired long before my time.'

'They never argued?'

Zoe laughed. 'William could cause an argument in an empty room. He was the sort of person who would wake everyone up in the house to tell them he was going to bed. Loved the sound of his own voice.'

'So they did argue?'

'About the work. I encourage healthy debate among creative people. Good art dies when all you hear is "yes, that's a good idea". You have to kill your darlings.'

'Was there anything about this book that could have been causing more friction than usual?'

She scoffed. 'You could say that. I hesitate to say this, because I know it will cause jumping to conclusions.'

'Try me,' said Lomond.

She sighed. Saying nothing now would only make herself look suspicious. 'William was going to kill off Roxburgh.'

'Going to? He changed his mind?'

'Yes. He sent through his final draft of the new book last night.' She showed Lomond her phone screen with the email and the attached file.

The time of the email was what caught Lomond's attention. He showed the phone to Ross and Donna.

Ross said, 'That must have been...possibly the last thing he did.'

CHAPTER FORTY-SIX

Lomond asked Zoe, 'Have you read this version?'

'I've read the last chapter,' she replied. 'To see what happened to old Roxburgh.'

'And?'

She laughed. 'I'm not going to give away the ending of William MacRae's final DCI Roxburgh book, am I?'

'This isn't an Amazon book review, Miss Hathaway. This is a murder investigation. I need to know. Did William kill off Roxburgh in that final draft?'

A long pause followed. She finally relented and answered. 'No. He must have changed his mind.'

Donna looked to Lomond for permission to step in. 'Why would he have killed off Roxburgh in the first place? Even in a draft?'

'It's hard to say. It's not like Hathaway could have done anything with the character if William left us for another publisher. The copyright is his.'

'As long as he was alive,' Lomond clarified.

'The notion that I or anyone in Hathaway murdered one of our most successful authors because he wanted to kill off a character is fanciful.'

Ross said, 'But William wanted to leave. He wanted to leave months ago, before you were even CEO. What if William knew he wasn't going to be around much longer after the book came out?'

'What do you mean?' asked Zoe.

Lomond nearly asked the same question.

Ross explained, 'I don't know nearly as much about books as you, or Donna. But it seems to me that if you knew you were going to die, killing off your character could either be a way of saying goodbye, or protecting your legacy: no one acting on behalf of your estate can give permission for anything to be done with the character.'

Lomond remarked, 'Even Sherlock Holmes came back from the dead.'

'Yes,' said Zoe, 'but his head wasn't lobbed off by a train like Roxburgh's was prior to the final draft. Say what you want about William. He was...thorough.'

'AD Sullivan, then,' said Lomond. 'Walk me through how that whole process happened. How did Hathaway find them?'

'We didn't. The author contacted my dad directly.'

'I thought authors had to contact publishers through an agent.'

'Normally, yes. Anyone who sends a manuscript in the post or by email to a publisher, will find their package sent straight into recycling, or the email binned without being read. Publishers need agents to act as quality control.

Think of them like bouncers at a fancy nightclub. They stop the riffraff getting in.'

'Then how did Sullivan manage to not only get picked up by Hathaway, but by going directly through the CEO?'

'That's how I know the author is an industry heavy-weight. My dad would never have taken a phone call or listened to anyone else with an unsolicited manuscript. The only way he would have taken a book like that on is if they were known to him, with a proven track record.'

Donna wrote down in her notes "industry heavyweight confirmed".

Ross asked, 'How did communication with Sullivan and you work once your dad had died?'

'When we organised the transfer of his email accounts, we found plenty of emails back and forth between them. I just used the same email address that my dad had used to contact Sullivan.'

Donna clarified, 'You never spoke to them on the phone?'

'No, it was always email,' Zoe replied. 'Or WhatsApp messages.'

Lomond said, 'Didn't it strike you as odd that this author was so keen to stay anonymous?'

'It's certainly irregular. Most writers are desperate to get their face in the media. But given the nature of how my dad had acquired the manuscript, I was excited about the prospect of pinching a bestselling author from a rival. We've lost big books by Hathaway talent to rivals in the past, and it isn't nice. With Sullivan, I saw an angle we could play. Instead of our PR team trying to flog someone for interviews everywhere, we created buzz by demanding secrecy for the author. It created intrigue. And it's worked. Social media's been churning for weeks now about who Sullivan is. The event tomorrow has sold out for a reason.'

Lomond said, 'This is the part I don't understand: if you don't know who Sullivan is, how will it work at the event tomorrow? Someone is going to find you backstage and tell you that they're AD Sullivan? How will you know you've got the right person?'

'It's a little bit James Bond, but I emailed a passphrase to them a few days ago. Whoever they are, they'll tell me the passphrase backstage. Then I'll know.'

Lomond scoffed at the lengths they were going to. 'Why do you think anonymity has been so important to Sullivan until now? And why break it now?'

Zoe said, 'Questions I've been asking myself ever since we signed the contract. An author of sufficient magnitude would come under a lot of heat if they were shopping around a book to a different publisher. Take someone like Tom Ellison, for example. His contract is worth north of thirty million. How do you think his publisher will feel if he's writing books under a pen name and selling them off to the competition?'

'Miss Hathaway, we desperately need any physical links to Sullivan that we can get. Do you have any emails or messages from them that I can look at?'

'Sure.' She scrolled to the relevant message. 'I emailed Sullivan, highlighting concerns for their safety in the aftermath of William's murder. You can see that I encouraged them to make contact with your team at Helen Street.' Zoe handed the phone over. 'I'll let you read the reply. I was a bit shocked by it, to be honest.'

Lomond read it silently, then he showed the phone to Ross and then Donna.

Both were too professional to give anything away of their honest feelings about the message. But they were stunned.

The message to Zoe said, *"If the choice is between giving the bastard an award or stabbing him in the heart then it sounds like he got justice, if you ask me.'*

'It's not just the language,' Zoe said, showing some vulnerability for the first time. 'I never told Sullivan what the police had said to me about cause of death. So how did they know William had been stabbed in the heart?'

Lomond exhaled heavily. He looked longingly at Zoe's cigarettes. God, he would have loved one.

'Miss Hathaway,' he said, 'If Ross gives you my email address, can you send me that actual email as an attachment? Don't just forward it to me.'

'I understand how email works,' she replied.

'Also, I might need access to that phone at some point. Would you be okay with that?'

'Of course.'

'Can you do something else for me, please?'

'What's that?'

'Tell Rebecca Hawley we want to speak to her.'

THE THREE DETECTIVES took a moment to consider the information once Zoe had gone.

Lomond was first to speak, pacing in front of the fire. 'Okay, what do we think about the Roxburgh thing?'

Donna said, 'He just happens to radically change the ending of his book less than an hour before he ends up with a knife in his chest?'

Lomond said, 'There's no way Moira will be able to be so precise on the timing that we can say one way or the other whether that email was sent before or after time of death. A window even of fifteen minutes would be plenty of time to use William's computer and send a previous draft.'

'What about Seth's motive, though?' asked Ross. 'He had a point in your conversation, Donna. It makes no sense for him to kill MacRae.'

Lomond stared into the fire, then gave the logs a poke. 'Unless MacRae knew something about Seth that he didn't want to get out.'

'Or,' said Ross, 'we could have it backwards. What if Seth knew something about MacRae? Something from his past that made Seth angry enough to want to kill him?'

Lomond looked at Donna, and she at him.

Ross said, 'Revenge is a powerful emotion.'

Lomond said, 'Ross, like a stopped clock that's still right twice a day, consider that statement right on time.'

CHAPTER FORTY-SEVEN

THE FIRST THING Rebecca did when she reached the library was point her nose in the air and sniff. 'Was Zoe smoking in here?'

'She was,' said Lomond, still miffed about how he and the others had been duped into coming there. 'And you should know that some of my superiors would consider what you've done here tonight as obstruction.'

'Don't be obscene,' she replied calmly. 'You should be thanking me.'

Lomond waited for the reason.

'I'm going to help you catch William's killer this way,' she said. She walked over to a console behind a cupboard door, revealing a large TV screen. On it was a multi-camera set-up showing the rooms on the ground floor. Including the lounge where everyone was currently drinking and arguing amongst themselves.

Lomond went over for a closer look. He pointed to the

screen. 'There are audio levels showing on these. How are you doing that?'

'The ceiling speakers,' said Rebecca. 'They're recording right now. You're not going to miss a thing tonight.'

'None of this will be admissible in a court,' said Lomond.

'It doesn't need to be. It just needs to point you in the right direction.'

'Funny,' said Ross. 'That's exactly what every bent officer I've ever encountered said about planting evidence or breaking into locked properties.'

Lomond said, 'Is this your way of removing yourself as a potential suspect, then?'

'Of course I'm not a suspect like the others,' said Rebecca. 'I wasn't in Glasgow last night.'

'You have an alibi?'

'Of course.' She paused. 'I was here. All night.'

'I think that would be stretching the definition of alibi to breaking point, Ms Hawley. Did anyone see you?'

'My security team throughout the day and twice in the evening.' Addressing Ross and Donna, feverishly taking notes, Rebecca said, 'The only way I could have got to Glasgow and back is via a time machine.'

Ross added, 'So your alibi is the team that you employ?'

Unfazed, she replied, 'That, and the video security system. I'll be all over it throughout the night. Check it if you like.'

'We will, Ms Hawley,' said Lomond.

She cracked a window open, which immediately caused a pile of papers across the room to shoot up into the air in a swirl. The wind whistled through the turrets above the window outside. If anything, the storm had worsened since they had got to the castle.

She said, 'There really should be a special automatic jail sentence applied for people who smoke in libraries with rare books. I didn't just buy all of these by the crate like a lot of people with more money than taste. They were all hunted down one by one.'

Lomond admired the endless shelves of leather volumes, old hardbacks, and paperbacks, and first editions. 'That must have been quite a task.'

She sat down in the seat in front of the fire. 'I would consider myself an expert in the field. I can only hope the smell of tobacco doesn't linger.'

Feeling responsible, he said, 'I was going to say something to her, but...'

'It's fine,' she said. 'You wanted her to feel comfortable. Keep her talking.'

Donna said, 'You've been researching interrogation.'

Lomond perked up. 'That's right. You're a crime novelist these days.'

'It should have been a much smaller affair than it's ended up,' said Rebecca. 'The kids books had overwhelmed my impulse to write anything else. I simply didn't have the time. Most people don't realise I actually started out writing crime. That's how I became acquainted with William in the first place.'

'How did it come about?' asked Lomond.

'I had just finished the first Sally Stroud book.'

Donna leaned towards Lomond. '*The Curious Case of the Goldfish Who Lost Her Bowl*. Absolute classic.'

Embarrassed at the thought of Rebecca thinking that he

hadn't heard of it, he replied through gritted teeth, 'Yes, thanks for that, Donna.'

'Sorry, boss,' she whispered. She gestured apologetically for Rebecca to continue.

'It's quite all right,' said Rebecca. 'As of last week, I've actually sold five hundred million, six hundred and fifty thousand, five hundred copies. That's up six per cent on last year. In many ways, I have William to thank for that.'

'How so?' Lomond asked.

'William had got his hands on a copy through his old editor at Hathaway and given it to his daughter Liz.' Rebecca paused, suddenly overwhelmed with emotion. 'I'm sorry! I don't know what's got into me...It still seems criminal that she's no longer with us. If it hadn't been for her, I wouldn't be in this...crazy *place*. Liz started reading the book at bedtime, and ended up in tears because she kept wanting to read another chapter.'

Ross said, 'I've got a one-year-old at home. I'm looking forward to those moments.'

'My three have long since grown,' said Rebecca. 'Bedtime stories are one of the real highlights, DS McNair. I hope Sally Stroud will be well loved in due course.'

Ross smiled politely but awkwardly. Worried how the conversational tangent would be affecting Lomond.

Lomond cleared his throat and looked at his notes. 'Let's crack on, shall we.'

'The point is,' said Rebecca, 'if it wasn't for William, and Liz, I probably would have been dropped by Hathaway. The first print run was only nine hundred copies. They weren't confident it would work. But after William had a word with Max Hathaway, things started to turn around. On William's insistence, Hathaway took *The Lightning Keeper* to the Bologna Children's Book Fair. It's the biggest of its kind in the world. Certainly the most important for selling foreign rights. A few months later, I was number one on the *New York Times* bestseller list.'

Lomond said, 'That sort of thing must make you intensely loyal towards William.'

'Certainly,' she replied. 'That's why I wanted to set this up tonight. Flawed as I know you believe it to be. In a way, I envied William's career. I know, I know...I've had the fame and fortune and yadda yadda yadda. For me, I would have taken his career over mine any day.'

'Like a lottery winner that insists on keeping their minimum wage job. I've got to say, I don't know where you still find the drive.'

'I'm a storyteller. It's what I do.' She sighed wistfully. 'William could walk around Kelvingrove Park all day and not be recognised. A guy who's sold over a million books. *That* to me is the real dream.' The smile soon vanished from her face. 'Unfortunately it's not worked out as far as my crime books are concerned.'

Donna asked, 'Can I ask what exactly happened there?'

'I wrote a crime book a few years ago, in the rare occasion I had a break of six months from the Sally Strouds. I always thought it was good, but I wanted to know. The problem was, the moment I put out anything under RJ Hawley it becomes something else. Critics can't keep Sally Stroud out of their heads. So I decided to try an experiment. I would submit the book through my agent to publishers under an alias.'

Donna, eager to let Rebecca know that she knew, said quickly, 'Robin Balfour.'

'Interesting,' Ross said. His head had been buried in his notes. He gave Rebecca a cryptic smile. 'That's exactly how Zoe Hathaway said AD Sullivan did it.'

'Is it?' Rebecca said, apparently uninterested. 'The point was, none of the publishers would know it was me. It was the only way to be sure that the reaction was totally about the book, and nothing else to do with my reputation. The only publisher I didn't submit to was Hathaway, in case they passed. I didn't want to embarrass anyone.'

'Did this Robin Balfour experiment work?' asked Lomond.

'For a while, yes,' she replied. 'It got great reviews, sold steadily. Didn't set the world on fire, but it was never about that. It was about proving to myself that I could still do it. And I did. I wrote another two in the series, and it was starting to do very nicely. Until...' She raised and then dropped her hand on her thigh. 'Bloody social media. Within a day of my name leaking online, the Balfour books had all three top spots in the book charts. The first hardback was selling for five figures on eBay. And critics lined up to declare that they always knew it was really me all along. What a farce.'

'That's a shame,' said Lomond.

'It's a damn sight more than that,' she countered. 'No one else can understand. Unless you've been in my shoes. The only thing I wanted in my life again was anonymity. That's why I moved here. Why I financed the festival anonymously. And then published under Robin Balfour.

That was stolen from me. And I can never get it back again.'

Lomond said, 'Maybe that's the reason your sales are up six per cent on last year.'

She ran her tongue across her front teeth. Her eyes withering. 'Sales aren't everything, Chief Inspector. What I care about at this stage of my career is legacy.'

'Are you going to continue the series?' Donna asked.

'Oh, yes,' Rebecca replied, relieved to be talking to an obvious fan again. 'I love the characters too much, and I have all these ideas for the series. I'll just never know how much of its success is down to me. Or Sally Stroud. To put it bluntly, would the BBC have bought the rights if I was plain old anonymous Robin Balfour? I doubt it. I'll never get that opportunity back again.'

Ross had looked so disinterested throughout, it was a surprise to hear him speak again. 'Unless you're AD Sullivan,' he said.

An icy silence followed.

Rebecca finally said, 'I'm not AD Sullivan. As will be proven at Sullivan's event tomorrow.'

Lomond asked, 'I highly doubt that anything will come of the event tomorrow. After all this noise we've caused, I doubt they'll show their face if it means being confronted about a murder.'

Donna sneaked away to the back of the room quickly to answer her phone.

'I don't know,' said Rebecca, rising from the chair. 'I'm confident that between us all we can get to the bottom of this.'

She was halfway to the door when Lomond asked, 'Was it William?'

She stopped and turned. 'William that what?'

'Leaked it to the press that you were Robin Balfour.'

She hesitated just long enough for Lomond to get his answer. 'I have no idea,' she said. 'Even if it was, it wouldn't mean he deserved to die.'

CHAPTER FORTY-EIGHT

As soon as she was gone, Ross pointed aggressively at the door she had just closed behind her. 'She could easily be Sullivan. You heard how much she wants that anonymity back.'

Lomond said, 'Except, she wasn't in Glasgow last night.'

'She could have slipped in and out of here without anyone knowing. She's holed up like *Citizen Kane* here. Those security guards would say anything.'

'We'd better check that security camera footage.'

Donna, coming off the phone, suggested, 'Except, she's also got the funds to hire someone to off William MacRae and keep her hands clean.'

Lomond pushed his lips out, unconvinced. 'I've seen professional hits before. MacRae's isn't one of them. The personal touches on display at the scene. You can't fake that. Especially little details like the photo of Liz turned down. Rebecca Hawley can't have known that such a photo was there, then given an assassin instructions on what to do with it.' He shook his head. 'I'll tell you what. She goes in the maybe pile.' He asked Donna, 'Was that Willie?'

'Yeah,' she said. 'He's got some things on Liz MacRae and Seth Knox. He said it's urgent.'

'Look,' Lomond griped, 'this whole Liz angle could be helpful at some point, but it was a suicide case nine years ago. Meanwhile we've got a guy who's been murdered twice yesterday.'

'Willie says it's about the murder. Specifically the poison.'

Lomond checked the video screens to make sure no one was near the door listening in. Then he put the outgoing call on speaker so that Ross and Donna could join in. 'Willie,' he said upon answering. 'It's me. I've got Ross and Donna here. What do you have?'

The connection wasn't great, but they could make out Willie saying, 'I'm sending you a video file.'

Lomond watched the file downloading from the sent email. 'Yep, got it now...' He opened the file and pressed play.

Willie explained, 'This is the drop-off shop that the poisoned whisky was sent from. Looks like you were right, Donna.'

'About what?' she asked.

Willie asked, 'Is it playing?'

'Yeah, it's playing.'

'Wait for it...'

Something about the simplicity, the banality of the scene, was chilling – even to veteran police. Knowing that someone was about to send off a substance that would cause or contribute to the death of William MacRae. It wasn't the same as having to watch footage of a fatal car accident, or a stabbing, as was so common in their line of work. But it wasn't far off.

Lomond, still seeing a vacant counter on the screen, complained, 'Is anyone going to–'

The sight of the figure in the video shut him up instantly.

Walking casually into frame and setting the whisky box down on the counter was Seth Knox.

'I bloody told you so,' Donna said.

Ross shook his head disappointedly at her as if to say, *now's not the time for that*. If there was a big no-no in MIT it was milking the moment when you were proven right. You never took victory laps. And you certainly never said words like *I told you so*.

Not that there was much time to take a victory lap. Lomond got up from his seat, hearing a commotion across the hall. 'Two secs, Willie...'

As the shouting intensified, Lomond rushed to the door.

'It's Seth and Zoe,' he said. 'It sounds like they're going to kill each other...'

CHAPTER FORTY-NINE

WHEN REBECCA RETURNED to the lounge room across the hall, she found everyone still arguing and drinking.

'I'm not sleeping here,' Charlotte maintained, pouring herself another glass of wine. 'You've got to be out of your mind if you think I'm staying.'

Noel wasn't feeling quite so dour. 'We're in a castle with a free bar. Outside sounds like the apocalypse. I'm going nowhere.'

Jim, sitting next to him on the couch, patted him on the leg in agreement.

Claire, standing by the door, said, 'I don't know how you can be so casual about this.'

'It's simple,' said Jim. 'Just don't go anywhere alone and you'll be fine. That's where the characters went wrong in *And Then There Were None*. They kept bunking off in pairs, hoping that they wouldn't be left with the killer. If everyone sticks together, we'll all be fine.'

'Easier said than done,' Seth retorted.

Zoe pointed to the glass in Brad's hand. 'Unless you drink poison...'

Brad considered the drink, then shrugged and downed it. 'I've had a good life.'

No sooner had he lowered the glass from his lips when he started to splutter a cough. He looked confused at what was happening. He grabbed at his throat, and his eyes bulged.

There were cries for help from the room as Brad gripped his neck tighter. He was choking, his face turning redder by the second.

Then he released his hands from around his throat, and started to laugh.

'Oh great,' said Jim. 'Very nice.'

Noel remarked, 'He's been hanging around with the great Tom Ellison too much. Turning into a proper arsehole.'

'Christ,' Charlotte groaned. 'It's like being back at university. Surrounded by silly silly boys.'

Brad said, 'I'm making the best of a bad situation, which I thought you'd all be in favour of.'

Tom decided to wade in. 'You could do with some escapism, Charlotte. Reality is clearly not your forte.'

'What's that supposed to mean?' asked Zoe.

'She wrote a hit piece on me,' said Tom. 'Accusing me of sexual misconduct with my co-authors. Alleging that I promised young female writers a chance at co-writing a book with me if they slept with me. Or did other...things.'

'Are you making a move into investigative reporting, Charlotte?' asked Brad.

'No. But I have personal experience of

what's...*expected* of a young female author when working with Tom Ellison.'

'I don't have to listen to his shit,' said Tom, wandering to the back of the room with a bottle of vodka.

Zoe shook her head as she got up to leave the room. 'That's the first wise thing you've said all night, Tom. I couldn't agree more with the sentiment.'

When she was halfway across the hall, Seth nipped out to chase her down.

'Zoe,' he said, checking that the others were still embroiled in their argument, which had now pulled in everybody.

Except for Claire MacRae, who was pouring herself a gin and tonic at the bar, but keeping a close eye on what the pair were up to.

'What did the police want?' he asked.

'What they want from everyone,' she replied. 'To know whether I killed William or not.'

'But I mean...details.'

She raised her eyebrows expectantly. 'Details? Like William's manuscript?'

For once, Seth was tongue tied. 'Do you mean...about Roxburgh? I tried to talk him out of it over the phone, and by the time I got there...'

'Fascinating that he did a complete U-turn on his previous draft and managed to send it to me mere minutes before he was killed. What astonishing luck. Or perhaps it was something else.'

'I...I didn't know that he had changed his mind,' he stammered. 'He never told me.'

'Is that because he had no intention of doing so?'

He stammered some more.

'Don't bother denying it, Seth. Oh, you mimicked his voice very well in the email, I'll give you that. You of all people should know it better than anyone. There's just one thing that you got wrong. Something that you could never have known. Never, since I've become CEO of Hathaway, has William addressed me in an email as "Zoe".' She chuckled, thinking about how deep down she really was going to miss the old bastard. 'He started every email to me as "Dear spoiled brat". You see, Seth, there are some things in life that you can't fake.'

Like any liar, when confronted with one of their lies, Seth doubled down. 'Zoe, I swear, I don't know what you're talking about.'

She was through playing around now. She had given him a chance to come clean. Now it was time to go nuclear.

'How's your mum?' she asked.

Seth's mouth hung open in shock. 'What?'

'Your mum, Seth? Still alive? Not actually dead from cancer?' Revelling in the look of terror on his face, she kept on. 'That's right. I've been doing some work on you the last few weeks. You might have pulled the wool over my dad's eyes, but not me.'

'Okay,' said Seth, stepping back, attempting to reset things. 'I don't know what information you've got, but it's wrong.'

Zoe felt months of doubts and fears now pouring out of her. It was like bursting open a dam. 'I can't trust a single word you say, a single thing you do, and I certainly can't trust a single thing you write.'

'I don't know where all this is coming from...'

'Seth, you never received a doctorate from Oxford. I checked. You went there, sure. But you scuttled off to Glasgow instead.

'All I've ever tried to do is protect the company. Protect William. And protect your dad.' He started to well up.

'Is this the start of a confession?'

Seth rubbed the tears from his eyes. They were certainly genuine. What wasn't clear was if they were for himself, or for the hurt he had caused. He moved around the corner, against the wall, so that he could see anyone coming. He admitted, 'I changed it. Yes. I changed the manuscript.' He took a long breath. Relieved at unburdening himself. 'I was going to his house to try and talk him out of killing Roxburgh. When I got there, he was already dead, just like I told the police. I checked his pulse, his breathing. There was nothing. You *have* to believe me.'

Zoe replied, 'I think *you* think that admitting to a smaller crime will help you get away with a much much bigger one. I don't *have* to believe anything.'

'When I finished checking for a pulse, I stood up and saw the manuscript. It was just sitting there on the screen. I don't know why, I...I thought it would be the best thing. For him. For us. The company.'

'You did what was best for you, Seth.'

Struggling to keep his voice down, he insisted, 'I didn't kill William, Zoe. I *swear*.'

'Without the Roxburgh series, without William's backing, your career was over. You knew that William has been the only thing keeping you at Hathaway. After Hathaway, no one would take a chance on you again. Or did William find out that you're a fraud? Did he threaten to expose you?

ANDREW RAYMOND

There have been rumours about you circulating for a while now. The guy who left his last job under a cloud. You wouldn't survive that twice. There aren't any Max Hathaways left in the industry to let you get away with it any longer. My dad was so naive. He never thought to actually check if you had been a junior editor, or a glorified intern. Guys like you, your time is up. Personally, I wanted to get rid of you when I found out about Oxford. But William wouldn't let me. Can you believe it? He actually threatened to walk if I fired you. Because it entertained him that Hathaway had been duped, and he was annoyed that I hadn't been as naive as he thought I was. You've spent your entire adult life lying and cheating to get ahead. It was so easy for people like you before. In my dad's time, it was all about whether he liked the cut of your jib. If you spoke the right way. If you were into the right kind of books. If you disliked the right kind of people. No one ever thought to check if you actually had a Ph.D from Oxford or not. Everyone was too busy being entertained. Flattered by your attention. Those eyes. That face. That smile. But it was all a lie.'

Seth had no response.

Zoe went on, 'We'll deal with the police privately. We have lawyers that can hush all of that up. But the book you sent me will never see the light of day.'

'Zoe, you don't understand...'

'William could be a bully and a bastard. But I'm not sullying his legacy by changing the last creative decision he ever made. He's dead, so is Roxburgh, and soon you will be too.'

She turned to go back to the lounge, then saw Rebecca

standing around the corner. Behind her, everyone else in the lounge had heard the final part.

So, too, had Lomond, Ross, and Donna, looking on from across the hall.

Undeterred, Zoe concluded, 'I'll keep you on until the book comes out. Then you'll leave quietly. In a twisted way, you actually hold all the cards here. Hathaway's reputation would be buried if it came out that we had hired and then promoted a sociopathic liar like you.' She pointed to the group. 'And in case I succumb to any tragic accidents in the next twenty-four hours, my lawyers have been instructed to make all of this public if that happens.'

The others froze with shocked expressions on their faces.

Seth hurried upstairs to take refuge in one of the many bedrooms.

Ross started towards the stairs, but Lomond stopped him.

'Let him go,' said Lomond.

Ross whispered, 'But he poisoned MacRae.'

'No. He sent a bottle of whisky. We still don't know who poisoned him. All we have so far is a loose thread. Now we need to pull on it.'

CHAPTER FIFTY

WHILE LOMOND GOT BACK to the call with Willie, Donna whispered to Ross, 'Aren't we going after him?'

'Not yet,' he replied.

Lomond asked Willie, 'What do you think?'

Playing devil's advocate, he said, 'We need to be careful. What if the poison was added to the whisky after it arrived in Glasgow?'

'That's possible,' Lomond replied. 'But William very rarely had anyone in the house. He'd been working on the final draft of a new book. According to everyone who knew him, he simply would not open his door to anyone.'

'Maybe that was why Seth was sending it rather than delivering it.'

Donna said, 'But he was coming up north in a few days' time. Why not wait?'

Lomond answered, 'He didn't know he was going to see MacRae yet. He hadn't read the manuscript where Roxburgh is killed off at the time of that video.'

Willie jumped in. 'Hang on, he was killing him off?'

'According to Zoe Hathaway,' said Lomond. 'And we just overheard a blazing row between the pair of them downstairs. Seth's stormed off in a sulk. We'll get to him later. God knows he's not going outside.'

Donna said, 'It's actually just like Seth said to me. He should have been the last person to want MacRae dead. The Roxburgh series made Seth's career.'

Ross, who had been pacing away from Lomond and Donna, raised a hand for permission to indulge in a thought. 'What if Seth sent the whisky – for whatever reason, we don't know yet – then read the manuscript, discovered MacRae was killing off Roxburgh, and panicked. Zoe said that MacRae had been threatening to leave Hathaway. That can't be a good look for an editor to have your star author kill off your character and leave the company all on your watch. So he tried to intervene. Rushed up north to try and convince him to change the ending. Then he either found MacRae already dead, like he said he did. Or he killed him.'

Lomond shook his head. 'I'm with you all the way, apart from him killing MacRae. I don't see it.'

'Well, *someone* killed him.'

'Yes, but Seth killing MacRae does nothing to bring Roxburgh back from the dead. He would have killed the one man who could change that.'

Donna said, 'Unless he got there and did a little post-mortem editing on MacRae's behalf.'

The room went quiet, and so did Willie. No one could think of a solid reason why it wasn't at least a possibility.

Lomond said, 'We've got Zoe here in the...I was about

to say house because I felt silly saying castle. But I suppose that's exactly what it is. Let's find out from her if Roxburgh lives or dies.'

Willie said, 'We can start looking into some of the other claims Seth made when talking to Donna. There's clearly something going on there. Pardeep and Jason have been doing some digging on this.'

Pardeep said, 'We got our hands on a copy of the student register for Liz MacRae's year at Glasgow Uni. Guess who she had three classes with.'

'Who?' asked Lomond.

'Seth Knox.'

It took Lomond a moment to get his head around it. 'What?...But how...'

Donna chimed in, 'He went to Oxford.'

'Did he?' Pardeep asked rhetorically. 'How do we know that? Because he told us? Not only was he there at the time, but he dated Liz MacRae for a while. Jason and I reckon he was the last one she dated. Some of the things Liz told her flatmate about him tie in perfectly with what he told Donna.'

'Hang on,' said Lomond. 'He dates Liz MacRae at university, then just happens to end up senior editor to her father years later?'

'It is a huge coincidence,' said Pardeep.

'And you all know what I think about those.'

Donna drummed her fingers on her leg, prompted by Pardeep's comment. 'If he's not been to Oxford, and withheld his past with Liz MacRae, then what else might he be hiding? We need to unpick this guy's life, one thread at a time.'

Lomond asked, 'Is Jason still there, Willie?'

He said, 'He's nipped out to Mordor for investigation files relating to Liz MacRae.'

Willie hadn't lost his mind thinking Jason was off to the fictional volcanic plain in *The Lord of the Rings* – home to the evil lord Sauron. Officers of Willie and Lomond's generation had always known Police Scotland's gleaming glass headquarters in Dalmarnock on the banks of the Clyde as Mordor. A gallows humour typical of officers who found themselves leading departments but still under the thumb of public relations-driven, blue sky-thinking ideal-ists, who had no idea how their mad policies operated in the real world. It didn't matter if their ideas were good, or even practical. All that mattered was that it looked and sounded impressive, cost little public money, and assured them of a few more rungs up the greasy ladder that led to the promised land of Police Scotland Corporate Headquarters in Tulliallan.

Willie clarified, 'The Procurator Fiscal had the judge-ment, but not all of the investigating officers' notes and Forensic Services photos.'

'Right,' said Lomond. 'Well, get someone to go through Donna's notes with a fucking highlighter pen. Go through it a line at a time, and fact check every assertion he makes. Every claim. Every title. Every achievement. If he misuses a fucking adjective. I want to know everything. And if any of it's bullshit, find out where he really was, what he was really doing. Because that could be the key to solving this thing.'

Willie exhaled gruffly. 'It's not going to be easy late on a Saturday night, John.'

Lomond checked his watch. 'No, you're right,' he replied, tapping his watch, lost in thought. 'What you can do on a Saturday night, though, is contact Google about that email from AD Sullivan to Zoe Hathaway. Pardeep, seeing as Jason isn't there, congratulations. Consider yourself chosen for volunteer duty.'

'Oh, man. What is it?'

'I'm going to send you log-in credentials for LERS. That's Google's Law Enforcement Request System. You submit a request through the LERS system to access user data. Sullivan used a Gmail account. Google can give us the IP address used to send the email to Zoe. Once we have that, we might be able to track down their location at specific times.'

Pardeep said, 'Wouldn't someone as secretive as Sullivan have been using a VPN?'

In a culture of increasing privacy concerns, the use of Virtual Private Networks was becoming more and more common. A VPN server was able to hide your IP address – your computer's physical location – by making it appear that you were somewhere else entirely. An IP address that you were nowhere near.

'There's all sorts of things they might have done to remain hidden. We can cross that bridge when we come to it. For now, let's go onto LERS and find out what they can give us.'

Willie asked, 'What are you going to do? Drink free booze with a bunch of writers? Tough life, eh.'

Lomond knew Willie long enough to know it was a gentle ribbing rather than a proper dig. 'I don't know,

Willie. The closer we get to finding out who AD Sullivan is, the more anxious I'm getting. It's something about being stuck in this castle with these people tonight. I'm worried about what we're going to wake up to tomorrow morning.'

CHAPTER FIFTY-ONE

By 3 A.M. the group's energy was wilting. They were all evenly spaced across several couches and armchairs facing the centre of the room – a suggestion by Jim. Tiredness was making them all much colder than normal. Claire and Zoe had tweed blankets draped over their shoulders even though the fire was still going.

Zoe said to Rebecca, 'I hope you're happy.'

'Excuse me?' she replied.

'We're all having to stay up through the night because of your little experiment. What have we learned so far? Seth can't be trusted. Tom can't handle his booze...' Zoe indicated the sleeping Tom, snoring soundly with his mouth hanging open. '...and this room badly needs a TV or some sort of device that plays music.'

'I thought it was at least worth trying,' said Rebecca.

Half-cut, and eyes drooping shut, Jim pointed his glass back and forth at himself and Zoe. 'I'm no businessman, Zoe...but I wonder what Hathaway's shareholders would make of you picking a fight with the author who made your dad's fortune.'

Zoe replied, 'They would probably ask me why an author who owes everything they have to Hathaway didn't even think to offer them a first look at a new crime series.'

Rebecca said, 'It was supposed to be a secret pen name, Zoe. That was the point.'

'You know that it was bound to come out sooner or later that you were writing the Robin Balfour books. And didn't you think that when that happened, Hathaway ought to be the publisher on the receiving end of the royalties rather than the competition?'

'You're rather sensitive to authors leaving for greener pastures, aren't you,' said Rebecca. 'William threatened to leave Hathaway months ago. I would say that after your dad's heart attack, I would like to know if you have an alibi for Friday night?'

'I was in my hotel room alone,' said Zoe. 'And I would be a bit more sympathetic about your alias leaking to the press if I thought for a minute you intended on keeping it a secret. Fortunately for you, someone did that before you had to.'

'Ah, yes,' said Rebecca. 'Straight to the conspiracy portion of the argument.'

'It's no conspiracy,' Zoe replied. 'I know who leaked your name to that reporter on Twitter. I think you do too. But saying that would give you a motive to kill William.'

Rebecca let out a short sharp laugh. 'Is this your way of deflecting questions about whether *you* killed William out of revenge for the heart attack that killed your dad?'

Zoe turned to address the rest of the room rather than

Rebecca. 'She knows that it was William who leaked her name to the press.'

'William?' said Claire in shock. 'Why would he have done such a thing?'

'In retaliation for not letting him ride on her coattails,' Zoe said. 'William and Liz are the reason she owns this bloody castle and has more money than God. Liz read her books when she was small and told her dad they should have been made into movies. William insisted that Hathaway promote them more – and we did. And once Rebecca climbed to the top of the charts, she pulled the ladder up. William would complain to my dad that she wouldn't take his calls. Then he accused her of ripping off his Roxburgh books. There he was plugging away at the genre he loved for decades, then she comes along with her name in lights and already known to millions. It was a slap in the face. So he took away the one thing she wanted more than anything: anonymity.'

'I've had it with this,' Noel announced, knocking back his drink and putting it down with finality on the glass table. He stretched his arms out with a yawn. 'I've been up since five thirty and I've got a headache.'

'You could end up with a damn sight worse than that if you go to bed on your own,' Crawford warned him.

Brad chuckled. 'Is that a proposition?'

Crawford blushed. 'You know what I mean.'

'If anyone's got a reason to do William in, surely it's you.'

Brad's directness took everyone by surprise. Not least Crawford.

'Why the heck would you say that?' Crawford asked.

'Are you joking? The man who bankrupted Crawford Bell Books?'

'This really isn't the sort of thing I want to talk about.'

'I'm not surprised,' said Brad.

Jim asked, 'What happened?'

Brad waited to see if Crawford would field it.

'You go ahead,' said Crawford. 'I have little interest in digging up old graves.'

Brad told the room, 'William told me the story back in the day when we were on a book tour together. He was struggling to find a publisher that would take on *The Long Dark*. His last chance was a tiny Glasgow publisher. Crawford Bell. Who, I think it's fair to say, hadn't exactly set the publishing world on fire.'

Crawford interjected, 'I'll have you know that we sold a travel guide called *Glasgow The Best*. We updated it every other year, and it always did a roaring trade with local Waterstones stores. We just hadn't had much luck with fiction.'

Brad said, 'No one would touch *Long Dark* except Crawford. But they didn't have any money in the bank. William told Crawford that when the book started to sell, he would hold off taking royalties as a thank you. But when it sold more copies than anyone ever dreamed, William reneged.' He said to Crawford, 'It should have made you a millionaire. Instead, you went bankrupt.'

'I don't understand,' said Jim. 'What about the contract between you and William?'

Crawford mumbled something.

Jim said, 'I'm sorry?'

Crawford repeated, louder, 'There wasn't one.'

'You had no contract?'

'It was nineteen eighty-five, Jim. Our business meetings all took place down the pub. We talked. We shook hands. That was how it was.'

'Must have gone over real well when your family found out,' said Brad.

'Money's always been very important to them,' Crawford maintained. 'Show me someone who doesn't care about money.'

Jim spoke up, 'I don't care about money.'

Noel added, 'Neither do I.'

It had been coming for a while. Since nineteen eighty-five, in fact. Crawford erupted. 'That's because you all HAVE IT! Of course I wanted to be rich. Is it great running from creditors your entire adult life? Changing mobile numbers every three months so they can't track you down? Eating ramen noodles four times a week, and stocking up on sandwiches at Costa when they get reduced in the early evening, just to cut down on food costs?' He directed his ire towards Brad. 'And as we're on the topic of old secrets, why don't you tell the story about the time you went on a book tour across the States, and came home to find William in bed with your second wife.'

Brad fumed silently. His potential motive had been exposed, and there was nothing he could say to neuter it.

Crawford looked around the room in disgust. 'You bloody people. Whichever one of you is AD Sullivan, and whoever killed William: I hope it was worth it.'

He promptly vanished upstairs.

Zoe said, 'I thought he was afraid of going up there on his own.'

Charlotte asked, 'How does he know which bedroom is his?'

'What does it matter,' said Brad. 'There's about a hundred of them.'

Seeing that he was heading for the bar, Jim held his glass up over his head for Brad to collect on the way. 'This was Laphroaig,' Jim said.

Brad ignored the demand. 'Good for you.' He then set about making a black coffee.

'You can't be serious,' said Noel. 'Coffee at this hour?'

'I'm not going to sleep,' Brad said. 'I'm taking this double-shot espresso upstairs and I'm staring at the inside of the bedroom door all night with an upturned brass candlestick in my hand. And God help anyone who tries to come in.'

Rebecca joked, 'You know it's Jack Law that everyone thinks is a badass, and not you, right?'

'Well, I don't give a shit,' said Jim through a yawn. 'I'm taking that bottle of Laphroaig upstairs and I'm going to drink until I can't see.'

'You're making it very easy for the killer,' Claire warned.

'What happened between William and I was our business. Frankly, I don't trust a single one of you. What I do trust, however, is a locked door.' Jim grabbed the bottle from the bar then raised it on his way out. 'See you in the morning.' He said over his shoulder, 'Most of you, anyway.'

CHAPTER FIFTY-TWO

LONG AFTER MIDNIGHT, conversation in the lounge had become more sedate. But the topic remained the same.

Brad had gone upstairs with his espresso. Jim had been upstairs for an hour by then, knocking back whisky and listening to Rolling Stones live tracks on YouTube via the castle's wi-fi.

Crawford and Rebecca sat next to each other, leaving Noel and Claire in their own armchairs. Zoe sat on a sheepskin rug in front of the fire, Googling self-defence tips and how to use household items as weapons.

Tom was still passed out on a couch in the corner, and Charlotte had fallen sleep on a chaise longue, tipsy but not nearly as drunk as Tom. Safe in the knowledge that Noel and Claire had promised to look after her when she confessed to feeling exhausted. What she didn't know was that while she slept, conversation progressed to a discussion of any likelihood that she might be the killer. No one knew of any motive. Except for Claire.

Lomond was outside in the reception hall, sitting on a leather chair, keeping watch – a position he planned to maintain throughout the night. He was listening in to the conversation via a set of earbuds hooked up to the ceiling speaker system.

In the lounge, Claire spoke quietly. 'Charlotte and William had been having an affair when William was teaching creative writing at Manchester University. We had already separated by that point. Charlotte was his student. It was so tediously predictable from William, falling in love with the first pretty young thing to show him any attention. Apparently Charlotte had been obsessed with him, and when William broke it off, she took it badly. You know the adulterous writer in *The Woman on the Stairs*?'

A few in the group nodded.

'That was based on William,' said Claire.

Zoe looked over at Charlotte, questioning if she was really asleep.

Rebecca said, 'Surely she wouldn't have killed William over that.'

'You never know,' said Crawford.

'I'd like to hear what Noel has to say,' said Zoe. 'There aren't many secrets left between us all. What's your William MacRae history?'

He lifted his hands, trying to communicate openness, honesty. 'Look, show me a friendship that doesn't have ups and downs.'

'But you're the nicest guy on TV. Everyone says so.'

'By that,' said Noel, 'they mean inoffensive.'

'How did you two know each other?' Crawford asked.

'William and I had once worked on adapting Roxburgh for TV – this was long before TV was considered a prestige showcase for character study. TV in the nineties was where books went to die. They were taken out the back of the studio and shot, then whatever remained of the carcass was dragged back inside and used as the script. Needless to say, William wasn't a fan. He had sabotaged every stage of the production, especially the writing. It had been at a time when he was drinking heavily.' He glanced towards Claire anxiously. 'It hadn't been long after Liz's death.'

Claire nodded. 'I remember.'

'William thought the production would act as a distraction. Instead, it just annoyed him. He found the channel executives dull and illiterate. He turned in all of his teleplays for six episodes weeks late each time. Production shut down before filming could even begin, as rumours of his erratic behaviour and ghastly temper drove away any talent that had stuck around.' He hesitated to say it. 'The process ruined me. It cost me tens of thousands of my own money. Wrecked my reputation in the industry. It took me years to recover.'

Zoe said, 'You've bounced back pretty well, I'd say. One of the nation's favourite TV quizmasters, and everyone and their dog has copied your cosy crime style.'

'It was William who encouraged me to write crime fiction,' said Noel. 'Because there are no budgets to worry about, and no one can tell you no.'

'Well,' said Rebecca. 'I'd say that now only Tom, Brad, and Claire are without a motive.'

'I'm sure it won't last,' Claire quipped.

CHAPTER FIFTY-THREE

CHARLOTTE AWOKE in the lounge an hour later, gripped immediately by panic. It hadn't been restful sleep. It felt more like she had been unplugged for a short while. Such a short sleep after four glasses of wine was never a good idea. Now she was still drunk, but all of the fun and mischief had been replaced by grogginess and fear.

Noel and Claire, who had promised to stay up, had abandoned her once Rebecca and Crawford went to bed. No one had wanted to fall asleep in the lounge, at the mercy of whoever else was in there.

Now Charlotte's only company was Tom, who was in the same position he'd been in hours ago.

He was still. And quiet.

Charlotte crept closer, wondering if he had perhaps succumbed to poison. Then, as she was about to touch him lightly to check if he was alive, she heard the lounge door creak.

She looked over with a start, then grabbed at her heart.

'Christ...you scared the shit out of me.'

Lomond raised his hands in apology. 'I'm sorry. I heard someone stirring and wanted to check you were okay. I've been monitoring everyone coming and going.'

'Aren't you going to sleep?' she asked.

'I can sleep tomorrow. Or the next day. It's a small price to pay to keep everyone safe. Think of me like a bike lock. I probably couldn't protect anyone from a really determined threat. But if I'm visible, I might just put someone off trying anything.'

The fire had burned out, now reduced to dull orange cinders.

Charlotte looked across the room, considering Tom. 'Do you think we should wake him?'

Lomond said, 'Leave him to me.'

Halfway across the hall, Charlotte stalled. 'What if *you're* the killer?'

'Then this would be the part where I promise you that I'm not. Which is exactly what a killer would say.' He pointed towards the pitch-black staircase. 'I can walk you to a bedroom, or you can take your chances. It's up to you.'

'You first,' she said.

The stairs were deathly silent as they ascended to the first floor. Outside, the storm raged on, pummelling the castle with relentless rain and wind. The ancient building moaned and groaned under the weight of the tempest.

As Lomond reached the corridor, Charlotte felt a sense of relief at having the company of someone she trusted. It was impossible for someone to sneak up on her. Or so she thought. As she moved down the gloomy hallway, she felt as though she was being watched.

Suddenly, a door creaked open and a figure emerged from the shadows.

Lomond threw up a fist, indicating for Charlotte to freeze. He backed up against the wall, hiding in the shadow of a deep doorway.

At first, it was just a silhouette, but as the door opposite opened, a shaft of light illuminated Seth Knox.

A woman's voice whispered urgently to him, 'Quick, before someone comes.' And with a wave of a female arm, he was ushered into the room before the door shut once again, plunging the hallway into darkness.

Lomond hesitated, unsure of what to do next. Charlotte was about to sneak into an empty bedroom when Seth's door opened again. A woman appeared, looking left and right for any witnesses.

In a heartbeat, Lomond grabbed Charlotte back into the shadows before she could be spotted. The pair held their breath as the woman scanned the hallway. 'Hello?' she whispered.

It was Claire MacRae.

As soon as Claire went inside again, Lomond directed Charlotte towards the nearest door. 'Lock it behind you,' he told her.

'Thank you,' she mouthed.

Lomond's heart was racing as he tried to process what he had just seen.

Why was Claire MacRae sneaking Seth Knox into her bedroom in the middle of the night?

The more Lomond thought about it, the more his mind raced with possibilities. Whatever was going on, it wasn't good.

CHAPTER FIFTY-FOUR

WILLIE HAD INSISTED that Pardeep and Jason take off for the night once Jason had returned from Mordor – which was why they were currently occupying a shared desk in the middle of a deserted Major Investigations floor. There was no way either of them would go home for a good eight hours' rest when there was work to do. White light from desk lamps cut through the diminished green night lighting above, installed to reduce electricity costs when the office was least occupied.

Pardeep had a Kindle open in front of him, reading book six in the Sally Stroud series to his youngest through his phone. An occupational necessity at times, as unfortunate as it was. But Pardeep wouldn't compromise on getting in story time.

When he was done, Jason asked him, 'Are you going to tell her that our boss had a sleepover at RJ Hawley's castle?'

'She'd never believe me, mate.'

'It could have been us up there.'

Pardeep was distracted by one of the documents from the Liz MacRae investigation that Jason had come back with. He gave it a sharp frown.

'What is it?' asked Jason.

Pardeep dismissed the fleeting thought with a rapid shake of his head. 'That's weird...' He handed a piece of paper across the desk divide to Jason. 'These are requests through William MacRae's lawyer demanding to know the whereabouts of the *Shattered Glass* manuscript that was in Liz's flat. His lawyer's accusing the investigation team of losing it.'

'I wonder where it could have gone.' Jason hunted through various stacks he had accumulated throughout the night. 'Here it is.' He thumbed through to the page he needed. 'Yeah, definitely no manuscript listed in property found at the scene. A bunch of textbooks, small notepads... No manuscript.'

'Strange,' said Pardeep, rifling through more of the files. 'Why would William have wanted it so badly?'

'Kate said that it was a good book. He probably wanted to get it published posthumously. A kind of tribute for her.'

'Yeah. Makes sense. Except for this...' He showed Jason two photographs still in their original plastic protective sleeve. He held two of them up side by side, then pointed to each in turn. 'See this one?' He showed Jason a photo of Liz sitting at her desk, bathed in afternoon sunlight. She was shielding her face from the camera. 'This is the last-known photo of Liz, taken by Kate Randall. Liz died that night.' He flipped the photo around to show the date written on the back. He then showed him the other photo. 'But this is an official Forensic Services photo taken no more than three hours after Liz was found dead.'

Jason shook his head. It had been too long a day for Spot the Difference. 'What am I meant to be seeing here?'

Pardeep pointed out the difference. 'This black box file in Kate Randall's picture is missing over here.'

'Oh yeah.' Jason peered at it. 'What does that say on the side of the box?'

'*Shattered Glass.*'

'Maybe Liz threw it away,' Jason suggested. 'Burned it as part of some sort of ceremonial thing before she killed herself. Claire MacRae told John that its lack of success could have contributed to her depression.'

'Possibly,' said Pardeep. 'Or maybe someone stole it.'

'Why would someone steal it?'

Pardeep sighed, then closed his eyes in frustration. 'I don't know! I've been up since six. I'm not thinking clearly. Have you got anything?'

Jason had been up since half five but looked twice as sprightly by comparison. Necking the remainder of an energy drink that had enough caffeine to power a herd of wildebeest, he showed Pardeep a financial document. 'This was in William MacRae's study. It shows that William wasn't the sole owner of the Park Circus property. He was co-owner. With Claire MacRae.'

'But they divorced,' said Pardeep. 'They divorced, like, a decade ago.'

'They agreed a settlement between themselves. There was no involving the courts to direct financial arrangements.' Jason handed over another document. 'Things get a lot tastier with this. It's called a survivorship destination.'

'What is that?'

'When two people jointly take the title of a property, they can choose to have the disposition – the document that transfers ownership from a previous owner to a new one – include a statement that the title is being transferred to them jointly, and to the survivor of them.'

'Are you saying that if one of the co-owners dies...'

Jason nodded away. 'Ownership passes to the other co-owner.' He raised his finger, asking for just a little more time. 'There's a semi-complicated statute that says if a property title is jointly held by spouses and includes this survivorship destination, that destination is terminated if the couple divorce. Unless they state otherwise in the disposition.'

'I mean, I *am* following all of this. It's just putting me to sleep. What's the point, Jason?'

'The point is that, because they were divorced, for the survivor destination William and Claire had to sign a provision that would allow ownership of the Park Circus property to fall to whoever survived out of the pair of them. They divorced ten years ago, right?'

His patience dangling by a thread, Pardeep said, 'Right?'

'But this provision was only signed last week. Without it, in the event of William's death, Claire wouldn't get the house.'

'What if William left the house to her in a Last Will and Testament?'

'After the divorce, they would still need a provision that said the house should go to Claire in the event of William's death. The provision had to be signed jointly. And it was. It's right here.'

'Why would William choose to do that all of a sudden?'

'Exactly,' said Jason. 'Something happened last week. To both of them. Something significant. We've got to get this to John and the others. They're the only ones that can find out from Claire MacRae.'

CHAPTER FIFTY-FIVE

LOMOND SPRANG from slouched in the leather chair to bolt upright in a violent thrust. He was still breathing heavily from the nightmare. The images etched onto his brain. At this point, there was no real distinction between memory and nightmare when it came to the Sandman case.

Not that he ever talked about it, but Lomond would have said that the stuff that stayed with him wasn't so much the crime scenes – though they were hard to forget. The crime scenes were reduced to single images for him. Like paused frames in a movie. What stayed with him were the human interactions that went with the crimes. The more benign, the worse it was. Drinking cups of tea in living rooms with parents of the missing alongside the Family Liaison Officer.

Or when news leaked that a body had been found. The family would inevitably hear the rumours before Lomond could make arrangements to come round and confirm the worst news imaginable to a parent. They knew what

Lomond was going to say before he said it. That their child had been found, and wasn't coming home.

No one else makes noises like the suddenly bereaved. They're noises that the person will never make again in their entire life. The shock – or sometimes the predictability – of having it confirmed. When your child is missing for five days, and three others have already been taken and killed by a serial killer, you can't deny what might be happening. But people tend to cling on to hope, Lomond always found. The only way to keep going.

It was the noises that he heard in his nightmares. When he had to tell them that their child was dead. It echoed in his head until his eyes opened, and he remembered it wasn't happening all over again. The Sandman case was solved. But in a way, cases like that are never over. Men like Lomond didn't get the luxury of walking away. That was his penance for taking on the job in the first place. You accept the likelihood that you'll be dealing with the most depraved, vicious, and cruel acts that humans are capable of.

He had never thought of himself as brave. But Lomond had chosen a life of lying awake at night. Of waking up in a cold sweat in the morning. To bear witness. To find the truth in a world of lies.

AFTER A COLD SHOWER, Lomond had been up and walking around downstairs on his own. He made a black coffee in the kitchen, then took it back to the lounge where so much conflict had arisen the night before. It was like visiting a movie set after seeing so much of it play out on the TV screen. He wanted to get a feel for the room itself.

Once everyone had gone to bed, Ross and Donna had stayed up to analyse the footage captured of the group. By the end of the footage, they were left pondering a curious contradiction: for a group of people pulled together to commemorate someone they were supposedly very close to, they all had deep and compelling reasons to wish harm on William.

It was after sunrise, and the sky had barely lightened because of the heavy cloud cover. The wind had died down, though. Without it, the castle was a much more peaceful place than the night before.

Then, from across the room, someone emitted a solitary grunt from under a pile of blankets. Lomond hadn't realised anyone was lying there. It was Tom Ellison. Before scuttling off upstairs, Noel had taken pity on Tom and covered him with the blanket he'd been using. At some point during the night after the fire had gone out and the temperature plummeted, Tom had pulled Noel's blanket all the way over his head for extra warmth.

Lomond jumped at the unexpected sight of him, spilling hot coffee all over his hand – which prompted cries of pain.

Having fallen asleep laced with fear, Tom woke up with a terrified gasp at the hazy sight of Lomond bearing down on him.

'Jesus, man,' exclaimed Tom, 'you scared the life out of me.'

'I was going to say the same thing,' Lomond replied. 'Have you slept down here all night?'

'Seems like it.'

If he had been on his own, Tom would have dozed for a while. But Lomond's company necessitated that he at least sit upright and engage in conversation.

Fighting off a yawn, Tom said, 'Has everyone survived the night?'

Thinking of the arguments and dark secrets that had come out, Lomond replied, 'That remains to be seen. Though you've come out of it relatively unscathed compared to the others.'

Tom might not have been the most stylish writer, but he was sharp enough to figure out how someone who hadn't been in the room all night could have known that. 'You know not a single word you've heard or recorded is admissible in a courtroom.'

'How did you know?' asked Lomond.

Tom pointed to the ceiling speakers. 'I've got them in my beach house in Malibu.'

'I wasn't looking for proof,' said Lomond. 'I was looking for clues. And I got plenty of them.' He paused. 'I just don't know what they all mean yet. Do you have any suspicions?'

'You'll probably be expecting me to say Charlotte.'

'Is it true what she said happened between you two?'

Tom took a long breath, looking out the window at the fog rolling over the clifftops. 'My marriage had been rocky at the time. I won't deny that her looks weren't a factor in me asking her to come out and write with me. But I never tried to take advantage. I just made it plain what I wanted. She didn't feel the same way.'

'Would you forgive a blunt question, Mr Ellison?' asked Lomond. 'What are you doing at Lochinver? The others all have a connection to William MacRae. But I've been scouring for a connection between you two, and I can't find any. How did you end up invited to speak at his lifetime achievement prize-giving?'

'Claire invited me,' he said.

'Was she using your high profile to throw light on William?'

Tom sniffed. 'That's a pretty cynical take, detective.'

'Detective isn't a rank over here, Mr Ellison. I'm Chief Inspector. Or John is fine.'

There was something about Lomond that made Tom want to talk. It felt safe, the two of them sitting there. As if you were talking to your one mate who can absolutely keep a secret. Even if what you have to say makes you look like a right prick.

'Years back,' began Tom, 'I brought William over to work on a story for me. He was five books in on the Roxburgh series...'

He pronounced it Rox-burrow, the way some Americans mispronounce Edinburgh.

'He'd had big success in the UK, but Hathaway wanted him to start breaking the American market. They approached me. My publisher was only too happy to bring him in. You see...I don't know if you know this, but I lost my son to suicide when he was twenty-one.'

Lomond pursed his lips in commiseration. 'I'm sorry, I didn't.'

'Christopher. He was in college. Smart kid. Big reader. Maybe too big. Couldn't handle the real world.' Tom stared into his hands and picked at a frayed bit of skin around a thumbnail. 'He took an overdose in the basement of his dorm. Like a dog that goes under the stairs to die. Quietly. No fuss. Despite my wife at the time's pleas not to, I demanded to see a photo of the scene. God help me, to this day I can't get the image out of my head. I don't know why I asked. I guess I knew he was in a lot of pain to want to do that. As his father, I felt a sense of duty to bear witness to what he did, even if it meant causing myself pain.' He shook his head. 'A pointless gesture in the end. Anyway, when William reached my house in upstate New York, I was a mess. Christopher hadn't been dead a month, and I was drinking from eight in the morning until I passed out at night. My publisher had no idea how bad it was.'

'What did William do?' asked Lomond.

'The bravest, most honourable thing anyone's ever done for me. He let me drink. For six straight weeks. This was two years after Liz had died. He understood. That a man needs to get certain things out of his system when he loses a child. If he wants to have any kind of life afterwards. William knew that. All I wanted was to die and be with Christopher. William covered for me. He wrote the whole damn book himself, and in the end he told my publisher to take his name off it.'

'I thought the point of him doing the job was to help him break the States?'

'No, that was Hathaway's aim. And I'm sure it was William's at the start. But it became about helping me get my life together again. I couldn't have done it without him.'

Lomond said, 'But then William wrote that article years later – the one exposing your so-called writing factory.'

Tom looked back in incomprehension. 'That never made it to print. My lawyers got an injunction on it.'

'Because William signed a non-disclosure agreement when he worked with you years earlier.'

'How the hell did you find out about that?'

'You're not talking to the caretaker, Mr Ellison. My question is, what made William turn around so spectacularly on you?'

Tom thought for a moment. 'There's this scorpion and a frog by a riverside. The scorpion wants to get to the other side, but it can't swim. So it asks the frog to carry it over. The frog says, no way. You'll just sting me once we're halfway across. The scorpion says, but if I stung you, we'd both drown. The frog figures that the scorpion has a point. It wouldn't make sense for the scorpion to sting him. So they set off. And of course, once they get halfway across, the scorpion stings the frog. As they're drowning, the frog says, why the hell did you do that? Now we're both doomed? The scorpion shrugs. What did you expect me to do? I'm a scorpion.'

Tom was relieved to see that Lomond understood the point of the story.

Lomond laughed and nodded his head. 'William was always going to be William.'

Tom said, 'And you can't judge a man for being a scorpion, when his entire life, he's been a scorpion.' He took a long breath, quivering through the exhalation like he was fighting back tears. 'I would have swum across the Atlantic to be here for his award. I would have swum across the Atlantic blindfolded with an arm cut off to be here for his memorial.' He pointed to the ceiling, towards the bedrooms upstairs. 'These other guys...they're chicken feed compared to William MacRae. And if any one of them is responsible for killing him, I wouldn't think twice about putting a bullet in their head.' Tom stood up. Then he addressed the ceiling, where he knew there were microphones picking up his every word. 'And *that*, you can put on the record.'

CHAPTER FIFTY-SIX

As soon as Tom opened the lounge door to leave the room, a loud gong crashed somewhere on the other side of the castle.

In the library, where Donna and Ross had been listening to Lomond and Tom talking, Ross bolted out of his chair.

'What the hell was that?' he exclaimed.

He and Donna charged out of the room, where they saw Lomond and Tom across the lobby.

One by one, the bedroom doors upstairs opened, and the occupants peeked into the corridor – some dressed and others less so. They silently assessed who was present and who was not, but it was too early to make any assumptions as there were so many other areas in the castle where people could be.

The gong rang out again, prompting a few jumps from people on the first floor.

Then a voice called out. Rebecca Hawley's. 'Breakfast's up!'

Holding his head in anguish, Jim groaned. 'Of all the choices, why did it have to be a gong?'

Rebecca led everyone from the lobby to the dining room, where silver serving dishes of bacon and eggs were laid out – steam rising invitingly from them.

'Get them while they're hot,' she said.

But all anyone could do once in the room was look around with trepidation and take a head count.

'Are we all here?' asked Noel.

Claire was the first to notice. 'Where's Seth?' she asked.

Crawford asked, 'Did anyone see him after he went upstairs last night?'

Charlotte, looking the most frazzled of the bunch, waited for Claire to say something.

But she didn't.

'Everyone stay here,' said Lomond, giving Claire a sceptical look as well. 'I'll check.'

He went upstairs and checked the room that multiple people had reported hearing Seth being in, talking on the phone. The door wasn't locked.

The bed hadn't been slept in – unless Seth had somehow emulated the crisp, precise way the bedding had been made up. There was no one there.

But there was a phone. Lying in the middle of the bed, beads of water sitting on the body of the phone.

Lomond tried switching it on, but it was dead.

He hurried downstairs with the phone, finding everyone emerging from the dining room notably quiet. Anxious.

Rushing through the hall, Lomond confirmed, 'He's not there.'

Donna asked, 'Was his phone lying on his bed? Soaking wet?'

Lomond halted. 'How did you know that?'

She said, 'Because I read the first half of *The Shortlist*, and you didn't. If you had, you would know that the first person whose body is found initially goes missing overnight. All that's left of him is his phone on his bed. He'd been drowned.'

Ross interjected, 'Hang on...you said that the killer turned out to be the first victim. They weren't really dead. That was the solution.'

Lomond said, 'Yeah, they were in cahoots with the person who checked their vitals.'

Zoe added, 'You might be forgetting an additional detail.'

'What?'

'That first victim is an editor to one of the writers. He comes back and kills the others.'

Claire put her hands to head. 'Oh, no! This is it. It's starting...'

CHAPTER FIFTY-SEVEN

Ross and Donna tried to calm her down. 'Mrs MacRae, we don't know anything yet.'

She gestured at the phone Lomond was holding. 'His phone was on the bed, soaking wet.' Incredulous, she said, 'You think all this is just coincidence?'

'No, I don't,' Lomond answered.

'Great!' Jim applauded sarcastically. 'So some maniac is running around acting out this bloody book.'

Rebecca had to step away from the proximity of the group. 'We're all going to get bumped off by Seth.'

Brad said, 'I get that life often imitates art, but this feels a little too deliberate.'

'What do you mean?' asked Charlotte.

'Come on, look at it. We've got the plot of this *Shortlist* happening in front of us. Don't you see? It's all AD Sullivan.' Brad scoffed. 'The bastard's advertising!'

'I'm a pretty cynical person,' said Zoe, 'but the idea that

a writer is going to start killing people to imitate their book is stretching things a bit.'

Crawford looked a nervous wreck. 'How do you know? You've never even met this person!'

Zoe fired back, 'Yet you were happy enough to give them a prime slot at this festival!'

The anxiety and paranoia were growing within the group. Even Noel was feeling it.

'This is all you, isn't it?' he said to Zoe. 'You were the only person to threaten Seth last night.'

Brad, pouring himself the first of the day's dozen black coffees from the sideboard, quoted her. 'Your words were, "he's dead, so is Roxburgh, and soon you will be too."'

Zoe replied, 'You know fine well that I meant he would be dead within the industry. Not literally.'

'Words matter, Zoe,' remarked Brad, then turned to the others. 'She could really do with an editor. Ironic.'

Claire snapped, 'I don't think now is the time for jokes, Jim.'

'I think it's the perfect time for a joke, actually, Claire,' he retorted, the threads of his composure starting to fray. 'We're stuck in the plot of that bloody book. We've got a homicidal maniac editor on the run who, once we find his corpse, is going to come back from the dead and kill us all!'

'There's a very simple solution to that,' said Noel. He was by far the calmest person in the room, arms folded, logically thinking it all through. 'If we find Seth's body, we all check his vitals.'

'Exactly,' said Charlotte. 'If we know what happens in the book, we can counter all the mistakes the characters make in it. We'll still have the upper hand.'

Zoe asked, 'Has everyone here read it?'

Lomond and Donna raised their hands. Then Zoe too.

She waited for more to go up, but none did. 'Is this a joke? You all gave me quotes to use for the hardback!'

'Don't be a child, Zoe,' said Tom. 'We gave you quotes so that our names were attached to a book Hathaway was going to make a hit. None of us wanted to miss out on that.'

Brad said, 'I believe my quote was "Reminds me of the classics of the genre." I left out the second part, "And how much better they are than this tripe."' He laughed to himself.

Claire said, 'I suppose you find that terribly amusing.'

Brad shrugged affirmatively. 'I do, actually. People take this industry far too seriously. I sit at a desk for a living. So I gave a quote for a book I haven't read, like the rest of you. Big deal. Do you know how many *Shortlist*s I've seen in my career? The next big thing that everyone's going to be reading? Giving a quote is win-win. If it's great, everyone thinks you've got your finger on the pulse of literature. It the book sucks, no one's going to remember your quote. The reader's much too mad about the book sucking.'

'Crawford, what about you?' Zoe exclaimed.

'Have you any idea how many books are sent to me in the months leading up to this festival? You promised me your lead thriller for the year, that was all I needed to know.'

'So what happens next?' asked Tom.

Rebecca suggested, 'Why don't we get into pairs, and we can search one floor at—'

'No, in the book! How is the second person killed?'

All eyes turned to Lomond, Donna, and Zoe.

Noel said, 'Yeah, if this book is being acted out, we need to know what's coming.'

Lomond had heard enough. 'Right, everyone just stop! Clearly, someone is playing a game with us. But if we're all going to get out of this castle alive, we need to deal with this methodically and professionally.' He pointed down a long corridor that led into darkness. 'Rebecca, is the kitchen down here?'

'Yeah,' she replied.

'Good. Because I need a bowl of porridge. A big one.' He turned and marched off towards the kitchen.

Jim asked, 'Is he taking the piss? Shouldn't we at least search for Seth?'

Claire replied, 'Great idea, Jim. And play right into the killer's hands by leaving one of us in danger.'

Rebecca struggled to catch up with him. 'I know everybody has to eat breakfast, Chief Inspector, but do you think that's really necessary right now?'

'Everybody does *not* have to have breakfast,' Lomond said, marching on. 'The whole "setting you up for the day" trope was invented by cereal manufacturers in the sixties who paid off scientists to cite studies that breakfast was important. The modern-day studies all point to a fasted state aided with a cup or two of black coffee and some water as being most optimal for both brain health and mood in the morning.'

'Then why porridge?' asked Rebecca. She looked over her shoulder to find everyone else following.

Lomond turned around but kept most of his speed by walking backwards. He held up Seth's phone. 'A drying agent.'

With Rebecca's help, he found a bag of porridge oats in one of the kitchen larders. He placed the sodden phone into a large bowl, then poured the oats on top.

'If I'm right about Seth,' said Lomond, pointing to the phone, 'when that dries out, we'll know once and for all who AD Sullivan is.'

In the crowd at the doorway, Crawford said, 'But the event is only a few hours away. How are we going to get out of here?'

Rebecca told him, 'My guys think they can clear the trees by lunchtime. If they manage that they can bring a long ladder to replace the bridge.'

'A ladder?' exclaimed Jim. 'Fuck that for a game of soldiers. I'll stay here until mountain rescue can land a helicopter on the roof or something.'

'Great idea,' said Tom. 'You can stay here. With Seth, wherever he is.'

Noel said, 'Seth has got to be somewhere on the grounds *right now,* Jim.'

Charlotte countered, 'He couldn't have survived outside.'

'And there's about a hundred rooms in this place.'

Crawford said, 'Then let's search it.'

All eyes turned to Lomond, Ross, and Donna.

'It's actually not a bad idea,' Lomond admitted.

Claire, came charging down the corridor that connected the kitchen to the main lobby. She beckoned everyone to follow her. 'You should come see this. Quick.' When she reached the dining room, she pointed out towards the driveway. 'Look!' she said. 'Someone's coming.'

Three Range Rovers were heading towards the fallen

trees that were blocking the road at the Crichton House end of the driveway, just beyond the moat. Despite the floodwaters having receded, it was still a perilous crossing that required caution.

Crawford and Zoe were first to join her at the window.

'Thank heavens for that,' said Crawford, taking out his phone for frantic networking with his staff. 'The Sullivan event might happen yet.'

Ross turned to Donna and Lomond. 'Yeah, but will Seth make it?'

CHAPTER FIFTY-EIGHT

Pardeep and Jason were comparing notes, standing at their shared desk, shaking their heads.

'I mean, this guy is a piece of work,' said Pardeep. 'If we can trust the contact at Hathaway.'

Jason replied, 'It's not just one contact. This is all–'

He stopped talking when he heard their names being bellowed from Linda Boyle's office.

'Get up here!' she yelled.

Jason sighed in resignation. 'Was that her I'm-going-to-give-you-a-bollocking voice?'

Pardeep replied, 'Naw…that's her give-me-everything-you've-got voice. You need to learn her voices, man. Or you'll be a nervous wreck working in here.'

Climbing the stairs to her office on the mezzanine often felt like trudging to the gallows. Everyone at MIT had experienced it at one time or another.

Linda was sitting at her desk eating from three little

bags from Greggs. Willie stood opposite, looking like he'd been taking a hiding for the last little while.

'Awright, boss?' said Pardeep.

With a mouthful of sausage roll, Linda pointed at the landline phone on her desk. 'John's with us. Say hello John.'

Lomond had gone upstairs in Inver Castle in search of a phone signal. He paced around an upstairs bedroom, holding his phone out in front of him on speakerphone. 'Willie and Linda have been catching me up, guys,' he said. 'You two think this survivor destination document's a winner?'

'Yes, sir,' said Pardeep.

'It's certainly motive, sir,' Jason added.

Lomond said, 'It's looking like we might actually get out of this castle within the hour. I'll have a word with Claire MacRae.'

Pardeep said, 'She's not the only one hiding secrets, though.'

Linda wiped her mouth with the back of her hand, then deposited the grease onto her trouser leg – an act she made no effort to hide. 'Are we now introducing artificial elements of suspense into the investigation?' She shuffled forward in her chair. 'I'm on the edge of my seat. Spill it.'

Jason consulted his notes. 'Quite a bit of progress on Seth Knox. Pardeep and I have been working through Donna's notes, and made annotations for every assertion or claim that Seth made. To do that, I called up his ex-boss from his previous publishing house, Cargo. The first thing he said to me was, quote, I'm amazed it's taken this long for the police to ask me about Seth. He's a piece of work. End quote.'

Linda held up the remainder of her sausage roll. 'I want the protein, Jason. Not trimmings and gravy and a fucking cheese board. Give me the protein.'

'Okay,' Jason said, taking an inward breath. 'Seth claimed to have a doctorate in English from Oxford that he earned while nursing his terminally ill mother. Soon after she died, Seth's dad apparently committed suicide. The administration confirmed to me that Seth never completed his doctorate. I couldn't find any record of the deaths of his parents. I then dug into HMRC and found that they're both currently paying taxes, and they both renewed their address on the electoral register.' Jason let Pardeep take over.

'He said he's the youngest editor in Hathaway history. Not true. That he was a senior editor at Cargo before coming to Hathaway. Not true. The people I spoke to – including his old boss – described him in terms of being marginally above the mailroom guy. When he was pulled up on a disciplinary for prolonged absence without a medical reason, Seth's boss started finding abusive notes directed at him left around the office. Seth denied any involvement, but from the day he left Cargo, no more notes were ever found.'

Jason couldn't resist adding, 'By the way, his nickname in the office – behind his back, anyway – was Tom Ripley.'

Linda snapped, 'That's fascinating news for someone who gives a flying–'

'Linda,' said Lomond by way of a warning. He was the only person who could get away with even attempting to recalibrate her temper.

Linda responded, much calmer this time, 'I've seen *The*

Talented Mr Ripley, Jason. Italy. Jazz. Poor guy impersonates rich guy. I get it.'

Pardeep continued, 'The terms of Seth's departure from Cargo are covered by a nondisclosure, but it's alleged that Seth told Cargo he had received a job offer from a rival publisher. Cargo gave him a raise and a bump in his job title. Two months later, the CEO of the rival publisher was having dinner with the CEO of Cargo, who realised that there had been no such offer made to Seth.'

'Why wasn't he fired?' asked Linda.

Jason said, 'UK employment law is very robust. It's hard to prove that a job offer was never made. Also, I think Cargo was embarrassed at taking so long to uncover his deceptions.'

Lomond cut in, 'But surely Hathaway asked for references when he moved on?'

'Nope. Not a thing. Just a chat and a handshake. Apparently it was common in London publishing compared to New York and elsewhere.'

'Old boys' network,' said Willie, frowning at his phone.

'Sounds familiar,' Linda remarked. She knew of a number of suits in cushy jobs and plush offices in Dalmarnock and Tulliallan. 'Okay, so Seth Knox has lied and blagged his way into Hathaway. I get it.'

Picking up Linda's trail, Lomond said, 'What's the next question, guys? Because I can't access the information you can. Did that lecturer ever get back to you?'

'He's not answering his phone,' Pardeep said.

'Well, keep at him,' Lomond insisted. 'If Kate Randall can't tell us squat about Liz and Seth, then we need to find someone else. Hang on...' He covered the mouthpiece as Ross knocked on the open door.

'What is it, Ross?' He showed him the phone to indicate that he was busy.

'Donna and I have searched high and low – at least, in any room that's unlocked,' Ross replied. 'There's no sign of Seth anywhere.'

'It's not looking good, is it,' said Lomond.

Back on the line, Pardeep said, 'It all adds up to Seth Knox having a lot of secrets to hide. Maybe William MacRae found out one of them. It may well have cost him his life.'

Jason added, 'He dates Liz MacRae for months according to her old flatmate. Years go by, then Seth gets a job as editor to William, and Seth's involvement with Liz never comes up?'

'We might never get an explanation for all that,' said Willie.

Lomond snapped, 'Guys, that's not good enough. I need more! I've got a killer on the loose up here. I need you to bring me something in the next few hours. Or I don't know how much longer it will be before someone else drops.'

Linda glared at Pardeep and Jason. She raised her eyebrows expectantly. 'What are you waiting for? You heard the man. Uni lecturer. Go.'

Lomond added, 'And Pardeep. I want that phone in your hand at all times. If a Google agent calls back and they don't get an answer, it could be hours before they try you again. And heads up, for crying out loud. This is Major Investigations. Keep digging.'

CHAPTER FIFTY-NINE

THE DINING ROOM had become the new battleground, watching Rebecca's security team struggling to break through the trees bisecting the driveway to reach the moat for repairs. Until the bridge was fixed, the group was at the mercy of a potential killer on the loose.

Recriminations about who said what, or did what prior to Seth's disappearance ping ponged around the dining table.

Jim was the only one eating, tucking into bacon and scrambled eggs, and happily dusting off anyone else's.

Noel wondered aloud, 'What's the old adage about the killer arrested and put in jail? He's relaxed and calm because he knows he's caught? While the innocent man in the same position would be shouting from the rafters that he hasn't done anything.'

Jim covered his mouth while speaking and eating crispy bacon at the same time. 'The innocent man also knows he has nothing to hide and could be tucking into some decent scran while everyone else worries themselves daft.'

Brad smiled and duly pulled up a plate of his own. 'Sounds about right to me,' he said.

'I don't know how you two can eat at a time like this,' said Tom, looking grey and like he might throw up at any moment. He couldn't even watch Jim and Brad eat.

Jim said, 'The fact that we didn't drink our bodyweight in booze last night is probably playing a part.'

Claire watched the security team buzzing through one of the tree trunks with chainsaws. 'They're on the second already.'

Crawford rubbed his hands together with glee. 'Great. We're going to make it!'

Charlotte stared out the window. 'It's so strange... people parking their cars, filing into Crichton House...no idea what's happened here.'

'They'll find out soon enough,' Claire replied.

Rebecca asked Crawford, 'Do you really think it's appropriate to go ahead with this event?'

Zoe stepped in. 'Of course! Look, no one is as worried about Seth as I am...'

That prompted some sceptical expressions around the table.

'...but for William's sake, we have to get back. Don't you all want to know who Sullivan is? After all this?'

Lomond, standing at the margins of the room next to Donna and Ross, unfolded his arms. 'I admire your optimism that you still think they'll appear.'

He gestured for Donna and Ross to join him in the hall

while the others were swept up in a debate about whether the Sullivan event should go ahead.

In the hall, Lomond spoke quietly. 'I need to tell you both something about last night. It's about Seth. And Claire MacRae.'

CHAPTER SIXTY

IN THE HALL, Lomond said to Ross and Donna, 'So we're agreed? I'll do this in the kitchen. It's more relaxed, and she'll have seen everyone being dragged over hot coals in the library last night. We could do with checking Seth's phone anyway.' He turned to leave.

Donna said by way of stopping him, 'Actually, sir...I thought the three of us should be in on this. To push her.'

Lomond looked mildly insulted. 'You don't think I'll push her?'

Without hesitation, Donna said, 'No, sir. Possibly not.'

Surprised, he replied, 'I respect your honesty. May I ask why you think I won't push a suspect in this investigation?'

'Perhaps you see yourself as having a bit too much in common with her. It's natural to sympathise, sir. Because of what you've been through.' She gulped hard in anticipation of what she was about to say next. 'Also, sir...is it possible that you may be thinking of her differently because of her resemblance...to Eilidh? She looks just like the photo of Eilidh you showed me a while ago.'

Ross didn't move a muscle. He couldn't believe that Donna was actually confronting Lomond on the subject.

But Lomond wasn't taking it badly. He was just too stunned to get angry about it. Now that Donna had pointed it out, he realised that he had felt a strong kinship with Claire from the start and not really known why. He had always been in favour of the adage, if one person tells you that you're drunk, they might be mistaken. But if everyone in the room tells you that you're drunk, then you're probably drunk. Lomond was big enough to understand that if Donna could see it, then there may be an issue there.

'You think this too?' he asked Ross.

Ross gulped. 'I...I do, sir.'

Lomond said, 'Fine. Let's do this. The three of us.'

Once he had gone on ahead, Ross said to her out of Lomond's earshot, 'You're feeling brave.'

'Glad it came across that way.' She showed him her hand, which was trembling.

CHAPTER SIXTY-ONE

LOMOND UNLOCKED the kitchen door with the key Rebecca had given him. He refused to trust anyone with access to the rooms where Seth's phone had been left – and he couldn't walk around with a bowl of dry porridge with a phone stuck inside for hours on end.

He took the phone out of the oats and blew the dust off it.

'Any joy?' asked Ross.

Lomond pressed the power button on the side to no avail. 'Nothing yet.'

Claire entered, hesitantly. 'John?' she said, about to knock on the open door.

'Have a seat, Claire,' he said, indicating a stool by the breakfast bar where Donna and Ross were already sitting.

Lomond was the only one standing, tending to the boiling kettle. As he poured four coffees and handed them out, he said, 'My team in Glasgow have uncovered evidence that's taken us by surprise.'

'Like what?' she asked.

She seems relaxed, thought Ross. *Trying too hard? Wouldn't anyone be nervous when invited by three detectives to a sit-down in the middle of a murder enquiry?*

'Were you or William aware that Seth attended Glasgow University with Liz?'

Confused, Claire said, 'But Seth went to Oxford.'

'He did. And failed to complete his doctorate. After that, he moved to Glasgow.'

'I had no idea.' Claire paused, then asked herself, 'Why wouldn't William have said something if he had known?'

'It's our belief that Liz and Seth were in a relationship.' He tried to soften the blow by delaying the next part. 'Towards the end of her life.'

Claire lowered her head slightly. 'The end? As in...'

Lomond nodded. 'I'm afraid so.'

'Then it was him? All this time, he had known Liz...' She began to doubt it though as the implications unravelled in her head. 'No, wait...then he and William just happened to end up working together?' It was too much of a coincidence for her to wrap her head around.

'You said that William was the one who plucked Seth out of obscurity at Hathaway.'

'He did...but then William did say he thought that Seth had engineered the situation with William finding his corrections that day.'

'You mean, he thought Seth planted them?'

'Maybe.' She froze, then pulled back from the breakfast bar. 'You think I did it, don't you?'

Lomond began to shake his head.

'No,' Claire went on. 'You think that I knew all this already, and now I'm the one acting out of vengeance...'

'There are no accusations being made here,' Lomond assured her. 'We're simply parsing information as it emerges. It's our job, Claire. If we're going to find out who killed William we need to have these sort of frank conversations with people like yourself. With everyone.'

Donna and Ross steeled themselves. They could tell that Lomond was laying the ground work.

Lomond said, 'Donna?'

She felt no such need to walk on eggshells around Claire. 'Mrs MacRae, were you in Seth Knox's company last night?'

'Of course I was,' she said. 'Everyone was.'

'I'm talking about your bedroom.'

You could have heard a pin drop in the kitchen.

'I was there,' said Lomond. 'I saw you both together.'

Claire said, 'He was checking on me. I mean...I had asked him to check my room.'

'You couldn't do that on your own?'

'I was scared.'

'Because you realise that this makes you the last person to see Seth alive?'

Claire turned to Lomond. 'You tell me that no accusations are being made here, John?'

Trying to appease her, Lomond put his hand out, 'Claire, it's a fair–'

Claire turned back to Donna. 'What motive could I possibly have?'

Donna didn't delay in presenting her phone, which

showed a photo sent through by Pardeep. 'Do you recognise this document?'

'I signed it with William last week.'

'This survivor destination gives you ownership of the Park Circus property.'

Losing her patience, Claire retorted, 'And William signed it in person in his own lawyer's office. Ask them! Are you really suggesting I managed to convince William to sign over ownership should anything happen to him, then I murdered him the very next week?'

Donna paused, struggling to find any other way of answering except for "yes". 'You asked what motive you could have, and this–'

Claire shut down. She got off her stool and turned her back on them while adjusting the long cardigan she had on. 'We're done here,' she said. When she whipped around, the others caught a glimpse of her face again.

Lomond grabbed a tissue from the sideboard and handed it to her. 'Claire...' He motioned at his nose.

She took the tissue and was surprised to see blood on it when she was done wiping. 'Damn it...Thank you.'

Lomond didn't take his eyes off her. It was the first time he had seen her lose composure. As if he was only now seeing the real Claire, instead of the presentation he had witnessed until then. This was Claire MacRae with vulnerability. And a hint of fear.

She held the tissue to her nose a moment to stem the blood long enough for her to say a parting shot. 'I think it's time I spoke to my lawyer if this is the route we're going down.'

'That might be for the best,' suggested Lomond.

He stood there quietly until Claire had gone, then he told Donna, 'Good job.'

'Thanks, boss.'

She knew that it must have taken guts for him to say it. Because it meant admitting that there was a chance that Claire MacRae was behind all of it.

'I'll give this phone a check,' said Ross.

Donna asked, 'What's with the nosebleed, do you think? Is she on the old Colombian marching powder?' She imitated someone snorting a line of cocaine.

Lomond shook his head. 'She hasn't exhibited any highs since she's been here. But she did nearly fall over when we were talking in the garden yesterday. She said it was low blood pressure.'

Ross called them over to the table where the phone had been drying out. 'I think I've got something...'

Lomond and Donna hurried over.

Ross showed them Seth's phone screen. It had lit up, but only to show the warning for low battery. 'It's working, at least. We just need to get it charged.'

Lomond patted him on the shoulder. 'We're getting there.'

CHAPTER SIXTY-TWO

A CRY of relief and joy rang out from the dining room.

One of the Range Rovers – an older style Classic model with a grunty engine – towed away a large piece of tree trunk that broke up the narrow flow of the flood waters. Now the other cars could get through and reach the moat.

'They're through!' Noel exclaimed.

Rebecca was at the window, looking on, as she hung up the phone on one of the security team.

Lomond barrelled in, quickly followed by Ross and Donna. 'What's the situation?' he asked.

'They think the ladder they have is long enough,' Rebecca said.

Zoe said, 'I assumed that they would be able to handle the dimensions.' She lifted a leg to indicate the elegant heels she still had on from the memorial drinks reception. 'I'm a little more worried about the actual crossing. The wind's still gusting out there.'

'It is, but not nearly as powerfully as last night. They're recommending we crawl over one at a time.'

Jim guffawed with laughter, then took a new bottle of Laphroaig from the bar area and poured a measure. 'Good luck with that,' he said. 'Let them know I'll be here.'

'Me too,' said Brad, sliding a glass over to Jim. 'Fill her up, Jim boy.'

There was a brief break in conversation as Charlotte came back, holding a cup of tea in both hands.

'What took you so long?' asked Zoe.

'I spilled it,' said Charlotte. 'I had to make another one.'

Zoe said nothing more about it.

Crawford asked, 'What if the wind picks up?'

Rebecca said, 'There's no getting around it. You'll need to hold on very tightly.'

'*Very*,' said Tom. 'You expect us to put our lives on the line on the basis of an adverb?'

'Surprised you know what one is,' Charlotte muttered under her breath, before taking a sip of tea.

Lomond said, 'If it can be done, we should all go. The longer we spend here, the closer we get to losing a second body.'

While the group descended into bickering once more, Ross had a quiet word in Lomond's ear. 'Boss, I don't know about this. Aren't we kind of playing Russian roulette here?'

'The killer is in the castle right now, Ross. The sooner we get everyone out of here, the safer they'll be. The kills in *The Shortlist* rely on proximity and breaking the group up. That's why I said no to search parties splitting up before.

Getting everyone over that moat and back to Crichton House disarms the killer's ability.'

Crawford, who had been listening in, corralled the others. 'DCI Lomond's right. It's risky. But not as risky as staying here. Not with Seth missing.'

'I'll take my chances on the ladder,' said Noel. 'I'm not staying another minute in this place.'

'Me too,' said Claire.

'Okay,' Lomond announced. 'Everyone staying, raise your hand.'

Brad and Jim raised their hands.

'Everyone leaving with me?'

Everyone else raised their hands.

Jim suddenly looked nervous. 'You mean, you're going too, Chief Inspector?'

'Of course I am,' said Lomond.

'What about looking for Seth?'

'Do you know how long someone has to be missing before they're declared a missing person? If Seth hasn't come to harm through an accident in trying to flee the grounds last night, then he may already be dead. It's not nice to say, but I have to confront it as a possibility. Maybe even a likelihood.'

Jim looked at Brad.

Brad at Jim.

'Then we're here on our own,' said Jim.

'Just us,' said Brad.

Rebecca asked, 'Are you really prepared to stay here and potentially leave yourselves in the company of a killer?'

Zoe added, 'That's a steep price for some eggs and bacon and a free bar.'

'Be smart, guys,' said Noel. 'Come back with us.'

Jim puffed. 'Brad, I love you, man. But I'm not staying here with *only* you. What if you're the killer?'

'You read my mind,' said Brad, standing up.

'Then it's settled,' said Lomond, about to lead the group outside.

CHAPTER SIXTY-THREE

In the lobby, everyone else was more than ready to get out of Inver Castle.

'No offence, Rebecca,' said Noel. 'This is a lovely place you've got here. But if I come back, it'll be over my dead body.'

'Same,' said Charlotte.

'Me too,' said Zoe.

The only one apparently not ready – still wearing her cardigan rather than a coat – was Claire MacRae.

'Tell me you're not staying here,' said Charlotte.

Claire folded her arms. 'I've no desire to find out who AD Sullivan is. I don't care. I'm done with all of this.'

Rebecca approached. 'Claire, you know that my home is always open to you. But as long as Seth is missing this place isn't safe.'

Donna added, 'If someone really is acting out *The Shortlist*, then Seth is still alive somewhere and could strike again at any moment. We know what happens in the book.

You're doing the one thing that's going to keep you in danger.'

'I would dispute that,' Claire replied. 'I'll take my chances.'

The group said their goodbyes – fragile, concerned for her safety. A few last-ditch efforts were made to try and change her mind – to no avail.

Lomond was the last to make an appeal. 'Claire, please don't do this. I know you're upset...'

She scoffed. 'That's not even close to what I am right now. I really thought you understood.'

'And I thought you understood what my job is here.' He knew that it was pointless. 'Okay,' he said. 'I'll see you back at Crichton House.'

Claire said nothing.

The wind howled, battering against the group as they huddled together like penguins against an icy gale. The moat was in front of them, still a raging torrent threatening to swallow anyone who fell into it. The ladder laid across it looked flimsy, unstable. But it was all they had. Survival was no longer a given, but a matter of luck.

'I don't know about this,' said Crawford, holding back.

'You can always take your chances back in the castle,' Rebecca told him.

The head of security barked orders. 'Crawl across, keep your centre of gravity low!' His team stood by, ready with ropes and life rings.

Jim said what they were all thinking. 'They look nervous, don't they? Why are they so nervous? What are they not telling us?'

Rebecca asked, "Who wants to go first?" But before

anyone could respond, Tom shoved his way past and started crawling across. His eagerness disappeared the moment he felt fresh air under his legs. The ladder rattled and shook under him, threatening to send him tumbling down.

Lomond brought up the rear, looking back towards the castle. Claire was standing on the front steps, tiny and vulnerable against the storm door and pillars. As she turned to go back inside, Lomond couldn't help but wonder if this was the last time he would see her alive.

CHAPTER SIXTY-FOUR

THE GROUNDS around Crichton House were buzzing with anticipation of the AD Sullivan event. Nearly two hundred people had packed out the main marquee, despite the weather. The marquee rattled and billowed in the wind, but the driving rain had at least subsided.

Chaperoning the group making their way across the gardens to the marquee, Donna and Ross overheard a couple rushing past. 'I just heard someone say that they saw Rebecca Hawley around the back of Crichton House...Do you think it could be her?'

Donna said to Ross, 'They have no idea the energy that's gone into finding that out in the last twelve hours.'

Ross replied, 'And it remains to be seen how many lives it's going to cost.'

The group made it to the green room backstage – where performers waited and prepared to go onstage. As fellow performers over the weekend, the group had reserved seats in the front row. Given the events overnight, they were as eager to find out who Sullivan was as the rest of the audience.

Off stage left, Crawford was with Lomond, awaiting the arrival of a familiar face to reveal themselves.

'How does this work again?' asked Lomond.

Crawford shook his head as he checked his phone for the hundredth time. 'They should have been in contact by now. They were going to message Zoe ten minutes before, then meet her here.'

Across the stage on the right side, Zoe was on her own, gesturing for Crawford to calm down.

As the lights dimmed, the murmur from the crowd turned to polite applause. Zoe was a big shot in the trade, but the readers in attendance didn't have a clue who she was.

She rolled out a pristine, rehearsed speech about the process of finding *The Shortlist*, and the uniqueness of its author's anonymity until now.

Crawford was a bag of nerves. Eventually he put his phone away, then took it straight back out again. 'They're not going to show, are they? What is she going to do if they don't show?'

Lomond peered at Zoe. He had been listening to her closely. 'Why do I get the feeling she already knows who Sullivan is? Something about the way she's talking. There's no uncertainty. No stalling.' He leaned forward to try to see around the curtain across the stage. 'No one waiting in the wings.'

Lomond was about to put his hands in his coat pockets when he felt something in one of them. The bulge of a small thin box. He heard it rattle before he took it out.

It was a box with tablets vacuum packed in foil inside. The name on the prescription sticker was Claire MacRae. The medication was called Everolimus.

He couldn't work out how they ended up there. Then he remembered she had taken pills after her funny turn in the garden. She had been wearing his coat, and must have slid the box back into his coat pockets instead of her own.

He opened up the instructions inside. The drug was described as "used in the treatment of renal cell carcinoma...' The drug acted as an inhibitor of a protein called mTOR, "which makes cancer cells grow and produce new blood vessels."

Lomond said to himself in disbelief, 'She has cancer.'

He turned the leaflet over for the side effects.

Tiredness and weakness.

Feeling or being sick.

Breathlessness and looking pale.

And in rarer cases, *nose bleeds*, due to a drop in platelets in the blood.

Lomond's mind was racing. Suddenly, he could see everything with a new clarity.

'Are you okay?' asked Crawford. 'You've been staring at the ground for a while.'

Lomond snapped out of his daze. 'I have to go back.'

'Back? Back where?'

Already on the move, he said, 'To Inver Castle.'

If he had waited only thirty more seconds, he would have heard what Ross, Donna, and the rest of the marquee had heard. Which was Zoe speeding towards the climax of her introduction.

Zoe said, 'This would normally be the point where I

welcome the author of the book in question out to the stage.' She lifted her hands and dropped them down sadly on the podium. 'Unfortunately, I can't do that today...'

'I knew it,' Crawford said to himself, pacing around backstage. He had visions of queues outside – everyone demanding their tickets be refunded.

Zoe said, 'It's with the heaviest of hearts that I can reveal the author of *The Shortlist* was indeed one of the industry's brightest lights, and most dazzling talents. We just never got a chance to find that out. I know a lot of you have you been anticipating this book as Hathaway's biggest thriller of this year. However, the book has quite a long history already. It was written over a decade ago. Formulated and plotted in meticulous detail in a student flat in Glasgow. Now, thanks to the efforts of crime-writing legend William MacRae, this long-lost book will no longer be lost. I'm sure it will surprise at least some of you to learn, then, that the pen name of the mysterious AD Sullivan, who wrote this most ingenious of murder mysteries is, or was, none other than...'

Jim leaned forward in his chair. 'Why does she keep using the past tense?'

'It's Seth,' said Brad. 'It's got to be.'

'I don't think so,' said Noel.

Zoe concluded, 'the incredibly talented daughter of William MacRae, and now imminently a posthumous bestseller herself. Sadly, both are no longer with us. Ladies and gentlemen, please give a round of applause for the author of *The Shortlist*...' Her voice cracked when she said, 'Liz MacRae!'

CHAPTER SIXTY-FIVE

THERE WAS a collective intake of breath around the marquee, and more than a few gasps. When the hardback image of *The Shortlist* was replaced with a photo of Liz MacRae, there was spontaneous applause from the crowd.

Ross turned to Donna in the wings of the marquee, close to the authors. 'Whoa...okay, I definitely didn't see that coming. Did you? Honestly?'

Donna smiled.

'Yeah, right,' said Ross. 'Then how come you never said anything?'

'I guess it kind of makes sense...except Liz MacRae is definitely dead and *definitely* not running around Inver Castle.'

Ross took Seth's phone out of his pocket. It had been attached to a mobile power bank to charge it on the move. He pressed the power button.

This time, instead of the usual black screen followed a large battery icon, the screen turned white.

'I think we're in here,' Ross said.

Donna crowded him, trying to see. 'Does it have a passcode?'

'Damn,' he said. The screen presented him with a keypad that they didn't have a code for. 'I don't even know what we're looking for now. If Liz MacRae was AD Sullivan, what use is Seth's phone? If Seth's dead, the killer's not exactly going to WhatsApp a picture of his body for us to find him.'

Donna hunted around for Lomond, but couldn't see him at the side of the stage anymore. 'Did you see the gaffer leave?'

Ross pocketed the phone. 'He was over there beside Crawford a minute ago.'

Donna then clocked Rebecca getting quietly out of her seat at the end of the row nearest the aisle, then heading for the backstage area.

'Where's she off to?' Donna wondered.

'Look,' said Ross, pointing through one of the plastic windows in the marquee wall. Lomond was running back towards Crichton House, the tails of his coat flapping behind him.

Lomond's mind raced, knowing that time was not on his side. He knew the risk of crossing the moat alone was high, but Claire had been without her pills for far too long since her earlier nosebleed.

Any thoughts of AD Sullivan faded into the background as Lomond quickened his pace, his work shoes slipping on the trampled, sodden grass. Finally, he made it to the castle driveway, but there was no time to search for drivers or cars.

Lomond's legs ached, and his belly felt heavy juddering around, but the urgency of the situation pushed him beyond his physical limits. The human body can always find a reserve of strength when it's needed most, and Lomond needed it desperately to save Claire's life.

He was her only hope of proving who killed William MacRae.

CHAPTER SIXTY-SIX

USING LOMOND'S CREDENTIALS, Pardeep had submitted a request through Google's Law Enforcement Request System the night before to access user data on AD Sullivan's Gmail account. Even as a police detective, there was no dedicated phone line for Pardeep to call up on. He had to submit a request through the LERS system, a log-in portal for law enforcement officers with official email addresses registered with LERS. Depending on the time of day and a little luck, he could get an answer to his query within an hour or two.

Turned out the wrong time was whenever the night shift in a Mumbai call centre was fielding requests, just as the entire west coast of America – and its police officers – were filing LERS requests in the morning.

With the lights turned down for the night in Major Investigations, Pardeep had fallen asleep at his desk. When the call back from Google's Mumbai call centre finally came through, he almost fell out of his chair he lunged for it so quickly. The remainder of his very late lunch spilled all over the floor.

'I'm here, I'm here,' he said.

The police didn't have to faff around with analysing email headers and other such technical stuff to narrow down someone's location. They just submitted a request through LERS. You had to know what to ask for, though. The first step for Pardeep was to find out the IP address of the computer or phone used to send the email from AD Sullivan's Gmail account to Zoe Hathaway.

For the Google analyst, Ramesh, that couldn't have been simpler. He was able to identify all the device information associated with the connection, even down to the make and model of phone used.

As he explained to Pardeep in impeccable English, 'The problem you have got, Detective Varma, is that a VPN has been used while sending this email. The IP address of the phone won't tell you where the sender really was. I can tell you who the VPN provider is, though. They are based in America.'

That then sent Pardeep on a series of phone calls to the States.

When it came to online privacy, a Virtual Private Network was a must-have. And if you were operating under an alias and looking to keep your location and real identity a secret while sending emails, a VPN was essential. As AD Sullivan clearly knew.

What Sullivan didn't realise, was that many VPN servers kept logs and were perfectly willing to give them up to law enforcement officials. Like Pardeep.

All he had to ask for was the IP address originally used

to access the VPN connection. That address would tell Pardeep where Sullivan had really been at the time of sending to the email.

Then there was one last hoop to jump through. To the mobile phone carrier that used that IP address. They couldn't give a precise location to Pardeep. For that kind of modern spy stuff, you had to go through GCHQ. The best Pardeep could get was the ID of the mobile tower the connection had gone through.

With the tower ID, he then went onto a popular tower tracking website that showed where every mobile tower mast in the country was, and its precise coverage with every network.

When Pardeep had put in the tower data, he thought he had done something wrong.

A red beacon showed where the tower was on a map. In a patch of wasteland in Ibrox next to a railway line. Directly across from where the M8 passed Helen Street police station. This was apparently where AD Sullivan had last communicated with Zoe Hathaway via email.

'This can't possibly be right,' he said to himself.

Willie, who had been monitoring Pardeep's flurry of activity for the last half hour, came over with a cup of coffee for him. 'What have you got?' he asked.

Pardeep pointed to the screen. 'I've been chasing up the location of that Sullivan email to Zoe Hathaway.'

'I've seen one of those searches before,' said Willie. 'It's not that precise.'

'No, I know. But look at the location of the tower the mobile connection went through.'

Willie was stunned. 'Sullivan was in *Ibrox*?'

'The email was sent on Friday night, Willie.' Pardeep waited for the penny to drop. 'AD Sullivan was within a few hundred metres of this police station at that time. It can't be a coincidence. Look...' He leafed through Donna's notes. 'Donna wrote down that after she returned with some water for Seth Knox he was messaging someone on his phone. Now, Donna obviously knows better than to secretly record a discussion like that. But we've got access to the interior cameras that show when Donna left the room to get water.' He maximised a window on his computer screen, showing a still of Donna. Pardeep pointed to the digital timer at the bottom corner of the screen. 'Ten twenty-seven.' He then showed Willie the email, highlighting the time sent.

Willie said in amazement, 'Ten twenty-seven.' He grabbed Pardeep by the shoulders and rocked him back and forth. 'Ya dancer, Pardeep. You've nailed him!'

'Unless Sullivan was standing outside the station at the exact same time, sending an email, then we've got our man.' Pardeep nodded with satisfaction. 'Seth Knox is AD Sullivan.'

CHAPTER SIXTY-SEVEN

LOMOND WAS beyond out of breath by the time he reached the moat. He cursed the extra weight he was carrying that he had promised to get rid of months ago.

But that was nothing compared to how he cursed the metal ladder he now had to navigate to get to the other side of the moat. The security team had left it there as it was far too cumbersome to be bringing it back and forth from Crichton House. The understanding, however, was that it would only be used under their supervision.

Lomond didn't have time for that. Nor did he have time to pluck up courage. Claire could have been convulsing, or bleeding out, somewhere in the castle. Lomond got down on his hands and knees and started the painstaking journey across a gaping chasm. The worst part was having no option but to look straight through the ladder towards your fate if you got a single hand or foot placement wrong.

He had never held onto something as tightly as he did

the ladder. Particularly when it dipped at its weakest point halfway across.

The ladder swayed. As he struggled to regain balance, his phone began to ring.

'You can leave a fucking voicemail,' he spluttered under his breath.

His heart was pounding at the thought of falling into the freezing water below.

He kept shimmying his way over, only allowing himself to relax even a little once both feet were on the driveway on the other side.

Behind, a Range Rover pulled up at the moat with a skid. Out rushed Rebecca Hawley.

'I saw you leave,' she called out to him. 'What are you doing?'

'I have to find Claire,' he explained. 'I think she's in trouble.'

'Stay there,' she yelled. 'I'm coming over.'

Lomond held the ladder down at the castle side with all of his weight to keep it steady. Rebecca was over in no time.

'Come on,' she said. 'We'll find her.'

It was only as they ran up the front steps to the castle that Lomond considered that he might have put himself in a precarious position.

Why had Rebecca followed him?

CHAPTER SIXTY-EIGHT

BEHIND THE STORM DOOR, the wooden door leading to the lobby was flapping open in the wind.

After failing to answer the first time, Lomond answered his phone when it rang again.

'This is Lomond,' he said, entering the gloomy lobby.

Wind whistled through the reception area, into the library where a window had been left gaping open.

Rebecca ran there, finding papers blown all around the room, falling like confetti from a great height.

On the other end of the phone line was Pardeep. 'Sir,' he said. 'I've got some news on the AD Sullivan email. It was sent by Seth Knox.'

Lomond, who had been stalking across the ground floor in search of Claire, came to a halt. A message pinged on his phone. 'Hang on, Pardeep,' said Lomond. The message was from Ross.

"We're locked out of Seth's phone but it's powered up.

Did you hear Zoe's announcement? Liz MacRae is AD Sullivan."

The message stopped Lomond in his tracks.

Returning to Pardeep, Lomond asked, 'What's going on?'

'Sir?'

'What's going on, Pardeep? Why am I getting messages from Ross telling me that Liz MacRae is Sullivan?'

'I have no idea, sir. But she can't be Sullivan. Liz only ever wrote one book. Claire read it, and so did Kate Randall. It was called *Shattered Glass,* and the story was nothing like *The Shortlist...'*

Lomond's thoughts trailed off, consumed by something that had taken up residency at the back of his head, and was fighting to reveal itself. He said in wonder. 'One lie reveals another...'

'Sir?'

'We had said that Seth's lie about attending Oxford was one lie that unlocked dozens of others. I think we've made the same mistake with Kate Randall.'

'I don't understand, sir. But if you want me to get you the proof you need about Seth, I need access to his phone. If I can get the IP address of the phone, I can prove that he was Sullivan.'

Lomond could hardly see as he navigated down a windowless corridor that had no lights on. It was as if there was a power cut.

'That might be difficult,' said Lomond. 'We still haven't found him.'

Then, from the ceiling speakers came a terrifying

sound. An orchestra at a deafening volume, playing a mournful symphony.

Lomond spun around and found that Rebecca was no longer there.

'Rebecca?' he yelled, trying to be heard over the music. 'Claire?'

No answer.

He threw open each door along the corridor, the intensely creepy music following him from room to room. 'What is happening?' he asked himself aloud. His skin was crawling with dread and fear.

Pardeep's voice was a faint whimper down by Lomond's waist.

Lomond had forgotten that he was still on the line to him. He held the phone to his face again. 'Pardeep, I might be in a spot of trouble here.'

'What is that music?' asked Pardeep.

'It's called Symphony of Sorrowful Songs by Henryk Górecki.'

'I didn't know you liked classical music, boss.'

'I only know it because I looked it up after reading about it.'

Pardeep paused while he rummaged through some paperwork. 'Hang on. Now that you mention it, that name rings a bell.'

'It should – if you've read the Liz MacRae files. The song was playing on repeat when her flatmate found her body.'

To be precise, it was the second movement. A tranquillissimo – in orchestral parlance, a movement that was very peaceful, very calm. The word that Lomond had thought of when he first heard it was "haunting".

A solo female soprano sang a libretto that seemed to hang in the air. Cinematic. Desolate. As a final track to hear before you died, Lomond could at least understand the choice. It was one of the most heart-breaking – and beautiful – pieces of music he had ever heard.

But in its current context, it was scaring the life out of him.

After a long pause waiting to see what was going on, Pardeep said, 'Boss, I think you should get out of there. I don't like this.'

Lomond didn't respond.

Pardeep waited again. He could hear a door creaking open. 'Boss? You there?'

CHAPTER SIXTY-NINE

LOMOND'S HEART raced as he pushed open the door to the bathroom. The bass from the music piped inside reverberated against the tiled walls. As he made his way to the far wall, his eyes widened in horror at the sight before him.

The overflowing bathtub was filled with deep red water, and Seth's lifeless body lay submerged inside. His arms were tied, and deep lacerations covered the insides of his arms. Lomond knew immediately that there was no way Seth could have done this to himself. The weight of a large black tie-top sack on Seth's torso had kept him under the water.

With the orchestra reaching a climax, the soprano peaked as well, hitting an almost miraculous A flat major.

Lomond ran quickly to Seth, lifting the heavy sack with all his might. When he dropped it, its contents spilled across the marble tiles – a dozen first-edition hardback copies of *The Shortlist*.

Lomond hauled Seth up out of the bath, then collapsed

back, holding the body. It was clear he had been dead for a while, his skin pale and pimpled from the cold. Lomond had never seen goosebumps in the dead before, but Moira had once told him about the phenomenon. As rigor mortis set in to the arrector pili muscles attached to the base of Seth's hair follicles, it caused what was known as cutis anserina – otherwise known as postmortem goosebumps.

Lomond cursed aloud. Cursed Rebecca for setting them up in that damn castle. Cursed the person that had killed Seth and William. And he cursed himself for not stopping it before.

No sooner had he pushed Seth's body off him onto the floor, a scream echoed from downstairs.

Lomond yelled back, 'Rebecca?' He scrambled to his feet, slipping and sliding from the blood on his shoes against the tiles.

He yelled again, sprinting as hard as he could down the corridor. 'Rebecca? Claire?'

Rebecca's voice cried out, 'DCI Lomond! In the dining room!'

He bounded down the stairs three at a time, expecting to find Claire MacRae dead.

Instead, he found Rebecca crouching over her, but she was still alive. Her face was pale. Her nose had been streaming blood. But she was trying to speak.

'Afinitor...' she croaked.

'What's she saying?' asked Rebecca.

Lomond put his ear close to Claire's mouth.

She repeated the word.

The only reason Lomond recognised it was because it

had been on the leaflet that came with Claire's Everolimus tablets.

Lomond fumbled through his pockets in a panic. 'Afinitor,' he said, struggling to release tablets from the foil packaging. 'It's the brand name of her pills.'

Claire lifted her hand, encouraging Lomond to feed them to her.

Lomond gesticulated wildly for the glass of water on the table nearby. 'Water! Water! Quick!' He fed her two of the pills and some water.

Claire used up every last ounce of strength remaining in her body to lift her head so she could get the pills down. Once she felt them slide down her throat, she lay back down and relaxed. She put out a weak hand and grasped Lomond's leg.

She closed her eyes in relief. The nearest she could get to saying thank you.

Lomond collapsed to one side in exhaustion. He had managed to save one person at least.

Rebecca held Claire's hand. 'Are you okay?' she asked.

But Claire had passed out.

'She has cancer,' Lomond said. 'Much longer and she might have bled out. Seth wasn't quite so lucky.'

CHAPTER SEVENTY

Donna had been tasked with keeping the author group where they were, while Ross made it back to Inver Castle – thanks to a more solid bridge solution constructed of long wooden boards provided by the local police and fire brigade. In the end, Forensic Services had to come from Inverness.

It was dark by the time the unmarked coroner van, marked as "PRIVATE AMBULANCE", arrived to take Seth's body away.

Now that they had access to Seth's fingerprint, Lomond pressed Seth's fingertip onto the phone's sensor. The process of finding the phone's IP address was so simple, Pardeep talked Lomond through it on speaker phone.

'It's a match,' said Lomond. 'God, you're right, Pardeep...This was the phone that sent AD Sullivan's messages. It really was Seth.'

Feeling like he had been blindfolded and then spun around a dozen times, Ross said, 'Then why has Zoe Hathaway just gone on stage and announced Liz MacRae as Sullivan?'

Lomond groaned with a realisation.

Pardeep and Ross waited for him to explain.

'What is it?' asked Ross.

'It's still just a theory,' said Lomond, thinking through the implications. A renewed focus behind his eyes, it was as if Lomond had just necked five espressos. 'Pardeep, get Willie to track that whisky bottle.'

'But, sir, he–'

'He already did that. I know. But there's a reason that this crime scene with Seth Knox was made to look like Liz MacRae's suicide. The music, the drowning in the bath, the torso weighed down by books. And the symbolism of using copies of *The Shortlist* only confirms it...Tell Willie to check where that whisky bottle had been *before* Seth took it to that drop-off point. I think there was step before it. And if I'm right about who was behind it, then it starts to explain all of this.'

'Are you going to tell us who?' asked Ross.

Lomond said, 'You know how I'm always telling you two when you have a theory, to press on it as hard as you can? As if you're trying to drive a truck through your own theory?'

'Sure,' said Ross.

'Opposition prep,' said Pardeep. 'You've got a theory, you've got to test it.'

'Well, the more I try to pick holes in this theory, the stronger it gets. And if I *am* right, let's just say that as murders go, I've never heard of anything else like it.'

CHAPTER SEVENTY-ONE

Ross HUNG up his phone and waved Donna over. 'That was John. He just found Seth Knox's body in a bathtub.'

'You're kidding. How did he die?'

'He's not sure yet. But the body was weighed down, and inner arms slashed and tied in front of his body. Toxicology should be interesting, but he didn't go peacefully.'

'Or voluntarily,' Donna added. Then a thought occurred to her. 'Was there any music set up in the room?'

Ross smiled. 'There was. Care to guess which piece?'

Donna's mouth slowly opened as the answer occurred to her. 'It was "Symphony of Sorrowful Songs", wasn't it? Just like Liz MacRae.'

'It seems like it.'

Energised by the connection, she said, 'We should keep a close watch for how they're all reacting to the news. It might tell us something.'

Ross looked down at his phone. 'That's the thing. John just told me that we don't need to worry about that.'

'Why?'

Ross waited for her to fill in the blank.

'Does he know who did it?' asked Donna.

Ross looked back at the authors, many of whom were trying their best to glean from the pair's body language what was going on. He led Donna away a little further. 'All he would say is that he just spoke to Willie about the whisky bottle package. Having to read between the lines until he gets back, I don't think we quite got the full picture of what happened there. Especially now that Pardeep has been able to match up the IP address on Seth's phone with an email to Zoe Hathaway.'

'It's definitely Seth?'

'It's undeniable proof.'

Donna looked down while she thought through the ramifications. 'But then...' Her gaze landed on Zoe Hathaway. 'That means Zoe...'

Ross nodded. 'Yep. And we'll get to that with her. But John says for now, the priority is not letting anyone leave.'

'Of course,' Donna replied. 'Do you want me to tell them?'

Ross sighed. 'No, I'll do it. We need to focus here, mate. John's relying on us. The next hour or two could make or break this thing.'

'I'm on it,' she assured him with a brisk nod.

Ross turned to the others and held his hands aloft for quiet. 'Ladies and gentlemen, could I have your attention, please. I'm afraid I need to deliver some news on behalf of DCI Lomond. A body has been found at Inver Castle...'

The group of authors were to be detained in the marquee. This time, no one could argue about the legality of holding them all at a single location. Unlike the previous night at Inver Castle, they now knew that one of the group was a killer.

After Ross made the announcement, there was speculation, fear, horror, and resentment, to name but a few.

'Right,' said Jim, getting to his feet. 'That proves once and for all that I've done nothing. You've all been with me all day–'

'But not all night,' Brad pointed out.

Jim looked more offended that his drinking buddy had been the one to say it than the fact he was still not officially cleared of any wrongdoing.

'No one has an alibi for the whole night,' said Noel.

Charlotte said, 'Apart from maybe Claire MacRae. Only trouble being, her alibi is about to be carried into a private ambulance.'

'What are you talking about?' asked Zoe.

'I saw Claire beckoning Seth into her bedroom late last night.'

Donna could already see where it was going. 'Right, everyone just pipe down. This sort of speculation isn't going to help anyone.'

'I don't get it,' Tom said to Zoe. 'You knew that Liz MacRae was AD Sullivan the whole time? And didn't tell anyone?'

'Yeah,' said Rebecca, 'not even the police?'

Zoe replied, 'I never withheld anything that endangered life.'

'That's not your judgement to make,' said Tom.

The only one not getting involved was Crawford, who

was so relieved at a satisfactory outcome to the Sullivan event, he was damn near smiling.

Donna then noticed a commotion at the entrance to the marquee, as two local constables tried to hold back a man in an immaculate pinstripe suit.

He had long silver hair, swept straight back. He had a thick north London accent and spoke like a street trader rather than someone in a £1000 tailored suit.

'Get out of it,' he complained. 'My name's Charlie Whelan. Ask the bloody festival director, Crawford Bell. He knows who I am.' Spotting Donna and her obviously-a-cop posture and demeanour, Charlie yelled the length of the tent, 'I'm William MacRae's agent! I've got every right to be 'ere.'

Brad and Jim shared a smile. 'Good old Charlie.'

They had once shared him as an agent before his legendary temper and even more legendary boozing broke up their relationships. The only writer to stick with him through thick and thin had been William MacRae – mostly because deep down, they were kindred spirits.

Donna motioned to the constable to let him through. 'Mr Whelan, why don't you take a seat down here...'

Charlie only had eyes for Zoe Hathaway. 'Zoe, you mug! What are you playing at? What is this bollocks about Liz being AD Sullivan?'

Zoe was used to being the most powerful person in any room she walked into. But Charlie Whelan had a way about him that made her nervous.

'Why don't you just calm down,' said Donna, stepping out in front of Zoe.

Charlie kept steaming down the centre aisle towards

the group. He thrust a thumb at his chest. 'I'm the one who told William who Sullivan really was.'

'You knew?' asked Donna.

'Course I bloody knew,' he shot back. 'If anyone had thought to actually ask me.'

Donna pulled out a seat for him. 'Why don't you start from the beginning, Mr Whelan.'

CHAPTER SEVENTY-TWO

Charlie duly ignored the seat. 'William told me he was trying to track down someone connected to a book about these crime writers who are on the shortlist for some prize at a book festival, and they start getting bumped off one at a time.'

'*The Shortlist*,' said Zoe.

'Right,' Charlie replied. 'William said he thought that Seth had written it. He wanted me to find out for sure.'

Ross thought he had misheard. 'That *Seth* had written it?'

'Yeah,' Charlie replied.

Donna asked, 'What made him think that?'

Charlie took out his phone and showed her messages exchanged between him and William. 'Look at these here. Editorial emails from Seth where he was giving out some-one's email address. Look how he spelled it.'

Donna took the phone. 'He put a full stop between e and mail.'

'Fairly unique way of doing it,' said Charlie. 'Now swipe left to the next one.'

'It's the same spelling.'

'Except that second email is from AD Sullivan.'

'How could you know that? Sullivan wouldn't have entered into contact with anyone else if they could avoid it.' Zoe came closer, holding her hand out, demanding a look at the email. 'Let me see that.'

Charlie relinquished the phone.

A look of horror and disgust rippled across her face. 'This email is to me. How did you get it?'

'That would be telling now, wouldn't it.'

She thought back to their last meeting. 'You bastard, Charlie! You fucking bastard. I left you for five minutes in my office. You went onto my computer, didn't you?'

Charlie gave a nonchalant shrug.

Zoe went on, 'I knew you had been up to something when I came back. You had this look.'

'Have you got any witnesses?' he asked with a smirk. 'That's a pretty incendiary charge to throw around. I'd say the more salient point is that email is from fucking Seth Knox.'

'That's pretty weak, if you ask me,' said Zoe.

'It's not actually,' replied Ross. 'We have the proof now, Zoe. We know that Seth was the one who sent that message to you on Friday night. The same email address that you've been using to communicate with AD Sullivan for months now. The same one that your dad used.'

Jim couldn't help wading in now too. 'Hang on, hang on...Zoe, you just announced in front of hundreds of people that AD Sullivan was Liz MacRae's pen name.'

She stuttered, 'Well...I...I...*clearly* William was communicating secretly with me to get the book published.'

Brad asked, 'Why wouldn't he just give you the book?'

Charlotte added, 'And why email you from an anonymous email address? Only to admit to you that the book was Liz's all along? You're a fucking liar!'

Ross already knew the angle Zoe had worked. 'You figured that Seth was already dead, didn't you? That's why you announced it as Liz. Because how could he argue if he was dead? We were in close quarters with someone acting out the plot of *The Shortlist*. In which case, Seth was either the first victim or the killer. You wouldn't have wanted Hathaway associated with either of those scenarios. Stop me if I'm wrong.'

Zoe said nothing.

Donna continued, 'So you took a punt. When did you decide? I'll bet you decided last night. When you had plenty of time to think when we were holed up in our bedrooms. You couldn't announce William MacRae as the author as it wouldn't fit with his branding. Then there was the email you had already given to us, which had been sent on Friday night after William was dead. So it couldn't be him. With Seth most likely dead too, you were free to announce whoever you wanted the author to be if they weren't around to deny it. So you chose Liz. Of all your options, it was the smartest one to go for: the way to associate *The Shortlist* with William was as punting it as the long-lost book by the tragic daughter of a bestseller who himself has just been murdered.'

Zoe was unruffled. All business. 'You have your story. I have mine.'

Everyone's attention was drawn to a grey van with blue flashing lights puttering through the muddy grounds. It was marked 'PRIVATE AMBULANCE' on the side. And it wasn't in a hurry.

Charlie said, 'You took a punt, Zoe. And you've missed. You've missed big time.'

Crawford was now suddenly troubled by something. 'Wait, wait, wait...Charlie, did you tell William that it looked like Seth was AD Sullivan?'

Charlie replied, 'I told him as soon as I found the email.'

Now everyone was wading in.

Clutching at straws, Brad called out, 'Is that why William was killed? Because he found out?'

'Seth killed him?' suggested Charlotte.

'No,' Tom griped. 'Why would Seth kill William over that? Why would anyone?'

'Exactly,' said Noel. 'Seth playing up anonymity might have been a great PR ploy for drumming up interest in his book. But why would knowing Seth was Sullivan be motive to kill William?'

The roll-down ripstop nylon door covering the marquee entrance flapped open. One of the constables held it aloft as Rebecca Hawley wheeled in Claire MacRae in a wheelchair, and Lomond followed close behind.

He called out, 'Because Seth wasn't AD Sullivan.'

His hands were stained with blood, and his face was wet from another downpour outside.

Jim walked away, holding his head in frustration. 'Oh, Jesus, I give up...'

Charlotte remonstrated at Ross. 'DS McNair just finished making this big thing that you had proof!'

'It *is* proof,' Lomond retorted, making his way down the centre aisle. 'There's no doubt that Seth Knox did an excellent job of pretending to be a writer called AD Sullivan. Because he sure as hell didn't write *The Shortlist*.'

Tom snapped, 'How exactly do you know that?'

Lomond turned to Ross and Donna with a glint in his eye. 'We've got Pardeep and Jason to thank for that.'

CHAPTER SEVENTY-THREE

PARDEEP WAS TRYING – and failing – to get his debit card to process via contactless on the coffee machine in the corridor outside Major Investigations. In sync with his complaints, he kicked at the machine. 'Come...on...you...piece...of...shit...'

Jason poked his head out the double doors. 'Hey, Pardeep. I'm just off the phone to that lecturer of Liz MacRae's. He says he can meet us.'

Pardeep sighed. 'Now?' The fact that Jason was clearly full of get up and go despite having been up since half five only frustrated Pardeep more.

'Yeah, right now. What's wrong?'

'I wanted a coffee, and it won't take my damn card.'

Jason looked at him like he was mad. 'We're in Glasgow. Is there a shortage of places to buy coffee around here or something?'

'Why do we need to talk to this guy anyway? We

already found out Seth was a student at Glasgow. What more do you think we're going to get?'

'I don't know,' said Jason. 'That's the point of what John told us: keep digging. The point is that you never know what you're going to find.'

'Linda told me to take ninety minutes for lunch because I caught the IP address thing on Seth's phone.'

'Yeah. And that was great.'

'I did that on three hours of sleep, man.'

'I get it. And it was great. But if John was here he would say the same thing. He would also say, great. What's the next question?'

'That's the point, Jase. There is no next question. We found out Seth went to Glasgow. That he was in a relationship with Liz. He read her book. They had a shitty breakup. She killed herself. And now he's dead. What else can we ask?'

'We need to find out if what Kate told us is the full story about Liz.'

'Why would she lie?'

'I have no idea. But until I have another source that says she's telling the truth...' he emphasised, 'we should *keep digging*.'

Pardeep was starting to get the message.

Jason said, 'Claire and William MacRae had no idea that Seth dated their daughter. Otherwise, why would they have allowed him in their lives for so long? Even if you say they were playing a long game. Biding their time before killing him in revenge for their daughter's suicide...Even if you say that, it doesn't add up that they would wait this long. Two, maybe, three years max, then surely you would strike. And remember, it was Seth who weaselled his way into William's life. Seth came to him. And William is the one who was killed first.' Jason shook his head. 'I'm telling you, I think there's more.'

Pardeep grumbled under his breath. 'God, I hate it when you're right.'

He pocketed his debit card. The only problem with having a work partner who had boundless enthusiasm and discipline for the job was that you had to keep up with their pace – not the other way around. 'Right,' said Pardeep. 'Where are we going?'

CHAPTER SEVENTY-FOUR

You could be forgiven for thinking that Lilybank Gardens, branching off from the steep hill of Great George Street was just another row of traditional terraced houses like the ones nearby. Overlooking Ashton Lane, the car horns and bustle of sound of static traffic on Byres Road were never far away. But the tree covered one-way street was actually home to many of the university's offices and teaching departments.

The university had acquired the houses one by one as they came on the market over a number of years. Now the whole street was the property of the university.

Halfway along, number 5 was home to the School of Critical Studies, where Creative Writing was taught.

The rest of the street was deserted, with no sign of activity inside or out. But at number 5, Dr Ken Dixon was stuffing a sleeping bag away on an old leather couch in his office. Through the front window looking onto the street,

Pardeep and Jason could hear muffled shouting on the phone.

'Honey, I promise,' Ken yelled, 'nothing happened with her. I swear!' He caught sight of the two detectives walking up the narrow front garden path. He said in a panic, 'Honey, I've got to go...'

He answered the buzzer once Pardeep and Jason identified themselves. He had hoped to be better prepared for the detectives' arrival, but it had been a sleepy Saturday.

After showing them into his office, a cramped little room that had once been a small bedroom in its residential days, Dixon hurried to remove a sleeping bag from the couch, then roll it into its stuff sack.

The electric toothbrush and pile of folded clothes sitting on the floor next to a holdall told its own story. It didn't take a pair of detectives to work out that Dr Dixon had spent the night there. And was preparing for possibly a few more.

'I'm sorry about the mess,' said Ken, taking a seat behind his desk. He motioned for Pardeep and Jason to sit down on the leather couch.

Jason recoiled and shuffled along a little: where he had sat down was still warm from where Ken had been sitting minutes earlier.

Ken explained, 'I meant to get back to you earlier, Detective Varma. It's been a bit of a manic morning.' He checked his watch. 'Well, afternoon, early evening, I suppose.'

When you've had the better part of a bottle of whisky the night before and slept until half eleven, it was easy to lose your sense of time.

Pardeep said, 'The reason we're here, Dr Dixon—'

'Ken. Please,' he said.

'Ken. The reason we're here is to ask a few questions about Liz MacRae. Do you remember her?'

He flashed his eyebrows up in surprise. 'There's a name I haven't heard for a while. Yes, I remember her. Awful what happened to her.'

'You must have been quite young at the time of being her lecturer.'

He paused to work it out. 'I would have been twenty-eight then. Working on my doctorate. I had published a novel that had garnered some attention two years before.'

'Oh, yeah?' said Pardeep. 'What was it called?'

He snorted ruefully. 'You won't have heard of it. Trust me. Not many people did even then. Teaching was supposed to be a temporary thing.' He gestured at his surroundings. 'Now look at me.'

Pardeep explained, 'We're trying to find out about Liz's relationship with Seth Knox. Do you remember anything about that?'

'I was aware that they were an item,' Ken replied. 'And I remember thinking that she was much too good for him.'

'You didn't like Seth?'

'He was very intense. Probably had a greater opinion of himself than what his talents would permit.'

'How so?'

Ken sniffed, aware that he was drifting into dangerous territory for a senior lecturer. 'I don't mean to speak ill of a former student. But when you leave a university in the manner in which he did, it's hard to not sound cruel when you're actually just relaying facts.'

Jason stepped in. 'In what manner did he leave the university?'

'You don't know about the plagiarism scandal?'

Jason and Pardeep exchanged a charged look of anticipation.

'We don't,' said Pardeep.

Ken said, 'I discovered that several short stories he'd written for class had been plagiarised from other published sources. He cribbed entire paragraphs from Raymond Carver short stories, swapping out the odd adjective here and there. Juvenile stuff. How he thought he could get away with it, I don't really know. What shocked me most was his attitude when I confronted him. Bear in mind that the university sets an incredibly high burden of proof when it comes to things like that. Students are no longer subordinates here to learn. They're customers buying the product of education. And lecturers like me are just sales assistants now. We used to be able to challenge students with difficult ideas. Now it's about providing safe spaces for learning. Which is well-intentioned. But the reality of a university is that if it's doing its job, it cannot be a safe space. It has to challenge your view of the world. Now a university's prime function is to keep students happy. It's simply incompatible to challenge someone and their assumptions and beliefs about the world and the arts, while making someone feel "safe". When all they want to learn is what they already agree with. But the university just wants them to pay their fees, to show up. Liz was someone who wanted to be challenged. From day one, Seth had an attitude of entitlement. That teaching staff were there to appease him, and tell him his work was great, when it wasn't. He routinely talked about becoming the next great novelist. I even overheard him once at the QMU chatting up some girl at the bar, and referred to himself as a novelist. At the time, he hadn't even had so much as a short story published. *That's* who he was.'

Jason asked, 'What happened after you confronted him about the plagiarism?'

'Oh, he had some therapist write him up as depressed and suffering from anxiety, which is the easiest way to get the university to fold over anything these days. The administration is terrified of being sued or causing a scandal. I know people who suffer from honest-to-God depression and anxiety. It's crippling. The only thing that crippled Seth Knox was his ego.'

'So he got away with it?' asked Pardeep.

'He would have,' said Ken. 'But he left voluntarily anyway. I never understood why. The day before I sat in a room with him and senior staff, debating what had happened with a short story that had ripped off Shirley Jackson's *The Lottery*. He argued vociferously about why he wanted to stay and why he should be allowed to. He even cried at one point. Three days later, he was gone.'

'What do you think caused the change?'

'Probably something to do with what happened to Liz. I mean, if your girlfriend commits suicide, that's got to break you, surely. Except, I can't imagine Seth being distraught about anyone but himself. He never cared about producing good work. He just wanted the afterglow of all the praise and attention that was the byproduct of doing great work. He was always asking me what it felt like doing interviews, attending book festivals, and going on the radio to talk about my book. Not once did he ask me a single question about the actual book. Which was funny, because he would talk to me about the book in a way that made me doubt whether he had actually read it. He used a ton of adjectives when he was blowing smoke up my arse about how good it was. But he never mentioned a single identifiable chapter or scene. He did the same with assignments. He could give me the first-paragraph-of-a-Wikipedia-article type of description. After that, it was just nothing. "Word soup" or "word salad" I used to call it. Sounded great, but there was no substance there. He was never going to make it, because he didn't have any talent. Certainly nothing close to the talent of someone like Liz.'

Jason said, 'We heard from her flatmate at that time that she had written a novel. Did you ever read it?'

Ken looked away, suddenly remembering. 'Oh yeah... what was the name of that again?'

Pardeep said, '*Shattered Glass*.'

Ken pursed his lips. 'Um...Yeah, maybe that was it. I can't quite remember the title.' His face brightened as his memory came back. 'What I *do* remember is that she was reluctant to show her work to anyone. She certainly would never show the novel to me, no matter how nicely I asked. And she certainly never showed it to anyone else in class. But I once met her dad William at a book event. He was a little drunk, and confessed to me that he had read long sections of Liz's book, even though he shouldn't have. I got the impression that he had actually stolen pages of it from her desk while visiting her.'

Jason asked, 'Was Liz really that private?'

'Oh, yes. Fiercely. Never let her mum or dad read her work. It was all I could do to get her to read her work in class for mutual critiques. She broke that rule once, I believe. She let Seth of all people read it. He, of course, was a scumbag about it. She told me he had called it "a fucking airport novel". After that, she never let anyone near that book again. That's why her dad...' Ken chuckled, 'look, he was a bestselling crime writer. He wasn't going to sit there knowing his daughter had written a murder mystery and not get his hands on it.'

Pardeep asked, 'Did he ever say anything about it?'

Ken smiled archly. 'He said that it was one of the best murder mysteries he had ever read...'

Pardeep and Jason were becoming experienced enough to tell when an interview was leading somewhere meaningful. They both had the same feeling as Ken spoke. They were both leaning forward further than they had been. As if the motion would get them to Ken's next sentence a little quicker.

Ken continued, 'It was set at this book festival – no, a crime writing festival. Yes, that's it. A group of famous crime writers end up stranded in this countryside mansion. You know, the classic locked room mystery kind of setup. Except this was more like *And Then There Were None* by Agatha Christie, where over the weekend they're all murdered one by one.'

Pardeep and Jason were aghast, and also fighting to hide the adrenaline rushing through their bodies at what they had just heard. But they couldn't react. Not yet. Not in front of Ken.

'Do you remember the name of the book?' asked Pardeep, trying to be casual.

Ken looked off to the side, struggling to get it right in his head. 'It was something like *The* something...*List*, I think. *The Bestseller List?*' Then he remembered. '*Shortlist!* Yes,' he nodded. 'I remember William particularly liking the title. Said he wished that he had thought of it first. Anyway, I always wish that I'd had a chance to read it.'

Pardeep, who had been tapping on his phone, rose from the sofa. 'Would you excuse me for a sec? I need to make a quick call.' He mouthed to Jason, 'Two minutes.'

Jason was beside himself at the thought of having to sit quietly on the sofa for two minutes after hearing such a bombshell. Fortunately, after a little small talk, Pardeep soon reappeared.

'Jase, we have to get back.' Pardeep said to Ken, 'Dr Dixon, thank you so much for your time.'

Ken replied, 'Uh, sure. You're...welcome.'

Pardeep was out the door in no time, and marching down the front garden path.

Jason hurriedly followed him.

Out on the street, Pardeep had Lomond on speaker. He waved Jason to come over. Quickly.

It was obvious from Lomond's voice that he was excited about the development. Progress – big progress – always added about five decibels to his voice. He explained with urgency, 'You two need to get over to that Kate Randall again as soon as possible. Find out what really happened with that book. This changes everything!'

Once Pardeep hung up, he said, 'I suppose that's why John tells us to ask the next question.'

'Yeah,' said Jason, impressed at his colleague's willingness to admit when he was wrong.

The pair dashed back to the car.

'Come on,' said Pardeep. 'We'll shoot up Queen Margaret Drive then over Craigmaddie Road. Milngavie will be a car park at this time on a Saturday.'

Jason was happy to be running to burn off the adrenaline pumping. He said to Pardeep, 'Kate Randall's got some big questions to answer.'

CHAPTER SEVENTY-FIVE

PARDEEP AND JASON weren't nearly as deferential as last time at Kate Randall's secure entry gate.

'This is the police, Ms Randall,' said Jason. 'We need to speak to you.'

'It's late,' she replied. 'You'll need to come back tomorrow.'

Pardeep shook his head, deeply unimpressed.

Jason replied, 'Ms Randall, I think the long driveway and being hidden behind a gate has given you a false sense of security. DC Varma and I have a warrant to enter the property.' He held it up to the camera.

Seconds later, the gates opened up.

She met them on the front steps, arms folded, her body language already on the defensive.

'What's all this about?' she asked, shielding herself from the pouring rain that was thwacking down.

'*Shattered Glass*,' said Pardeep.

'Or should we say *The Shortlist*?' said Jason. 'Or maybe no book at all, seeing as Liz never let anyone read a thing of hers.'

In that moment, Kate knew that the jig was up. Her body language eased. She unfolded her arms. It was pointless fighting it any longer. If she pushed them, they would simply take her to Helen Street and interview her under caution.

'You'd better come in,' she said.

ONCE THEY WERE in her living room, Jason started by showing her the acknowledgements in *Dead Hearts* by William MacRae on his phone app. 'You, regarding William MacRae on our last visit. Quote, I never met him before. End quote. Would you care to revise that statement?'

'Not without a lawyer, no,' she replied.

Pardeep said, 'There won't be any perjury charge, Kate. You weren't under an oath when we spoke. But wasting police time? Bet on it.'

She might have been busted, but her attitude was still intact. 'You two should have talked this out before coming in here, because right now you're both playing the bad cop.'

Pardeep began, 'Kate–'

She interrupted him. 'I'll take the hit on wasting police time. I can manage for the sake of Liz.'

Jason asked, 'How was this for the sake of Liz?'

Kate paused. 'I won't say anything else until I've

spoken to Claire MacRae on the phone.' She widened her eyes to convey she was serious. 'Really. Get her on the phone. I won't say another word until it happens.'

Pardeep retreated to the hall to call Lomond. 'Boss, we've got a stumbling block here...'

CHAPTER SEVENTY-SIX

WILLIE WAS HUFFING his way along Woodlands Road in the pouring rain in search of a post office. He held a pathetically weak umbrella over his head, that was far too short for him. It was his wife's that she had left in the car. Willie didn't care. He'd take some sniggers from men in white vans and construction workers if it meant he didn't get soaked for the third time that day.

He said to Lomond down the phone, 'All of this on a hunch?'

'I don't like that word,' said Lomond. 'It's synonymous with guess. What I've got is stronger than that.'

'Oh yeah? What's that?'

'Instinct.'

'You actually think that William MacRae originally sent the whisky?'

'I do. Because it explains the other half of my theory. Just go with me on this. If I'm right, it will all make sense in the end.'

Willie thought he had found a post office when he saw a red awning ahead. But when he reached it, he found yet another cheap chicken-based takeaway store. 'Who the fuck are all these people eating chicken these days? It's everywhere around here. Nando's and KFC knockoffs. I remember the days when you could still get an actual fucking post office on its own. Now they're all buried in the arse end of a newsagent...'

Lomond remarked, 'If you've been this cheery the whole time since we've been gone, then I'm glad we're at opposite ends of the country.'

'Hang on,' said Willie. 'There's a Mail Boxes shop here.'

'So there is,' said Lomond. 'Next to the garage with the world's tiniest Sainsbury's inside.'

'Aye, that's it.'

'Right. I've got Pardeep and Jason on hold. Call me when you know something.'

Willie found a queue of ten people when he went in. A miniature United Nations of locals, students, and immigrants, all carrying multiple parcels and looking like they were going to take forever.

A single harassed employee with a name badge reading 'Kyle' manned the till, flapping about under the pressure of heavy stares of the queue.

'Fuck this,' Willie muttered under his breath, then barged to the front. He showed his badge. 'Son, is the manager in? I need to see some CCTV footage.'

The three nearest the front of the queue groaned and shifted their weight in preparation of an even longer wait time.

Someone called out, 'Dude, get someone else out to help.'

The hapless Kyle replied, 'There isn't anyone else!'

Willie rapped his knuckles on the countertop. 'Hey, son. Look at me. This is serious.'

'I don't know,' Kyle said. 'Do you need to look through video files, or do you have a photo?'

'I need to watch the files,' Willie said. Then he had a thought. 'Wait a minute...' He threw his shoulder bag containing his laptop and paperwork on the investigation onto the counter. He took out a copy of *The Long Dark* and showed Kyle the author photo on the back. 'How about this guy? Maybe a week ago.'

Given the pressure of the situation and the stress he was under, Willie expected Kyle to respond with something noncommittal. I don't know. Maybe. I can't be sure...

Instead, Kyle nodded his head affirmatively. 'Yeah, he was in. He had to buy some "fragile" stickers. Said he was sending glassware.'

'Right, Kyle,' said Willie. 'I'm going to need to see the video.'

After Kyle set him up in the back, Willie scanned through the video files on a battered old desktop computer. After running through three separate days, Willie had the awful feeling that he had gone too fast and would need to rescan the files again. He didn't even understand why Lomond was so convinced that William sent the whisky to begin with. It didn't make any sense. But he knew better than to question Lomond's logic.

Willie was on the verge of giving up and trying the previous week as the current video file was racing towards the closing time for the day on the screen. Then, like a mirage, William MacRae appeared.

Willie slowed the video file to standard speed. 'Come on, come on, do it,' he said to the screen.

MacRae seemed to be having an ordinary conversation with the clerk when he reached into a tattered bag-for-life and produced a long narrow box the shape of a whisky bottle.

Willie burst out the dingy room to find Kyle. 'I need the sending address for a transaction.'

Kyle was like a burst couch after racing through a seemingly endless queue that had only just let up for the first time in ninety minutes. 'What do you need?'

He pulled up the details on his computer screen by matching up the date and time with Willie's video.

'Okay, got your address, DI Sneddon,' said Kyle. 'It was going to a Seth Knox. Care of Hathaway Publishing Mail Office.'

Willie's face went tense, his mouth curling tightly inwards on itself.

For a moment, Kyle thought that Willie had gone insanely angry about something. Then Willie's face turned to wide-eyed joy.

He let out a wild cackle of delight. 'Seth Knox at fucking Hathaway. Ya dancer, Kyle!'

After arranging for a copy to be sent to his Police Scotland email address and confirming on his phone that it had landed, Willie hurried out of the shop.

He waited for Lomond to pick up his phone at the other end. 'Come on, Johnny boy, pick up!' Willie pleaded. He paced around at the traffic lights, begging for a green man or a break in the traffic. Attempting to cross without the lights at that point of Woodlands Road was a dangerous game. But Willie couldn't wait any longer.

He ran – or as close an approximation to running as he could manage – out into the traffic with his hand held out at oncoming traffic. Just as a double-decker bus came charging towards him, Lomond picked up.

'Willie? Where are you?' Lomond asked.

Willie had to stand in profile in the middle of the road as the bus squeezed past him, and a van passed in the opposite lane, prompting a friendly response from the driver.

'Get out the fuckin' road, ya dafty!'

Lomond spoke up to be heard over the din of the shouting and traffic ambience. 'What's going on, Willie?'

'We've nailed him, John,' Willie cried. 'We've bloody nailed him.'

DONNA AND Ross watched Lomond intently as he hung up the phone. He strode out from his spot at the side of the stage where he'd got the full story of what had happened at the Mail Boxes shop.

'What do you think's going on?' asked Donna.

Ross could see Lomond's face morphing from quizzical to delight. 'Beats me. But we're about to find out.'

Tom called out, 'How much longer are we going to be stuck here, Inspector?'

'It's Chief Inspector,' Lomond replied.

Jim asked, 'What are you such a rush for, Tom? You

really think the killer is going to come running through here with a Tommy gun?'

'I just seem to be the only one worried there's a homicidal maniac on the loose.' He gestured at Lomond. 'And this guy's more than happy to leave us dangling here.'

Lomond replied, 'I won't be keeping you much longer at all. Not all of you anyway. One of you is going to be staying with me.'

Crawford asked, 'You know who did it?'

Tongue lodged into his cheek, Lomond called out to Donna and Ross in a loud voice – loud enough for everyone to hear.

'Ross, Donna. I reckon I might as well go full fucking Poirot on this one. It's a risk. But without the evidence we need, all I've got is a shot in the dark that the killer will give us some answers along the way.'

'Why would they do that?' asked Ross.

'If I'm right about who's behind this, and why they've done it, they don't care about getting away with it. In fact, they'll probably want us to know why they've done it.'

'But–'

'But why? I know, Ross. You're going to have to just trust me on this one. Can you arrange the chairs at the front of the stage here, so I can address the group with the solution to the murders of William MacRae, Seth Knox.' He then added, 'And the truth about what happened the night that Liz MacRae committed suicide.'

CHAPTER SEVENTY-SEVEN

AT THE FRONT of the marquee, the group of authors and acquaintances of William MacRae sat on foldaway chairs, eagerly awaiting the solution they had been promised.

Ross got up at the front of the stage and raised his hands. 'Ladies and gentlemen, I'd like to ask you for your cooperation one last time, while DCI Lomond makes his statement. In order to stop this descending into a free-for-all, I'm going to have to ask everyone to remain quiet until DCI Lomond has concluded.'

Lomond patted Ross on the small of his back, then took up his position front and centre of the stage. It was fairly low to the ground, meaning the group didn't have to crane their necks to see him. But the subtle added height gave him an authority that until now had often been in flux.

At a drinks reception, it was easy to forget he was there. In an unfamiliar castle surrounded by strangers at each other's throats, he had to remain in a different room to the group most of the time. But now – for one person especially – Lomond very much had everyone's full attention.

'I'll keep this as brief as possible,' Lomond began. 'The reason we are all here is because of William MacRae. Before meeting you all, it seemed that there could have been no writer more admired than William. But the more time I've spent here with you, the more secrets that have come out about how you all really felt about him. Was he a kind man? Was he a good man? It's not for me to make those judgements. But someone here this weekend did make those judgements on William. And that's why I now find myself,' he looked left and right of the stage, 'somewhere I never expected to be. Standing in front of some of the world's bestselling crime writers, and publishing professionals. Despite your celebrity, your notoriety, the element I kept coming back to in this investigation was not why did someone want to kill William. It was why did someone kill him twice? Were we dealing with two killers working independently of one another? Because it would have been perfectly possible to plant the poison in his whisky and have it delivered to his house. Only for someone else to arrive there and deliver the fatal blow to his heart.' Lomond paced from one side of the stage to another. 'Or were we dealing with one killer operating to ensure beyond all measure of doubt that William would die on Friday night?'

As he rhymed off the suspects, he counted them on his fingers.

'Was it Seth Knox, the man whose career would be destroyed by William MacRae killing off DCI Roxburgh? Or, by William threatening to expose a dangerous secret from Seth's past? Zoe Hathaway, who faced losing her publishing house's most-prized asset mere months into the job of CEO, not to mention blaming William for the death of her dad? Crawford Bell, whose publishing house went bankrupt thanks to William? Brad Carr, whose second wife had an affair with William? Charlotte Fount, whose affair with William was prematurely ended against her wishes? Rebecca Hawley, whose secret pen name was leaked to the press by William? Noel Redmond, whose TV career was derailed by William's drinking and temper. Tom Ellison, who William attempted to attack in print until Tom's lawyers stopped him. Jim Provan, who no longer has to pay William royalties on his earlier books due to similarities to the Roxburgh series. Or is it Claire MacRae, who stands to benefit financially from the house on Park Circus once William was gone?'

Everyone waited for the answer.

Jim was first to lose patience. 'Well, who was it?'

Rebecca shushed him.

Lomond shrugged in a desultory fashion. 'None of you. Technically. Sort of. You see, I was looking at this murder the wrong way from the start. Because I had been led quite masterfully to look at it as a murder.' He paused. 'Suicide. It's hung over this case since we found that photo portrait of Liz MacRae lying face-down on William's desk. Who had done it? And why? Was someone trying to draw our attention to Liz's suicide? Was it the killer? Or was it William? There could only be one answer to that. Once you accepted that answer, a lot of other things began to fall into place. It wasn't the killer who placed that photo down. That would have taken a particular care that was lacking elsewhere at the crime scene. The scene in the study was so carefully composed. Yet elsewhere in the house was evidence of impulsiveness: a bloody knife slowly trudged down a long staircase, then dropped near the front door. Why? A burner phone used to phone the police anonymously from the back lane. Why? Who made the call? No, this killer didn't turn the photo down. It had to be William.'

'What does it matter?' complained Tom.

Donna raised a hand for quiet, but Lomond waved it off.

He smiled. 'I know you're used to shorter chapters, Tom. So I'll cut to the chase. In order to understand what happened to William, we have to unravel what happened to Liz the night she died. Because that's what William wanted us to do.'

Even patient Noel's curiosity got the better of him. 'Why?' he called out. As soon as he did it, he winced and mouthed an apology to Lomond.

'It's okay, Noel,' Lomond replied. 'William wanted to finally expose someone involved in Liz's death. Someone that until very recently, had gone unpunished. We only learned in the last twenty-four hours that not only did Seth Knox attend Glasgow University at the same time as Liz MacRae, but that they were also in a relationship. What, according to those who witnessed it, was intense and tumultuous. With Liz and now Seth both dead, we can only speculate on the finer details about what happened the night she died...' He paused, almost out of respect for Liz. It had taken nine years for someone to uncover the truth. Too long, in Lomond's book. 'But on the bigger picture, I now have a fair idea of how it went down.'

CHAPTER SEVENTY-EIGHT

NINE YEARS AGO

Liz DIDN'T KNOW what else to say because she and Seth had been having the same argument for two hours now.

He was standing at her desk, peeling pages of her manuscript out of the box to remonstrate at her. 'With a few tweaks, this could be a great book, Liz!'

She was sitting up in bed, knees pulled up to her chest. 'You called it an airport novel. No, actually you called it a bloody airport novel.'

Seth looked to the ceiling in frustration. Yes, he had absolutely called it that, but he was never going to admit that. 'I just don't know why you put so much stock in what your dad thinks about books, and so little in what I think of them.'

'I don't let my dad read my stuff,' she replied. 'I don't let anyone. Apart from you. And look at what happened.'

Seth huffed, then placed the manuscript pages back down in the box. 'Is this about that girl at the QMU? I know that it was that weasel Ken Dixon who was in your ear about that. He just wants you for himself, Liz. Can't you see that? I never chatted anyone up at that bar. This is exactly the kind of thing that my friends keep warning me about you.'

Liz leaned forward in disbelief. 'Warning *you*? About *me*?'

He pointed towards the door. 'They all think you're crazy. But I'm the one who defends you, Liz. Me!'

She swung her legs down off the bed and headed for the studio kitchen. She took out a bottle of white wine from the fridge, then tossed out a packet of pills from a drawer. 'Because you love me so much, right?' she said. 'That's what made you disparage my book. When you knew how fragile I was about it. You tore it to shreds anyway.'

He held his arms out towards her and came slowly closer. 'I did not tear it to shreds. I gave you honest feedback because I knew it would make you stronger. I did that because I *love* you, Liz.'

For a moment, her expression softened. This was how it always went. She stopped listening to the actual words he was using, and heard only his tone. It sounded genuine. Remorseful. Even kind.

Then there was his face. And those eyes. You could get lost in them.

But the words...then she thought about the words.

As he reached out for her arm, she pulled hers away. 'No,' she said. 'You're completely toxic, Seth. You've been gaslighting me for months. You make me question my own memory. You always cite your friends as authorities on how and what I do. You want me to only accept your reality.

Not anymore.' She stormed towards the door then held it open. 'I want you to leave.'

Seth shook his head and scoffed with disdain. 'You really are a piece of work,' he said, gathering up his things. 'I try to help you, and this is the thanks I get.' He balled up his jacket in his hand and shoved it towards her. 'Well, good luck finding someone else who'll put up with all this sort of shit. I'm done! And good luck hawking *The Shortlist* around agents. If it ever gets published it will only be because your dad is William fucking MacRae...'

Liz pulled her hand back and slapped him.

The pair stared at each other. Both in shock.

Seth remained leaning over to one side in suspended animation, then slowly brought himself upright again. 'I'm the best thing to ever happen to you. And now this is me walking away.'

The sight of him striding down the long corridor towards the stairs prompted a sudden wave of emotion in Liz. She burst into tears and called out his name. Twice. Three times.

He didn't look back.

She was crying too hard now to run after him. Instead, she went back inside, slamming the door behind her. She put her hands to her face and cried harder than she had ever cried before.

It amazed her that you could feel so lonely and still be breathing. Loneliness like that should have meant that you simply expired on the spot.

The one thing that kept her going through her whole depression was the idea of being a writer. Of somehow creating something out of all the darkness, all of the torment she had felt in her young life. Then she handed it all off to her characters. It helped spread the load. Share the burden of being twenty-one, suicidally depressed, and alive all at the same time.

She couldn't do much about the first part. But she could certainly do something about the last part.

It had been in her head for a long time – about how to do it. She had visited websites, Reddit forums, Facebook groups, where there was open discussion about methodology, technique, dosages. Everything necessary to get the job done.

The main thing was that she wanted it to be over. And to not hurt. After all, hurt was what had got her there.

The solution she had decided on was pills and alcohol to take the edge off, and to give her the confidence to go through with it. Liz couldn't imagine killing herself while sober. She needed a little help to get over the line.

Months of Seth's gaslighting and abuse helped. As did her broken relationship with her parents.

The one person she felt bad for was Kate. She would have to cope with finding the body.

———

LIZ RAN the bath and put on the music she wanted to hear one last time. Henryk Górecki's Symphony No. 3. Otherwise known as the Symphony of Sorrowful Songs. She had originally planned on listening to the full piece on repeat, but landed on just the second movement.

The libretto for the second movement was taken from a prayer to the Virgin Mary inscribed by an eighteen-year-old

Polish girl on a Gestapo prison wall. Gorecki had visited the prison and found the wall screaming with inscriptions from people begging to be saved, to be set free. Then here was this teenager, who didn't despair. Didn't cry or demand revenge. She didn't think about herself. She thought only of the sorrow her mother would feel.

There was a courage there that astonished Liz. Mostly because she knew she would never be capable of such clarity or bravery.

She put the second movement on repeat, then climbed into the bath. She pulled the sack full of books up into the bath with her. Then she downed the last of the pills and the wine – being careful not to drink so much that she would throw everything up. She had the internet to thank for that nugget of wisdom.

The flat was quiet now. Peaceful. Just the music and the gentle sound of lapping bathwater.

She wondered if anyone would even notice the song she had chosen. Would the person who found her body simply switch her phone off before they registered what song she had played out her final moments to?

The manuscript box file was left on her desk with a note on it.

"TELL MUM AND DAD I'M SORRY. I WANTED TO BE BETTER. TELL DAD NOT TO BLAME HIMSELF. IT'S MY FAULT. ALL OF IT. TELL HIM I TOOK HIS BOOKS TO BED WITH ME ONE LAST TIME. THIS WAY WE'LL ALWAYS BE TOGETHER. I'VE LEFT MY BOOK HERE. IT'S THE ONLY COPY. DO WITH IT WHAT YOU WILL. GOODNIGHT. GOODBYE. – IN CASE ANYONE'S WONDERING

WHY: THINGS JUST WENT WRONG TOO MANY
TIMES."

She had pointed her desk lamp on the box and dimmed
the lights elsewhere. She knew that the book was probably
special, and maybe even could have been a success. But it
was too late for thoughts of success to save her. There was
no choice now in Liz's eyes.

Suicide was no more a choice than a trapped person in
a burning high-rise will eventually, inevitably choose to
jump from the window. The fear of falling and hitting the
ground is just as big as for anyone else standing on the
pavement. The difference is that in the burning building
scenario, there is the addition of fear. Because the fire is
coming to get them too. When confronted with the fear of
both falling from a great height, and a terrible fire, falling
becomes the lesser of two evils. No one else can understand
it unless you're there with them, feeling the heat of the
flames getting closer by the minute. The terror of falling is
nothing, when those flames come to find you.

CHAPTER SEVENTY-NINE

NINE YEARS AGO

Liz had left the door unlocked. She knew how Kate could get when she had been out drinking. But it wasn't Kate that came back first.

Seth knocked on the door tentatively at first. 'Liz? You there?'

There had been time for a few drinks. Enough to take the edge off and just try the door. When it opened, he followed the sound of the music coming from the bathroom.

Upon opening the door, he was met with a ghastly sight: Liz was submerged in the bathtub, and the water had turned a deep shade of red. Her head was intentionally held underwater, and the weight of a sack of books on her chest prevented her from resurfacing. To ensure her demise, Liz had also slashed her arms from the inside with a knife.

Killed twice, had been her last thought.

Something that would occur to her dad in the coming days.

Seth gagged and turned around quickly. He had never seen a dead body before. He knew without touching her that she was already gone. The paleness of her skin. The stillness of the bathwater.

He retched, though nothing came up.

He had to get out of that room as fast as possible. He shut the bathroom door behind him and tried to steady his breathing.

The lighting pulled his attention towards the manuscript box file. And the letter next to it. Not the suicide note.

The letter marked 'To Seth.'

He read it, of course. It laid out in stark terms how Liz had felt about their relationship, and his role in her demise.

For anyone walking in off the street, there would be little room for interpretation in who to blame. It wasn't even a choice.

He folded up the letter and put it in his pocket.

Then his eye was drawn to the manuscript. He couldn't help it. The lighting had made it the focal point of the entire room.

The decision to take it happened quickly. The justification could come later. What mattered more in the immediate was the calculation that he could get away with taking it.

Liz herself had said that no one else had read it. She certainly had never read any of it in class.

He didn't know yet what he might do with it. But the overriding emotion he felt was that he was somehow entitled to have it. That no one else would care for it or tend to it the way he would. William would only butcher it, or hide it away in a desk somewhere like an urn of ashes.

He grabbed a carrier bag from the kitchen and slid the box file into it. Then he stood at the inside of the front door and did a final visual check of the room. What had he touched? What had he moved?

He pulled his hand up his jacket sleeve to turn the door handle, using the same motion to wipe it down – though he figured that if his prints remained anywhere, it wouldn't matter greatly. He had been her boyfriend after all.

As far as grief went, he didn't feel much of anything. What he did feel, though, was panic, when he saw Kate Randall exit the lift doors and come walking towards him.

It just wasn't necessarily straight towards him. It was bouncing off one wall and then the other. Then a brief pause. Then a stagger forwards again.

She was absolutely off her face.

He kept his head down and barrelled straight past her. She only took in the merest of glances. Barely enough to register that a somewhat human shape had stomped quickly past. The fact that he was carrying a bag with a box file in it would go unnoticed.

Seth waited by the lift doors, hearing Kate take five attempts to get her key into the door before realising it was unlocked.

He got into the lift, his heart pounding now. What the hell had he done? What was he doing? He couldn't just steal Liz's book, could he? Why didn't he sound the alarm? What if Liz was still alive, and those five minutes of him being there were her last chance to survive?

He couldn't answer any of those questions. What he did know was that there was no going back. There was no way of explaining that he had been in the flat, taken the book, and was now returning it, and hadn't noticed the music playing and Liz lying dead in the bath.

There was no going back.

He reached into the bag for the suicide note. What really stood out was Liz telling her dad she forgave him. Seth wasn't a monster – he didn't want to deny William the knowledge of what Liz really thought of him in those final moments. It was simply bad luck for William. Seth figured what William didn't know couldn't hurt him.

How wrong he was about that.

As the lift doors started to close, Seth heard Kate scream.

Again and again.

Then it grew faint as the lift doors closed fully.

It was a scream that would haunt him for the rest of his days.

CHAPTER EIGHTY

As was to be expected, Claire MacRae was in tears by the end of Lomond's summary. Rebecca put her arm around her for comfort.

Lomond's voice was gentler now. More sombre. What he had to say next was directed at Zoe. 'When you announced Liz as the author of *The Shortlist*, you thought it was a lie. But you had actually stumbled across a grain of truth: Liz wrote the book, but AD Sullivan was Seth.'

Jim sighed as the truth was finally revealed. '*Liz MacRae* wrote that book?'

'Of course,' said Brad, turning to Claire. 'I wondered why you reacted so angrily when I criticised it last night. You were defending it. Your own daughter's book.'

Lomond said, 'It was Liz's book, but AD Sullivan was Seth's invention. A mask to hide his theft behind. A man who, as my colleagues back in Glasgow have been discovering, had no real talent of his own. Only for correcting or rearranging others' work. He thought he was in the clear, because he couldn't exactly get Liz's book published under an assumed name if William MacRae was going to recognise it the moment he found out the plot, let alone read any of the prose. Liz's guarantee had been an honestly held one. She didn't know that William had secretly read the book. At least parts of it. He confided in Liz's Creative Writing lecturer that he had done so. Without knowing that, little else of what we have would make sense.' Lomond paused for a sip of water. 'I can only imagine what must have been going through William's head when he read the opening pages of *The Shortlist* proof, sent to him by Zoe.'

Claire glared at her. 'Tell me you didn't know that Seth was behind AD Sullivan.'

Zoe shook her head. 'Claire, I promise you. I didn't know a thing. All I ever did was pick up what my dad had signed off on.'

Lomond said to Zoe, 'Seth was always your dad's golden boy. Wasn't he? He plucked him out of obscurity and gave him a senior position. When Seth brought the book to him, he treated it as if a major writer had given it to him. That's how an otherwise anonymous writer got a manuscript in the hands of one of the most powerful publishing CEOs in the world. It came from one of his own senior editing staff.'

As one of the few non-writers in the room, and having been out of the publishing game for a while, Crawford asked, 'Why didn't Seth just submit the book to other publishers? It was clearly good enough to be picked up.'

Ross answered, 'Because his reputation was in the toilet. He had burned his bridges with Cargo. And after that word of that got out, he had a black mark against his name in the trade.'

Lomond added, 'That's why anonymity was so vital to Seth's plan. The minute his name was put out there as the real AD Sullivan, the blowback would be huge.'

Donna said, 'He had been taken to task during his time at Cargo for taking lots of unaccounted-for leave. Given the timing of that, it's likely he was at home working on the manuscript of *The Shortlist*.'

'Yep,' Lomond agreed. 'He had waited more than long enough to know that he was in the clear. Sure, William asked the police about what happened to the manuscript, but Seth never heard about that. It took him thirteen years before deciding the time was right. The market was shifting to cosy crime and whodunit mysteries. Noel's success last year was likely the catalyst. Murder mysteries bring comfort at times of crisis or uncertainty. Because they provide closure. And make sure the culprit doesn't get away with it.'

Jim, getting used to being unofficial group spokesperson, called out, 'Speaking of which, what about William's killer?'

'It was obviously Seth,' said Charlotte.

'It had to be,' said Brad. 'He found out that William knew he had stolen the manuscript.'

'How?' asked Lomond.

There was silence.

'Seriously,' Lomond went on. 'How could Seth have known that?'

Noel suggested, 'What about when the proofs were

sent out. Seth would have found out that William had been sent one.'

'Yes,' said Lomond. 'For a book that Seth thought no one else in the world had read. As far as he was concerned, *The Shortlist* would be a completely unknown quantity to William.'

'Okay,' said Tom. 'Say William reads the proof, and he *does* recognise it as Liz's book. What does he do that gets him killed?'

'Oh, that's simple,' said Lomond. He turned to his left, towards Claire MacRae in the wheelchair. 'He called *you*, Claire.'

She was weak. But that wasn't why she didn't argue.

Everyone turned to her, their estimations of her switching wildly around.

Doing their best to hide the transaction, Brad quietly slipped Jim a twenty-pound note.

Horrified, Zoe said, 'You killed William?'

Claire turned her head towards the ceiling and shut her eyes. It was going to feel like the weight of the world was leaving her shoulders. 'I did.' Tears filled her eyes. Enough that she had to wipe them away. 'I killed William.'

Lomond turned his head slightly, indicating doubt. 'Oh, that's only a fraction of the story. Correct me if I'm wrong, Claire. Because this is the part where speculation defeats me. What I do know for sure is that my guys in Glasgow are currently accessing you and William's phone records for the week prior to his death. I'm betting somewhere in there was a very long conversation, or an arrangement to meet face to face.'

Claire steadied herself. 'We met face to face. William

called me at first, but he said that what he had to tell me he couldn't do over the phone. We met at his bench in Kelvingrove. That was when he told me what he was going to do.'

'I'll need you to fill in the blanks,' said Lomond. 'Provided you're open to a confession.'

'The plan was never to get away with it,' said Claire. 'Not totally. The plan was to get away with it just long enough to get rid of Seth.'

'Wait,' said Noel. 'She killed Seth as well?'

Tom asked, 'Why would you kill William *and* Seth?'

'It's complicated,' Claire replied.

Keeping his hand below the level of his seat, Jim made a gimme gesture with his hand to Brad.

With a grumble, Brad took the twenty out of his pocket and handed it back to Jim.

Lomond peered at Claire. 'Try us.'

CHAPTER EIGHTY-ONE

Claire explained, 'I can't take credit for much of it. It was William's plan. He had it all figured out.'

'The catalyst must have been *The Shortlist*,' Lomond said.

'Of course,' she replied. 'Without William reading that book, none of this would have happened. Seth never knew anyone else had read the book. So when he stole it and plenty of time had passed, he thought he was in the clear. He might have been an egomaniac, and borderline sociopathic liar, but he was a very decent editor – and he knew what he had. Even back in university days. Something instinctually told him that he should take it. It certainly wasn't for any sentimental reasons. As everything he did in his life, he did it to get ahead. Because he knew that he wasn't capable of writing something like that himself.

'The fatal flaw was that William had read the book. He pulled his hair out for months trying to convince Liz to let him read even a chapter or two. He managed to find out from her that she was done with it for a while, so he knew he could safely take it for a few days without her realising. He told me that he stole it while she went to the bathroom. He hated himself for doing it, but it was the writer in him: he couldn't stand that his daughter had written a book – a murder mystery no less – and she wouldn't let him read it.'

Lomond said, 'Kate Randall told my colleagues that William was hard on her. I expect he never admitted to Liz what he did.'

'He couldn't,' said Claire. 'William read some of her short stories, and after he gave her notes, she vowed to never let him see anything else of hers ever again. If only she had known that the book he read was one of the best mysteries he had ever read – not just by a debut author, but by anyone. He did everything he could to encourage her to take the book out and submit it to agents – any way he could think of telling her the book was great without admitting he had secretly read it. But she was broken. By Seth. By the criticism and attention that she knew would come her way. She was savvy. She understood that there would be enough cynical fascination in a mystery written by William MacRae's daughter to at least find the book a publisher. From there, the press would do what they have always done to children of successful writers: savage them. It took Martin Amis decades to step out of the shadows of Kingsley Amis. There isn't much of a history in literature of famous parent-child novelists. The assumption would always be that Liz only got published because of William. He could never turn her around on it. Then once she died and the manuscript went missing, William was helpless. Neither William nor I even knew there was a boyfriend on the scene at that time. Only Kate knew about that, and she had no idea that the manuscript had disappeared. The fact that Kate couldn't identify with any certainty who had passed her in the corridor the night Liz died, became immaterial. Liz had committed suicide. That was it. The book was gone. And so was Liz. It was over. Until William read *The Shortlist* in proof.'

Lomond asked, 'But at some point you must have brought Kate into this. Because when we first spoke, you knew that Liz had been seeing a boyfriend around the time of her death. Only Kate could have told you that.'

'That was William's idea,' said Claire. 'After he read the AD Sullivan proof, he knew that someone somewhere had stolen Liz's manuscript. What William didn't know yet was that it had been Seth. So he tracked down Kate, who told him about a boyfriend. Seth Knox. The moment he heard the name, all the pieces fell into place about what had happened. And who the mystery person behind AD Sullivan must have been. After that, it was about forming a plan.'

'The Kelvingrove meeting,' said Lomond.

Claire shook her head in amazement. 'It all happened so fast. But then it had to. William made it clear that we didn't have a choice. There was a rapidly closing window that we had to operate in. So when he told me the plan, he didn't hold back.'

'What was the plan?' asked Lomond.

'The first thing was to get Seth to walk into the building. He couldn't be framed for William's murder otherwise. Knowing what William did about Seth, he told him the one thing that he knew would guarantee to get him to show up.

First of all, he killed off Roxburgh. Which broke his heart as much as losing a true friend. But the nature of the plan was predicated on the assumption that William wouldn't be around much longer. He didn't care about leaving Roxburgh alive for someone else to continue with. That was part of the bargain that he made. Then he had to add a cherry on top. He didn't just tell Seth that he knew who Sullivan really was. He was smarter than that. Saying that could scare Seth off completely. Instead, he told him something to intrigue him. Tantalise him. The only thing better than telling Seth he knew Sullivan's identity, was telling Seth that he knew it *wasn't* him! How could Seth resist that? Add in Seth's professional obligation to show up to convince his author not to kill off one of the most profitable characters in crime fiction history, and William got what he really needed.' Claire stabbed a finger on the armrest of the wheelchair for emphasis. 'To *make sure* Seth Knox walked into that building.'

Lomond said, 'What happened *after* that, only Seth, William, and you know about.'

Claire smiled, looking into her hands. A picture of relief. Of resignation to the inevitable. 'Say what you want about William. But he knew how to put a good murder together. Even his own.'

CHAPTER EIGHTY-TWO

EIGHT DAYS AGO

THEY MET at William's favourite bench in Kelvingrove Park, next to the Lord Roberts Monument. William was sitting down already, hands stuffed into the pockets of a long woollen overcoat. He had on a tweed flat cap to keep the freezing air off his head.

There was a light dusting of snow on the ground already, and it was starting to fall again.

Claire came similarly wrapped up, with a cashmere scarf doubled around her neck.

William stood up when she arrived and gave her a hug. 'How are you feeling?'

'Still dying,' she replied. 'You know, the usual.'

William couldn't believe her fortitude in the face of what she was dealing with. Four months to live, and here she was cracking jokes about it.

She sat down and held her hands to stop them trembling. 'Billy, I'm really worried. Will you tell me what all this is about?'

He sat down next to her and looked out over the park, towards the grey clouds that had covered the sky. He said, 'I'm sorry about the cloak and dagger, but this couldn't wait. And it couldn't be done over the phone.'

'Whatever it is, I promise you, I'm here. We can deal with it.'

'I'm glad to hear you say that, because I need to ask something of you, and you're not going to like it.' He gave a light chuckle. 'Maybe you will.'

'Anything,' she assured him.

'I need you to kill me,' he replied.

The sentence seemed to hang in mid air for a few moments, while Claire figured out how she was supposed to react. 'Is this a joke? All of this, for a stupid bloody joke, Billy?'

'It's no joke,' he replied, stony-faced. He couldn't look at her. Not yet. 'There's this book coming out, you see. A week ago I was sent a proof copy. I didn't think much of it, apart from the title. It's called *The Shortlist*.'

Claire didn't recognise it.

'It's the same as Liz's book.'

'I'm sure it's just coincidence. In any case, you can't copyright or protect book titles.'

'I know, but it's the same book, Claire. The text. I've read it. What's going to be one of Hathaway's biggest books of the year is actually Liz's. And someone is publishing it under a pen name.'

Claire was dumbfounded. 'How can that be possible?'

'Someone stole Liz's manuscript the night she died. Remember? I kept getting the lawyer to go back and find it. It was stolen. And I know who did it.'

'Who?'

'It was Seth. He went to university with Liz. They were an item, if you can believe that.'

'But that's crazy,' said Claire. 'Liz would have told us.'

'She didn't. I spoke to Kate, her flatmate. She told me that she was seeing someone called Seth Knox. The man she described is the same Seth we know, Claire. He wormed his way into my sphere at Hathaway. Trying to get close. To check how much I knew. He's waited all of this time. And now it's getting published under a pen name.'

'We have to stop it!'

'We can't,' William assured her. 'We can't prove a thing.'

Explaining the details of exactly why that was the case, took him a while. Eventually, Claire agreed that it was indeed impossible.

'I can't let him get away with it,' said William. 'He's the reason she...' He pressed his lips firmly together, hesitating at the mere thought of Liz's death. 'He's the reason she's not here anymore. She died blaming me, too.'

'You don't know that, Billy. Don't do that to yourself again.'

He snapped, 'It wasn't a bag full of your books that she used to weigh herself down, Claire!'

'You don't know what she meant by that.'

'Of course I do. She was a smart girl. It was a metaphor. Of the weight I put on her with my criticism. My expectations. I won't let her death be in vain.' He waved a finger in front of him. 'This is something I can do for her. It might be too little, but it's not too late. All sins are eventually revealed.'

'What are you talking about?' asked Claire.

'Seth's going to be arrested for murder.'

Claire sighed. 'Billy, Liz committed suicide. The police have–'

'I'm not talking about Liz. I'm talking about me.'

She shook her head in confusion.

He said, 'I'm going to frame him for my murder.'

'*Your* murder? And who's going to murder you?'

He didn't reply.

She could tell just from his face what the answer was. 'No,' she said, getting to her feet. She backed away from the bench. 'No way. This is insane. You've lost your mind. You're angry about Liz, I understand that. But this isn't the way you fix it. You can't fix it, Billy. It's too late.'

'It's not,' he retorted. He got to his feet too, beseeching her. 'But it will be soon. Once this book comes out, Seth could disappear forever. We might only have one chance to do this. Let me do this, please.'

'Billy, I'm not going to...' She looked all around to check no one was there. Still, she lowered her voice. 'I'm not going to kill you. Get a bloody grip of yourself.'

'Calm down. You won't actually be killing me,' he explained. He looked down into his hands again.

This time, Claire grabbed them and forced him to look at her. 'Hey,' she said. 'Talk to me.'

'We lost everything when we lost Liz. We lost each other. We didn't stand a chance after that. Everyone gave us a free pass when we told people we were separating. When you lose a child...how do you come back from that? Everyone understood. But I gave up too easily. I gave up on us, and I'm sorry about that. I already lost Liz. I'm going to lose you before the end of the year. Instead of me sitting here on my own, powerless, let me do something. One last act of love in Liz's name. The boldest thing that any parent can do for their child: sacrifice themselves.'

Claire's head was spinning. William seemed so sure about it all, but he had been grappling with the prospect for days. Claire hadn't had nearly as much time.

William said, 'Think about it: Seth pays for the lives he's destroyed. And Liz is given her book back. You're the last piece of my life, Claire. I don't want to just go on and on without you.'

She couldn't believe that she was actually entertaining his idea. 'But I could never hurt you, Billy. How do you expect me to kill you?'

'You won't be,' he said. 'Not really.' He fetched a boxed bottle of Lagavulin by the bench and brought it over. 'I'm going to poison myself. As part of the framing device. I'll make it look like Seth sent it to me. And for added effect, I'll make it so that he's the one who finds my body. But you're going to have to do something for me. It will need to look convincing. Like a real murder. That means the weapon can't just be left at my side, otherwise the police might speculate that I did it myself. If I die of a knife wound upstairs, and the weapon is found downstairs, and there's no evidence of my body having been moved, then it could never have been self-inflicted. If there's any suspicion it might have been self-inflicted then Seth might walk.'

'Billy, I can't stab you!'

'You don't have to. I have a plan. But we also need a back-up.'

'What sort of back-up?'

'If Seth is found at the scene, he'll for sure come under suspicion. But we can't frame the forensics. It's too hard. We need to make sure Seth doesn't get away with it.'

'How?'

'The only way we can.'

'You want me to kill Seth?'

William's emotions came flooding out now. He needed Claire to get onboard with the final part, or everything before it might disintegrate. 'He stole our daughter, Claire. Our little girl. She had her whole life ahead of her. And he poisoned her. Poisoned her against life. Against joy. Against finding a way out of her depression. He only drove her deeper into it. And then he stole the one legacy she left in this world.' There was nothing else for it. He had to raise the stakes on Claire. 'If you can't do this, I'll understand. But if you don't, then I'll simply get a gun and kill Seth myself. I'll do it in broad daylight, I don't care. This is the ideal solution where everything Seth did is exposed. But if I can't have that, then I'll accept the lesser option. He doesn't get to walk the earth while Liz can't. As a dad, I simply won't allow it.'

Claire took a long breath and exhaled towards the sky. She knew that it was pointless debating with him. He had made up his mind. Now she had to decide if she could stand blithely by while he got himself arrested for murder.

'You won't have to do it alone,' he promised her. 'I've already spoken to Rebecca. She's agreed to help us.'

Claire exclaimed, 'You've told Rebecca Hawley about this?'

'AD Sullivan is holding an event at Lochinver Book Festival in a little over a week, Claire. Rebecca owns Inver

Castle. It's like the planets have aligned on this for us. It's perfect. Rebecca's going to invite all the speakers for my event to the castle for the night. By then, the police will have wound everyone so tight in suspecting the killer is among the group, you'll need to get Seth to trust you.'

'How?' asked Claire.

'Appeal to his vanity. Invite him to your room. Jab him with a sedative that knocks him out. Then you dispatch him the same way that Liz died. He'll already be drugged. Then you weigh him down in a bath with a bag full of hard-back copies of *The Shortlist*. Then cut the arteries in his arms.' His voice cracked. 'Just like Liz did.'

Claire was staggered at how forensically William had thought it all through. She said, 'Billy, even if Seth is drugged, I'm not strong enough to carry him into a bath.'

'You don't need to be,' he said. 'Rebecca's going to help you. No doubt there will be a proposal to search the property at some point the next morning once Seth is confirmed as missing. You and Rebecca will have to do your best to dissuade people. You'll need to keep the body hidden somewhere until the AD Sullivan event the next day. The police won't want to miss that. You'll need to find an excuse to stay behind at Inver Castle to prepare the scene, so that it looks just like how Liz was found.'

'But the police will realise Seth's been killed in a similar fashion to how Liz died. I'll be a prime suspect.'

'That's the point, Claire. If we're to draw the police's attention to Seth's crimes, we have to make the parallels obvious. We should go all the way. Even down to playing the same music as when Liz was found. The Górecki symphony. If you can get away with it, or maintain some deniability, then great. But the priority is ensuring Seth's crimes are exposed. We get to avenge Liz's death in the most poetic way possible. It will be like Seth is stuck inside Liz's own book. I want him to feel terror like Liz must have felt that night. Of knowing that you don't have long left. I want to hurt him. I want him to suffer. And I won't stop until it happens.'

Claire started to sob. It was enough that she had to deal with her own terminal illness. Now William was laying all of this on top of it. 'I need some time,' she pleaded.

'That's the one thing we don't have, Claire. I'm sorry. I need to know if you'll do this with me. For us. For Liz.'

CHAPTER EIGHTY-THREE

Lomond said to Claire, 'The voicemail was a nice touch.'

'That was mine,' she said.

'I must say I fell for it hook, line, and sinker. Just as I was supposed to.'

'William said that the police would need a helping hand at the start. A bit like a hook at the start of his books.'

Lomond looked to Rebecca, standing stoically by Claire's side. 'Little of this seems to be shocking you, Ms Hawley,' said Lomond.

Rebecca said nothing. She reached down over Claire's shoulder and grabbed her hand to console her.

'Without you,' Lomond said, 'the final part of this plan would have been next to impossible. Claire needed someone she could rely on. Someone who would do anything for William.'

Charlotte turned to Rebecca, mystified. 'But you hated

William. He leaked your name to the press. Everyone knows it!'

Lomond asked Rebecca, 'And that was exactly what you needed him to do, wasn't it?'

'I don't know what you mean.' She said it in such a way that declared that she absolutely *did* know what he meant.

'You would have done anything for the man who backed you when no one else would. Without William and Liz, the Sally Stroud series becomes just another pulped print run of kids paperbacks. He also came through when you needed your name leaked to the press as the author behind the Robin Balfour crime series.'

'We *did* go over this, Chief Inspector,' said Rebecca. 'I wanted anonymity more than anything.'

Unconvinced, he said, 'Yeah...not so much. The sort of author who has sold the number of books you have, yet still knows weekly sales numbers rounded to the nearest five hundred, cares plenty about popularity. I think when you started you wanted the anonymity. But it got boring after a while. Too quiet. You wrote a book you were proud of. You wanted it in the hands of as many people as possible. That's only natural. The only thing worse than the anonymity was having to live silently with it. Then you had an idea. If you could get someone else to leak your name then you'd have the best of both worlds: the freedom to write a new series, and the satisfaction of watching it become the sort of success that you had become accustomed to. You might hate being RJ Hawley. But you still *need* to be RJ Hawley.'

The last part landed like a gut punch on Rebecca. It was hard to hear someone state so baldly what she could barely admit to herself.

'What I don't understand,' Brad said to Claire, 'is why you're giving all of this away? Am I alone in thinking I haven't heard a single piece of evidence so far that hasn't come directly from you?'

Claire answered, 'Brad, I'll be dead by summer. I'd sooner spend a few months in custody than live in freedom, and not have the world know what Seth stole from me. And from William. And Liz.'

Noel asked, 'Why not just go to the police? Have Seth arrested?'

'Have you even read a Roxburgh book, Noel?' she replied. 'Roxburgh *is* William. Justice doesn't exist in his world. Only right and wrong, with Roxburgh in the middle. Who was going to testify that Seth was at the flat that night and stole the manuscript? A drunken twenty-something who needed two attempts at giving her name to the police that night? Seth could always say that Liz had simply given him the manuscript. It would never make it past the CPS.' She checked with Lomond.

He nodded. 'It's true.'

'In any case, what we decided we wanted was real justice. And William, bless him, figured out the most poetic way to do it. He used Liz's own book to destroy Seth once and for all. Frame him for a murder, then set him up for a murder of his own in the setting of Liz's own story. What could be more appropriate than that? I'm dying anyway. William was the one willing to make the sacrifice. My only regret was that I couldn't be there to see Seth's face when he realised what William had done.'

Lomond explained, 'The background had been fleshed

out. The details honed and refined. The help had been organised. The stage was set. On Friday night, Seth walked into that house on Park Circus not knowing that it would be the beginning of his end.'

CHAPTER EIGHTY-FOUR

FRIDAY

WILLIAM MACRAE TOOK up his usual spot on the bench at the Lord Roberts Monument. He cried gentle tears at the thought of killing off Roxburgh the previous night. It was out of his hands now. The manuscript had been with Seth for hours now. It was only a matter of time before he would have to confront it.

He took out a silver hip flask with the poisoned Lagavulin, and took a long swig. It stung the back of his throat. Harsher than usual. 'Well, Billy,' he said. 'I guess it's over.'

He had already taken more than enough of the poison to be fatal. All that was up in the air was the timing when it would take full effect. The dosage he had worked out from his 19th Century encyclopedia of poisons in his library suggested his body would go into cardiovascular shock in about twelve hours' time.

Which was fine. He would be long dead by then anyway.

He took one last look at the city he loved. God, he was going to miss it. But for Liz's sake it would be worth it. He had to be strong now and see it through. Liz's legacy was dependent on it.

HIS FINAL MINUTES WERE SOMBRE. Quiet. It wasn't particularly arty or impressive, but one of his favourite films was *A Shot at Glory*, about a second-tier football team fighting for survival. It was a little sentimental, but what William liked most about it was the soundtrack by Mark Knopfler. The end of the film used a version of "Wild Mountain Thyme", featuring a gentle mix of whistle, piano accordion, and Knopfler's trademark fingerpicking on acoustic guitar.

His mum and her sisters used to sing it every Christmas when it came time to do a tune. His dad's was "Peggy Gordon". But it was "Wild Mountain Thyme" that always hit him the hardest. Maybe it was the three-way harmony they sang, and the memory of losing his mother before he was a teenager, that kept the song close to his heart all those years.

Now, as he sat in his leather chair, surrounded by decades' worth of books that he had dedicated his life to, it was now the photograph of his daughter Liz that consumed him. Everything else fell away into the background.

'I'm sorry I didn't do more, Liz,' he cried, wiping tears from his eyes. 'I should have done more.'

He could have said so much more. But he wanted to just sit and listen to the song. He thought about his mother.

About Claire. About the weight of what he was about to do. And he felt a sense of calm come over him.

He lifted the knife up off the desk in front of him. He had one last dram. Then he turned the photo of Liz down onto the desk.

'For you, sweetheart,' he said tearfully. He lay his hand on the back of the photo for a moment. Then he stood up and took his position.

He called out, 'I'm ready, Claire.'

She came in tentatively. She was crying as well.

William took her by the hand and told her, 'Hey, it's okay. It's okay.'

She threw her arms around him. 'I don't want you to do it. Don't leave me. I've changed my mind.'

William pursed his lips. He took her hand and squeezed it. He didn't have any words left. There had been enough of those for one lifetime.

She stepped back and turned away, shutting her eyes tightly.

She was relieved that William had put music on. She did her best to focus on "Wild Mountain Thyme", and how beautiful a composition it was.

Behind her, William held the knife with both hands and pointed it straight towards his heart. He said, 'Be strong, Claire.'

He shut his eyes and let himself fall forward. When his hands hit the floor, the full weight of his body forced the knife straight into his heart. For the briefest flash, William's entire body lit up in agony. He felt nerve endings he never knew were in his body. His brain was on fire, every last synapse firing like nuclear explosions.

But as quickly as the pain appeared, it faded to black.

Claire recoiled at the groan William emitted upon impact. She lowered her hands that were covering her face. She didn't want to turn around, but for the plan to work she would have to do a great deal more than that.

She cried harder now at the sight of William's lifeless body. Blood was pouring out of his chest, creeping out across the floor.

It was her job to lift him enough to remove the knife – which was every bit as hard as William had warned her it would be. Once it was out, she touched the back his head, then she kissed it.

'Liz would be so proud,' she sobbed. 'I'm so proud.'

She laid out the copy of *The Shortlist* as planned, and took a finger of William's blood. She wrote on the book, "*JUSTICE*".

She went to the hi-fi and switched off the CD, as William had asked her to do. He didn't want the name of the song or the artist noted in any police report. It was between him and Liz and Claire, as far as he was concerned.

Claire could only take slow steps down the stairs, still covering her mouth with her free hand. She kept trying to tell herself what it was all for. But it didn't lighten the load of what she was carrying.

She placed the knife on the hall floor as planned. Then she slipped out the back door to the gardens, where she took out a burner phone that William had purchased online a few days earlier.

It took everything she had to control her emotions to

make the 999 call. It was vital that they understood what she was saying, so she could flee as quickly as possible.

Once the call had been made, she tossed the phone in the lane behind William's building. The home they had once shared. All three of them.

Now Claire had to return to Hotel Devonshire Gardens and act like nothing had happened.

Seth would be pulling up in his taxi in no time. And that would only be the start of what was to come.

WHEN SETH FOUND THE BODY, he discovered a note that Claire had left on top of William's body. A note that the police would never discover.

"*I KNOW WHAT YOU DID, SETH. AND NOW YOU'RE GOING TO PAY. WITH LOVE FROM LIZ.*"

William had wanted Seth to know that he had arranged all of this. To know that he was being framed. It would make it so much more satisfying.

When Seth read it with shaking hands, he said, 'You fucking clever bastard, William. Well played.' He pocketed the note, then quickly set to work on William's computer.

He found the most recent file of William's manuscript, and reverted it to the previous version where Roxburgh had survived. Then he emailed it to Zoe, as if William had sent it. Seth knew enough about forensics that they could pinpoint the timing too exactly. He wasn't going to let William take him down that easily.

Then he watched with horror as the flashing blue lights of police cars danced across the study ceiling.

CHAPTER EIGHTY-FIVE

WHEN CLAIRE FINISHED, there was silence.

Outside, the wind was calming down. The marquee no longer billowing so hard.

Lomond said, 'I've seen a lot of murder investigations in my time. But this was a new one on me. There have been a few murders made to look like suicide. But I've never seen a suicide made to look like murder.' Lomond caught sight of the constables by the door, who had been waiting for his signal. He whistled then pointed at Claire MacRae. He said to her, 'In many ways, this was William's last masterpiece.'

'No,' she said. 'It was Liz's masterpiece. It always was. Always will be.'

She then lifted her hands, offering them for handcuffs as the two constables from the entrance approached down the centre aisle.

While Donna put the handcuffs on Claire, Ross somewhat reluctantly explained, 'Claire MacRae, I am arresting you under Section One of the Criminal Justice Scotland Act, twenty sixteen for the murder of Seth Knox. The reason for your arrest is that I suspect you have committed an offence and I believe that keeping you in custody is necessary and proportionate for the purposes of bringing you before a court or otherwise dealing with you in accordance with the law. Do you understand?'

It was word for word out of Police Scotland's Standard Operating Procedure – something that pleased Lomond to hear.

'I understand,' Claire replied. She started to get up out of the wheelchair. 'I don't need this,' she said. 'Thanks to John.'

Lomond looked away awkwardly. He preferred when confessed murderers didn't highlight in public what friendly terms they were on.

Ross and Donna led Claire away.

Rebecca looked surprised. 'What about me?' she asked Lomond.

He paused. 'I'm betting that Claire MacRae, once under caution, will suddenly suffer a fatal loss of memory about your involvement in any of this. Your legal team could drive holes through any case we could bring.'

'That's very honest of you,' she said.

'The truth is all that matters, Ms Hawley,' he replied. He then left to catch up with Ross and Donna.

Once Claire was handed over to the local station for holding, she asked to see Lomond privately. He went through to her cell where she sat on the edge of the concrete block cutout that formed the bed.

'I wasn't sure when I would get to see you again,' she

said. 'I wanted to apologise for lying to you. You should know that I didn't take any pleasure from it.'

'I obviously can't say that I approve of what you and William did...' He paused. 'But I can understand it.'

'I thought you might. As a dad.'

'I was nearly a dad.'

'It doesn't work like that. You were a dad. I can tell. Being a dad is about more than statistics of when a heart did or didn't beat, and whether it happened inside or outside the womb. You were a father.'

Lomond had never thought of it that way before. No one had ever pulled him aside and explained whether he had ever qualified. The baby's heart wasn't beating when he came out. Did that matter? No one had ever referred to him as a father until now.

He could feel the first waves of a tear working its way up from the pit of his stomach. But he fought it back down. Now wasn't the time.

'If what happened to Liz had happened to my boy, I would probably have done the same as you and William – given the opportunity. I don't know if that's worth anything.'

'It is.' She looked down, satisfied that it was as close to a compliment as she could expect in the circumstances. 'What happens to you now?'

'To me?'

'Yes, you. How will you move on?'

'I hate to shatter any illusions you might have about you and me,' said Lomond. 'But I expect there will be another murder for me to solve pretty soon.'

'That's exactly my point. I'm not talking about work.

I'm talking about moving on with your life. After such a terrible loss.'

'Well, I don't plan on committing any murders anytime soon, if that's what you mean by moving on.'

She took a moment to just look at him. His sad, narrow eyes. 'You're in a million kinds of pain, and you don't know how to get out. Your only answer is, more of the same. I hope that you don't do that to yourself forever, John. I hope that you can find some peace wherever you go.'

Lomond looked over his shoulder. No one was there. 'If you deny everything you've said today, this will be the only day that you see the inside of a cell. We've got nothing else to go on. Maybe some forensics with Seth, but I expect you took care of that at the time.'

'Are you being my lawyer now?' she asked.

Lomond turned to leave. 'No,' he said. 'Just some advice. From one parent to another.'

CHAPTER EIGHTY-SIX

THE WHOLE MAJOR Investigations Team reconvened the following day, early evening. Claire MacRae had been arrested and taken to the security suite at Helen Street, ready for questioning. She would be one cell along from Kate Randall.

Lomond raised a paper cup of coffee. 'A quick shoutout...' he turned to Pardeep. 'Am I saying that right?'

'Yes, boss,' Pardeep said with a generous grin.

Lomond went on, 'A shoutout to Willie, Pardeep, and Jason. We couldn't have brought this home without you.'

'What are the chances of any of this sticking?' asked Willie.

'Honestly? Slim. Somewhere between slim and none. But you all did your job, and that's all I'll ever ask of you.' He raised his coffee. 'To asking the next question.'

Pardeep and Jason smiled at each other. 'To asking the next question,' they both said.

'Anyone fancy a pint?' asked Lomond.

'I can't, I'm afraid,' said Jason.

Pardeep nudged his ribs. 'Tell them why, Jase. Tell them why!'

'Jeez, Pardeep. This isn't high school...'

Pardeep said, 'He's got a date.' He held up his phone. 'I got him a Tinder profile.'

'About time too,' said Linda. 'Can I say that? Fuck it. Yes, I can.'

Lomond asked Pardeep, 'What about you?'

'I've got four girls at home that are desperate to make fun of me again.'

On that note, Ross added, 'I should get back to Lachlann and Isla.'

Willie looked at his watch by way of leading up to an excuse. 'Sorry, John. I promised Jean I would be back as soon as.'

In a last-ditch effort, he turned to Donna and Linda.

'Don't look at *me*,' said Linda. 'I've got a conference call with the Chief Constable in half an hour about whether to arrest Rebecca Hawley or not.'

Pardeep said, 'If she sues us and wins, maybe she'll have her little child detectives running the place.'

Lomond asked Donna. 'What about you? I know you can't be desperate to get back to Paisley on a Sunday night.'

'Can I stick a pin in this one tonight, boss?' she said. 'I've got something I need to take care of.'

Lomond grumbled, 'Fine. I get it. Go have fun without me.'

The group dispersed, leaving Linda and Lomond alone as the others filed out, yelling goodbyes from a distance.

'What's Claire's lawyer saying?' asked Lomond.

'They'll fight it all the way,' said Linda. 'Without her confession, we're dead in the water. A full recantation and she'll be clear. Rebecca and Kate, too.'

'I should be angrier at the thought of a murderer walking free.' He shook his head. 'But I just can't get there. If you ask me, the real murderer got tagged in a bathtub in Inver Castle.'

'You know who would approve of all this?'

'Who's that?'

'DCI Bob Roxburgh.'

Lomond did his best to smile. A laugh, though, was beyond his reach.

Linda went on, 'I'm just glad I didn't have to send divers in to pull you out of that moat.' She watched him carefully, monitoring his reaction. 'Take tomorrow off, John. You need it.'

'Nah, I'm good,' he said.

'Nah, you're not. Take the day.' She patted him on the leg and went home to her family.

Lomond stayed there for a while, standing under the muted lights. He didn't envy everyone else their family and social lives. That was how it was meant to be. Sometimes there had to be a watcher prepared to make sacrifices that others couldn't. It wasn't even that he had made sacrifices, so much as the opportunity for a normal life had been taken from him. Now, this was all that was left. And he decided he would make the most of it.

Across the office, a solitary phone rang. It wasn't even his section of Major Investigations. But as he looked around, he was reminded that no one else was there.

So he dashed across the room and picked up.

'DCI Lomond, Major Investigations.'

Donna drove over to London Road police station, where the Specialist Crime Division's Organised Crime team had made a base for the money laundering investigation.

She had been toiling with the decision about what to do the whole weekend. She had the proof she needed that the owner of the burner phone the money launderers were using had been her estranged dad. The only reason she knew his address was because of the totally illegal means she had used during the Sandman investigation. Admitting to it would inevitably lead to a disciplinary. It may even cost her a place on Major Investigations.

The choice was stark. Either give up the address to Specialist Crime Division and face a barrage of questions about how she acquired knowledge of the address, and risk her career in the process. Or say nothing, and let the investigation fritter away, and miss out on snaring much bigger criminals higher up the food chain who were running amok in the city.

In essence, she had to choose between her career, and the chance of a conviction that would be credited not to her but to Specialist Crime. In Donna's line of work, she couldn't face a stiffer test of selflessness.

When she was shown through to their hub in a separate area far away from CID and Major Investigations, she felt like she was back in the cliques of high school. The dozen or so officers in the room were all male. Alphas the lot of them. They took their weight training seriously. And their tight black t-shirts were like an unofficial uniform.

They sat up on their desk and used chairs as footrests. They were a different breed. At least, that was how they saw themselves compared to street detectives like Donna.

A cocky DS called out from across the room, 'Can I help you?'

'Yeah,' Donna replied. 'I've got some information on an address you're after.'

'Oh, aye? Who's that?'

Donna could feel her entire career – and her childhood – flash before her eyes as she said, 'Barry Higgins.'

CHAPTER EIGHTY-SEVEN

LOMOND WAS WALKING down Sauchiehall Street, when he saw a full window display for "*The Shortlist* by Liz MacRae."

Zoe Hathaway had caught the luckiest break of her brief career in announcing Liz as AD Sullivan. It seemed only right to strip away Seth's pen name if Hathaway was to press on with publication. The author name change had happened a few days too late though. And over five thousand copies with AD Sullivan's name on the front cover were pulped.

A fitting end to Seth Knox's authorial career.

Seeing the books piled up into tidy pyramids, it got Lomond thinking about the damage the past can do to someone if you hold onto it for too long. William and Claire had blamed Seth for Liz's suicide, but that was only part of the story.

For some reason, it made him think of Loch Garry. Next thing he knew, he was in an outdoors shop looking at hiking jackets. He tried on an Arc'teryx and a Fjällräven, then realised that they each cost close to £400.

Lomond joked with the sales assistant, 'Does it come with a car?'

He didn't get Lomond's sense of humour. 'It's just a very very good jacket.'

Lomond puffed. 'Okay, then. Thanks.'

Thinking that it was a sign from the gods that he was not meant to be in the great outdoors, he saw a Mountain Discount store over the pedestrian walkway. Lomond didn't know much about the shop, except that it seemed to have been running an "Everything Must Go!" sale for the past five years. He had never gone into one before. His wardrobe was simple. Jeans. Plain tees. Navy suits. Not too flashy. A long wool coat for winter. He had no need for gaiters or base layers or sweat-wicking trousers.

In five minutes, he grabbed a fleece, waterproof jacket, and walking shoes all for half the price of the fancy jackets next door.

As HE DROVE north in his car, he found himself muttering under his breath, convinced that what he was doing was stupid. Why wasn't he still in bed, or hitting golf balls at the driving range on Great Western Road.

But as he arrived at a lay-by off the A9 near Dalwhinnie and crossed the railway line, he followed a path leading him towards the mouth of Loch Garry.

He had no map and no plan. Only the recollection of having wanted to visit the area with Eilidh. He hadn't expected to have a 4G signal, so he had downloaded Henryk Górecki's Symphony of Sorrowful Songs before he left Glasgow. With earbuds in, and Górecki's symphony as his soundtrack, he wandered on, overwhelmed by his majestic surroundings.

The music had originally piqued his interest as a professional curiosity, as he sought to uncover the reason behind Liz's choice of the symphony as her final song – beyond its obvious sadness. But soon he was entranced by its beauty.

In the midst of the second movement, Lomond felt a glimmer of hope. A sliver of light breaking through the ominous and haunting first half. The musical equivalent of light breaking through a dark cloud.

As he paused to take in the view of the surrounding hills, he heard Eilidh's voice in his head.

Nothing is irredeemably lost. It always returns.

Though he would have once been overcome with emotion at the thought of her voice, this time he felt only a sense of peace, as if he had found his rightful place after all these years.

He stopped briefly halfway along the loch, taking in the view before him. It was not the most breath-taking sight in a country spoiled for natural beauty. But it was his and Eilidh's place. That was what mattered most.

He spoke to her as if she were there beside him. 'We made it, Eilidh. We finally made it.'

After waiting for a few minutes to take in the view they had always dreamed of seeing together, he reminded himself that he couldn't stay for long.

He had to keep moving forward, chasing after the light before it slipped away.

DCI Lomond and the team will return in 2023...

Until then, why not catch up on all of my other books here on Amazon:

https://www.amazon.co.uk/Andrew-Raymond/e/B07FBJGNV3/

ACKNOWLEDGMENTS

This book is dedicated with love to the Prowse, Parks, and Virlogeux families. Thank you for making me feel like a son and a brother.

This book would not have been possible without the incredible support of my loving wife and editor.

Thank you to my baby son, for lighting up my life. I used to think I was put on this earth to be a writer. I wasn't. It was to be your dad, matey.

Thank you particularly to DW and JP for being early readers of the book when it was in embarrassingly poor shape. It is so much better for your input.

And, finally, thanks to you, dear readers,

If you enjoyed the book and have a spare minute, I'd really appreciate it if you could leave a review. Even a sentence or two or just a star rating is great. Every single one honestly helps writers a lot.

Thank you for all of your lovely emails, Facebook comments and messages, and anything else. They are truly appreciated. As I always say, a writer is nothing without readers, and you lot are the best out there.

Your good humour and encouragement really keep me going.

- Andrew

ALSO BY ANDREW RAYMOND

Printed in Great Britain
by Amazon

28077443R00265